PRAISE FOR THE MERCY SERIES

'A sinister and rather fabulous world' — *The Age*

'Gripping ... by the end, you can't help but wonder who this angel of Mercy will become next' — *Sunday Herald Sun*

'This thriller has a creepiness that keeps the pages turning.' — *Kirkus Reviews*

'Mercy['s] sarcasm, courage, and determination will hook readers.' — *School Library Journal*

'Subtly beautiful and utterly intriguing, Rebecca Lim's Mercy series brims with mystery and romance that pull readers through the veil between worlds real and mythical.' — Andrea Cremer, *New York Times*-bestselling author of the Nightshade series

'A page-turning mystery with touches of romance ... beautifully written prose; and a dark and twisting plot that kept me guessing' — Laurie Faria Stolarz, bestselling author of *Touch* and the Blue is for Nightmares series

'What is compelling about this novel is not only its tightly constructed plot but the lyric quality of the writing ... Not to be missed' — *Reading Time*

'In her U.S. debut, Australian author Lim opens her planned series with a dark and chilling mystery, where the supernatural meets every parent's nightmare. Vivid prose highlighting Mercy's sense of isolation will draw readers in ... while dramatic tension and the mystery of Mercy's *Quantum Leap*-style body-hopping ought to keep their attention' — *Publisher's Weekly*

'A racy story of good and evil in a world where angels aren't all sweetness and light' — *Sunday Herald Sun*

ALSO BY REBECCA LIM

Mercy
Exile
Muse
Fury
The Astrologer's Daughter
Afterlight

FOR YOUNGER READERS

The Sweet Life
Cover Girl
Sista Fashionista
Star Style
Whiffy Newton in the Case of the Dastardly Deeds
Whiffy Newton in the Riddle of the Two-Tone Trousers
Whiffy Newton in the Affair of the Fiendish Phantoms
Whiffy Newton and the Mystery of the Marble Beach Mugger
Five-Minute Tales Messiest Monster Ever
Five-Minute Tales Bravest Princess Ever

Love transcends worlds ...

WRAITH

REBECCA LIM

THE HIGH STREET PUBLISHING COMPANY

To the readers who loved *Fury* — *Wraith* is dedicated to you.

First published in 2017 by The High Street Publishing Company

A Cataloguing-in-Publication entry is available from the National Library of Australia www.trove.nla.gov.au

ISBN 978-0-6480392-2-8 (paperback)
ISBN 978-0-6480392-1-1 (ebook)

Cover design by Karen Scott
Cover photograph by Subbotina Anna/Shutterstock
Typeset in 11/15.5 Minion

10 9 8 7 6 5 4 3 2 1

Oh sinners let's go down
Let's go down, come on down
Oh sinners let's go down
Down in the river to pray

— **Traditional**

PROLOGUE

My memory is a cracked and treacherous thing, but I remember —

The silence of thousands as the sun went dark above the Andaman Sea and an aurora flamed across the hot noonday sky in vivid bands of red and green. The ground had begun to shake beneath our feet — as fluid as the skin of some vast, waking animal. People fell to the earth. Then the screaming began.

And as Ryan and I crossed the equator, chasing the heat, chasing life, I remember —

The evening sky suddenly peppered with light: hard, bright flashes filling the horizon from end to end. One after another, *pop, pop, pop,* high overhead as if the stars themselves were exploding. Cars, buses, people — everyone stopping to see, to wonder at the signs.

I recall that some days, whole streets ruptured without warning. Overnight, buildings shook to pieces without cause, inland waterways drained dry, small atolls vanished without trace; the earth, the sky, everything was chaos, and we would all draw breath in terror, then pick ourselves up and move on. Because that's what humans do. We survive. We...evolve.

It was a new world to which we were confined: Luc and his *daemonium*, all of us. Confined forever to this sphere because of a bargain I'd made with Death himself; no paradise for Luc and the exiled, and none for me. No return.

I would do it all again to save my brothers, the Eight.

And Ryan, who loved me when I did not know myself — or what I was.

But the moment I made my choice, I was marked for sacrifice, as was he. A price was settled; a debt, escalated.

Time. There would never be enough.

I gasp now as a hand draws me up out of black water, the liquid heavy, hot and viscous as blood. It streams off me, and I cry out to see my exposed skin glow once again, luminous in the half-light that falls across the wide, dark river in which I kneel.

It must mean —

I look up into the Archangel Azraeil's glorious face, youthful, everlasting — a power unto himself, a power greater even than evil — and know that I have entered the kingdom of *Sheol*, and that I am dead.

PART 1

You ever at a loose end, you look me up, you hear?

1

I know that angels and demons exist. I've seen them.

Now? I'm nobody.

But once, I knew people.

I was never beautiful — I just spoke the language. But everyone around me *was*, and they were surrounded by so much beauty that after a while they failed to see it. Or be it.

I'm short, and thin. Sharp-featured, sharp-tongued. Most people remember me by my eyes — the right one is brown; the left one, blue. I used to dye my hair jet-black and have it cut into these razor-sharp lines to suit the person I had to be because I worked for a monster — one of the one-name It girls, Irina. A model so infamous and lovely that her life was a revolving torment of appearances and commitments, walk-outs, bitch-fights and broken stints in rehab. I don't know who she's sleeping with these days, or what she's putting up her nose now, and I'm so *glad*.

I made things happen. I got people places. I was the one who made sure the bookers and the rivals, the luxury conglomerates, the excommunicated lovers and the baying paparazzi, never pressed assault charges or sued for breach of contract or slander.

But I walked away from all that after Lucifer himself appeared at an internationally-televised fashion show beneath the glass and iron ceiling of the Galleria Vittorio Emanuele in

Milan — and tore it down around my ears. There was death and fire that night, administered by shining, winged giants who walked among us with flaming swords and burning eyes.

I blame Mercy for what happened. But a part of me misses her too, because she *got* me. It's weird to say this — because we knew each other for such a strange, brief time — but she was my friend. She actually cared whether I lived or died. And she brought Irina back because I asked her to — when no human power on earth could do it.

These days, I manage the general store for an organic farm outside a small town called Craster on the English far north coast. All you need to know is that it's as far removed from my old jetset life as it's possible to be. There's sea and there's *space*. When it's cold, nobody comes around unless they're lost — which suits me just fine because I'm permanently over the people and the crowds. Nobody here calls me *darling*, or wants me to hold their stingray hide bag, or their thirty-thousand-dollar jacket. I've let my hair go back to the nothing-brown I was born with, and it's long now, and snarled at the ends. I wear it in two plaits — just like a real farm girl — and I've got calluses on my hands from mucking out the animal pens, and corns on my feet from all the walking. I can also list hangnails and moles, freckles and wind-burnt lips. I've even dropped that stupid cut-glass high-class accent I used to affect. I'm unrecognisable.

Or I thought I was.

See, Sunday morning, I was bagging up new potatoes behind the shop — the wind cutting straight through me the way it always does here — when I imagined I felt a breath of fire: just a hiss of energy.

I imagined that I saw someone standing right at the peripheries of my sight, by the goat pen. No joke, just a flash:

of someone tall, male, powerful-looking, with dark red hair, wearing a worn Barbour coat over an unremarkable assortment of farm clothes. Little details I was once paid to notice. When I turned to look and there was no one there, I told myself it was a fast-moving tourist and kept right on weighing and bagging.

But I *knew*. Because once you see them, you can't ever unsee them. You're just never the same.

Then yesterday I was at the post office, sending a parcel of mixed preserves to an address in Buckinghamshire, when I saw him again, the same one; he was standing in the doorway of the butcher's shop across the way. When I turned to look at him properly, all I saw was the winter sun reflecting off plate glass. Kid you not.

'You're bloody mad,' I said out loud to make myself feel better. As mad as all the things that had been happening in the news lately: tidal waves and heatwaves and unseasonal snow, UFOs and mass shootings and cavernous blowholes at all ends of the earth. The whole world going to shit, and me in the best place to avoid it all: on a small hobby farm just outside Craster. *Safe*, the way houses used to be safe, solid rock used to be safe, safe as the sun rising of a morning.

But something catches my eye now, in the darkness outside my kitchen window. I'll never get used to it: 3.19 pm in the afternoon and it's as black as pitch out and I've closed the shop early and walked home to my humble stone gatehouse beside the main road in my five-pound wellies, because no one's coming to look at jams and artisanal cheeses on a biting, howling dark afternoon in the north, are they?

But as I glance outside at the wind shaking all the branches of the trees, my heart stops. I drop the saucepan full of cold water I'm holding. It hits the slate-tiled floor with the force, sound and feel of an icy, drenching bomb, spraying up the legs of my mud-encrusted jeans, the ends of my dark-green plaid flannel shirt.

Out under the row of towering pines that separates my home from the road, there's the giant figure of that man, still wearing the same picture-perfect, broken-in Barbour coat. He's not attempting to hide from me now. He's the tallest, most perfectly proportioned person I've ever seen, with long, dark red hair spilling in waves down his broad shoulders, emerald-green eyes that are as piercing as jewels, and long, muscular limbs, pale as marble. He's standing beyond the reach of the kitchen light, in the very face of the gale, but nothing about him is moving, not one hair. His arms are crossed. I can see him as clearly as if he's standing in a patch of sunlight, or is lit from within, I can't explain it. But I *know* what he is.

Mercy was the same way. She didn't announce herself the day she took over Irina Zhivanevskaya's body. She remained oblique — was simply there — until I caught her out, play-acting at being someone else. She gauged the world silently before making her move, the way *he* is now doing.

He's an *archangel*, I realise, my skin tightening. Them with the burning swords. He was right there in the thick of it when the roof fell in Milan, wings shredding curls of energy, hair like living flame. Unforgettable.

The old me would have rushed out there shrieking, all claws and bravado and outrage. But now I'm so paralysed by fear and wonder that I can't move away from the window. I touch my fingers to the icy, brittle glass, as if in doing that, he will feel it on his skin. Across my straggling kitchen garden we stare at each other, the giant and I. The burn scar on the back of my neck, in the shape of a crescent moon, begins to pulse with remembered heat.

Around me, the room suddenly grows so bright I am forced to turn, shielding my eyes.

And then I understand, at last, why he is out there.

I turn to confront her —

The one the watcher is really guarding.

'*Mercy*,' I whisper.

2

Gia, she says, her lips clearly moving to form my name, but I don't hear it.

It's been two years, but she looks exactly the way I remember her from the catwalk in Milan when that ice-blonde demon — Gudrun — grasped her by the throat, ready to strike the fatal blow.

It's Mercy's true form, what I'm seeing.

She's still tall, far taller than me — that's a given, almost everyone is — but human-scaled now. Still beautiful in that strong-nosed, sombre way that always reminded me of a girl from a Renaissance painting. Broad-shouldered and long-limbed with big brown eyes and long brown hair hanging down past her shoulders: every strand straight, even and perfectly the same. Pale and luminous — light coalesces on her skin like she's somehow made of it — but she's clad all in black now. The absolute black of mourning.

But it's a black that's strangely insubstantial. All of her is. I catch the faint outline of my kitchen table, the out-of-date calendar hanging by the light switch, right *through* her. It's the way the kitchen fluorescent is hitting Mercy that is somehow a little bit...wrong.

'What *happened* to you?' I say, stepping closer, and there's real fear in my voice. I find that I'm shaking.

Her lips move as if she's answering me, but I can't hear the words. We could be separated by soundproof glass, or by a medium so dense that her reply is lost to it.

So I say again, 'Mercy,' reaching out to do those stupid double air-kisses the way I was programmed to for years and years. But my hands pass right through her and, as they do, I feel a brief and terrible burst of intense pain and see colours, images, hear my name — *Gia!* — uttered inside my own head in Mercy's anguished voice.

When I look up from my stinging hands in horror, I see that the great sadness she carried with her in Milan, before Ryan found her again, has returned.

She seems made of sadness. Sadness and light.

Mercy holds her hands out, palms up, asking me to take them properly. I shake my head, remembering the terrible heat all along my nerve endings when I tried to touch her; like putting my hands on a lit stove. Her lips tighten with that familiar flash of impatience I recognise, and she squeezes her hands into fists then opens them again, palms up, demanding.

Her eyes say, *There is no other way to make you understand.*

Mercy makes fists of her hands again, opens them, palms up; the gesture is emphatic.

I've never been a coward. I'm a multiple foster-home survivor, a fighter, an iron-plated *bitch*, and proud of it. I made myself out of nothing. I'm still here because of *me*.

My eyes snapping to hers — *challenge accepted* — I reach out, my fingers closing on air, and she courses through me.

She's pure energy — energy without boundaries — and it's as if I've been plugged into live current.

Rigid with pain I see, hear, feel —

Creatures with names like songs: *K'el, Nuriel, Gabriel,*

Uriel, Michael, Jegudiel, Selaphiel, Jeremiel, Barachiel, Raphael, Azraeil.

Each, each, each.

I see them and know them and understand that some are gone from this world, will never return.

Archangels all, Mercy's voice roars through me. *Elohim. My brethren.*

I twist in her grasp, convulsing in the stream of her broken memories —

Of countless human lives lived without recall of what she once was.

Of archangels protecting her from Lucifer, life upon life.

Of *Ryan* and re-awakening.

Of archangels in chains and demons of cloud.

Of cities and ghosts of the ancient dead.

Here, inside my tiny kitchen, I am swept by unearthly waves and see a great battle, fought in her name and her image by an army of angels: *elohim, malakhim, ophanim, seraphim* in order to give Mercy — I can hear myself shrieking thinly in agony — time to contain Lucifer, the Accuser, to this earthly realm forever.

I gasp as I see Lucifer plunge his hand deep into Ryan's chest; watch Ryan fall to the ground.

Then I witness Azraeil — the only archangel with the power to give life or take it — sundering Mercy from her immortality in order to bring Ryan back from the dead and keep Lucifer earthbound, forever.

A decision at once elegant and simple — irrevocable.

I look up into Mercy's face; my own contorted in pain.

I kept my bargain. Her voice is in my veins. *Those that fell from Heaven and sought to retake it will never leave this world again. Those of my kin that Lucifer had found and enslaved I avenged and freed — every one.*

I suffered, Gia, and I deserved happiness. But Ryan and I were only one step ahead. Always.

I fall to my knees sobbing, unable to bear her touch or break from her grip. She's burning me alive in order to make me understand, but I still can't see —

I'm suddenly lost in the roar of taxis and buses, tourist rickshaws and cars, the cries of flower sellers thronging a temple complex entrance. *Asia* — somewhere. I *am* Mercy, and I'm in her memory. The air is heavy with petrol fumes and the smell of wet foliage, incense and warm bodies. We're crossing beneath a temple roofline which is a riot of pinks, sky-blues, ochres. There are human figures and monsters upon it, bulging-eyed deities and things with no name, all writhing and dancing, tier-upon-tier towards heaven. One figure is repeated among the rest: a blue-skinned, four-armed goddess, garlands of skulls and flowers around her neck, long, fanged teeth in her mouth, a skirt of human arms about her waist, holding a bloody scimitar and a severed head.

'*Kālī*.' I feel Ryan breathe against my long, unbound hair, his warm hand in mine as we gaze on a twenty-foot high statue of the fanged, blue-skinned, raven-haired goddess. For a moment, leaning into him, feeling his dark, laughing eyes on me, I feel a surge of longing so powerful I don't know if it's coming from me, or from her.

Ryan continues reading the inscription before us in his deep, spine-tingling drawl, 'Goddess of Time, Change, Power, Destruction: merciless, bloodthirsty, forbidden, a vicious slayer of demons…'

He throws his head back and laughs and I see the strong,

sleek column of his throat. 'More than a little like you, then, Merce!'

And I can feel it — how mortal she is, how her heartbeat flutters in the smooth column of her neck, the sweat where both their human hands are joined tightly together, the way Mercy is wearing her long straight hair forward across her shoulders, how her plain yellow sundress with spaghetti straps is sticking to the back of her legs in the heat. They're just two people who love each other, among billions.

Joy, I feel her joy.

Then the world is just... gone. It's no longer there, the way Ryan is no longer there — there's just an aching absence.

Then: a sudden flare of pain so terrible and obliterating that I wake — as she must have done — floating facedown in a wide black shining river, beneath the hand of Azraeil, the silver-haired Archangel of Death himself, the water as hot as blood against my skin.

He raises me up now, choking, out of the black water, before a vast and gleaming crowd which stands silently watching upon one bank, and cries, 'And she shall be my right hand — the right hand of Death. Once was archangel, then human — then *wraith*.'

I hear myself gibber, 'I can't bear it, I can't bear it, make it stop, Mercy, *please*.'

Then she lets me go, and I crumple forward onto the kitchen tiles.

3

I feel warm hands lifting me, laying me down gently on my hard and narrow bed. The room is unusually warm, too; the light beyond my closed lids a pale gold. I can feel him there, just out of reach. The watcher.

Feverish, sensitised with remembered pain from Mercy's touch, I whisper, 'Archangel,' because I know who he is now, the one of all her brothers Mercy loved best and who loved her best in return. 'Whatever she wants, I can't do it. Tell her... I'm not strong enough.'

I open my eyes with difficulty into his brilliant, emerald gaze and am suffused instantly by love, longing, *desire*.

Looking at them changes you. Being with them changes you and makes you want things that are impossible. I can't look away from where he's standing at the foot of my bed, somehow shifted in scale to fit beneath the ceiling of my tiny house, but still maybe seven, eight feet tall. He's dressed in proper antwacky, top-to-toe farm clobber complete with thigh-high wading boots, just like one of the local lads.

Everything's too... correct. So much thought and effort has gone into the human authenticity of his 'outfit' that I can't help the laughter that bubbles up suddenly. As if he could ever blend in; be one of us. Then I'm suddenly laughing so much and so hard I can barely breathe, I'm almost crying into my hands.

Rolling from side to side on the bed, racked by laughter, I peer at the glorious farm-angel creature through my fingers and see answering humour flare in his bright emerald gaze.

He has a sense of humour, too, I think. *He's perfect.* But then, of course he is.

'It's the clothes,' I gasp, filled with a pure, real joy I can't ever remember feeling. I've never been a happy person; I don't *do* happiness the way I don't do camping or Pilates or raw oysters. But here I am, howling with laughter. 'They're too much! As a former 'stylist-to-the-stars', I should know. Those boots! Hasn't anyone ever told you to take one thing off before you leave the house?'

Then he laughs — the archangel Mercy calls Gabriel — and the sound is as ringing and golden as the light pouring off his skin. Without warning, the farm clothes he's somehow fashioned of his own energy melt away, and he is himself. In sleeveless raiment so bright, so terrible and beautiful to look upon that I have to turn away sharply for a moment to shield my eyes.

My laughter dies as abruptly as it began. 'Where are your wings?' I say softly, so dazzled I can barely make out the curve of the smile still lingering about his wide, mobile mouth. 'You're supposed to have wings. You did in Milan.'

Gabriel's reply is quiet. 'Pray you never see them again, for they are mere symbols of our fury and serve only as a warning of the terror to come.'

I sit up straighter, pulling myself up against the cracked wooden bedhead. 'I'm a results-oriented person,' I drawl, hating the hard, sarcastic edge that's come back into my voice, 'and Mercy knows that. That's why she came looking for me, I suppose. I used to get things done. But I've sworn off your lot for good. And I'm not that person any more — the *fixer*.'

My hand flies up automatically to the puckered edges of the scar on my neck and I have to force it back down. But Gabriel sees the gesture, because he sees everything.

'I can't even fix myself,' I say lightly, crossing my arms to hold in the pain. 'I'm permanently damaged.'

There is a catch in my breathing when I think of Ryan holding Mercy's hand, and about how there is no one like Ryan, on this whole earth, for me. *To want* and *to have* are two very different things. And I can want all I want. But I will never be fit to have, or to hold. Broken girls never are.

'I just want to be left alone,' I insist fiercely around the hard ache in my chest. '*Tell her.* Mercy will listen to you. You more than anyone.'

Gabriel's eyes are unbearably kind, but he continues as if I never spoke a word. 'Lucifer has clothed himself in human flesh —'

I raise my hands to ward him off.

'I don't think you're quite comprehending me.' We both hear the brittleness, the anger. '*I can't help you.* Mercy gave up what she was to keep Lucifer here. She showed me that. She did what you wanted. You got your way — he's our problem now, the way he's always been our problem since the moment the Archangel Michael cast him down. Satan's been contained for good, and the universe is safe again, right? But after everything Mercy did for you, even with all the powers she once had and your lot possess — *something bad still happened to her anyway.* She never got her happy ending. And if *you* can't protect her, what chance do I…?'

Suddenly, there is steel in Gabriel's green gaze as he says, 'But your world —'

I stare him down, even though I'm quaking inside. '— Is a world of ants and monsters. We're all like ants to you: plenty of ants to go round, plenty of monsters, too. I can't help you, and I can't help her. I told her once, I said —' My voice is high and shaky, 'that none of you were ever, *ever*, to come after me. All I offered her was a beer, if she ever came around again. One lousy beer. And yet, here you are, breaking promises.'

Gabriel drifts forward until he is beside me, and I am so blinded by the heat and light of him — like golden summer in the room — that I focus on the edges of the rag rug on the floor instead of on that heartbreaking face. The air hums with his power.

'Please go away,' I whisper.

'But don't you want to get him?' Gabriel murmurs above my bowed head.

I shake it so forcefully that my long hair falls down around me like a sheltering curtain. 'He's not *my* enemy,' I mutter. 'Lucifer.'

'But he is.' Gabriel's reply is swift. 'He is horror and destruction, degradation, abasement and pain.'

Every word he utters falls on me like a stone, for I know each word well.

'He is the enemy of all life,' Gabriel insists.

I'm not looking at him — I'm refusing to look at him — so that when he touches me, just the lightest point of contact, like a feather drifted down across bare skin, I am wholly unprepared for the way the room vanishes around me and how time itself reels backwards.

❧

Not many people can tell you exactly where they died.

But when I close my eyes? I'm right there — in this clearing filled with long grass and twisted yew and oak, the air dense with the scent of resin and the drone of insect life. When I came to, there was this sharp crust trapped between my skin and the cold, cold soil.

Twigs and acorns, someone told me later. *Like lying on a bed of nails, I'd imagine.*

Mama Kassmeyer had only just taken me in. I hated her — because she was obese and kind and cheerful and it was standard practice to hate everyone I'd ever been sent to — and I especially hated the long walk to a new school through a mile or so of dense woodland.

She lived out on a farm built in 1912 with a cast of desperadoes — animal and human — that I pretended were all invisible. I didn't learn their names; I looked away from all their faces, misshapen or otherwise. Two months more and I'd no longer need any of them, anyway. I'd be eighteen, and in fine family tradition, I'd vanish. That was the plan. The second my birthday rolled around? I'd shoot through without a goodbye and no one would have the power to stop me any more.

So I came and went like an angry ghost when I was sent to Mama K's, quickly committing another grid of village streets to memory, convinced I'd soon leave it behind for a new one because people always ended up saying I was *Difficult* and *Trouble* and *Unable to play nicely with others.*

Two weeks, and I never saw a soul during my slog from the Kassmeyer farm towards Scenic Road and civilisation. But that morning, I recall the distant figure of a man coming through the trees, the already searing early-morning sun burnishing his shaved head, striking off the barrel of the slender silver torch he held in one hand.

Lone guy with torch. Heading towards the river.

I dismissed it, even though it made no sense, the torch, on such a bright summer's day. All sorts of weirdos gravitated to the village where my school was; it was a sore point with the locals. It was a river town with a grand past and the summer tourists were easy pickings. Strangers everywhere in the summer taking all the good parking spots and tables, looking every which way, speaking every language under the sun. The same scenic river ran through the boundaries of Mama K's farm.

So I figured: *sightseer.*

I paid the man no mind, striding on grimly, ignoring his soft *Hey, baby* as our paths intersected. I've replayed that a million times since. The steady closing-in he must have done; the oblique path he must have taken away from the river and through the trees to circle back around: to me.

If I'd started running earlier, well, maybe it would have been different.

But only metres from the main road I looked up to see him facing me across a clearing — a big man, big as a wrestler, biceps, calves, forearms all corded with thick muscle — and that blazing look he gave me with his pale blue eyes was what sent me dodging through the tree trunks, trying to make it back towards the river bend where Mama K's farmhouse stood. Some part of me knew that if I just made it back, Mama Kassmeyer would die trying to protect me and I would be safe.

Back then, I weighed maybe fifty kilograms soaking wet, and sprinting — hell, sport — had never been my thing. I had no thing, like, literally.

I had no breath left in me to scream when he ran me down. He just touched me on the soft skin at the back of my neck with the end of the silver torch. And I crashed to the ground in agony.

That thing was no torch.

It gave out *pain*, not light.

He shocked me on my neck, my face, between my breasts.

Any place with bare skin showing, he let me have it with that thing until I was suffocating inside my own body.

When I close my eyes now, all I choose to see is the way the sunlight moved upon the flaming death's-head moth tattooed across the man's thick neck, stretching below his jaw from ear to ear, etched in reds and blacks.

I do not admit sounds, I do not admit sensations.

There was a woman's skull, right in the middle of the moth's jointed thorax. What was unusual, people told me later, was the fact she had long black hair twining out of her bone-white scalp. The long, twining hair forming an integral part of the wings on either side was what made the tattoo unique. There was no one on record, people told me later, with a tattoo *exactly* like that. I'd done well to remember, the officers said. *It must have been bespoke, made-to-order, absolute murder to have done.*

Jump cut to the moment he rolled me facedown into a shallow pit with my hands tied behind my naked back, my own tank top the restraint. Someone told me to be grateful for that.

If he'd used cable ties, well, you would've been a goner for sure, love, because no crackerjack ring's ever gonna to cut through flex cuff, right?

Soil rained down into my hair, the crevices of my body, onto the handle of the huge hunting knife he'd plunged just to the left of my spine, puncturing a lung but just missing the frantically beating heart he'd been aiming for.

I've since paid to get that particular memory removed, but it's stubborner than a bloodstain. It just won't go away.

As I look up into Gabriel's burning eyes now, I see that he has seen everything I have held inside me for years — all the filth and darkness and despair — and that he pities me.

4

'You have no right.' Now there is loathing in my words, where before there was only anger.

'Don't you want to get him?' Gabriel repeats, his voice stern.

I draw myself into a tight ball, the tears coursing down my face. All the years I spent growing spiky armour — the bullying charm and ruthless efficiency I was known for first as a dogsbody, then stylist, model booker, manager, *fixer* — it's all been stripped away. And I am that girl again — soil coating my tongue and teeth, blood running down between my legs, into the soft cavities of my body, blood everywhere — blindly sawing away at the seams of the cheap tank top he'd hogtied me with because I wanted so desperately to *live*. I hadn't hung on so long, through all the beatings and abuse and foster shit, to go this way.

Life was supposed to *start* one day.

Just start. That was all.

'Of course I want to get him!' I howl, reliving all the ways I've imagined killing the man with the death's-head tattoo. *First I'll cut out his eyes*, I've told myself, nights when I couldn't sleep. *No, no, his balls.*

A cheap purple gemstone cocktail ring with a sharp, clawed setting saved my life that day. Vanity was my salvation. When I clawed my way out of that hole in the ground, dirt and stones and leaves streaming off me, I was a new animal. Metal, studs, safety pins, needles, piercings — for years after, I couldn't get enough of things I could hurt people with, hurt myself with. I adorned myself with pain because, in my mind, vanity and pain equalled salvation. I would remake myself completely. And I did.

'It's unfair, to make an offer like this. You know it. It's blackmail,' I hiss through my fingers. 'What answer could I possibly give you but *yes*?'

Gabriel doesn't deny it, but his voice is almost unbearably gentle. 'The one you seek dwells with Lucifer.'

I smear the heels of my palms into my eyes and glare up at him through wet lashes. 'Literally or figuratively? I don't speak Old Testament.'

Gabriel favours me with the ghost of a smile. 'After Mercy's bargain with Azraeil contained Lucifer here forever, a new age began. There was no longer any reason to hide — the rules had changed. No longer content with the dark, burning places that gave him the energy to survive indefinitely in this cold, hostile world, Lucifer moved swiftly to build a mortal empire guarded by beings both demonic and human. The one you seek is one of these.'

'So what you're saying is — Lucifer's always been scared of the cold, but now he's come up above ground and put together a personal army of rapists, torturers and murderers because if he can't leave, he might as well be king.' My voice is flat. 'Even saying it out loud sounds loony. I'd be just one woman going up against, what, The Prince of Darkness? And men like that, like…that…'

I see the tattoo, moving.

Swallowing down the urge to vomit, I whisper, 'And she's…*what* is she? I can't even say what Mercy is now. You couldn't even give us odds — the two of us against all of them. She's got no body to do murder *with.*'

Gabriel's green gaze is unwavering. 'Those who first fell numbered one hundred and began to make for themselves an army of *nephilim*, of wraiths and monstrous remnants. But the first fallen were the strongest. No more like they are will ever be made again. And Mercy herself took *six* of them in her quest to find and free Nuriel, Selaphiel and Jegudiel; with six more destroyed because she and Uriel saw fit to find and free *me* after Lucifer himself had imprisoned me in stone.'

'Those still aren't fantastic odds,' I say hoarsely.

'They *can* be destroyed,' Gabriel insists. 'Kill the human shell and you kill the succubus inside it. Help her, and you help yourself.'

I know my expression is hard, closed, unfriendly. 'If she needs my help, why can't she just ask me herself? What's wrong with her? Why can't I hear her when she speaks to me?'

It's unmistakable, the sorrow that moves across Gabriel's face like the ripples created when a stone is flung into a still pond.

In reply, he extends one gleaming hand and — God help me — I take it.

⁊

I can barely breathe for the shock, let alone speak, my neck craned up in the darkness to take in what stands before me.

I *know* I'm at the isolated headland outside the village of Craster, because I'm looking at the ruins of Dunstanburgh Castle. I'm facing the two crumbling, drum-shaped towers of the Great Gatehouse, a structure over seventy-nine feet high, but I can't understand how I came to be standing here, in the dark, in a stained shirt and jeans, socks, no shoes, the sea crashing far below and to the right of me. The Castle is almost four miles from home and can only be reached by a winding walking trail that hugs the line of the Northumberland coast. It's looked the same way for centuries and there's not a soul around.

Even Gabriel's shining form beside me cannot pull my astonished gaze. Around us, a howling north-easterly is in full force; I see what it's doing, but I can't feel it, because around *him*, time — everything — is somehow separate and apart.

'*How —?*'

In between *there* and *here* there was no means of knowing which way was up or down, forwards or back. It felt like some kind of veil had been thrown over me; that I'd passed through a searing eternity of ice and fire — a limitless, soundless, bleak black void laced with acid-bright starbursts and pinpoints of colour. There was no way to call out or thrash around or even frame a conscious thought, because everything that I *am* felt as if it was breaking down, piece by piece, and reassembling.

Gabriel turns and regards me gravely. 'Tell me.'

Suddenly, I'm gabbling. 'It punches you inside out finding yourself *there* and *here* almost instantaneously. It's like you, you leave some part of yourself behind and arrive just a fraction diminished, a fraction...awry. When you took my hand, it wasn't a feeling of falling, exactly, there was no real sense of momentum. It's more that I'd shivered into something sharp, hard, *inhuman*, and everything I'd ever taken for granted just, just...fell away.'

Gabriel's eyes are very green as I add in a rush, 'You become the barest essence of what you really are. And moving through seems to take forever, but it also takes just a heartbeat.

It's supposed to be fast, right? But it's like the *slowest* fast you will ever experience.'

I can see that not a word of what I'm saying really makes sense to him because this is how they move: they just do it. Will it, and it is done. The ability to go from place to place in less time than it takes to click your fingers.

But it's indescribable what I just went through. None of what I tried to tell Gabriel even got close to how it felt: taking his hand, travelling here in the space between heartbeats. I wonder how many before me have done it and survived, or whether I am the first.

'Something in me has changed.' My admission is hesitant and I look down at the ground, feeling strangely afraid. 'I can't... measure the change, but I just know that I'm different, and it's, it's a forever thing.'

Gabriel tilts my face up gently so that I am forced to look at him. 'Though Azraeil will not thank me for saying this, his realm and Lucifer's are not so very different. One rules and emanates that which we call Death, the other that which we call Hell. Doorways, fissures, lakes, pathways, structures natural or unnatural — all may open onto one or the other realm *from this world*. Nothing is fixed, nothing is solid. Everything is connected. A line joins us all. Understand that, and you will have a measure of our understanding.'

'I don't believe you,' I shoot back, but he can hear the uncertainty in my voice.

'Hell, Sheol, Earth — and all that reside in them — all connected,' Gabriel repeats. 'Between them nothing is ever lost; there is only ever change.'

He places a hand on my right shoulder then, and the promontory before us, the curtain walls and structures within the ruined castle grounds, all are instantly transformed.

The sound of the howling gale cannot drown out my terrified screaming.

We two are not alone in this place.

Gabriel's touch has lifted some kind of blindness in me.

There are palely shining forms everywhere: moving in a steady stream into the castle ruins, standing in the long grass around us, beneath the trees. Many surge towards us eagerly, coming as close as they dare, as if drawn to his light. But then I realise with horror that they are drawn to *me*, and if Gabriel were not here, they would surround me, maybe touch me. The looks on their faces are almost hungry; each one was once a man, woman or child, that much is clear. Not one of them is the same.

'If I were not with you,' Gabriel murmurs, almost to himself, 'these ones would break themselves upon you like the waves. They crave your living energy. It draws them. Some part of them still yearns for what you are. Most don't even comprehend what they have become.'

I can't breathe as I whisper, 'Where are they going to, all those...others?'

The others that can pass through the solid walls of the castle.

'Sheol.' Gabriel's whispered reply is reverent. 'Where freed souls reside and no demon is welcome. It is Azraeil's domain; the boundaries of which are strange and porous. A great river runs through it, from which Mercy now draws her power in the same way Lucifer once drew his strength from molten rivers beneath the earth. She is charged to do Death's bidding — she was marked and she was called by Azraeil himself — but she resists, because she would not be herself if she did not...question. In us from the beginning was *the choice* — to turn against our own natures, or be what we were made to be. Mercy understands this now in a way that none of us — not Raphael, not Michael, not even the Great Adversary himself — ever will. She has seen both sides of that choice for herself — for better or worse.'

Gabriel turns and looks down at me. 'The newly dead are very strong, for they have not forgotten who they once were, what it meant to be alive, to love. And Mercy is Azraeil's now. She will not be allowed to forget.'

My skin goes icy as I realise what he is saying.

'Once she has come to terms with what she has...become,' — I hear the slight catch in Gabriel's voice — 'and torn that place apart looking for Ryan Daley, she will bring down the walls of Lucifer's empire to find him and finish what none of us — no archangel alive — could do. But she needs your help to do it, Gia Basso. This is *your* world Lucifer hides in, not Azraeil's. You are the survivor here; there is no horror in this life you have not seen or borne. And yet you live and thrive. You see how *necessary* you are?'

Gabriel places a finger against my mouth when it looks like I will argue, and then the clustering silver wraiths, the haunted castle on the promontory that is some kind of strange gateway to a world I cannot comprehend, they all vanish.

5

It's as if someone bends low and whispers deep into my ear while I'm still asleep: *Go now.*

I open my eyes suddenly, waking fully clothed, but stiff with cold, on the narrow single bed inside the stone gatehouse. I uncurl the tight fists I must have made in the night and see that my nail-scored palms are thin and bloodless and weak-looking. Not the hands of a demon-killer.

But I push myself upright, filled with a new, restless energy I've never felt before. Can I really believe it? That I'll finally get what I need?

I rise — still wearing the mud-stained plaid shirt and jeans from yesterday — and stuff my frozen feet into another pair of thick socks, following them with a pair of waterproof hunting boots. I pull my hair back from my face, dividing it into two hanks and plaiting each of them roughly, before going all around the gatehouse and placing my meagre clutch of belongings into my navy duffle bag.

A PTSD psychologist I'd been forced to see had once counselled me to ask myself, *What am I in the business of?* I'd glared at him like he was barking. The cheerful reply to that question was supposed to be, *The business of living!*

I was supposed to ask and answer that question daily. It was supposed to help me heal.

'And it *is* a business,' the man told me solemnly, 'and you must treat it as such. There will be days, young lady, where the ledger will not balance. But given time, with careful work, the pluses will outweigh the minuses.'

I've never been any good at arithmetic. I have not asked myself *the question* for many years. The worlds of fashion and mathematics always seemed mutually exclusive, to my mind.

But I say aloud now to the icy, empty house, 'What am I in the business of?' as I shrug on my navy hooded oilskin coat and slip the front door key into my pocket.

Taking one last look around the kitchen, I shoulder my navy duffle bag and open the door onto the frost-covered garden, replying fiercely, 'I am in the business of *vengeance*.'

ॐ

The farmer and his wife were regretful to see me go, but it was winter after all, and I could see them thinking my wages were a drain that could be better spent on feed or fertiliser as I handed back my key and wished them all the best for the remainder of their lives.

I sprang for a taxi to Alnmouth Station — the first luxury I'd allowed myself for months. The rest of the three-hour train trip back down the east coast to Kings Cross Station passed in a blur except for the moment the old Scottish woman sitting across from me poked me in the knee to tell me that they should have put an Angel of the South on the way down to London, the exact same as the one to the north.

'Big as a jumbo jet, them wings, love,' she insisted. 'Over sixty feet high, the Angel of the North. Copper and steel. Largest angel statue in the world. No one hae ever seen one, the maker said, which was why he put one there: tae remind us tae *believe.'*

Fearing the launching into of something, I gave her a quick glance and tight-lipped smile, before looking down again at the newspaper I'd been pretending to read.

They don't look anything like that, I wanted to tell her. *Nothing ever as rigid or fixed.* But I didn't. I looked mad enough in my dirt-covered farm slicker, with the shadow of black soil under my fingernails, and my cracked lips and bloodshot eyes. I probably looked like I badly needed saving.

When I caught her still staring at me, I folded my newspaper into a fat, pillow-shaped rectangle and placed it between my head and the window. Then I pretended to doze for the rest of the trip down from Newcastle to London.

At King's Cross station it's only a few minutes on the Tube to Shaun's place. I don't know what I'll find, or even if he's still there. But when I walk out of the station and hurry past council flats nestled hard up against trendy new apartment complexes and shabby storage warehouses, the clatter of an eastbound train in the distance, I could be that kid again: the one who couldn't talk properly for weeks after being let out of rehab, just a jumpy bundle of bones and nerves and skin.

It was a month before I could bring myself to look Shaun Kassmeyer in the eye. After I left him and the East End, I never went back again. Model friends used to joke I was the world's biggest snob because you couldn't pay me good money to set foot north past Whitechapel Road. But it wasn't snobbery that kept me away. It was the risk of bumping into Shaun — who knew me at my lowest, when there were moments it seemed I was ready to die.

My steps slow as I enter the small asphalt car park packed with rusting early-model cars. I look up at the swinging metal sign hanging outside the red-brick Victorian public bath-house with its arched windows and pitched roof that is now one of the most famous boxing gyms in London.

The sign says simply *The Pound*, stark white on royal blue, exactly the way I remember it.

Everything is.

I shiver, but not from the cold. It's as if I've fallen through a black hole and gone back in time seven years. I even look the same way I used to, before I cut off all my hair and dyed it midnight and walked out of the East End in a pair of studded, high-heeled combat boots, someone shiny and new.

I push through the swing doors and the familiar sounds and smells hit me immediately like a boxing glove to the face: the squeak of trainers on the floor and the hammering of speedballs, the humid stink of worn rubber and men forever trapped inside the huge, echoing, tiled space. Back then, I was ready to throw up, or run screaming, and Shaun had placed his big, muscular body between me and the doors, knowing I was that close to trying.

'Why *the Pound*?' Shaun had asked rhetorically, showing me around beneath the slanting glass skylights in the pitched ceiling. 'It was an in-joke, see? A place for lost dogs. Like me and my business partner Danny Alizhad. But also,' and I heard the fierce pride in Shaun's voice, 'it means that pound for pound we've some of the best fighters in Britain. None finer.'

My lidded gaze was furious and wary as I took in the hanging punching bags being given a steady workout by lines of young men and women, the sets of chin-up bars all occupied by sweating, straining bodies. In the middle of the room there stood a raised, old-style boxing ring where two women were gloving up in separate corners: blue gloves versus red gloves. To my immediate right was a large, gym-matted area where a man in a white *jujutsu gi* was throwing another man onto the ground.

Surveying the room from the doorway, it hasn't changed much. Maybe there are a few more photos crowded in among the Hall-of-Famers, but the cavernous chamber is packed with men and women of every age, size, colour, all moving, restless with energy, bravado, nerves. The boys on the chin-up bars nearest the door — maybe Pakistani or Indian — ease themselves down, curiosity written all over their faces at the sight of me. One makes his way immediately into the tiny office off the main training area with the graceful, gliding step of a trained fighter.

Two seconds later Shaun Kassmeyer is standing in the doorway looking out at me over the heads of some mixed martial arts fighters — a hardcore-looking group of men and women — throwing huge Soviet-style kettle bells around on the gym mats like they're plastic beach toys. Shaun doesn't make a move forward, just crosses his arms and glares across at me with burning amber eyes, and I feel a wave of hot shame. I almost turn and go back out the front door. Why would I even think he'd want to help me after all this time?

When it looked like the hospital was finally going to let me out after weeks of setbacks and rehab, I refused to go back to Mama Kassmeyer's. It was her fault that I'd been smack bang in the wrong place, at the wrong time; that's what I'd told myself.

So one of her former foster sons — who'd loved and respected her so much he'd changed his surname to hers by deed poll — arranged to have me taken in by a female friend for the remaining few weeks of my legal guardianship. He also arranged for daily self-defence classes and a place at a local comprehensive school but, on my eighteenth birthday, exactly the way I'd promised myself, I cut and dyed my hair jet black, got myself some new kit, and walked away without saying goodbye. New me, new life. Easy as pie.

The kid who called Shaun out of his office wraps his big hands back around the chin-up bar beside me now. 'G'wan,' he tells me, grinning, 'the man's waiting. Won't bite. Not hard, at least.' A few guys, eavesdropping nearby, snigger.

As I step forward hesitantly, Shaun turns and goes back into the little office with the chipped blue door. But he doesn't shut it. And I take that as a sign that he'll at least hear me out.

He doesn't look up from the blizzard of paperwork on his desk as I come through into the tiny space that's little more than a broom cupboard. It hits me again how big Shaun is — shoulders, neck, powerful forearms, quads like a wrestler, six four if he's anything. Would have been a sensation on the catwalk with his bright eyes and hard cheekbones if he didn't think 'fashwan' was some kind of collective mental illness. I'm looking down now on his head of short, dark-gold corkscrew curls, the smooth, coffee-coloured skin on the back of his neck, and the pit of my stomach lodges somewhere in my throat. It's been too long, and there are no words.

He skewers me finally with a quick upward flick of his unusual amber eyes — the legacy of an Afrikaner father and mixed-race mother. 'Caught you on the news once,' he growls, his teeth very white and even, the mark of his personal prowess as a boxer. 'Danny pointed you out a few years ago. Said he was sure the woman in the front row of that fashion show on the news where the famous Russian supermodel fell straight down on her bony arse, was *you*. Didn't look like you.' He gives my mousy plaits, dusty oil-slicker, jeans and muddy leather boots a dismissive, up-down glance.

Wordlessly, I sink into the visitor's chair crammed in on the other side of Shaun's child-sized desk and lick my cracked lips.

'Before then,' he adds crisply, 'I thought you was *dead*. You were this feeble, bruised-looking little thing with no skills, and when you did a runner you still had none. You had *future murder victim* written all over you.'

He gives me that quick up-down look again and I can see him thinking, *Nothing's changed.*

'I did stop by before I...left,' I almost whisper, 'but you weren't in. I told Danny to tell you I was going. Didn't he tell you?'

Shaun pushes away from me abruptly in his lumpy black office chair like he finds me mortally offensive, and the thing creaks in violent protest.

He points a hard, callused finger at me. 'Because Danny took off on tour with some of his boys to Belfast right after you left here, he failed to mention how you'd struck out in a new direction for *three whole days*. Faiza thought you'd been abducted. She actually reported you missing to the police. You can imagine how Mama Kass felt about that. It was *my* watch you were on. I promised no harm would come to you — but you took off.'

It hurts me to swallow. 'I'm really sorry,' I mumble finally.

'Just a postcard or a fucking phone call would have sufficed,' Shaun snaps, his entire body rigid with anger. 'Now you're six years too late. Get lost.'

He pushes his chair back in towards his desk and returns his gaze to the balance sheet in front of him. When the silence grows truly uncomfortable, he says quietly, but with no less menace, '*Go.*'

I scoot my own plastic chair forward until my knees are touching his desk and reach out with trepidation, putting one of my small hands over his. The knuckles of Shaun's left hand are misshapen and covered in scars, but it's not pain that makes him suck in his breath. It's shock — because I'm touching him. He stares at the point where our hands meet, and it hits me how far I've come. I was never a touchy-feely person, couldn't bear anyone to even come near me, or give me direction — for good bloody reason — and I see him remembering that.

He looks up at me, his amber eyes darkening, and mutters, 'What are you doing here?'

I say with a tremor in my voice that I can't keep out, 'It's been *seven* years, Shaun, not six. I've been keeping track too.'

Then I tell him a story that makes his golden eyes widen, makes him forget profit and loss statements, rostered-on trainers, the sound of men and women pushing themselves to the absolute limit, just for a little while.

6

After I finish describing Dunstanburgh Castle to him — I even get him to look it up on his phone so that he can see the sheer scale of it — Shaun is very quiet. All the way through my potted summary of the last seven years he asked me question after question. But when it came to the part about Ryan, Lucifer, Azraeil and the Archangel Gabriel — and how it might be possible that I'd be required to assist some kind of bodiless creature to commit murder — he listened with a mounting look of anger on his hard, handsome face.

'I'm *clean*,' I insist, knowing exactly how it must sound. 'The only thing I ever got remotely dirty on was champagne, ciggies and lager. Oh, it was on offer: Irina was a cokehead most of the time I was with her. And she tried everything: speed, ice, crack, liquid meth. But it was the hospital, actually, that kept me straight all these years. I never liked how the painkillers made me feel. I wasn't myself when I was on them, and I never wanted to feel that way again. I'm telling you the *truth*, Shaun. Scout's honour.'

I make the sign of an X over my heart and my slicker rustles.

Shaun pushes away from his desk again, this time so far back that his tight curls brush against the whitewashed brick wall behind him. He replies, with scepticism and that touch of anger that's tightening all his features, 'But we don't have a specific training program here regarding *satanic* beings. I'm not sure how you think I can *help* you.'

I told myself the same thing, the whole time I was packing up my stuff, all the way down from the North in the train: no martial art existed on this earth, right, that would guard against attack by malignant and/or demonic creatures. Who was I kidding?

But it was almost instinctual to seek Shaun out. He knew things 'normal' people didn't. Faiza told me as much when I found myself sleeping on the sofa in her tiny studio flat. 'I know Brick Lane's just around the corner, Gia, but he can speak *fluent* Pashto, Farsi and Urdu,' she told me once over a TV dinner. 'These are not languages you just pick up at the laundrette, darl. And especially not when you've been raised in a series of foster homes all over the South of England because your abusive father brutally bashed your mother to death when you were five. Shaun doesn't think I know he can, but I do. People…talk. Before he opened the gym with Danny, the two of them used to disappear for months at a time. Then suddenly they're home again and Shaun will be standing on a train platform at two in the morning and "disabling" — barehanded, mind — three drunken hoons who've come at him with knives because they don't like the colour of his skin. He's not normal, love. Best to do as he says.'

Shaun hasn't aged a day since I've been gone, and he doesn't appear to have gotten any softer or slower either. 'Just make me strong, make me fast,' I say quietly now. 'Teach me the things I was supposed to have learnt from you after I left the hospital. That's all. I'm making up for lost time with a vengeance. Anything that comes at me — and let's assume for simplicity it'll be human in appearance like they always are on the telly

— I need to be able to handle myself.'

Shaun stretches suddenly and rolls his head in a couple of quick circular motions that don't disguise his weariness.

He looks up at the old clock hanging above the door of his office and I glance at it, too, meeting the curious eyes of at least half a dozen young men peering in through the open doorway. Most are pretending to do sets of barbell curls or dead lifts, but some are just openly staring at us. On the mats, the MMA crowd has just finished their kettle-bell workout and I know I look nothing like the female fighter with the grey dreadlocks and pronounced biceps, pecs and lats, nothing like the broad-shouldered, whippet-lean young woman in the corner warming down with a set of goblet squats using a kettle bell the size of a bowling ball.

'It's late,' Shaun rasps finally, pulling my gaze back to him. 'And Danny's away in the Midlands at an exhibition boxing match. As you know, this place never stops. I can't just drop everything to help you get strong enough or fast enough to take down the, like, Devil, yeah? You'll just have to fit in around everyone else's programs. But there's no sense in wasting time…since you're here now.'

Lifting his gaze into the middle distance abruptly, Shaun calls out, 'Summer?'

The younger MMA woman stops mid-goblet squat, butt almost touching the ground, and fires back, 'Yeah, boss?'

Shaun gives me that up-down look again, shouting back through the door to the woman who has now straightened up, kettle bell cradled easily against her hard abdomen, 'Start with five-kilogram handweights for this one, progressing up to tens if she can bear it. I want a program of swings, squats, lunges and farmer's walks for the farm girl — says she needs strength and speed training, like, yesterday. Make it happen.'

The woman innocuously called *Summer* looks across at me with her dark almond-shaped eyes, flicks her ponytail of Goth-black, poker-straight hair out of her face, and gives me a grin full of rose-gold grills that makes me recoil.

ॐ

It's well past my dinnertime. At the farm I sometimes ate my evening meal when it got dark and then went to bed — because there was nothing else to do. And then I'd wake well before dawn, cursing, because I was hungry and needed badly to pee.

It's exactly the way I feel now.

I groan as I roll over onto my side on the gym mats, my borrowed gym gear soaked through with sweat, every part of my body trembling and on fire.

'He hasn't said you can stop, love,' Summer says, almost kindly, in her strong Manchester accent. She helps me sit up and I almost flop over again, unable to control my neck, arms, hands, face, spine.

'What are you hoping to achieve?' Summer asks, abruptly pushing my head down towards my outstretched knees so far that I let out a loud groan. I thought the farm had hardened me up plenty, but it's clear it hasn't. Carrying two-kilogram bags of heirloom potatoes for short distances has done nothing for my flexibility or my strength. I'll probably just die right here, and never mind what Mercy wants.

Gasping as Summer finally lets me up, I rasp, 'To take and give *pain*.'

Summer flashes me that disconcerting mouth full of rose-gold grill work again and sits down on the gym mat facing me, pushing the dusty soles of her bare feet up against mine. 'Well, you've come to the right place,' she says as she lunges forward and grabs my hands, starts pulling them down towards my own toes. I can't help shrieking. Nearby, heads whip around; there's a scattering of laughter and catcalls.

'To be strong, to be a good fighter, you need to be flexible, loose, *relaxed*,' Summer breathes as the sweat pours off me. I feel like the backs of my thighs, my hamstrings, are going to snap. 'And you have to believe you can do *anything*, because anything is guaranteed to come at you in a street fight.'

Shaun looms suddenly and Summer lets me go so abruptly that the momentum causes me to fall over. I lie on my back and all I can see is Shaun's silhouette standing over me, his muscular shoulders and head of short, tight curls blocking out the light from the industrial pendant lamp overhead.

Summer's voice is wicked. 'Can I go now, boss? The farm girl's just about taken all she can stand today, I reckon.'

I can't summon the strength to move, let alone sit up. Summer springs lightly to her feet and joins Shaun, who is looking down on me with the shadow of a puzzled frown on his face. 'You heard what she wants?' Summer asks him.

By way of an answer, Shaun murmurs, 'We are very much in the business of dishing out pain, so she's come to the right place. Jamie's agreed to take her in.'

Summer turns and stares at Shaun in open astonishment. 'Jamie? You can't be serious. She's not ready for a house guest. She may never be ready.'

'What about Faiza?' I say hopefully, not liking the look on Summer's face. I loved the kind-hearted young Palestinian woman who took me in years ago, and didn't thank her properly when I left. If Shaun and Summer are anything to go by, Jamie will be some kind of ex-military, cage-fighting hard-arse.

'Faiza's got three kids now,' Shaun replies absently, still frowning down on me. 'And Jamie is an expert on pain.'

Shit, is my immediate reaction. 'I could go to a hotel,' I say as I reach for my discarded slicker and shrug it on; so shaky I miss both sleeves first time around.

Shaun continues staring at me in silence.

'I'm good for it,' I insist. 'Working in fashion almost did my head in, but the spoilt freaks of nature I fetched and carried for pretty much set me up for life. I've got cash. I can take care of myself.'

Shaun bends and helps me sit up. 'No,' he murmurs. 'This will be good for both of you. Jamie *needs* this. And her place is practically spitting distance from here. It's perfect.'

Summer looks at the two of us as she pulls her ponytail higher and shrugs on a hot pink track top. 'You be kind to Jamie,' she growls at me menacingly, 'you don't upset her — or I'll beat you up tomorrow, good and proper, yeah?' She gives us both an ironic *later* half-salute and stalks away.

'What did she mean, "be kind"?' I ask Shaun as he pulls the hood of his black puffer jacket up over his bright hair and ushers me outside the Pound, handing me my duffle bag.

Shaun looks at me quickly but doesn't stop walking. 'Let's see how much you've changed in seven years,' is all he says as I struggle to keep up with him on my shaky, burning legs.

&

It's past 9 pm and the streets are freezing and deserted as we pass a Sainsbury's Local then a Tesco Metro. After stopping to buy takeaway curry and chips at a hole-in-the-wall place called Curry Dhaba where everyone greets Shaun with loud affection, we duck out of the high street strip and into a residential street called Derbyshire Row that is filled with narrow, post-war two-storey terraces built shoulder-to-shoulder, only a low fence and small square of tired grass separating house from pavement. One window down, two up.

There's a porch light on beside the front door to Jamie's house, which is dark brown brick with white window frames, just like everybody else's.

What sets Jamie's place completely apart from the surrounding terraces are the metal bars across all the street-facing windows, the heavy steel mesh security door and the glass shards cemented along the edge of the roof. The security camera mounted above the front entrance moves when we do.

'It's like Fort Knox with all the charm of a supermax prison,' I say dryly as Shaun rings the doorbell. 'Good choice.'

'You'll understand why in a second,' he says quellingly as he stamps his worn trainers on the footpath to keep warm.

The lights on the inside stairs come on, but no one comes to the door.

'What's taking so long?' I complain, my breath coming out in a cloud of white.

'I expect she's regretting the call she made me,' Shaun says quietly. 'I had my hand on the phone, about to ring around to see if anyone wanted to take you, when I picked it up and...' he looks at me and his eyes are wide with remembered shock, '*she was already on the line.*'

The cold is clearly making me stupid. 'What do you mean, she was already on the line? So what if she was?'

'So I'd just lifted the receiver to punch in her number and she was already waiting to speak to me. No rings, nothing. It's like I thought of giving her a call and she just...called.'

I shiver inside my clothes, and not from the icy air.

The same shiver is in Shaun's voice as he adds, 'And Jamie said immediately, "Tell that girl I'll take her. She can stay here." Those were her exact words. Not even a greeting. I hadn't even told her *about* you yet. She had no way of knowing why I was calling. And you've got to understand — Jamie hasn't wanted to see anyone, or go anywhere for over a year. Not since it...happened.'

I shake my head, completely lost.

Behind the security door, the front door opens slowly and there's the sound of a security chain being tested.

'Shauny?' The voice is husky, young, female: with a slight babyish lisp as if the woman's tongue is too big for her mouth.

'Hello, Jamie love,' Shaun says gently, and she opens the inner door wider, then the heavy steel security door, and something in me flips over. I actually raise my hands to my mouth, covering it in horror.

Her *face*.

My god — her face.

7

I swallow hard, fighting back the urge to be violently sick.

It's hard to tell what colour Jamie's skin used to be because it's mottled all over with patches that are different shades of white and pale brown. She doesn't have a mouth, more just a darker, mouth-shaped smear. One of her hazel eyes is gone, the lids fused shut. And what's left of her nose is a misshapen dab of flesh, like something's chewed on her face.

I have to tell myself to force my hands back down, casually, to my sides, swallowing to get rid of the bitter taste flooding my mouth. I wrench my eyes away from the woman's ruined features and stare hard at the tops of my boots. All of me is hot and sick and sweaty, where before I was almost rigid with the cold.

I have been tortured to the point of death, so I *recognise* pain. When I see someone in pain, I can feel it: it takes me over. It's like a communion of anguish; everything hurts. I could be them, they could be me; it's hard to explain.

The woman makes an unhappy sound low in her throat, turning away and trying to scramble back inside her house because of me and my stupid, knee-jerk reaction. But her frantic movements still the moment Shaun gently places a huge, scarred hand on her shoulder. Jamie doesn't turn back to look at me, though she isn't trying to bolt any more. But her head is lowered, like she's listening for sounds of danger on the wind. And I recognise that, too, because I would find myself doing the same thing for a long time afterwards. Anything would startle me: a sound, a smell, a movement.

'You don't have to take her if you don't want to. You're allowed to change your mind, Jamie,' Shaun says quietly into the back of the woman's shoulder-length, synthetic brunette wig.

The woman's narrow, rigid shoulders suddenly slump. I find that I am hugging myself tightly, as she pushes open her front door finally, and leads us inside.

Behind us, Shaun locks up: twist lock, deadlock, chain. The house is mostly in darkness except for the light spilling down the stairs, and a desk lamp in a study filled with humming computer equipment to my immediate right. What's clear, as I follow the skeletal woman down the dim central corridor into a sitting room in the back, is that there are no mirrors in the house. As we pass a small washroom, I notice that where a mirrored bathroom cabinet should be is just a blank expanse of wall. The hallway walls are also bare of reflective surfaces.

Jamie turns on the kitchen fluorescent and waves over her shoulder at Shaun and me to take a seat while she hurries into her cramped galley kitchen and bangs mugs and plates together, filling and switching on an electric kettle. Shaun dumps the plastic bag of takeaway on the edge of the kitchen bench before taking the sofa nearby. Scanning the sparsely furnished space, I take an overstuffed velour armchair beside the TV on the far side of the room for safety, sitting right on the edge of it, knees pressed tightly together to stop myself visibly shaking.

Under the sound of the boiling kettle, I hiss accusingly, 'You should have *told* me.'

'She didn't want me to tell you.' Shaun's reply is even and

very low. 'She was quite specific about that.'

The kettle goes quiet and a moment later, Jamie is handing me a mug with a green tea bag in it, together with a fork and a plate piled high with a soft lentil curry, rice and chips. It had all smelled heavenly when we walked out of Curry Dhaba, but now my jaws are clenched so tightly together I can't eat. I put the plate down beside my chair and cradle the mug of tea.

Jamie sees me looking down at the surface of it because I don't want to seem like I'm staring at her face. 'Sorry,' she says huskily, misunderstanding my hesitation. 'I wasn't really...prepared for visitors. Usually I wear a mask.' She clears her throat, adding, 'Actually, I've got two — one for day, one for night. You kind of caught me between costume changes.'

I feel my eyes fill with sudden tears. 'You have *nothing* to be sorry for,' I reply fiercely, taking a sip of the scalding tea to hide the tremor in my voice.

Jamie hands Shaun his own dinner and steaming drink before sitting down gingerly beside him clutching her own mug.

'Neither do you,' Jamie lisps. 'It wasn't your fault.'

She sounds so sure about that that tears actually fall out of my eyes then, into my tea. I put it down on the floor beside the plate of food, grateful for the low lighting in the room as I sit forward, resting my crossed arms on my knees.

I take a deep, shaky breath. 'I've never wanted anyone to know.'

'Everyone knows about *me*: it's all online,' Jamie replies as I look up in horror. 'Copped a face full of acid in broad daylight, didn't I?' Her voice is matter-of-fact. 'Morning rush hour, like. Was just sitting there, at the bus stop, when this bloke come up with an open bottle I thought was fizzy drink. As he walks past, he just nailed me with it.'

Jamie makes a throwing gesture with one hand, then runs her palm down over her ruined eye and her throat. Appalled, I see that the skin disappearing into her pink mock turtleneck pullover is a puckered mess of hardened, shiny scar tissue that doesn't even resemble skin.

'I don't really remember what happened after that. They showed me on the news, I think, running into this newsagent across the road, screaming my head off. Lost both my shoes, my handbag, dropped the lot. My clothes, my skin — all melting off my body. All these strangers throwing bottled water on me. I don't remember any of it from the point where that man *smiled* at me — like I was his friend. But I can see it whenever I want, because it's all out there, forever, innit?'

Jamie goes silent, takes a small sip of her tea. She looks across at Shaun suddenly as if she's just remembered him being in the room and urges him to, 'Eat up, love, before it gets cold.'

Shaun gives her a little squeeze-pinch at the point where her shoulder meets the top of her arm and starts obediently shovelling the soft, cooling mess into his mouth quickly and efficiently like someone might take it off him at any moment. He eats like a little kid, wanting to get it over and done with so that he can go out and play, not even really chewing properly. I have to remember not to stare in open fascination. Seven years ago I didn't want to look him in the face, let alone watch him do anything as intimate as eat.

'Please,' Jamie tells me, indicating the plate at my feet.

'What about you?' I counter, picking it up off the floor and taking one or two experimental bites. It's delicious, but my throat feels too tight to swallow and I put it down again.

'Maybe later.' She pulls an expression that tightens the smear of her mouth sideways, and I realise that she's trying to smile.

'Was it a…random?' I murmur.

'The way it was with you?' she says, and I go cold, wondering again how she can sound so sure. Apart from the hospital and the police, no one's ever known — beyond the barest outline — about what happened to me because I've made sure of it. My policy all these years has been that if I don't talk about it, it never happened. I'm not someone's bloody *victim* and especially not that bastard's.

'No and yes,' Jamie rasps. 'The guy who did it was a friend of an ex-boyfriend I had a restraining order against. Never seen him before in my life and now I'll never forget what he looks like, not ever.'

Her laughter is harsh, like the squawk of a bird. 'I was a pin-up girl, grid girl, ring-card girl, did promotional work at nightclubs, local events, you know? Everyone knew me; my face was my calling card. It's how I've still got Shauny looking out for me, because I was on the scene, you know? Worked loads of his fights.'

'You were beautiful,' I say without thinking.

'*Are* beautiful,' Shaun interjects, still chewing.

'I wasn't even that.' My voice is stony. 'I was a flat-chested seventeen-year-old with the body of a child and freaky two-tone eyes. *Random* doesn't even begin to describe what happened to me. How that man and I crossed paths that day? How he happened to find *me*? Me, and not some other poor bitch? I will never know.'

I don't give Jamie any more detail of the devastating crime that put me on full life support for three weeks after a raging lung infection took hold. But I do tell her about what happened in Milan two years ago, and about how Mercy and the Archangel Gabriel reappeared in my life, 'Like, yesterday. And all I could think was: *Shaun can help.*' I don't look at him as I say the words, but they can both tell I'm speaking the truth. Jamie is silent for a long time. I catch that faint look of disgusted disbelief again in Shaun's expression as he turns and slides his empty plate and mug onto the kitchen bench behind him. He crosses his arms behind his head, his stern gaze on me bringing unaccustomed heat to my face.

His voice breaks the silence. 'If you believe a word of any of that, Jamie, I'm supposed to get her hard enough to take on *Satan*.'

'The other one will take him on,' Jamie responds calmly. 'That's not Gia's fight to have.'

I actually drop my mug of tea in shock at her words, and scramble around on the floor with some dirty tissues from my pocket to try to soak up some of the wetness and hide my confusion.

Jamie adds, voice thoughtful, 'Gia just wants the man with the two skull tattoos.'

Still on my hands and knees on the floor, I go rigid. I've never told anyone that part other than the police, and it was information they decided to hold back from the public — that the man who attacked me had another tattoo of an undone zipper running down from his collarbone into his pelvis. When you looked at it, you got the horrific impression he'd been split open somehow, just to show you the darkness inside. From the edge of the 'unzipped' area around the man's abdomen a skull peered out; as if someone dead was trying to climb out of his warm entrails.

'And he's very much *human*,' Jamie muses, as if from a long way away. 'Something you can definitely prepare Gia for, Shaun.'

For a second, the room goes black in front of my eyes. Shaun surges forward and deposits me back into my armchair before I can hit the carpet face-first.

'How do you even *know* any of this?' I say fearfully. 'Apart from the people assigned to my case, I never told anyone about the other tattoo. The police said not to release...' I swallow. 'Even Mama K and Shaun never knew. I never said.'

Shaun gives my shoulder a quick squeeze.

Jamie doesn't answer my question and her reply is brisk. 'You don't have long, Gia, love. When they come for you, you have to be ready. There are no second chances. Which means you need to get your rest now; you've got some big days ahead of you. There's bags to do if you want to get proper beastly, girl, before you meet the Rebel bloody Prince of Darkness himself.'

Jamie bustles Shaun out of the room on the promise that I'll attend the Pound bright and early in the morning. I hear the murmur of their voices out in the hall before there's the sound of all the locks being opened and then armed again. After taking the plates and cups back into the kitchen, Jamie leads me upstairs. And it kills me how everything about her seems so normal until she turns around and the horror is written right there on her skin.

She lays a towel, facecloth, soap and shampoo out on the end of the single bed in her spare room, pointing out the shared bathroom between her room and this one, before vanishing back downstairs into her study.

When I turn out my light, I know she's still down there, working on her computer, because the thin strip of light under the door, the sound of tapping, tell me so.

⁊

When I wake, it's still dark. For a long moment, I'm completely disoriented. I know I'm not in the little stone bedroom in

Craster any more, but the way the bed's oriented I *could* be in that shared loft packed with fashion people in Gramercy Park, or in the heritage palazzo apartment near the Via Veneto that Irina's management insisted we use when she had editorial work to do in Rome. But then I hear the sound of a clock radio going off, followed by the familiar musical intro of an early-morning London talk show that's been going for years, and I realise where I am and sit bolt upright.

When I walk out into the upstairs hallway I see a flash of shocking pink go past the partly open bedroom door across the hall.

Jamie — in a skin-tight, hot-pink ski mask that hugs the shape of her face and skull and extends all the way from the top of her head into the neckline of her cotton pyjama top, just one hazel eye and her mouth showing — freezes as she turns and catches me gaping in the darkness of the hallway in my tee-shirt and bare legs. Tight fingerless bandages of the same hot pink extend up under Jamie's sleeve cuffs.

Without a word, she raises a bandaged hand and gently shuts her bedroom door in my face.

Feeling numb, I pivot on one heel and stumble into the bathroom, shutting the door and throwing freezing water on my skin. There's no mirror in here either, but I'm sure my eyes look huge and bruised and fearful.

When I come out, there's a tumble of shiny lycra exercise gear on my bed — mostly pink, because pink appears to be Jamie's favourite colour and nothing's ever going to change that. I pick out a black tank top and a pair of black compression tights before pulling on a heavyweight navy jumper and some trainers from out of my duffle, topping the mismatched outfit off with my dusty navy slicker.

By the time I make it downstairs, Jamie is already sliding

a plate loaded with eggs, bacon, beans and tinned sausages across at me, together with a cup of instant coffee. In place of the bright pink pressure bandages, she's wearing a tight, clear plastic face mask with holes cut out in it for her eyes, mouth and nostrils and her brunette wig is centred firmly on her head, looking almost natural. But even the dreary early morning light can't hide the full-thickness burns beneath the plastic. I have to force my breakfast down under her steady gaze.

She doesn't drink her own coffee, and she doesn't eat anything.

'Sorry if I gave you a scare last night,' is all Jamie says huskily. 'Sometimes I forget what I must look like to other people.'

'Does it…hurt you to eat?' I blurt out, suddenly realising why the woman's so thin and her voice sounds the way it does. The damage isn't just on the outside. The smiling son of a bitch probably got acid right down her throat.

'It hurts to be alive,' she says briskly with her twisted smile, before clearing my plate away and sending me out the door with the cheerful exhortation, 'Go get militant, all right?'

∂כ

No one gives me a second glance when I reach the Pound. There are kids everywhere doing their morning workout, coming and going all the time. I can't see Summer today, and Shaun is running a hardcore personal training session on the mats with a muscular man-mountain who has shoulders like a woodworking sawhorse. A bit self-consciously, I commandeer an empty chin-up bar by the door and hang there pathetically for as long as I can take it, straining to count to twenty before dropping down, exhausted, the skin on my palms burning.

I do that a few more times until the West Indian guy doing muscle-ups on the bar beside me says disgustedly, 'Don't let it lick you up, girl! Where your head be at?'

For emphasis, he shoves his own head of tight black curls up and over the bar to show me what he's talking about and I roll my eyes at him before managing just one trembly almost-chin-up — more like a desperate forehead lunge — before I move on to a punching bag in the corner.

A girl with a heavy Slavic accent and light brown hair in tight cornrows grabs the bag while I'm jabbing at it and I freeze warily. 'I spot you,' she growls and I let her hold it steady with her bandaged hands while I rabbit punch away at the bag until I can't lift my jelly arms any longer and I've got stinging grazes across my knuckles. As soon as it looks like I'm done, the girl takes my place despite the disgruntled catcalls of the men and women who've been waiting in line, watching. I can hear the sound of her drilling it — hard and clean, the steel chain rattling, no let-up — as I cross to the drinking fountain in the corner.

A passing Asian boy with a sculptural undercut and pecs bursting out of his tight, shiny red singlet says, 'He wants you to do some box jumps next,' indicating a bunch of wooden boxes of different shapes and sizes with a jerk of his head. I look around, but Shaun is back inside his poky office, arguing loudly with someone on the telephone.

As I reluctantly drag out the shortest box — which is twenty inches more than I feel like jumping off the ground — and start leaping onto it from a bent-kneed, standing start, I can't even see Shaun any longer. But it's like that all morning: no sooner am I wiped out from one thing than I'm directed to continue with an entirely new activity by a complete stranger. No one's exactly friendly, but no one's paying me out too badly, either. It's more that I'm some pathetic group project people have agreed to take on but not really talk about.

'Everyone's got a right to be bangin', love, and at least you're trying,' a man in sweat-soaked boxing gear tells me kindly as he loads weight plates onto the end of the twenty-kilogram cylindrical steel bar I'm struggling to hold straight in front of me.

Just before noon, after a wobbly round of baby deadlifts, Summer glides over out of nowhere whispering gruffly in my ear, 'Go grab some lunch, yeah? After my kickboxing class, we'll work on your blocking and side-stepping.' Even the question isn't a question. Bouncing off the walls because I can't walk straight, I head out into the surrounding streets looking for something fatty and deep-fried because that's what my entire body is screaming out for.

After I return, Summer teaches me the basics of blocking. ('Both hands up like blades! Protect your head! Watch my elbows to see where the hits are coming from! Keep it loose! Move, move, move, move, *MOVE*.') She gets a crowd of eager young men to come at me from every angle — front, sides, back — teaching me the basics of side-stepping and deflection until I stop tripping over my own feet in my rush to get out of striking range. When I don't think I can stand it a moment longer, Summer then cements all the theory by rushing me repeatedly with a red body-length punching shield until the act of defending myself, and maintaining my stance, is almost automatic. If I don't defend, I fall to the ground. Simple as that.

There's stinging sweat running into my eyes, pooling between my clavicles, but it's like Summer is made of solid iron. She's not even breathing hard as she pummels me with the shield, repeatedly driving me right off the mats so that I fall on my arse on the hard ground. The thought occurs to me more than once, as I'm flung off balance, that Irina Zhivanevskaya, with her sharp *pivot-turn-flounce* manoeuvre, aggressive hip and shoulder moves and bitch-slapping tendencies, would have been a natural at this stuff.

I don't always manage to stay on my feet, but I'm finally throwing both arms up to protect my centre line, my head and my 'gates' the way Summer's been screaming at me to do all afternoon. I'm not quick enough to sidestep everything that's coming at me, or turn the deflections into attacks — mainly because I've broken through the zero-energy barrier — but I think I'm starting to understand the basic mechanics.

Shaun doesn't appear again until the light coming through the glassed-in ceiling begins to fade and all the fluorescents snap on, one by one.

'Walk you back to Jamie's?' he offers casually.

I'm too exhausted even to snarl, 'And where have *you* been?'

We don't really talk on the way into or out of Curry Dhaba, although I do make him stop at the Tesco Metro so that I can pick out every flavour of pre-made blended soup I can find, for Jamie to try.

It's a re-run of the night before when we get to her place. But at least I manage to coax her into having some of the soup and am rewarded with the fleeting, twisted grimace that passes for her smile.

ౡ

Every day, over the next few weeks, I feel myself getting stronger and faster. I can use a short wooden baton now — without much elegance, admittedly — and Summer's taught me a clutch of illegal raw combat moves like how to crush someone's elbow and shoulder joints, or fracture the knee or the ankle, to slow the attack. She's got me doing weird combinations — *punch, knee, sweep* or *block, knee, elbow-to-the-base-of-the-skull* — and I've even perfected the flowing *tai qi*-looking move that's supposed to result in twisting someone's head right off their spine.

The day I manage to tip Shaun's best mate and business partner, Danny Alizhad, right off his feet — just for a second, before he rolls over and springs back up as lightly as a cat — I get even Shaun's grudging respect: a single grunt from the sidelines before he walks away. Danny is the same sleek, darkly handsome, Iranian-born troublemaker weighing over two hundred pounds that I remember from seven years ago, and I feel a burst of fierce pride before he comes right back at me with a series of aggressive hooks and crosses like the professional boxer he used to be.

'And here I was thinking you was all mouth and no trousers,' Danny grins as I duck and weave, one of his fists glancing painfully off the side of my face because my block is just a fraction too late.

But it's true — I'm not all talk now. I feel stronger. I can handle a level of pain the old A-list me wouldn't have tolerated for a second.

'You're a beast,' Summer puts it one night as I'm leaving. 'You've officially attained beast status, bitch,' she grins at me through her grills, 'and you owe me a bloody big beer, for starters.'

ॐ

I'm in my tee-shirt getting ready to climb into bed, everything aching, bruises up the wazoo, when there's a light tap at my closed door. Glancing at my clock radio, I see that it's just before eleven.

Jamie's always downstairs working on her computer at this time of night, so whatever it is she wants to tell me must be important.

I open the door warily to Jamie in her loose cotton pyjamas and bright pink pressure bandages, which over the last few weeks she's taken to putting on before I even walk in the door.

'I have to show you something,' she says, and there's a strange hush in her voice.

I start for the stairs leading down to the study thinking the *something* must be on her computer, but Jamie stops me with one of her pressure-bandaged hands. 'No, *this* way,' she urges.

I watch as she walks into her dimly lit bedroom, past her neatly made-up double bed. She heads for the barred window that looks out onto the street below and hitches up one corner of the heavy blind.

Instantly, my skin goes hot. 'Is someone hassling you again? Is he out there right now?' My voice is shrill with tension.

I pivot immediately, crossing the landing for my phone, about to call Shaun, maybe the cops, when Jamie says hoarsely from behind me, 'He's not here for me, Gia — he's here for *you*.'

I stop dead and turn back slowly and, I swear, my heart skips a beat before I feel it pounding again, faster than before. Being back here with Shaun, training at his place in the East End, I've almost convinced myself that I've been in London all along these last seven years, and that Irina and Mercy — and the rest of it — are all things my diseased mind had made up.

As I drift back into her bedroom, Jamie draws me to the window and says gently, 'It's not my angel that's here. It's yours. Mine only ever told me you were coming and would need my help. But he said that when *yours* showed up...'

The woman in the skull-shaped bandages looks at me gravely with her one good eye as she indicates the street below. 'It would be time: *to do your best*.'

8

As Jamie lets me out of her house, I catch sight — through her open study door — of a bright humanoid blur on one of the monitors in the bank of computers. It's the thermal image of an exceptionally tall, well-proportioned man, picked out in a blazing spectrum of reds, oranges and yellows.

A man made of fire. No — of pure *energy*.

When I get outside, and cross over to where he's standing, he nods at me gravely but doesn't speak or try to take my hand, and it's a relief. My heart is too full for words. Seeing him again, feeling the crackle of energy that the Archangel Gabriel sends into the air around me, sends waves of feeling across my skin. It soon becomes clear that we're headed back towards the Pound and it has to be a miracle of some kind that the streets we walk to get there are completely empty. No one sees me limping along beside a flame-haired giant whose outline seems to shift and blur and curl into the night air. Part of me could walk beside him forever this way — just the two of us — the unyielding world beneath our feet.

My angel. If only.

The stars are cold and brilliant in the sky as I push through the swing doors of the boxing gym. As I walk across the gym mats, my trainers making small scuffing noises, I see that the place is in darkness save for a thin sliver of light shining from the partially open door of Shaun's tiny office.

'Hello?' I call out, stopping in the centre of the mats, wondering what it is that I'm supposed to be doing here just past eleven o'clock at night; if it's someone's idea of a joke.

Behind me, as Summer had done, Gabriel suddenly breathes, *Be kind.*

When I turn towards him in confusion, I see that he's gone, and that the air between me and where he was standing has begun to tease apart.

I step back in horror from this small point of *nothing* that's growing in the air before me — first along the vertical, then the horizontal, as if something's gone wrong with my eyes, like maybe I'm going blind — only to see a flash of colour that should not exist, within it.

As the rift begins to grow — sucking any remaining heat out of the air — I get a glimpse of an overarching, dark violet sky scattered with bright stars in formations I don't recognise, the gleaming bend of a serpentine black river winding below. The river, the sky, the stars, all obscure the wall of the boxing gym that I know should be right there.

Blinking rapidly does not dispel what I'm seeing: one world inside another.

Just over my left shoulder, a familiar figure throws wide the door to the office and my heart plunges as I hear him gasp.

I raise my hands frantically to indicate he should get back inside immediately and bolt the door.

But Shaun never does anything Shaun doesn't want to do. He moves closer to me protectively so that when *she* comes through — stepping out of the black river like a vengeful siren, the water sheeting off her body and leaving a sheen of silver in its place on her skin, in her long dark hair, in her eyes — Mercy sees him first.

And these burning blades, I swear, they come out of her hands and she surges towards him through the gap that shouldn't be there and before she can kill him with them — I can feel it in her, *Death*, moving — I throw myself straight at her.

Subsuming her.

᠌

The pain. I can't describe it.

There's a sharp, awful flare deep inside me — as if something damaged in me recognises the same thing in her — and we come together as if we are magnetic.

There's a clash and a convergence.

She's stronger than she was before, at the farmhouse in Craster. I can feel it. In the intervening weeks, she's evolved into something new, she's come fully into this new state, and every muscle in my body is straining to keep her in check because it's her and me both trying to be in the same place — the same body — at the same time. And I feel like I'm dying all over again, but I'm somehow also holding her back so that she can't touch him because I know that if she touches Shaun he will no longer *be*.

I feel her twist within me, her banshee scream pouring from my own mouth, and I catch Shaun springing away from me — *us* — looking up and up at a point well above my head, as if I'm over seven feet tall. Whatever this thing is that I'm doing, it's imperfect. She's bleeding through me, or she's trying to, because the feel of Mercy moving through me is like the feel of the blades she was holding in her hands.

But with every muscle of my body, with that strange scar that's somehow knotted deep in my soul that *sees* the scar in hers, I keep her anchored.

'*He's a good man*,' I pant. '*He's done nothing to you. He's. Not. The. One. You. Want.*'

The flare inside me pulses like lungs drawing breath as her scream echoes from the rafters. '*Then who is he to me?*'

She tries her best to shake me loose and the world becomes monstrous: every sense taken over as if by electricity, the world amplified and reverberating in waves of discordance as I thrash in place like I'm fighting my own nature.

But somehow I do it: hold her away from Shaun with every inch of my being.

'*Leave. Him. Alone*,' I gasp, imagining that I am the net in which she is caught. It's all I can do.

A net made of remembered pain.

Caught in the weave of me, shrieking, we burst into flame.

A kind of pale blue fire laced with silver is pouring off my skin now, lightening the air around me. I stagger backwards, away from the breach that opens onto the black river that runs through Sheol, struggling to keep Mercy from Shaun; who's retreated to the edge of the gym mats, fists up around his face, eyes huge as he tries to take in this *thing* that I've become.

I am flesh and blood fused with a cold, pure fire.

How is it that I'm still alive?

I know Shaun can somehow see her within me or around me because his eyes are darting everywhere, taking in distances and potential weapons, escape routes. All the things he's had his people drill into me for the last few weeks has been made absolutely real in this moment — except he's the one under attack now. She fights me every inch of the way, trying to get away from me to get to him.

For a moment, it's *me* speaking, me in control.

'*Shaun* —' my breath comes out in short, painful bursts, cloudy-white in the icy air, '*get out while you can. I can't…hold…her…for…much…longer.*'

I feel the net — made of my own remembered agony — beginning to slip.

Through me, I feel Mercy pause and study Shaun — really *look* at him, seeing him — and then she…stretches.

I get a shocking sense of how it would have felt to *be* her when she was alive. How incredibly strong she was, the way she would have stood, breathed, laughed, used her hands — everything so very different from me. There's some kind of shift, too, in her mood and her restless, questing energy, as she continues to look at him.

I am suddenly flooded with a cold clarity so powerful it's like a drug: I can feel the short blades she wields as if they are in my own hands, feel how they are *made* of her somehow, how she can see down into every particle of everything in this room in a way no human being ever could. I can't read her thoughts exactly — she won't let me in — but I know that she is calculating…something, I can feel it. Consequences.

Something here is being tried and tested.

Faster than I can believe, Mercy pivots — so I do, too — making a gesture of negation with the blade in her left hand. The rift in the air behind me just closes and the heavy, purple, star-filled sky, the black river of Sheol, all wink out of existence and there is only *one world* again.

Mine.

Immediately, the air seems ten degrees warmer, the vast space lit eerily by the electric light spilling from the open door of Shaun's office and by the hypnotic fire that's rolling off my skin in waves.

Suddenly, Mercy springs back into motion and I cannot stop her — *me* — lunging again towards Shaun with a hyper-fast, predatory grace.

Like a sprinter leaving the starting blocks, Shaun explodes across the room — arms and legs pumping — vaulting discarded weight plates, wooden boxes and mini tramps, throwing himself up and under the triple layer of ropes surrounding the boxing ring. Before he's even managed to scramble across the surface of the ring she — *we* — have sliced our way clean through the ropes, almost catching Shaun by the ankles before he has time to slither and fall out the other side onto the floor. Vaulting over the nearest turnbuckle and landing easily on the ground, we duck the gloves and hand weights Shaun throws in our path with negligent ease, sidestepping the peanut-shaped double-ended punching bag he slings in our direction, destroying a small army of freestanding bags on stands, stalking him calmly and deliberately as he tries to lose himself in a forest of suspended speedballs, heavy bags and wrecking balls.

It's like her blades are made of some corrosive element. Everything they touch — leather, synthetic, steel — shears through. We leave an exploded trail of sand, pebbles and dry maize in our wake, broken chains rattling as we pass.

Finally, in the far corner by the battalion of armless human torsos mounted on pedestals, Shaun has nowhere left to run.

We stop mere inches away from him and raise the short, luminous blade in our left hand so that the wicked point is levelled at his jaw. Flames lick from it in waves of silver-blue as if drawn towards his living energy. 'These blades were a demon's weapon of choice once,' she whispers through my lips. 'And now they are mine.'

Shaun's wild-eyed gaze flickers from point to point as he tries to take in me, her, the blades, the shattered room. I can feel his thoughts like trapped birds, beating against my skin. And then he surprises even Mercy — I feel her surprise — by dropping out of reach of the deadly point of the blade in her left hand with a swiftness that makes me catch my breath, sweeping me off my feet with a powerful kick.

Pain explodes through my legs. I feel the unyielding concrete rush up to meet me as I crash to the ground, badly winded, sending the forest of human-shaped torsos around us jittering on their stands. But Mercy laughs; a terrifying sound with such a strange, sonic afterbite to it that Shaun staggers, clutching at his ringing ears, as he struggles to regain his footing.

Mercy propels me to my feet — the room tilting crazily — in one fluid move, like a gymnast. But at no speed any earthly gymnast could match.

And I am standing again.

Shaun grasps at the only weapon within reach — a long steel bar discarded by the base of the wall just like the one I was deadlifting only hours ago. He grips it like a staff, putting it between me and him. But Mercy lunges forward abruptly, hissing like a snake, and it's me swinging the blade at Shaun's head only to have him duck and sidestep instinctually with only millimetres to spare. With preternatural speed, Mercy forces me to lunge again and the second blade we're holding catches Shaun's steel bar on the upswing, slicing it neatly in two, just nicking him across a cheekbone before he has time to fling his head backwards. For a shocking moment, the cut ends of the bar glow bright red before Shaun drops the burning steel rods with a cry, reeling backwards into one of the dummies, fingers curled over his scalded palms, blood running from the small cut on his face.

'On your knees,' Mercy growls. And I am suddenly

light-headed, imagining it to be *him* at last — the one who cast me down unto this earth — that I have him within my power after all these years of searching. I am giddy with this feeling of power and it's hers, too, because I am in her thoughts now. If only for this moment, *we are one*; as is our need for vengeance.

'I have waited so long,' we murmur aloud, our words sibilant, resonant, threatening. 'So very long.'

I'm shocked to find myself breathing heavily above Shaun's kneeling figure, his head of damp curls bowed in exhaustion. Both Mercy's blades are held crossed beneath his chin; I am holding them, my hands steady as a surgeon's.

In a single move, her whisper fills me, *we could take off his head, and have we not always wanted this?*

Mercy laughs again. And it is a kind of madness, to hear that vast sound rising through me to fill the cavernous room.

Shaun raises his head and looks me in the eye without flinching as she — *we* — take our crossed blades wide on either side of his neck to administer the killing blow.

I hear her think: *I could use a man like this at my side, and would it be so wrong to reap him now?*

There's a roar; I don't know, a blast of...coalescence? Of rising?

Something bright — brighter even than the sun — bursts into being in the space where Shaun was a moment before, and I rock backwards, shielding my face.

Gabriel takes form before me, his giant wings unfurling soundlessly, in one hand a flaming broadsword that burns a clean, bright blue.

Before I can move, he grasps the blade of his weapon in his right hand, bringing the great pommel and crossguards up in one smooth move from below and catching Mercy's crossed blades with a *crack* so powerful that all three weapons are snagged together. The room fills with light — blue and silver — and so much pressure that I can't tell whether it's in me, or around me.

'I can't, I'm sorry — ' I gasp tearfully into Gabriel's wrathful, beautiful countenance, so very close now. '*I can't hold her* —'

The net is breaking, it is true.

I'm breaking.

Gabriel gives me a smile to stop my heart. A smile just for me before he snarls at Mercy, '*Let her go. It is* enough.'

His words hang there for a moment.

'*Soror.*' His tone is dangerous, without a hint of strain, as he pushes us back easily with just the hilt of his flaming broadsword.

Sister. That's what he's called her — though they are equals in memory only. Now, they are beyond compare.

I feel a brief burst of sorrow before Mercy grates, looking up and out of my eyes dangerously, 'Your sister is *dead*, Gabriel, and this is all that remains.'

The last word rises like a scream, and I'm buffeted from inside; I'm brought to my knees by a sharp, stinging hail of feeling that I can only compare to a sandstorm, or needles of glass, piercing my soul.

I'm writhing on the ground.

Then this cloud of fine, silver-blue mist: it just swarms up and out of me, slipstreaming up towards the skylights before dispersing completely.

As I lose consciousness, I can sense Shaun there, smoothing the damp hair back off my face with his burnt hands, murmuring urgent things to me in a language I can no longer hear or understand.

And, I swear, there's an echo of laughter, of exultation.

9

I find myself walking beside that wide black river under a lightening violet sky. Whatever passes as day here — it's coming.

And she's waiting for me; she's seated on the riverbank, fragrant green-gold rushes crushed beneath her body. Her long legs are tucked beneath her chin, straight dark hair fallen down across her oval, strong-boned face. She's still dressed in black: the suggestion of a shirt, flowing trousers and soft black boots that seem to change shape, swimming in front of my eyes the longer I look at them, as if what she's really clothed in is shadow.

Mercy pushes back her heavy hair — as though to see me better — and gives me the kind of wry half-smile I remember from when she was Irina. It's weird to catch the same sardonic expression on a completely different face. I don't think I'll ever get used to it.

I'm pierced by an inexplicable happiness to see her like this. She seems younger and freer than I ever remember her being. She could be just a girl by a river, somewhere.

I sit beside her and she casts the smooth, round stone she's holding into the slow-flowing mass of black water. As it hits the surface, the water sprays up briefly, with that strange sheen of after-silver, before the stone sinks out of sight, concentric rings forming before the current swallows them.

'The Valley of the Shadow of Death,' I whisper, not knowing where the words come from, but knowing that it's true. It's where we are.

'Yes,' she says simply, then adds, 'For what it's worth, I'm sorry. I had to know if you could do it. And you *can*. You're stronger than you know.'

Her grin is fierce, then it fades. 'But next time — don't fight me so much. It will seem... easier. More bearable. He was very brave. Your Shaun.'

I shake my head to deny that he's my anything, but I finally understand what the test was and, strangely, feel no anger. Perhaps it's impossible to feel that way here.

'If that was supposed to be a dry run,' I say cautiously, because it's Mercy I'm talking to, and she's still capable of anything, even terrible violence beneath this gentle violet sky, 'Luc will see us coming a mile away. The flames, you know? That general sense of being on fire? It's a little hard to disguise.'

Mercy studies my face for a long moment and one corner of her mouth quirks up again before smoothing out. 'Raphael has ways to circumvent that. If Gabriel can find him, that is, and Raphael can be persuaded to... help,' she murmurs, almost to herself, with a fleeting expression that's close to pain on her face. 'How do you think I was able to hide in plain sight for so long? With Raphael's help, you could find yourself naked in Luc's bed and he would not know that *I* was also there.'

I go hot, thinking of Luc's golden, flawless beauty, revolted by my own brief flash of intense desire.

Mercy reaches for my hand and I scoot backwards in shock, putting some distance between us. She laughs, throwing her head back so that her long, heavy brown hair ripples down between her shoulderblades.

'Give me your hand,' she insists, holding out her right, palm up. It is smooth and unmarked, like luminous marble in the soft, violet light; as solid and real as this place is. 'I want to show you some... magic.'

Tentatively I take it, and she closes her fingers around mine. They feel warm, and there is no pain. 'I'm different here,' she murmurs. 'I am myself in this world in a way I can no longer be in yours. There's no distortion, no feedback. I can think, see, hear, feel — clearly.'

It's true. She seems realer and more alive than I do. She's no longer insubstantial and voiceless, the way she was in my kitchen in Craster.

'Only you're technically *dead*,' I can't stop myself from blurting out, remembering what Gabriel had showed me at Dunstanburgh Castle. 'And he's not here, is he? Ryan, I mean. So what good is that?'

I regret the words immediately, because her grip tightens and a flash of real grief passes across her face.

I look down at where our hands are joined. Mercy's skin gleams in a way mine does not. Mine is flat and matt and opaque against this place, as if I am the wrong frequency.

I look up at her soft, 'No, he's not. And I know Luc has him because I have torn through two worlds, searching, and Ryan remains in some way shielded from me. He can't be allowed to remain in Luc's hands. Every second Luc has him, Ryan is in *Hell*…'

'How do you know then,' I say hesitantly, 'that Ryan's still…alive?'

Mercy releases my hand abruptly, clasping her own together in a gesture of anguish. 'Ryan is *alive*, or he would be *here*. Azraeil claimed him until the end of time — I was there. The bargain was mine; *I* was the consideration, willingly given.'

Mercy looks out over the water. 'Ryan still serves some purpose for Luc. He keeps him close to punish us both. Luc will never let us just *be*. He will keep Ryan alive forever, if it means I cannot have him.'

I can't keep the horror out of my voice. 'You understand that if Ryan's still alive and Luc has him — Ryan's not going to be the same as…as when you left him.'

He'd be better off dead, I think.

Her eyes flash to mine as if I've spoken out loud.

For a moment, I recall the two of them — Luc and Ryan — physically identical at first glance until one's shocked eye took in the detail: one so golden, so dazzling, with eyes as pale as ice, and the other pale-skinned, dark-eyed and dark-haired, undeniably mortal.

So very different: like her and me.

'Not so very different,' she insists, again responding to words I haven't said aloud. 'Azraeil has marked us both — you felt it the same way I did. And we know what it means to be utterly friendless; to start again from nothing. You and I are more alike than you know. Gia, we had no ability to strike at those who hurt us before, but *together…*'

She stands and moves towards the water, so I do too, and the smell of this place is suddenly dizzying as I breathe it in. There's the clean, green smell of the wild grass of the valley, cut through with the scent of wildflowers — jasmine, honeysuckle, rose, and a mass of other blooms there might never be a name for — the fresh, cold, metallic tang of the black river at our feet. It seems bottomless when I look down at it, made of an absolute absence of colour.

'I am charged to do Death's bidding. I need your mortal body to help me find — and kill — Lucifer,' she says and Mercy's voice has a ringing, formal quality to it. 'Will you help me?'

My reply is fervent as I turn to look at her. 'You know I will. There's no peace, anywhere, if do nothing. I know that now.'

I feel myself sway dangerously in the fragrant air and she puts out a hand to steady me.

Her voice is strangely urgent. 'It took *eight* of the most powerful beings in creation to hide me inside a living body without trace. Not even an archangel can do that alone — remain hidden when they take someone over. Something always seeps out; there are always *signs*.'

The waters are hypnotic and my ears are filled with their dull roaring. What she's asking is impossible. What she's asking me to do might kill me.

But isn't that what I've already been, for years? A dead woman walking?

Mercy shakes me gently. 'Luc, his *daemonium*, they are the same: they cannot remain hidden for long inside those they possess, though they hold on as desperately as they can, clawing heat and life out of the body until there is nothing left to draw from. *There are always tics and tells*. Gia, it's important. Listen to me.'

But it's like her words are coming at me from a great distance. I take a step closer to the river's edge and the metallic tang of the water is stronger than ever in my nostrils; there's a ferrous taste on my parched tongue. Heat is visibly rising off the surface in the form of a clinging silver mist, and it twines around my ankles now as if it possesses sentience, is somehow reaching for me. I bend for a moment, trailing my fingers through it, and my sense of vertigo worsens.

I'm not meant to be here. No one has to tell me that. I just know it.

Mercy places her warm hand on my shoulder from above. 'Work out *who* Luc is, Gia. If you can work out who he is, then we will know *where* he is and where to strike. And if Luc keeps Ryan close, then...'

She grips my shoulder harder. *'Azraeil deals in death.* There is no human on earth whose passing Azraeil does not see and judge, and he *saw* Luc take human form because a multitude died for that to happen. Azraeil himself walked among the dying that day. But he could not act in time because Luc is well-protected; the man you seek, the one who almost took your life when you were a child, *he was there.* We can't be sure if Luc has already moved on — in the same way *I* once did, from body to body, life to life — having learned well from his long pursuit of me. But unlike me, there is no Archangel Raphael to keep Luc hidden. There will be markers: there will be demonsign. Upon the face of the world you cannot hide the passage of the *daemonium.* They are accursed and always will be. They chose to turn away from first light, and that choice will follow them all their days. *Luc is not content to be just anyone*, remember that.'

I try to straighten, but stumble forward instead, as Mercy adds, 'There is nothing in this age that is not known. Nothing can stay hidden for long. Ask yourself, Gia: in all the world, given the choice, *who would Luc be?*'

I close my eyes, her words beating at me like giant wings, and I'm unable to stop myself toppling headfirst into the swell of the moving black water that bears me away.

I sit bolt upright with the feeling that I'm drowning. Choking and clawing at my throat, it takes me a few seconds to work out that I'm perfectly dry and that all I appear to be wearing is a man-sized tee-shirt and borrowed underwear. I'm also lying in an unfamiliar bed in a darkened room, flashing red and green neon from a street sign outside playing rhythmically across the walls through the partly open curtains.

Fear grips me tight.

The room smells of sandalwood and citrus and male sweat.

Turning my head gingerly, I catch sight of Shaun folded untidily into an armchair beside the king-sized bed I'm lying in. My skin goes icy when I realise that his amber eyes are wide open and fixed on me. There's a stark fear in his gaze — something I've never associated with Shaun — but then he sits straighter, shaking it off, and it's the same old Shaun I remember, except that his palms are tightly bandaged as if he's getting ready for a fight and there's a tiny cut on his face.

'Where am I?' I say huskily for something to do, but I've already worked out where I am, and the awareness that this is *his bed*, *his tee-shirt*, further tightens my skin.

'Water?' I plead. The taste of that black river, I swear, is still on my tongue.

Shaun unfurls his cramped frame from the armchair and crosses the room to a dresser with a jug and a glass resting on it and pours me some, holding the glass for me to drink from. I can barely lift my arms and curl my fingers to support it. Everything aches.

After I indicate I've had enough, Shaun puts the glass down on the bedside table nearest to us, his movements unusually clumsy because of his bandaged hands. He clears his throat. 'I'm not a...believer,' he says cautiously and I see his eyes dart around the room for a second, as if he's worried someone might be listening and there might be immediate consequences. 'The world has always been brutal to people like me,' he continues, 'and I've come to expect it. *All you know is what you're taught* and you learn to avoid the hits because in the end: there's no one to save you but *you*. That's the *only* thing I believe.'

'I believe that, too, you know that. But they're *real*,' I rasp. 'And I saw, through Mercy's eyes, in all her memories, how they care — they care very deeply — but there just aren't enough of them to...to get to everyone. Except Azraeil, who's special in some way I haven't quite worked out.'

When Shaun gives me a look of sheer incomprehension, I clarify, 'Azraeil — the Archangel of Death. He's...different from the others. He *has* to get to everyone. It's his job to work out who goes and who stays.'

When Shaun shakes his head, still bewildered, I say, '*Who dies.* Azraeil works out who dies. If he doesn't do it, it doesn't happen. There's this place most of the dead go to...'

I hesitate to name it aloud, not telling Shaun that I was apparently just there—by the river that is Sheol's heart's blood. The river at the start, and end, of time.

I pull the bedclothes higher, feeling chilled to the core. 'Azraeil is — what was the word Mercy used? — "charged" to *see* everyone who dies. He's got to make some kind of judgment. No one else can do that. But he's also "charged" Mercy to kill Lucifer. She's his right hand now: Azraeil's weapon. And this thing between Azraeil and Lucifer goes deep: Lucifer's been trying to prove that evil is greater than Death, greater than all of it, his entire existence. And in all this time, *none* of them — not Gabriel or the other archangels — have ever been able to get Lucifer. They've never even been able to get close enough to touch him — until now. Mercy changed all that. When she gave up her...*life*,' Shaun's eyes widen, 'she made Luc vulnerable in a way he's never been before. He's here, she says, walking among us, wearing someone's face and body. If we can work out who he is, she says, we can work out where and then...'

Shaun shakes his head disbelievingly. '*Luc*, you call him. As if he's someone you can actually take down. If the, uh, angels, can't do it, then what chance do you...' He waves one bandaged hand at me and I know how delusional I must appear.

'If the body Lucifer is in is anything like mine is — something made of flesh and blood and bone — it can be done,' I say fervently. 'It's his weakness. You showed Mercy that when you kicked my legs out from under me. Being in our world without someone to feed off, without someone to…to *house* him —' Shaun's eyes flicker with revulsion, 'would kill Luc before long. Whatever he is can't stay unprotected in our world for long. They can't abide the cold, demons. They need a constant source of energy to survive. But there are over six billion of us. He could be anyone. Given the choice —' I parrot Mercy's question back at Shaun, *'Who would he be?'*

I turn, pulling my pillow upright behind me, leaning back into it carefully. Every action sets a carillon of pain ringing in my head. Even the surface of my skin hurts, as if my collision with what Mercy has become left me riddled with unseen exit wounds.

Shaun pulls his armchair closer, sitting so near I can feel his warm breath on my bare forearm. 'The Pound is a mess,' he says carefully. 'It looks like we're going to be out of business for the next month while repairs are done, and the kids aren't happy. I might even lose some of my best fighters permanently to the other boxing gyms who've been circling. The only reason the insurers are coming to the party, Danny says, is that there's indisputable CCTV footage of me being chased around the joint — clearly in fear for my life — by a sword-wielding crazed intruder who appears to be *on fire.*'

He leans back in his chair and puts his bandaged hands behind his head as if he's relaxed, even though I can feel his tension radiating from where I am. 'You've been out for two whole days and Jamie's beside herself; she keeps ringing to find out if you're conscious yet. It's the most she's said to, or about, anyone for months. Soon as you're strong enough to get up, I'm taking you back to hers. Then you can tell us how the hell we're supposed to help you find — and get — the Anti-Christ.'

10

We make it back to Jamie's house as soon as the sun's up and I have to laugh at how long it takes us to get there, even though it's a block and a half at most from Shaun's place.

At Jamie's doorstep, Shaun gives my shoulders a reassuring squeeze and drops the arm he's had around me the whole way. 'For support, that's all, don't get ideas or get all defensive now,' he told me cautiously — like he was scared I'd bite — when we set off from his man-cave located above an Indian grocery store.

With the weight of Shaun's arm gone, I have to push down the sudden cold feeling of abandonment. I force myself to stand straighter as Jamie studies her security cam feed from inside the house before cautiously unlocking her front door and letting us in.

Once I've had a hot shower and pulled on one of Jamie's bedazzled pink tracksuits with trembling hands, Jamie has Shaun help me back downstairs into an armchair in her study while she goes to fetch a fleecy blanket to tuck around my legs.

'You've got the shakes,' she says firmly, when I try to fight her off.

'This is hopeless,' I mutter, looking down at where she's

got my knees tucked up under fluffy pink fleece. 'I'm still as weak as a baby and it's been more than forty-eight hours since Mercy…' I almost say *landed through me like a bomb* but finish weakly with, 'It's like a whole body/brain flu thing. Even my skin hurts.'

'Let's just assume what's required will be a once-off,' Jamie says briskly, settling into her office chair and turning to look at me, the tight plastic face mask over her skin glistening under the bright study lights. Her mouth crooks up wryly. 'Just like the last time was. All "once-offs"; that's the way I look at things these days. Shaun and I will get your strength back up — for when it's needed.'

'Speaking of which,' Shaun sighs, running a hand through his curls, 'can't do that till I've got a working boxing gym again. I'll be at the Pound for the next few hours, supervising the clean-up, all right?'

His look is sombre as he backs out the study door. 'Tell her exactly what you told me, Gia, word for word. Don't leave anything out. I've come to realise that she knows things the same way you know things — by impossible means.'

After Jamie locks up her front door again and returns to the study, I tell her about the 'test' Mercy put me through at the Pound. When I come to the part about the scar that was somehow *inside* me, Jamie rubs her breastbone absently, as if she knows exactly what I'm talking about.

When I get to the part about working out who Luc is 'wearing' these days Jamie leans down and switches on a series of computer towers on the floor under her desk.

She straightens up and swings around in her office chair to face me. 'I figured it would be something like that. So I took the liberty, pet, while you were away, of preparing a slide show of sorts for you to look over.'

In that instant, all the lifeless, black computer screens come to life, and I give a high, breathless shriek of surprise. There are eight screens set up side by side across the long workstation that takes up one whole wall of the room. Apart from the terminal directly in front of Jamie — which only has a single blinking cursor on it — on each of the others is the face of a dangerous man.

I shuffle my wheely chair closer to the terminals reluctantly, skin prickling in apprehension. On the screen closest to me is the image of a tanned, smooth-skinned, black-bearded man in a beret and white military uniform with epaulets and loads of gold trim. I would say Middle-Eastern based on the desert backdrop and brilliant background light; maybe late fifties, early sixties.

The next one along features a chiselled northern European businessman. It's a sharp, professional head-and-shoulders shot — like a portrait taken by an official photographer at a business or political summit — and I see that he's got white-blonde buzz-cut hair, pale grey eyes and cheekbones you could julienne vegetables across. The backdrop to this guy is the flag-filled lobby of some rolled-gold hotel I faintly recognise that only stratospherically rich people can even enter.

There's an exceptionally tall, handsome, clean-shaven African man in military fatigues thundering oratory from a podium, fists raised; a short, moustachioed South American in an open-necked silk shirt with flashing eyes and facial scars; a white-haired elderly gentleman of average height and slender build in an impeccable morning suit and top hat at an English garden wedding; a heavy-set Greek or possibly Italian with wind-tousled hair in off-duty mogul-wear of sports coat, polo shirt, slacks and loafers, standing on the deck of a large yacht.

The last computer screen features a dumpy Asian official in olive drab surrounded by a battalion of sharply dressed generals. He's the only one of the lot who looks familiar.

As I scan the seven faces, each image begins to dissolve into a new one: of the man in question opening a new bombing range, say, or single-handedly shooting an assault rifle into the air from an open jeep.

'What do they all have in common?' I ask tentatively, not really wanting to know.

'They're all mass murderers,' Jamie replies grimly as images dissolve and appear before our eyes. 'They each control enormous global networks that do a lucrative sideline in businesses ranging from arms dealing, drug trafficking, human slavery, torture, money laundering and state-sponsored genocide. They are far and away the current worst-of-the-worst for sheer numbers: in dollars, foot soldiers, lives, countries and territories affected.'

I look at Jamie, in her neat wig and pale pink cashmere pullover, blue jeans, bare feet, meticulously pink-painted finger- and toenails, the livid scars on her face and neck like a crazy roadmap.

'What *are* you?' is all I can manage as I return my awed gaze to the shifting and dissolving images. I don't doubt her for a second. She knew things about me before I even came into her life. Whatever she used to be — dolly bird, glamour model, lads' mag fave — that person is long gone.

Jamie begins to type furiously into the keyboard in front of her, the screen with the blinking cursor filling up rapidly with scrolling lines of text and code. 'Not just a pretty face these days,' she rasps. 'Like your friend Mercy, I've been forced to adapt. I've had to learn to tap into the river that allows you to move between the world you see — and the one you don't.

There's a whole load of people out there, just like me, who still love a good gossip and a project. When I asked my friends who the most powerful, evil men on earth were *right now*? This was the consensus. Evil knows no boundaries: not culture, not faith, not geography.'

'It's a smorgasbord,' I agree lightly, but we can both hear the tension there.

Jamie shoots me a sideways glance. 'So where should we start, do you think?'

I look at the seven faces on the screens before me and my reply is immediate.

'The obscenely wealthy Teutonic ice-blond,' I say tiredly. 'Start with him. Luc's got a definite type. I saw it for myself, in Milan. If these guys are like suits for hire? Then the "businessman" — is the best...fit.'

ℬ

Jamie starts digging down into the life and times of a thirty-eight-year-old Russian resources, telecommunications and logistics multi-billionaire called Spartak Arkady Skorobogatov, fetching and retrieving information from all across the Clearnet and the Deep Web with the aid of others in her hazy, anonymous, friend-to-friend network of wounded people.

When she spots me nodding off in my chair an hour later, Jamie sends me back upstairs to bed, but not before I remind her woozily of the date that Mercy appeared to me in the farmhouse in Craster. 'Assume that's close to when she, uh, died — give or take a few days — because time doesn't seem to run in the same way for her kind.'

I can still feel Ryan's warm hand in mine — from that last memory of Mercy's when they were still together, still whole, so in love it almost hurt me to look at him — and I close my eyes momentarily to block out the pain.

'And Mercy…died,' I falter again on the word, 'somewhere in Asia. So see if there are reports of a young woman losing her life at a temple that was popular with tourists where the Hindu goddess *Kālī* featured heavily — maybe a temple in Malaysia or Bali or India? And if Luc assumed the body of that man between the date Azraeil and Mercy made their bargain for Ryan's life and *now*, look out for some kind of catastrophic event during that time which killed loads of people in one hit that the Russian somehow miraculously "survived".'

My mouth is suddenly dry and I have to swallow hard a few times before I can get the words out. 'The man who, who, hurt me — he was there, Mercy said, when Luc took the body over. He's some kind of human agent for Luc these days. They're tight — wherever Luc is, he is. So look out for him, too, in your travels. An image, a snatch of video, he must be somewhere…'

I describe the man's tattoos to her again in shuddering detail, and Jamie nods as she jots down the descriptions on a notepad. 'There must be a picture with him and the Russian in it,' I insist, backing unsteadily out of Jamie's study. 'Find it for me.'

ॐ

I sleep for hours. The house is dark again when I roll out of bed to the rumble of Shaun's deep voice downstairs answering Jamie's lighter one.

When I shuffle back through the door of the study, Shaun and Jamie are staring at the central computer screen while spooning soup out of giant mugs.

Shaun leaps to his feet when he sees me. '*Sit,*' he commands, taking Jamie's mug with him as he leaves the room. 'I'll get you something to eat, yeah? You must be starving, G.'

Only a couple of computer screens are on now, the one in front of Jamie still filling rapidly with letters and code, the other populated with a hazy black-and-white image of an airport tarmac somewhere, littered with dead bodies. All the people are lying where they fell between a clutch of sleek private jets, their legs and arms at impossible angles. Standing at the very far end of the shot, to the left, are two men: one very tall and well-built, impeccably dressed in a tailored suit and heavy overcoat, the other blocky and muscular in typical international thug-wear of wraparound sunnies, form-fitting leather jacket, muscle tee, jeans and boots. The second man is big, but still dwarfed by the first.

From the way they're standing it's clear what they are to each other: master and servant.

I go hot. It's impossible to tell, but something about the shorter one with the shaved head seems ominously familiar.

When Jamie sees me staring, she hastily clicks the image closed and turns to me just as Shaun comes back in, handing me my own mug of hot soup and a spoon.

'You sure you're ready for the highlights, darl?' Jamie says worriedly as Shaun hunkers down beside me, sitting in the chair that's still warm from his body. He takes the mug and spoon out of my nerveless hands and starts feeding me from them until I suddenly snap to attention and grab them both off him with a snarl. I find I am shovelling the soup into my mouth because I'm ravenous.

But also because I'm suddenly hugely, absurdly *afraid*.

'It's him,' I whisper as I continue taking huge, gulping swallows of my hot soup. 'Isn't it? The tattooed man. I'm sure it's him. You found him.'

Shaun's dark gold eyes search mine and he rests one hand briefly on my arm before standing and stretching.

'It's bad,' he warns, looking down at where I'm sitting hunched over my mug. 'I've been part of combat operations that weren't as brutal as some of the footage Jamie's pulled together. Spartak's on your hit list for good reason.'

I lick the last of the thick, creamy soup off my spoon. 'Play it,' I tell Jamie grimly, my legs already beginning to shake. 'I'm ready.'

But I'm not, not really.

Oh, it starts off innocently enough, with an aerial shot of a massive 200 metre-wide, 80 metre-deep sinkhole crater that inexplicably opened up in Siberia eighteen months ago with a vast, icy lake deep at its heart. Like the earth expelled something noxious into the air, and the wound then filled with rank water. But that's quickly followed by real-time video footage taken at an explosion at a coalmine complex in the nearby Ural Mountains where I can see actual human body parts littering the foreground, to a soundtrack of continuous, tortured screaming. It sounds like people are being torn apart *alive*.

I kind of lose track of my sanity after the photo montage of eighty-one dead people crammed into a refrigerated truck abandoned on the side of a freeway in Serbia, oil tankers packed with scores of suffocating slaves and the Spartakex-branded shipping container brothel-town filled with dead-eyed, emaciated teenage girls of Middle-Eastern appearance. There are images of burnt bodies inside a Spartakex-operated 'alternative energy' research facility and follow-up shots taken in and around the radiation-affected ghost town near the Chinese–Russian border. Jamie skips quickly through those, but I know I'll never unsee the picture gallery of livestock born with six legs or no heads, the flash-burned, cancer-ridden survivors of the fallout, or the miles of dead pine forest to the immediate north of the failed power plant.

I don't ask how Jamie got hold of all of these images, or the snatch of video of Spartak himself giving a fiery motivational speech at a private, invitation-only billionaires' business symposium in Geneva fifteen months ago. But I don't doubt for a second that it's all real.

When Jamie's Spartak montage finishes on that haunting black-and-white image of two men standing calmly at the edge of a private airfield littered with dead people, I have to leave the room for a moment to heave into the powder room sink. When I get back, dropping into the empty seat beside Shaun, Jamie reaches out and gives my knee a quick squeeze before asking if there's one more thing she can show me.

Voicelessly I nod, and she opens a new file as she says, 'He's got deep sea gas and oil drilling interests, coalmine and fracking concerns, freight, tanker and trucking companies, satellite and wide dish arrays, telecoms towers and huge retail networks. Everything it takes to make this world tick, Spartak Skorobogatov has a piece of it. He's the perfect human "cover", wouldn't you agree?'

I think of Mercy's words — *Luc is not content to be just anyone, remember that* — and nod. 'Luc's always going to pick outliers: good-looking, off-the-charts wealthy, super-connected *freaks*.'

Jamie nods, then brings up the same snatch of video from the fancy business symposium in Geneva and I snap, 'We've already seen that. It's the least offensive bit and I don't really need to see it again.'

But Jamie silences me with a look and clicks *play*.

This time, the footage has been slowed down to an

excruciatingly slow number of frames per second. There's nothing new for several seconds and I shift restlessly in my chair until Shaun clamps his warm hand over mine and murmurs, 'Look, look, it's coming up, right...*here*...'

I suck in a shocked breath. When Spartak Skorobogatov appears to shrug his broad shoulders mid-sentence, there's the faint silhouette of another person around him, or rising from him, like a dark halo: who is taller, broader; inhuman in proportion.

'Just a flash,' Shaun breathes, his hand holding me steady, 'like a shadow, but then at the two minute thirty-nine second mark, there it is again.'

Leaning forward, I see Skorobogatov shrug again, and there's another weird after-image of a dark, man-shaped halo stretching for a moment, as if trying to shake itself free of Skorobogatov's body. But then the dark halo disappears completely and there's nothing else for the rest of the sample. Jamie finds and plays the same snatch of video at normal speed and there's nothing more than two flickering changes in the light moving across Skorobogatov's face. And the two weird shoulder shrugs.

What had Mercy called them? *Tics and tells.*

'One of my girls cleaned the video up for me,' Jamie lisps. 'Her exact words were: *Fixed lighting, internal conference room, no windows, no blinds, so there shouldn't be any shadows playing across his face that way.* Plus, those two involuntary shoulder movements of his. Skorobogatov isn't listed anywhere as suffering from a motor tic. He's always been written about like some prototype man of the future: always the smartest, best-looking, best-dressed, richest, most physically threatening guy in the room. So maybe it's something new. Good pick-up, right? Scared the pants off me when I first watched it, too. And

I know for a fact that Skorobogatov's going to be in London in a couple of weeks for a Titans of World Logistics business summit. Every billionaire logistics magnate in the world will be there. Mega deals are done at this thing. But the real reason Skorobogatov will be in town is that he's negotiating for valuable oil and gas interests in the North Sea off the Shetlands. The financial press have been talking about it for months. So he's confirmed for the summit's opening night black-tie function at the Argo, a private club in Pall Mall.'

'I need to see him,' I reply without hesitation.

'Get into the Argo?' Shaun exclaims. 'It's members, guests and bodyguards only. I've had mates run personal security there. It's like a fortress. What you're asking is impossible.'

Searching my memory hazily, I say, '*Logistics* has to do with the movement of things or people…'

'Sounds about right,' Jamie replies.

'Well, where have I heard that word or seen it before?' I mutter.

Shaun shrugs in a *search me* kind of way.

'I can bring up broad schematics for the Argo,' Jamie says, doubt in her voice. 'That's simple enough. It's an architectural landmark — there's plenty been written about it that's freely available. But it's still not going to help you get inside, love. You don't — if you don't mind me saying, Gia — look like a *titan* of anything.'

My throat is so tight I can't seem to draw breath.

'Anyway, what will seeing Spartak actually *do*?' Shaun queries.

'I don't know,' I whisper, distracted by a thought that refuses to come to the surface of my brain. 'I just know I need to see him…'

I suddenly sit up, electrified. 'Can you find out if Bianca

St Alban is confirmed to have a representative at the opening night function? S-T, A-L-B-A-N.'

Jamie nods, mystified, and starts typing.

As I back out of the room with my empty mug, I add, 'And ask your, uh, friends, Jamie, if they can clean up that photo at the airfield. I need to *see* the faces of those two men.'

Shaun — about to take the seat I've just vacated — looks across at me with troubled eyes before I leave the room completely.

11

'Bianca St Alban,' Jamie says, bringing up a photo gallery of images the moment I return to her study at the front of the house.

There are hundreds of pictures of a young, slender woman with an oval face and elegantly arched brows, light olive skin and unbound dark, glossy hair with the most startlingly pale blue eyes, framed by long, dark lashes. She's pictured emerging from six-star hotel entrances, limos and parties, always serenely beautiful, usually surrounded by crowds of people being held back, away from her.

Beside me, Shaun whistles in appreciation.

I think about the last time I saw Bianca in Giovanni Re's private haute couture fitting rooms in Milan. She'd just been very publically dumped by her fiancé, Felix de Haviland, because Mercy's corporeal 'ride' at the time and my boss, Irina, had done the dirty with him right before Mercy took Irina over. Bianca didn't even given me a second's notice as she prepared to tear strips off 'Irina' only to come out of the locked fitting rooms with a look on her classically beautiful face like she'd just seen a monster.

'Bianca was in Mercy's memories,' I tell Jamie huskily, studying images of Bianca with sunglasses and without, Bianca at work and Bianca at play on the French Riviera. 'She was at

Giovanni Re's design atelier before the disaster in Milan, but she also met with Mercy and Ryan at a large private house somewhere in Lake Como a few days after the Galleria roof collapsed. I remember, because Bianca wasn't at the fashion show and I was expecting her to be there, front row, centre. You know how half the towns around Lake Como went up in flames? Bianca's house was somehow spared. Something happened out there that made Bianca help Mercy, because I saw Mercy and Ryan get onto a plane with the legend *StA Global Logistics* on the tail fin.'

Jamie nods as if all this makes perfect sense as she brings up a new window with names and dollar values on it. 'The St Alban family holding company, StA Global Logistics, is one of the top ten logistics firms in the world by revenue, in billions, based out of Switzerland. But Bianca works as some kind of roving international women's wear editor for a prestige fashion magazine. So what do you want me to do exactly?' Jamie queries, hands poised over her keyboard.

'I need you to get Bianca on the line,' I say as Shaun rises wearily to his feet, preparing to leave for the night. 'She and I need to have a little face-to-face talk. Just *her* — not her PA, PR firm or a corporate flunkey, tell her that. Say whatever you have to. And make sure you bring Mercy into it; her name always gets people's attention.'

༂

I'm deeply asleep — dreaming that I've just stepped into the temperamental 1970s-era shower at Mama Kassmeyer's farm fully clothed for some reason, ready to turn on the taps and wash myself from head to toe, clothes and all — when Jamie touches me lightly on the shoulder.

I'm immediately awake, eyes wide, and Jamie yawns and says, 'I'm off to bed now, love, but she's waiting for you to dial through. You'll see the link to her private account on the main screen downstairs, all right?'

Jamie trails into the snug little bathroom between her room and mine and starts tugging off her wig just as she closes the door. Suddenly sick to the pit of my stomach with nerves, or excitement, I can't be sure, I throw on a cardigan over my ratty sleep tee and race downstairs.

The clock on the screen says it's 2.01am. I have no idea where Bianca is, or what time it is there, or how Jamie managed to get hold of one of the world's richest, most sought-after young women and convince her to talk to me.

I see Bianca's avatar exactly where Jamie promised it would be and I dial it.

It rings only twice before she picks up. It really *is* Bianca framed in the screen — dressed in a simple white linen shift, skin tanned gold from the sun, dark hair in loose waves around her shoulders like she's just taken it down from a topknot, wide-set brilliant blue eyes staring back into mine.

Do I imagine that they seem slightly afraid?

She's framed by a chic all-white suite — high ceilings, the suggestion of a feather bed and a mirrored vanity behind her, gauzy curtains moving in the breeze from open windows, brilliant sunshine. I wouldn't be surprised if I'd somehow dialled her up in actual Paradise.

'Gia Basso?' Bianca says in her faintly French-accented English, a small pleat appearing between her immaculately arched dark brows. 'You were —'

'Yes,' I cut in eagerly, 'Irina Z's general dogsbody. We met at Giovanni Re's Atelier just that one time.'

Bianca St Alban's frown deepens. 'I don't see how we have

anything new to discuss —'

And I interrupt her again before she can close the connection, the words tumbling out of my mouth about somehow *seeing* her with Ryan and Mercy through Mercy's memories, and how Lucifer did something to Ryan that made Mercy give up what she was forever, and how they were so happy, 'Really happy,' I say, my eyes welling with sudden tears. 'After they left you, they travelled everywhere; they were never without each other for a second. That is, until Mercy... died.' I choke to a stop.

Bianca rears back. *'What?'*

She leans in close so that her heart-shaped face looms into the screen, and I'm flapping my hands in front of my eyes to try and stem the tears, disgusted at myself, blurting out the rest through the pain squeezing my throat shut. I'm crying and speaking so fast that a thousand emotions seem to flit across Bianca's face at once: pity, frustration, revulsion, shock. But she just lets me cry and ramble, and I get it all out and finally all that's left to say is, 'I need you to get me into the cocktail party for logistics magnates. In London — in just over a fortnight. I need to see him. *Spartak Skorobogatov.*' I practically shout the name.

When Bianca remains silent, sitting back a little and crossing her arms, I say gruffly, 'You don't know me, and you don't owe me anything, and Mercy's probably used up all her favours so that we're in negative favours territory and I should be the one doing *you* favours, but I need to *see* him. Up close. Not just on the street, separated by a bloody great wall of bodyguards and reporters.'

'You need to *touch* him?' Bianca asks, a shrewd look on her face, and I wonder again what happened between her and Mercy inside the haute couture fitting rooms at Atelier Re.

I've been too afraid to admit that to myself until now. 'I don't know,' I say truthfully. 'There's no, uh, rule book for any of this. But touching is...bad.' I don't tell her what it feels like, when Mercy takes me over — as though I'm filled with an energy that is also slowly tearing me apart. 'I'd rather not, if I can help it. I think, if I look at him, I'll just know if there's something not, well, right — I'll know if he's *the one*. I know I'm not making much sense here. But if I can see him, Bianca, then I can figure out what to do next.'

Bianca looks off-screen for a moment as if she's searching for something across the room, before refocusing her pale gaze on me.

'My father and my uncle mostly send some ambitious office elf to these functions. I didn't even know there was a "thing" in London, to be frank. I have little to do with the day-to-day running of StA Global, just the odd board meeting. But if it's as important as you say it is, well, one of them, Papa or Uncle Tony, will usually flip a coin to work out who needs to make an appearance for appearance's sake. Let me make some enquiries.'

I see her hands already busy with something beside her keyboard as her gaze grows distant, a slim hand rising to cut the connection between us.

She flicks her remarkable eyes back to mine for a moment, her hand still upraised between our two faces. 'I wasn't very nice to you, the last time we met,' she says stiffly. 'And I apologise for that. I was in a lot of...pain.' Then she gives me the cool, measured gaze beloved of so many paparazzo long lenses over the years. 'I'll be in touch.'

The screen goes blank.

I don't hear back from Bianca St Alban until a pale blue, gold-embossed envelope shows up in the mail at Jamie's place a few days later, inviting me to accompany Bianca St Alban to drinks in the Grand Saloon at the Argo just over a week from today. *Dress: black tie.*

I telephone the number I'm advised to telephone and a professional-sounding, young male voice informs me that a limousine will pick me up precisely one hour before the start time. He double-checks Jamie's street address without a hint of warmth and hangs up before I can say anything else.

'Everything all right?' Jamie asks over breakfast the next morning.

I start laughing, ruefully. 'I never thought I'd hear myself say this, but I've literally got nothing to wear that you can't shovel manure in. It's not quite the tone the Argo's after, is it?'

Jamie's face tightens sideways in answering amusement. 'When you get back from the Pound today, we'll have you put on a little fashion parade. No spandex or sequins, love, I promise.'

ॐ

I wasn't appointed the door bitch for the most difficult supermodel in recorded history for no reason. In between sessions of weights and stretching, self-defence and cardio, Shaun has me cajoling, sweet-talking and downright harassing the Pound's insurers, tradesmen and equipment suppliers in ways even he doesn't have the stomach for. All the traffic management and crowd control I have to do mean the day flies by. But the second it gets dark outside, Shaun comes out of his office with a telephone handset jammed between ear and shoulder, and indicates with a jerk of his thumb that I need to get going.

Jamie studies me as I come through her door, hair plastered to my head by a charming combo of sweat and sawdust, plasterboard powder all down the front of my sweatshirt and staining the knees of my jeans as if I've rolled around in an exploded bag of flour.

'I'm no expert in fashion,' she says cautiously, as she leads me upstairs, 'you only have to look at some of my old promo shots to have a good laff, love, but I've got a few ideas about your general look.'

On her bed is an assortment of shoulder-length wigs from ash blonde through to raven, a pair of candy-pink spectacle frames with clear lenses and a two-tiered, brushed-metal beauty kit the size of a carpenter's toolbox. The kinds of things you'd need for a radical makeover.

I'm suddenly reminded of the last time I saw Tommy Taffin, the genius brand manager for Giovanni Re. I'd put him in charge of giving Ryan Daley a 'make-under' inside Irina's hotel suite in Milan to make Ryan less recognisable. The plan was to keep Ryan and Mercy safe from Lucifer.

I swallow a laugh that sounds like a sob.

Jamie looks at me strangely. 'Sit,' she tells me briskly, patting the end of her neatly made bed.

'Since I'm assuming this has to be a stealth job, has Lucifer...' she pauses delicately and we both clock how weird that sounds, 'ever *seen* you before?'

I nod as she flips open the top tier of her beauty case, rubbing some kind of cool ointment into my face as she peppers me with questions.

'How many times?' she asks, 'and for how long?'

And I tell her just the once, at the fashion parade. 'But then the sky fell on my head right after. It really did. And I saw *him* — you couldn't help but eat him up with your eyes, it was like Lucifer drew all the light, all the energy, from the room *into* him somehow, he was the most perfect-looking creature I've ever seen — but I doubt he saw me at all. There was a raised catwalk between us, the floor was at eye-level, and I had black hair then, in this sharp, razor-cut kind of asymmetrical cartoon geisha ninja bob with slanting bangs…'

'The complete opposite of the way you're wearing your hair now?' Jamie muses, as she puts the cap back on the tube of primer, before reaching for another tube.

I nod as she starts delicately blotting concealer over the dark circles I know are beneath my eyes. 'Were you wearing dark glasses?' she queries my closed eyelids.

I shake my head.

'So he may have seen your eyes,' she replies, rubbing foundation into my skin. There's a pause as she discards the piece of cotton she's been working with, picks up another. 'You've got very memorable eyes.'

I open them now. 'Luc only saw Mercy that day. He didn't care about anyone or anything else in the room — not even the blonde goddess demonoid creature he was holding hands with — because he'd been hunting down Mercy for centuries, right? And then, suddenly, there she was. *Bang*, in the room with him. Jamie, you've got to understand, there was this whole *kiss or kill* thing going on, like dry lightning in the air, before he even left his seat and went full, raving Prince of Darkness. I can't describe what being at that parade felt like. For all we knew — all of us trapped in that building — it could have been the end of the world. It certainly felt like it.'

'Still,' Jamie muses, 'he may have noticed you for your eyes. I've never seen anyone in real life with eyes like yours. They're both so different — it's like you're wearing contact lenses.'

And then she makes a small surprised noise, dropping the tube of mascara she's holding onto the open lid of her makeup kit before rushing out of the room.

I'm so exhausted from the day's heavy lifting that I slump on the end of Jamie's bed and close my eyes again. I hear her rummaging around in the cupboard under the sink in the bathroom before she walks back into the room and drops something hard and plastic into her beauty case. I don't even open my eyes while she fills in my eyelids and paints my lashes extravagantly with mascara, tilting my chin up and telling me to pull a trout pout while she contours the lines of my mouth with something sticky.

'Hair colour?' she queries and I say, eyes still closed, 'Hell, let's go blonde, I've never been a blonde. It's always felt like too much effort. Even for someone in *fashwan*. Couldn't sit still long enough to have it done. And the regrowth phase? *Please.*'

I feel Jamie pin the ends of my plaits tightly to my head so that they hug my skull, Bavarian milkmaid-style. She follows this up by tucking the whole mess into a scratchy wig that hangs like straw around my neck and brushes my shoulders.

'Now for the *pièce de résistance*,' Jamie giggles huskily in a fake French accent, striding out of the room for a moment to wash her hands before returning and fumbling around inside her beauty kit. 'Open your eyes,' she says softly as she tilts my face up again with one of her claw-like fingers. 'It might sting a little, but I have to keep them open to do this — so try not to blink.'

Jamie holds one of my eyes wide before clumsily tipping a soft contact lens into it, repeating the gesture for the other eye. Immediately, I feel them beginning to water from the unfamiliar sensation.

'I still have loads of these,' Jamie says quietly as I blink and roll my eyes around in their sockets, trying to get used to the feeling. 'I bought a bucketload of different colours because people had me doing all sorts of kinky cosplay. Fan conventions, you know, where I had to dress up like a sexy Viking or a fantasy robot madam with a whip and silver eyes. Some of the jobs I used to book were wild.'

Jamie hesitates with her hand in the beauty kit for a moment, then hands me a closed compact before turning away sharply so that she's staring out her bedroom door into the hallway beyond. 'Open it,' she says quickly. 'Tell me what you think.'

I look dumbly at the sleek black gold-rimmed compact in my hand for a second, not sure what to do with it. 'Open it,' Jamie repeats hoarsely.

I open the compact to find pressed powder in a neutral beige tone, but my eye is immediately drawn to the reflection of my pointed chin in the small round mirror on the inside lid.

Mirror. My eyes flick to Jamie's averted face. She must want so desperately to look into it, but the knowledge, at the same time, would destroy her.

I raise the mirror up high and gasp as I take in my reflection: two bright emerald-green eyes surrounded by strong cat's-eye makeup, almost geisha-white skin, glossy red lips and straight platinum-blonde, shoulder-length hair.

'The most arresting feature of your face now, poppet,' Jamie says, still facing away, 'are them eyes of yours. If forced to describe you, people will remember seeing a green-eyed, red-lipped, white-blonde in the room. And that's *all* they'll remember, because we'll put you in something tasteful and unmemorable. Like a black pantsuit with a discreet V-neck. Nothing vulgar for a business affair like yours. Low-heeled shoes. So you can run — if you have to.'

I'm still staring in shock at my altered reflection, unable to answer, when she turns around and places her fingers over mine, firmly closing the compact in my hand and defusing the temptation — to see and know — for the time being.

'Even the Devil himself wouldn't recognise you now.'

12

Bianca herself comes to the door of Jamie's house and rings the doorbell. Even the distorted, fishbowl quality of the security cam feed can't disguise how ethereally beautiful the woman is in her loose up-do and sleeveless, ankle-length white Grecian-style shift, accessorised only by a blazing pair of diamond earrings, and killer heels in a rich tan colour.

When Jamie opens the security door wearing her tight, clear plastic face mask, Bianca's gaze is direct, and her Swiss-finishing-school background doesn't allow her to flinch in shock the way I did at the sight of Jamie. 'You're Jamie Suggitt, aren't you?' Bianca says warmly.

Taken aback, Jamie nods and I see a deep red flush stain the unscarred places on her neck.

Bianca holds out her tanned, slender hand and Jamie grasps it, only to withdraw it quickly when she recalls the skin on her twisted fingers. Bianca doesn't let her pull away, though, instead shaking Jamie's hand firmly and naturally before releasing it and looking over her shoulder at me.

'Ready?' she says and I nod, giving Jamie a quick squeeze on the shoulder as I go by.

Jamie stops me, holding out a piece of paper folded down the middle so that the black-and-white image on it is on the inside. I fold it over again so that it fits into my palm, and slip it into one pocket of my suit jacket. The knowledge of what it must be burns against my hip. I don't want to look at it. But then again, I do — so desperately it's the only thing I can think about.

'Be careful, Gia.' Jamie's light, rasping voice is almost severe. 'You know I'm going to worry myself sick about you every minute you're gone. Be quick on your feet, love.'

I give her a lopsided smile. 'Shaun's armed me with every trick in the book, Jamie. I'll be in and out before anyone even knows I'm there.'

'Shauny's coming straight over after he finishes pouring concrete at the Pound tonight,' Jamie adds. 'Said he's anxious to see how you get on mingling with the billionaire jet set — so don't be too late. And he said, whatever you do, don't get into a fight. You do your *reconnaissance* — that was the word he used — and then you get the hell out of there. *Looking, no touching*, he said, that's the deal we all agreed. Shaun says, if something's screwy about Spartak, we'll work out a plan to tackle him once we're all back together.'

Bianca forestalls Jamie saying anything else by interrupting smoothly, 'I have every intention of returning her to you, in one piece, before midnight.'

Jamie gives us the quick grimace that passes for her smile and Bianca studies her face for a long moment. 'I know an excellent plastic surgeon, Jamie. There's nothing that can't be fixed if you know the right people. I'm going to send you his details and advise him to expect a call from you.'

Touching Jamie lightly on the arm in farewell, Bianca lifts the hem of her brilliant white gown before turning and heading back towards the middle of a three-car convoy of identical black town cars hugging the kerb outside Jamie's modest home. The passenger side doors are being held open by a man the size of a small outbuilding.

Feeling light-headed, I shoot Jamie an apologetic *this is what she's like* look before clomping out to the car in my functional black pantsuit, scratchy platinum wig and ugly, low-heeled black pumps.

Inside the sleek town car, Bianca retrieves her phone and sends Jamie her plastic surgeon's details before the doors are even closed behind us. When she sees that I'm shaking — because not much escapes her notice — Bianca orders her driver, through the intercom, to turn up the heating.

Suddenly, it's almost tropical inside the car, and I look at Bianca's bare shoulders in renewed admiration.

She shrugs. 'An overcoat would completely spoil the line of the frock,' she says as the car pulls away from the kerb.

I recall what I'd heartlessly told Mercy when she'd woken up, disoriented, inside Irina's body a lifetime ago. 'Beauty hurts,' I repeat now, numbly.

The lush sweep of Bianca's mouth turns down at the corners for a moment as she stares into my eyes. 'And *we* would be in a position to know, wouldn't we?'

We travel for a while in silence, our car equidistant from the glossy black town cars in front and to the rear. Lights seem to magically go green as we approach them, and I see faces at the windows of the cars we pass, all wondering who could possibly be behind the dark-tinted, bullet-proof glass of our imposing convoy.

The ends of my fingertips prickling, I jam my right hand into my jacket pocket and pull out the folded piece of paper Jamie had handed to me with the blown-up photographic image on the inside. I stare down at the square blindly for several blocks until Bianca takes it gently out of my hand and unfolds it for me, the image still facing away from my eyes.

'It only gets done if you get it done,' she says quietly. 'My mother used to tell me that so often I wanted to throw myself down on the floor of whichever house we were living in at the time and scream the roof down. But now I find myself saying it too. God help me, I'm *becoming* my mother, could there be anything more terrifying?'

Bianca studies the smoothed-out image for a moment before turning it to face me, and it's like a fist to the guts.

I fold myself down around the pain, wrapping my hands around the back of my head and placing my head on my knees, struggling for air. The familiar all-enveloping panic, when I think about the man who attacked me, is like the feeling of his huge hands around my throat, pressing down. It will never go away.

'One of these men is clearly Spartak Skorobogatov,' Bianca continues softly. 'I've seen him across enough crowded rooms to know that. But who's the other one? I have an excellent memory for names and faces. But I don't know him at all.'

'I do.' My voice is muffled, from where my face is still pressed hard into my knees. 'I am alive despite having been buried facedown in a hole made by that man. I am *alive.*'

Bianca doesn't break her appalled silence as I explain who that man is to me, and what he's done. Smoothing stray strands of synthetic hair back from my face, I finally sit up.

From her rear-facing seat, Bianca studies me with her unnervingly blue eyes and I imagine I see the shine of unshed tears in them. 'Drink?' She indicates the mini bar taking up an entire wood-panelled door of the vehicle.

I shake my head, sitting straighter and uncrossing my arms. 'I never thought I'd have to enter this world —' my eyes dart around the car's luxe interior, 'ever again. And I never thought that someone would offer me the chance to drive a... *blade*

—' Bianca blinks, but otherwise betrays no emotion, 'into the heart of that man, the same way he tried to do to *me*.'

I stare blindly at the image still clutched in Bianca's hand. 'But Mercy knows me too well. I've never been the type to do something for nothing, so she promises me the one thing I can't turn down if I help her. Access to *him*. Every street, hotel lobby and airport lounge in the world, I've searched for that animal. If I'd seen him, I would have committed murder in broad daylight with whatever I had in my hand. But I never did find him. And then Mercy offers him to me on a plate.' Bianca studies the face on the paper for a second before her eyes flick back to mine.

'The *Lex Talionis* is one of the laws the *elohim* — the archangels — live by,' I murmur. 'It means *an eye for an eye*. I even looked it up. Harm no one and no harm will come to you. Do evil, and they'll get you in the end. There will be an accounting. And Azraeil wants Lucifer dead, and Mercy wants Ryan safe, so...'

'So it's a kind of celestial three-for-one offer?' Bianca says drily, shifting in her seat, her white column dress whispering against the leather. 'That makes good operational sense. Get Lucifer, get his human enabler at the same time; rescue Ryan. Efficiencies of scale. It speaks to me. I knew I liked Mercy for a reason. We think the same way. Isn't that funny?'

I strive for the same light tone, failing miserably. 'So I'll do what it takes to help Mercy bring Luc down. How could I not when there's so much at stake? And if it means I have to be some kind of living...weapon for her, for Mercy, so be it.'

I turn my eyes away from the wide, pixelated grin on the face of the man who ground me into the dirt when he was done with me, like something you'd scrape off the sole of your shoe. 'If he's there tonight, and all I have to defend myself with is a canapé fork — he's still going to buy it.'

'You're a brave woman.' Bianca's voice is suddenly sober, with none of its usual sardonic, mocking quality. 'But remember that the cardinal rule for tonight appears to be *Look, don't touch*. So here's what I think we should do,' she continues briskly.

སྡ

When we reach the imposing canyon of Italianate nineteenth-century and *fin de siècle* stone facades lining Pall Mall, we join a slow-moving tide of limousines and armoured town cars jostling for position along the south side of the road.

'I'm still not happy about your plan,' I repeat as our car draws to a stop outside the black-carpeted front entrance of the Argo, crowds of gawkers being kept well back by a series of black velvet ropes and two parallel lines of burly men.

Skin crawling at the sight of so many faces, and feeling a panicky *déjà vu* from the madness of the Irina days, I frown up at the four-storey, palazzo-style façade faced in intricately chiselled stone and tall casemented windows.

'Tough,' Bianca says briskly as the passenger doors closest to the kerb are flung open by matching grandly-dressed concierges. 'You wouldn't be here without me, and I need my curiosity satisfied. I lead such an otherwise boring and sheltered life. Since Mercy burst into my world — not once, but twice, I might add — some part of me has always longed for her to come back. Three's supposed to be a charm. I want to see her again. She gave me so much hope. Who doesn't want to believe in real *magic*?'

Bianca looks back at me before she places one foot on the pavement and, I swear, her blue eyes are luminous. It strikes me then — that Bianca *wants* something to happen tonight. The thought makes me shiver.

I almost to tell her *Be careful what you wish for*, but before I can, two of Bianca's unsmiling security guards hand us out onto the black carpet as a hail of camera flashes lighten the darkening sky around us.

'Bianca, darling, who are you wearing?'

'Bianca, Bianca, over here, love! What's in your clutch?'

'Ms St Alban! What are you *thinking* right now?'

'Miss St Alban, can you give us some background on the recently announced StA Global takeover of the Precision Group's premium aerospace subsidiary?'

'Bianca St Alban, are you as drunk as you were at the opening of the Berlin International Film Festival?'

Bianca doesn't respond to questions as she sails down the carpet with me scurrying behind her like a puppy, Bianca's three-man, three-woman security detail flanking us on all sides. 'Remember,' I hiss at her artfully bared back as the inane-as-hell questions concerning Bianca's brand of g-string, Bianca's personal nail artist and Bianca's views on the next presidential candidate of the United States rain down on us from everywhere, 'all I need from you is an *intro*. That's all. Get as far away as you can the moment Skorobogatov and I make contact.'

If Bianca's heard me, she pretends she hasn't, raising her dazzling eyes to acquaintance after acquaintance and flashing her flawless white smile in every direction. As I continue following Bianca's sculpted shoulderblades down the black carpet, I say insistently, 'I'll find my own way back later. You don't need to do any more. You're just my golden ticket, got that?'

She doesn't reply to any of this either. But she suddenly

turns and, as if we're the best of friends, links her tanned, slender arm companionably through mine before bearing me beneath the high stone architrave carved into sprays of acorns and oak leaves, and through the front door of the members-only club.

We are greeted in the gilded front vestibule by a series of liveried porters and I can't help gasping as we enter the towering space and a red-faced, uniformed man haughtily booms in our faces, '*The Grand Saloon.*'

I can hardly take it all in at once. The Grand Saloon is filled with a crowd of men in black tie and birdlike women in an eye-watering array of jewel-coloured gowns and discreet but priceless gems; all gossiping to the strains of a string quartet playing Vivaldi. Less an innocuously-named 'saloon' than a vast rectangular void that rises several storeys, the Grand Saloon is surrounded on all sides by soaring marble columns in a riot of reds, greens, blacks and golds, which are mirrored at each upper level so that it feels as if I'm standing inside a hollowed-out wedding cake. There are rooms with closed doors leading off the Grand Saloon floor and off each of the upper galleries. It's unashamedly magnificent, one of the most beautiful buildings I've ever seen, and I shiver again; a feeling like somebody is dancing on my grave moving through me.

I crane my neck up at the spotlights illuminating the octagonally-pieced domed ceiling created almost entirely from struts of concrete and thousands of lozenges of sparkling lead glass. An enormous crystal chandelier is suspended in the centre of the dome, and the whole of the ceiling is ablaze from the combination of manmade light and the rays of the setting sun. The scale of the entire building is overwhelming, filled with the roar of voices and the clinking of crystal.

'I've been on the land too long,' I murmur aloud, only to be brought back to my immediate surroundings by Bianca's voice in my ear. 'He's over *there*.'

I follow her hand as she points out a sweeping archway directly across the room from where we're standing. The archway frames a grand carpeted staircase that leads to the three upper galleries above our heads. There's a red velvet rope suspended across the base of the stairwell and I go cold as I spot the broad-shouldered ice-blond man in the form-fitting tuxedo standing in front of the rope. He's already looking our way.

Skorobogatov is surrounded by an eight-man security detail so impressive no one seems game enough to breach it. Though I'm pierced by disappointment because not one of them is *the man* — the one with the death's-head tattoos. A quick scan of the entire saloon confirms that he's not here at all; part of me is so giddy with relief that the mosaic floor seems to undulate beneath my feet. Looking down, I imagine there are tendrils of silver mist twining about my ugly black shoes, around my ankles, as they did by the river in Sheol.

I blink, and the illusion is gone.

At Bianca's muttered order to her own people to *stay back* to give her a chance to speak freely with the Russian magnate, I look up hastily, rearranging the lines of my face into something blank and bland and subservient. As I watch, I see several other people try to approach Skorobogatov before us, but a single raised eyebrow from one of the bodyguards is enough to send people scurrying in another direction.

Leaving her uneasy security team stranded in the centre of the floor, Bianca lifts the hem of her gown with her free hand and hauls me across the room by my left arm. 'Spartak!' she calls out, waving, her face breaking into a broad smile. 'Здравствуйте!'

I know she's just said *hello* in the formal sense because I have more Russian in my arsenal than Bianca does, but as we push through the eveningwear-clad, face-lifted crowd towards Skorobogatov, I am struck dumb.

The man looks *sick*. He's twitching on the spot, the muscles of his face and shoulders moving independently of each other, the hand holding his crystal glass visibly trembling so that the amber-coloured liquid slops from side to side.

For a moment I dig my heels into the floor, and Bianca looks back at me with impatience. 'You're like a mule tonight, Gia,' she complains through gritted teeth, her polished smile never faltering. 'Isn't this exactly what you *wanted*?'

We're only a few feet from the man now, but it merely confirms that there's something very wrong with the individual who calls himself Spartak Skorobogatov. My eyes are telling me he's the exact same individual who gave that motivational business speech in Geneva fifteen months ago, but my brain is screaming at me to *run away*.

Up close there's an unhealthy pallor to the man's skin, a faint, sickly grey tinge. He seems to be perspiring heavily for such a perfectly temperature-controlled room. But the worst thing is how *broken* he looks. All the lines of his face and neck are gaunt and withered, as if they belong to a much older man. His white-blond hair is thinning in uneven clumps and he has the hollow, cadaverous look of a young man with a terminal illness. His tuxedo seems slightly too big for him, as if he's sinking into it second by second.

He's dying. I don't need to get any closer to know that. It's almost a smell rising off him. I can practically taste his decay.

'I've seen enough,' I mutter, turning to go, 'it has to be him. I need air. I need to think. I'm not sure what to do.'

But Bianca's grip on my hand is suddenly crushing. I can

feel her perspiring, too, and for a moment, I can *feel* her fear. But I can also feel her excitement. It's like a presence in the air between us.

Pasting that dazzling smile back on her face, Bianca draws us closer until only a few feet separate us from the tall, hard-faced men standing warily in a loose ring around the Russian billionaire. They look healthier than their boss does, but there's something about every one of the faces — moustachioed, bearded, clean-shaven — that also looks... wrong. To a man, they're all staring at Bianca, and I know, deep down, that they're drawn to how *alive* she is. Bianca radiates health and wellness and wealth. None of them are looking at me, for which I am grateful. I can barely breathe. There's something oppressive wrapped around this group of men like an invisible canopy, and we're *entering* it.

'It's like a cancer,' I find myself mumbling under my breath, unable to walk forward another step. 'They all have it, to varying degrees.'

'What are you talking about?' Bianca murmurs impatiently through her brilliant smile as we stare like lovestruck autograph hunters through the cordon of bodyguards at Skorobogatov himself.

'*Him*, his men,' I mutter, 'it's all coming from them. Some kind of light. Can't you see it?'

Bianca shakes her head, dragging me onward as if she's walking into a strong headwind, her hand upraised in greeting.

But I find myself stumbling forward as if I've been pushed, stepping onto the back hem of Bianca's gown and causing her to almost fall to her knees.

'What are you *doing*?' she cries out, exasperated, turning and looking at me. Then her eyes widen fearfully as she looks into my face.

Around him, Skorobogatov's security men suddenly search the air around us with their eyes, their heads questing as if they can smell something, like hunting dogs.

If I reached out now, pushed forward through that circle, I could touch him, Spartak — and our eyes lock onto each other at last.

'It's *demonsign*,' I whisper in a low voice that is not my own, and Bianca reels away from me in horror as I feel something move within me — quick and sinuous, like a serpent, or a fist of iron suddenly filling a chainmail glove — and I roar in a voice like sounding brass, *'Ejicie eum!'* — *Cast him out!* — and all Hell, it then breaks loose.

13

Out they pour from their wretched human casings, like a sea of grey-silver, writhing worms, and I watch as the bodies, the tuxedoed husks of men fall to the ground, chests faintly rising and falling to signal that they yet live.

The distant string quartet grinds to a confused halt as the screaming rises and I feel the swords flare to life in my hands, flames of blue-silver playing across the surface of the blades.

I roar, *'Go!'* pivoting and pushing Bianca away with such force that she flies across the room in an arc, coming to rest against the base of one of the marble columns by the entryway to the Grand Saloon.

I turn to face the eight pale columns of boiling smoke beginning to take shape before me. Everywhere, like ants, the people in their finery scatter, wailing; I laugh, the sound tolling like thunder through the room. *'Flee!'* I snarl in warning at the scrambling human forms. *'Fly!* No one dies on my watch.'

Just beyond me, creatures of vapour at least eight feet tall and vaguely humanoid, but lacking distinct features, are forming. They pour down through the icy air like columns of living smoke. They still loosely ring this cloud of buzzing, seething energy that is struggling to reform and I move closer, hope and hatred rising in me, that it might be as simple as this.

That it could all end here between Luc and me; now and forever.

Bianca told me herself once. *To save someone you love from Lucifer could never be wrong.* And to destroy the one who sought to destroy you twice over — first as archangel, then as human — would be a thing beyond rubies, beyond pearls.

'I am *owed*,' I shriek.

In reply, the *nephilim* — half-human bastard spawn of Luc's earthbound *daemonium*, giants of cunning and smoke and malice — let forth a collective, wordless howl, raising their vaguely armlike appendages as one. As I watch, the appendages shift to form vicious blades, keeping me away from the roiling mass of energy at the centre of their circle: the thing they are protecting.

But I can feel it, immediately — the difference in the signature — and my disappointment is as great as my rage. This one is not the one that marked me. I would know Lucifer's singular energy anywhere. I would have died for him, once. And I did.

'Who *are* you?' I hiss at the raging, formless, buzzing thing at the centre of the circle, which is still deaf and blind and vulnerable to its surroundings.

The nearest of the eyeless *nephilim* lunges forward suddenly — toothless mouth drawn back wide in a scream — seeking to spear me with its swordlike arm. In a kind of trance, I feel Gia's body sidestep the stabbing blade, only to have me cut the creature in half on the upswing with the blazing weapon in my left hand. The *nephilim* shatters with a blast wave of heat and energy, pushing us back momentarily.

As if the death of their brother is a signal, the seven other *nephilim* surge forward in a vengeful tide as the demon that possessed Spartak Skorobogatov's body continues to struggle to take shape behind them. He has been too long away from the dark, hot places that kept Luc and his fallen alive for millennia. Without the human life source that has given him constant protection these last few months, the demon will be compromised and disoriented. I know I need to strike quickly.

But the *nephilim* leap and fall over each other like ravening wolves to reach me first, and I am forced to scramble backwards, away from the roiling, shrieking shape by the stairs. I know that if any of them so much as touch Gia, they could kill her, and I will be cast out; I feel it keenly — in every straining fibre of our shared body, our shared flesh — how little time I have, how good it feels to live again, if only through another.

Like beasts of nightmare, the *nephilim* separate, scrambling across the tiled floor on four loose, long limbs to close the gap between us. The leading creature flies forward, bladelike arms extended, and I feel Gia's inchoate, wordless terror as she hits the ground on her back.

I slice upwards with my blades, sending that one, and then the next, back to God in a blast wave of dark energy. Rolling, Gia shakily regains her feet, scanning the room wildly, only to be surrounded by four more.

Only four.

Where is the last?

I feel Gia's heartbeat escalate as she swings around in a wild arc, outnumbered.

Beyond us, I see a lethally muscular male demon with short auburn curls and dead-looking midnight eyes begin to lift his head at last, the shining imprint of an archangel's punishing hand in the centre of his bare chest. His lower body is barely clothed to mid-thigh in the manner Lucifer used to affect before he fell; so that his beauty might be better displayed.

The moment the surrounding *nephilim* swivel their heads toward their master expectantly — like dumb pack beasts seeking orders — I leap forward among them, cutting them down so swiftly that the heat of their dying is like standing at the centre of a fiery blast. I feel more than hear Gia's scream of pain as she shields her head and face, momentarily, with her crossed arms. Every moment we share this body is causing her terrible anguish. I am conscious of that. And I am sorrier for it than she will ever know.

I will the blades in my hands to vanish, hooking myself deeper into Gia's flesh, pulling her about me like a cloak, so that the demon will not spy the ghost in the machine; what he is truly facing. Or the element of surprise will be lost.

For a moment, I sense the monster struggling to focus: on the room, on me; taking all the heat from the air only to leak that cold, grey energy that signals the baleful presence of the *daemonium*.

But then he raises his densely muscled arms, as if in triumph, and two giant, glorious wings, taller and wider than the demon himself, unfurl behind him to sweep the floor.

When he lifts his head at last and fixes his dead, dark gaze on me, all he sees is a frail and frightened-looking green-eyed blonde in an ugly black pantsuit and pumps, the faint nimbus of silver-blue light she is giving off lost in the silver-grey mist enshrouding the room, seeming to rise out of the very floor itself.

Te gnovi, I think with a surge of bitter heat. *I know you.*

And I do. I last saw this one screaming like a missile through the skies above a gothic stone cathedral rooftop in Milan, baying for my destruction. But I don't react. I don't let even a muscle on Gia's face change from fear to recognition.

'What *are* you?' Hakael growls through bared and glistening teeth. 'There is something about your energy, human, something muddy, yet familiar. But *weak*. And strange. As if you are already one foot inside the grave.'

I have to suppress a smile at that.

The cavernous, echoing space seems entirely empty of human life now. Outside, I can hear the wail of multiple sirens drawing closer, the shouts of the terrified and confused. But in here, it is just Hakael and I, and that one remaining *nephilim*, wherever it might be lurking. I can feel it, circling, at the edges of my awareness, just out of reach. Two against one; the odds, as always, against me.

Hakael draws himself up to his full height, wings spread wide like the hood of an enraged cobra. My gaze goes up and up as he shakes off the last vestiges of his cramped humanity; Gia's breath comes in short, pained bursts in the crackling, icy air. A layer of frost snakes across the tiled floor towards me, spreading outward from Hakael like a slick of grey rime that climbs the pillars of marble, one by one, until the air is filled with the sound of cracking stone.

'Where is Ryan Daley?' I bellow through Gia's chattering teeth.

Hakael covers a moment of real confusion with harsh laughter. 'The pet lapdog of Lucifer? *Nowhere on this earth*, woman. He is a special guest in Lucifer's own kingdom. *In Hell*. Where you would least expect to find it.'

My challenge is swift and contemptuous. 'Narrow it down for me. I'm guessing Hell's no longer in Russia these days, but somewhere warmer — judging by your patent inability to maintain a steady core temperature.'

Hakael's dark gaze flares in anger, but he counters with, 'How were you able to best my *nephilim*, woman?'

He darts forward at an oblique angle before vanishing and reappearing beside one of the gaudy pillars of Candoglia marble across the room. 'You have no power,' he snarls.

I suppose it's an advantage, that they have always misjudged me.

I taste sudden bile at the back of Gia's throat. To look upon Hakael directly is to look upon sickness and beauty, co-mingled. A shimmering, incarnate madness.

'Still,' Hakael sneers, reappearing at the banister of the first-floor gallery, looking down at me looking up at him, 'You are no match for a first-order demon, whatever you are — nothing my Lord Lucifer need fear. We had grown tired of the Russian, in any case. He was past all usefulness. We have taken all there was to take.'

Without warning, the last *nephilim* surges out of the shadows of the pillars to my left, bounding upward towards its master in defiance of the laws of gravity. It leaps straight over the balcony railing, halting beside Hakael with an unconscious woman in dazzling white slung over its shoulder.

As I look up through the green contact lenses covering Gia's mismatched eyes, her heart seems to stutter in her chest in recognition: *Bianca*.

Hakael receives Bianca almost gently from his servant, cradling her glossy dark head against his scarred and gleaming chest as he moves forward and holds her body easily over thin air, beyond the safety of the stone guard rail.

'Awaken,' he murmurs solicitously into her perfect ear, his gaze never leaving mine.

Bianca's eyes open into the burning eyes of Satan's right hand.

She is screaming even before he opens his arms wide over the balustrade ... *and lets her go.*

Time seems to stop in that moment.

Bianca's falling — I can see her doing it — her physical body seconds away from splitting open before my eyes on the hard mosaic tiles like ripe fruit. But she's frozen now — arms and legs at frantic angles — the same way I am. The same way Hakael and the *nephilim* are, their mouths stretched wide with laughter, high above me.

In moments, master and servant will be gone, escaped into other mischief, other bodies, and she will be dead.

As if to confirm this, I catch movement to my right and beside me stands Azraeil, his feet not quite touching the tiled floor laid down almost two centuries ago — whose instance of eternity this is.

I turn because I still can, inside this silver-limned bubble of stopped time. I am his handmaid now, after all.

'Bianca St Alban has been marked for many years.' Azraeil's deep voice is thoughtful. 'She has attempted more than once to take her own life, splendid as it is in human terms. But something has always stayed my hand with her. Perhaps it was for just this moment.'

'Please, Azraeil,' I beg. 'Not like this. She has been a friend to us. Not this way. Not *now*.'

Azraeil studies the demons standing above us with eyes as blue as the daytime sky, as blue as the sun on the sea, his gleaming silver hair spilling like moonlight made real across his broad, black-clad shoulders; incorruptible as time, youth and eternity in one shining form. 'You know I have one true power only,' he murmurs, still gazing upward at our bastard kin. 'Alone among all the *elohim* am I charged to take human life or give it. I cannot take *them*. Demonkind are beyond my power and my remit. I know that as if it is written inside me in lines of fire.'

He turns and looks at me, his blue eyes blazing out of his

youthful, flawless face. 'But not beyond yours. You straddle *worlds*, Mercy.'

'But what do I *do*?' I answer hoarsely. 'Take them or save Bianca? I cannot do both. Hakael knows it. He can't be sure what I am, but he will not let me get close enough to find out. Her death enables his safe passage.'

'She's not dead yet,' Azraeil snaps. '*Think.*'

I gesture wildly at the dense human body that is my instrument and vehicle in this world. Gia's mouth is set in a rictus of pain, her body stuttering and failing as she valiantly struggles to give me what I need: heat, energy, shelter, *time*.

Azraeil bends low and places a finger, smooth as alabaster, beneath Gia's heart-shaped face, tilting up her trembling chin to meet our gaze more clearly.

'*You* are elemental,' Azraeil's voice is like a breath of wind from the afterlife. 'As fire and water are, as are air and earth, iron and stone and wood. Everything that you were is still in you but is merged, at this moment, with everything that *she* is. Two energies, two sets of consciousness, two Selves, two kinds of Light to counter the darkness. Channel this convergence *to regain what you once were*. With powers so very different from those granted me. My hands have always been empty. I alone of all our brethren am wingless and flightless, indentured to go where human life or death must be decided. *You* are the weapon I have craved since first I *lived*.'

Azraeil kneels and grips Gia's narrow shoulders and his face is our sun, his ringing voice our whole horizon. 'Tell me, you who call yourself *Mercy* — do I reap her now?'

Horror engulfs me momentarily, to be presented with such a choice. I look down at where Azraeil's hands rest on Gia's shoulders and know with a cold certainty that they have rested there before.

All of us — Gia, Bianca and I — all already marked by Death and weighed in his balance.

'We have always known it — that there are too many to save,' I breathe through the tightness in Gia's chest. 'It's impossible — what you're asking me to do.'

'*You're* impossible,' Azraeil counters harshly. 'Remember. You were made to be that way.'

For a moment, raw power surges through me and it's as if a door to an endless library — hallway upon hallway disappearing down into others — flies open. I see how it is done. To hold a moment of time separate and apart from all others so that none but you are outside it — only Azraeil can do that. The others can suspend time, yes. But Azraeil can suspend life.

His bright blue eyes see that I see.

And then he vanishes.

Time recommences.

Bianca continues falling, screaming as she falls, and I feel something inside me shatter open, feel giant wings I never thought I would know again unfurl across my back, spreading wide, the outline of them drifting and fraying in the frigid air, taller and wider than me.

I am different, it is true. But I am still myself and always will be...because of Azraeil's intervention.

I plunge forward, catching Bianca before her body can fragment upon the hard ground, laying her down safely on the icy tiles before soaring upwards in the same breath. Terrible laughter pours from me, silver-blue flames licking across the surface of the guns I find nested in my two hands, made of my own fury. The same weapons that did murder the demon Jetrel upon a high, lonely mountainside half a world away.

Haud Misericordia! I roar down into the faces of my

enemies as they once did to me.

No mercy.

And lines of silver-blue spread from the sudden crater in Hakael's chest, another fiery projectile made of my energy, my wrath, obliterating the creature of cloud and malice beside him...

PART 2

I was wondering when you'd get around to remembering me.

14

The voices are hushed and indistinct.

'Did you see it?' the man says.

'On the telly?' the woman replies.

There's a *plash* of water, the rough feel of a washcloth against my skin, the drag of it over my face and neck setting off little explosions of pain everywhere. 'I saw it from here. Over the rooftops. Something made me stand up and go to the window. It looked like a bloody mushroom cloud going off.'

'I was there,' he replies across my closed eyelids. 'The heat — I can't describe it — just this incredible *spike*. It almost knocked me flat.'

I feel myself sliding lower in the water, coughing and spluttering as it begins to enter my mouth and nose, too weak to push myself upright.

I'm thrashing now and he's saying, 'Whoah, *whoah.*'

And she's scolding, half sobbing, 'Oh Gia, you gave us both such a *scare!*'

Then Shaun and Jamie are hauling me, naked, out of her bathtub that's filled to the brim with burning hot water.

I'm still shivering uncontrollably inside my cocoon of clothing and blankets in Jamie's study as she replays footage of the moment a lone blonde woman in black appears to leap barefoot off the shattered roof of the Argo into a service alley running behind the four-storey building. Minutes later, the woman — I only vaguely recognise her as me — still hasn't reappeared.

Shaun and I haven't seen the clip before, even though versions of it have been running non-stop on international news services since it happened last night.

'I don't even r-remember doing that,' I say through jittering teeth, 'and I *detest* heights. S-sorry about your shoes, Jamie. I don't know h-how I lost those when I managed to keep the wig on.'

Jamie wrinkles her nose good-naturedly. 'Didn't like them shoes anyhow. Just glad you're in one piece, love.'

'Police still haven't found the body!' a female voice says excitedly as the unsteady eyewitness footage comes to a close.

Shaun sits back in his chair, studying me with glittering amber eyes beneath a furrowed brow. 'You're lucky to be alive,' he mutters. 'You completely ignored orders not to engage.'

'They engaged *me*,' I reply through still-chattering teeth. 'Though I honestly don't remember a great deal of it. One minute I'm telling Bianca St Alban I've seen enough and we should go, and the next I wake up in a bath full of literal hot water.'

'Are you *serious*?' Shaun's voice is incredulous. 'How could you not remember being right in the middle of a complete shit storm? This is what the situation looked like from out front.'

Jamie presses *play* on another snatch of video. Taken from a point below the soaring façade of the Argo, there are sounds of violent breakage from inside the building. Intense, bright light is roving across the lower storey windows when, without warning, *all* of the front windows, and parts of the Argo's centuries-old leadlight domed roof, suddenly blow outward, showering the screaming throng outside with debris.

The explosion is so bright that the screen is filled for several seconds with nothing but light. 'It's not really white.' Jamie's voice is thoughtful. 'We ran the spectrum. There's pale blue at the heart of it, and silver. A luminous grey. And there's this —'

Jamie flicks out of that footage, starts running something else: the same snatch of video she first showed me and Shaun. Me standing on the roof seventy feet off the ground — but drastically slowed down and re-filtered the same way the footage of Spartak Skorobogatov speaking in Geneva was.

Shaun and I gasp at the same time as Jamie adds softly, 'If you muck around with the filter and the speed, that's what you get — the vague, dark outline of a very tall, winged woman somehow *around* you while you're standing there. It's still there as you're falling. Mercy is probably the reason you're sitting in that chair right now with a mild headache and not much else, Gia.'

'How —?' I begin, but Shaun interrupts. 'As soon as the news came through that there was some kind of developing hostage crisis at the Argo and for people to avoid all the streets around the area, I went straight over there and found you propped up behind a skip in an alley a block away. It was the platinum-blonde wig against the darkness that gave you away.'

'Good choice,' Jamie murmurs approvingly.

'Survival of the blondest,' I reply absently, thinking of all the fashion shows I've ever been behind-the-scenes for. 'It's a law of nature.'

Shaun rolls his eyes. 'You didn't appear to have a scratch on you,' he continues, 'and you were breathing okay, so I just brought you back here. I'm pretty sure no one even looked twice. Man carries an unconscious, barefoot woman through central London and —'

'No one gives a toss,' Jamie snorts. 'That'd be right.'

Shaun moves his chair around so that he can catch hold of both my icy hands and look into my face. 'I know it's hard, but what happened?' he says. 'Try to remember.'

His gaze is so full of affection and concern that I close my eyes with a shiver.

He's a kind man, that's all he is, I tell myself. *Don't read anything else into it.*

'It's as if she...took over,' I whisper. 'There was less of me this time, more of her, even without me choosing to fight it. She was so *strong*. Like I was still there, but trapped under thick ice, looking out. I could hear myself saying things, feel myself doing things, but it was her driving everything, somehow *drawing* on me, as if I was some kind of...battery. It was like I was sleepwalking, but at the same time lit up like a dashboard, all red with pain...'

I frown, remembering a burning great handprint on a perfect male torso. Seeing it had been shocking. I tell Jamie and Shaun of the disembodied memory, hear the rustle their clothing makes as they look at each other, disturbed. 'The mark of the exiled,' I murmur, not knowing how I know.

'Was it — I can't believe I'm saying this — uh, *Lucifer*?' Shaun asks. 'Was he there?'

With my eyes still jammed shut I shake my head.

'She was...disappointed, I think. I remember that. Mercy knew him though — she called him by name. Something beginning with an H. And she screamed, in this voice to make your skin fairly leap off your body, *Where is Ryan Daley*? Just point blank like that. And the giant with the handprint across his chest, he just...laughed.'

'Didn't give a bare-faced answer in reply, I suppose?' Jamie's voice is hopeful. 'Preferably with GPS coordinates?'

I try to remember what the scarred and shining giant had

boomed in reply, but my eyelids are heavy and I struggle to open them. '*The pet lapdog of... Lucifer?*' I mumble. '*Nowhere... on this earth...woman. He is a special guest in... Lucifer's own kingdom. In Hell. Where you would... least expect to find it.*'

'Got all that down?' Shaun asks Jamie.

'Got it,' is Jamie's reply as her study, and all the world, recede around me.

ॐ

I wake myself in the early hours of the morning screaming, '*We have taken all there was to take.*'

Sweating and shaking, I sit up. Jamie comes to my bedroom door a moment later, a concerned, skeletal shape in pink compression bandages and cotton sleepwear, like a mummified woman in a bathrobe. She sits gingerly on the end of my bed and studies me intently with her good eye through her skull-shaped face mask.

'I'm sorry I woke you,' I rasp, still aching from my dream of being trapped and stalked inside the Argo. 'But it's hopeless. We're never going to find him. I mean we've got no leads. Mercy *blew up* Lucifer's second-in-command. That was the blast you all saw: all our clues evaporating in an instant. Dead demons don't end up in Sheol. They're just... gone.'

I frown, unsure how I know that to be true. But it is. 'Demons and angels — they just cancel each other out.'

'We have plenty of leads,' Jamie says briskly. 'We've had actual confirmation that Mercy's Ryan is still alive, for one thing.'

'But he's *nowhere on earth*,' I retort.

'That can't be true,' Jamie rasps. 'They can't leave now, right, them demons? They're stuck here. No Paradise ever again for the wicked; Mercy saw to that. And your angel — didn't he say Lucifer and his lot have come up from underground for good now? That the main game was no longer any fun being run from downstairs? So they're here among us and, judging by what you told me and Shaun, there are real moments where they're...vulnerable. They can actually be destroyed. You and her — you did that. You got one together. An old one, from the sounds of it. One of the original fallen. Almost as powerful as His Nibs, yeah?'

I'm silent for a long time, racking my brain for more memories I can use. But all I get is impressions: intense light and pain and fog.

'I'm thinking demons aren't inclined to tell the truth,' Jamie adds. 'So it will be some play on words. Like Ryan's being held on a boat because that's not *on* earth, is it? Well, not technically...'

Her words cause my eyes to widen in appreciation.

'...or in a hot air balloon. Or on an aeroplane that's, like, continually circling the world.' The idea of it actually makes Jamie laugh out loud.

'Mercy *did* say Ryan wasn't anywhere inside Sheol,' I muse.

'Which takes us right back to my first point,' Jamie says patiently, 'that he's still alive somewhere here in *our* world; he's still reachable.'

'Don't be so sure of that,' I mumble, wrinkling my forehead; the simple act of doing that setting off painful Catherine wheels inside my skull.

'What happened to Skorobogatov and his goons anyhow?' I add, turning on my side to face the open door in an effort to stop the pounding in my right temple. 'Bianca St Alban?'

As I'm closing my eyes again, I hear Jamie say through the pressure in my head, 'Bianca got out — her family issued a press release saying that she's been discharged from hospital and is recovering at the family compound on the Italian–Swiss border, privacy requested at this difficult time et cetera. And the Russians are still alive too, but the press is saying there's a real chance all of them — including Skorobogatov — will never regain consciousness, and that there's not even any money left to take care of them. Skorobogatov's whole empire is a sham and has been for months, they say. Because someone's taken everything, they've transferred the lot out of his name, lock, stock and barrel...'

It's late morning by the time I wake again, and the minute I set foot on the stairs, Jamie pops her head out of the study to tell me that Bianca St Alban has just surfaced and needs desperately to chat and that Skorobogatov's asset trail goes stone-cold the moment it reaches a small tax haven just off the east coast of the United States. 'It could take weeks to unravel!' Jamie lisps cheerfully through the mouth-shaped gap in her mask. 'But there *is* one odd, outright transfer of twenty million dollars — *twenty mil*, love! — to an indie folk singer who calls herself 'Cibyyl' on the intertubes. She's very young, blonde, beautiful, all long spindly legs like a baby deer, skin like peaches, as yet unsigned by a record label. Possibly a straight business deal, possibly a hush-money pay-off because she's a Skorobogatov ex. Hard to tell from a transfer narration that just says *Beaut music*. Although there's no connection been made in the press between her and the Russian anywhere — and believe me, I've been digging. It could be a way in — or it could be nothing.'

'Coffee,' I croak, stumbling to the kitchen to get a jumbo mug of Jamie's vile brand of instant with extra sugar in it, before re-entering her peculiar arena of battle where the players are unseen, their allegiances unknown.

Jamie shows me a shortlist of company names and countries of domicile. As she describes each one, I see that the transfer amounts originating in Skorobogatov's company bank accounts are stratospherically huge — each one more money than a normal person would ever see in a lifetime — and that all of the transactions leapfrog through the same chain of companies, though not necessarily in the same order. All of them end up in the same bank account listed as held by an entity called Charybdis LLC. Except for this one, very recent, transfer of twenty million US dollars into the personal bank account of a fragile-looking waif-woman whose stage name — according to the few videos she's posted online — is the unrevealing *Cibyyl*.

Jamie plasters the girl's face across one of the terminals and Cibyyl peers at us through her wispy, honey-blonde bangs; her big, dark doe eyes shimmering like huge wells of meaning.

There's nothing much about Cibyyl out there. Apart from a handful of live performance videos of poor sound quality that predate the Skorobogatov money transfer by roughly a month, she's nowhere to be found — no email address, no agent, no website, no social media: a beautiful ghost.

'She's not even very good,' I mutter as Jamie plays a simple cover the girl has done of an old Beatles song. As she sings in an idiosyncratically breathless voice — enlivened by weird, unexpected runs of notes that end in eerie, discordant ways — we lean in and look at the girl's pillowy lips with the winsome dent right in the centre of the lower one.

'But you've got to admit, she's got *something*,' Jamie muses. 'She's almost… incandescent. *Tiger, tiger burning bright*, and all that. You can't tear your eyes away from her. It's like she has her own personal filter. The room's just a room; could be anywhere. But around her...'

It's true. Standing there singing to a simple off-screen guitar accompaniment that could be just a pre-taped recording, Cibyyl is all bangs, big dark eyes and wispy, bum-length, sun-kissed hair. She's wearing a body-skimming marle grey tee-shirt dress that ends just below her hips and knitted rainbow-striped fingerless gloves that reach her elbows. Her face is a gleaming oval of intense feeling, as if every word she's singing is resonating in some deep cavern of her soul. And she *could* be standing under her own spotlight. Whatever it is that's making her seem to glow is moving with her.

'I wonder how she's doing that?' I mutter. 'Clever lighting? Maybe a boyfriend standing on a milk crate holding a videocam in one hand and a flashlight in the other? She looks luminous.'

And that *mouth*. Jamie and I lean forward, mesmerised, watching it move.

'You kind of forget about her voice after a while, you're just so busy drinking in her *face*. Do you think those lips are... natural?' Jamie's gravelly voice is wistful.

'Who cares what she sounds like when she looks like *that*?' I agree.

Cibyyl finally stops her mournful warbling, stepping back from the camera and bowing her head just before the video stops so that her long hair falls around her face. Jamie pushes away from her workstation and looks at me. 'What do you think the money from Skorobogatov was *for*?' she asks.

'Maybe it was supposed to function as the world's biggest electronic bouquet of flowers?' I shoot back, but my interesting train of thought is interrupted as Bianca St Alban dials through on another terminal from her private account.

We look at each other for a long time.

Bianca's sitting so close to the screen that her head and shoulders block out most of the room she's in. She's wearing what look like fawn-coloured cashmere pyjamas buttoned right up to her neck. Because she's wearing her hair scraped back in a severe topknot today, the huge dark purple bruise blooming across the right side of her face is clearly visible, and her skin is unusually bloodless under her golden tan.

'I can't seem to get warm,' are Bianca's first words.

'Me neither,' I reply immediately. 'To do what she did, Mercy had to take whatever energy she could from wherever she could get it. I'm physically wrecked.'

I'm suddenly hit by the vague recollection of Bianca flying away from my outstretched hand, and it occurs to me that *I* might have had something to do with the damage to her face.

Bianca wraps her long, elegant arms around her slim shoulders and, before I realise what I'm doing, I find myself mirroring her actions.

We sit there digitally hugging each other for a while, with entire countries and oceans between us.

Finally, I ask Bianca what she remembers and she says sombrely, 'I remember I was about to die. I remember falling through the air like a bomb and thinking, *This is it; this is all you get to do.*'

I tell her what *I* remember — which still isn't enough to explain much — and about how Jamie seems to have found one loose thread in the wholesale takeover of the entire worldly possessions of the shell formerly answering to the name Spartak Skorobogatov.

Bianca frowns, diverted. 'I'll have my people look into those companies right away, see what they can find. And that girl — C-I-B-Y-Y-L, right? — for what it's worth.'

She reels off an email address and Jamie immediately sends all the information she has across as Bianca and I lower our arms and sit straighter, still staring at each other.

'I'm not going crazy, but Death was in the room,' Bianca mutters. 'I felt him the same way I've... felt him before. There's only ever been this thin veil between us, my whole life. Sounds crazy, I know.'

Beside me, I feel Jamie stiffen.

'Did you see him?' I reply, relieved not to have been the only one to sense him there, stalking the room. 'No matter how hard I try, I can't recall his face. But I get the echo of his voice — deep, you know, like a snatch of glorious music you're desperate to remember.'

Jamie turns and stares at me for a moment, as if she wants to say something, before frowning and re-focusing on Bianca.

'I don't know what to do,' I tell Bianca finally. 'It's *our* world, sure, but there are an awful lot of places for monsters to hide.'

My words seem to snap Bianca awake. She suddenly sits straighter. 'Let our global investigative team analyse the company data,' she replies briskly. 'I'll try to have something for you on Charybdis LLC as soon as I can. Our people are unparalleled at sniffing out money and the identities of foreign counterparties who wish to remain anonymous. You keep looking for the singer — our lot aren't so good at finding singers. Find out who she is, where she is. After all, you found me, and that's supposed to be impossible.'

Bianca abruptly cuts the connection.

15

Cibyyl proves to be as elusive as the grey mist that the demonic bring with them. Apart from a handful of photos online — fuzzy stills from her own lo-fi video clips — and a single cryptic, three-day-old tweet from someone called *@therealKit* — which says, *Cibyyl, I will hunt you by night forever you burn in my soul* — we have nothing. No address details, no appearances past or scheduled, not even a country of residence. Just that mysterious bank account number that showed up inside a braindead Russian mogul's electronic funds transfer history.

Jamie has a closer look at *@therealKit's* profile. His avatar is a heraldic lion with its teeth bared in a roar, and his profile description is equally cryptic. It reads simply, *The dagger or the poison?*

After scrolling backwards and forwards through the tweets for a few days either side, Jamie says with disgust, '*@therealKit* has a lot to say about his man parts to anyone who'll listen, I'll give him that. But most of it is rubbish. He's just some pervert who fancies himself rotten.' She points to a shambolic insult about the size of a rival's package before dismissing *@ therealKit's* profile from the screen.

'Are you sure we shouldn't look at him a bit harder?' I query. 'I mean, it's the only recent thing with the name "Cibyyl" in it. You'd hunt someone down too, if you handed them twenty million dollars and they didn't come through for you. Maybe that's what *@therealKit* is referring to.'

'It could have been any old Cibyyl he was talking about,' Jamie mutters. 'And, anyway, Cibyyl never replied. No one did. It was just another 3am ramble in the dark.'

'How many Cibyyls do you know in real life?' I insist. 'I think this is important.'

Jamie pretends she doesn't hear me as she clicks onto an indie music fan site and starts searching through the Next Big Thing gossip forums for mentions of our elusive blonde.

Hours pass in which Jamie sits hunched over her keyboard, doggedly typing. I'm woken from an uneasy doze in my armchair when Jamie cries out, 'What kind of indie folk singer doesn't want to get bloody *found* these days?'

As the light disappears from the day, I get up to fix us more soup while Jamie continues shooting off queries to everyone she can think of who owes her a favour, real or otherwise. It feels like a breakthrough when we work out that Cibyyl's bank account is held at a small agricultural bank domiciled in Switzerland, but after a bit more digging, that's all we've got.

The firewalls on the bank's databases are like nothing you've ever seen, someone called *$$yber* messages Jamie, *but I'm working on it for you.*

'*$$yber* is good,' Jamie mutters, 'but it could still take days. And I hate waiting. It's all I ever bloody do now. Wait.'

She shoots off an email to Bianca with the details of what we've managed to glean about Cibyyl's bank account, but nothing comes back. 'Probably because she worked it out hours before we did,' Jamie sniffs.

'Ryan Daley's not the only person who's impossible to find,' I snarl as I get up to turn on more lights throughout the house.

The darkness feels more oppressive than usual today. 'I can't stand much more of this, Jamie. My head's pounding.'

When I shuffle back into the study, I find Jamie staring intently at the video of Cibyyl singing that wistful song by the Beatles again. Of the handful of covers, it's the one with the most *likes*, which isn't saying a lot; Cibyyl might look the goods, but she's a little bit crap. There's something about her that's just the slightest bit off; like her heart isn't really in it and she's going through the motions.

Finally, in exasperation and all out of fresh ideas, Jamie creates an account and leaves a comment under the video clip.

Message *Mercy* via Rabbleknowledgenet with whatever it is that you want, is all the comment says.

'Uh,' I say uncertainly as Jamie's comment pops up onscreen, sitting right above a list of crude *Hey, baby*-style invites to get cosy and naked. 'Mercy isn't available right now to take your call. Plus, Cibyyl won't know who Mercy *is*, will she? And Mercy's hopeless with technology. I've witnessed her trying to work out what to do with a cell phone, and that was when she *had* a body. I can't just "channel" her, Jamie — Mercy does what she wants; she always has. Even if I could, I'm pretty certain Mercy couldn't find or use Rabbleknowledgenet — excuse me? — even if you set a howling demon in front of it with a sign on its head saying *Type message here*.'

My heart twists at the sudden memory of the call Ryan made to my phone in Milan when Mercy was still holed up inside Irina's slinky size zero body. Mercy didn't even know how to hold or speak into the thing properly, let alone kill the call to Ryan without fumbling and crying. It was pitiful to watch. *I* almost teared up — and back then, making me cry was a huge deal.

Jamie's face tightens briefly in a smile. 'From what I've

learnt about her, Mercy isn't averse to a little identity theft to get what she wants. We're just going to do the same thing and see what happens. If Cibyyl's looking for a major record deal or a reality TV show of her own, she'll play. If she doesn't, no harm done, and we ask Bianca to show us hers. It won't be a dead end. I've got a good feeling, darl. Trust me.'

Then Jamie sets her computers — all eight of them — to hibernate, solicitously puts a scarred claw under my elbow and ushers me out to the kitchen.

☙

This time, I'm woken by the sounds of gagging and terrible struggle across the hall. Like the noises a woman would make fighting for her life.

Sitting bolt upright, a cold bright light spills across the carpet outside my door, just for an instant. I leap out of bed, terrified that maybe Jamie's angel has come for her. From the expression on Jamie's face while Bianca and I were talking this afternoon, I have a feeling I know who he is.

I fall across the threshold of Jamie's bedroom only to see her rise slowly out of her own bed with a sightless look in her wide-open eye. There's no one in the room besides the two of us, but every hair on my body, I swear, is standing up the same way it had around Skorobogatov at the Argo.

Something's in here, with us.

'Jamie?' I say aloud, too scared to reach out and actually touch her. She doesn't answer. Walking straight past me as if I'm not there — in her knee-length tee-shirt nightgown, head in its usual casing of livid pink pressure bandage — she goes down the staircase in the pitch dark, her movements surefooted and her tread oddly heavy for someone so slight.

'What are you doing?' I call after her, turning and grabbing up a pair of thick socks and my phone, plus a cardigan and beanie because the night air is frigid. It's like breathing in ice.

But Jamie doesn't turn or stop, and by the time I'm headed downstairs at a run, she's already reached the lowest tread in the darkness. I watch her walk straight past the umbrella stand full of umbrellas she never uses because she never goes outside anymore.

She opens the battery of locks on her front door with calm deliberation.

Twist lock, deadlock, chain.

Then Jamie steps outside — feet, legs and arms completely bare — shutting the door behind her. Right in my startled face.

In the time it takes me to jam my hunting boots on and get outside, the weight of my phone inside my cardigan pocket banging against the top of my thigh, Jamie's almost all of the way out of Derbyshire Row. A few turns later and she's leading me straight through the western edge of Weavers Fields, which are deserted and eerie at this hour. As she makes her way unerringly in the direction of Spitalfields, the few people Jamie passes on the street actually leap aside when they register what she looks like.

She's striding with purpose through badly lit areas I've never been into before — past darkened primary schools and church rectories, cat emporiums and health centres, pubs and tattoo parlours — taking brisk shortcuts with absolute indifference up smelly back lanes and alleys that are pitch dark and could harbour anything. I can't be sure, because she's moving so quickly, but the bare skin on the backs of her arms and bare legs appears faintly luminous from a distance. Although I could be imagining things, because I'm seeing phantom smears of light everywhere, as if they're painted on my retinas.

The air feels like dry ice, like it could freeze your heart inside you. It's hurting my ears, nose and lungs just breathing in and out as I limp along, struggling to keep Jamie in sight.

When a drunk rears up out of someone's half-open garage door and tries to put his arms around Jamie in a crushing bear hug, I run forward, hands outstretched, shouting a warning. But Jamie — a woman with the build of a malnourished fourteen-year-old girl — just does something quick with her clenched fists and a twist of her slight hips and the man's on his back on the slick cobbles, roaring in pain. I'm past him before he can try anything else, only to see Jamie stride without pause into the thin traffic moving along the A10 into Shoreditch.

We pass more fitness clubs and cafés, but now their darkened windows are interspersed with upmarket dance fitness studios, real estate agencies and art galleries. I'm as fit as I'm ever going to be, but Jamie's just powering ahead, not even looking back to see if I'm following or bothering to stay to the lighted areas. She's completely indifferent to her surroundings.

Jamie emerges out of a laneway, passing the side wall of a closed Boots chemist into a wide thoroughfare lined with parking garages and billboards, business colleges and finance houses. She suddenly freezes in an attitude of watchfulness in the centre of the footpath, so I freeze too, just inside the mouth of the laneway.

Something about Jamie's complete stillness, her attitude of single-minded focus on the five-storey, redbrick art deco building across the road reminds me of the giant attack dogs Irina employed the one and only time we returned to Russia to visit her mother. 'If anyone tries to touch me,' Irina murmured at the dog handlers as her beast-led entourage stepped out of a series of ostentatious black armoured Mercedes Benzes outside a falling-down housing estate near the Novosibirsk train station, 'you tell them to rip out the face.' She made a circle with long splayed fingers around her own ethereal visage — just in case her instructions hadn't been clear enough — and laughed.

Barely able to breathe around the painful stitch in my side, I watch Jamie stare at the building as if she could set fire to it with her gaze. Coming up tentatively behind her right shoulder, I struggle to make out the name of the building we're looking at in the gloom. There are a couple of huge potted trees in stainless steel planters on either side of the looming glass double doors that make up the entrance with one stainless steel D facing the right way and another facing the wrong way for handles. The building's signage is so discreet it's almost non-existent.

I puzzle out the name, *Bar Darlie*, in simple letters just above the long steel and wood bar that's visible through one of the ground-floor windows, figuring the place must be some kind of boutique hotel. Even at this hour, there are seriously built security guards in dark suits and overcoats posted on either side of the potted trees, who wouldn't be out of place modelling for Ralph Lauren on the side.

Well to the left of the front entrance I make out a cordoned-off area, overseen by a few more well-groomed security boys. It's packed with pubescent girls and a scattering of mums and young women, all bundled up in heavy coats, down jackets and beanies. They're all sitting on camp stools or huddled in sleeping bags, makeshift tents and cardboard shelters, alone or in groups, packed in like sardines as if they're having an outdoor sleepover on one of the coldest nights in winter. It's almost 4am, but there must be hundreds of them penned in there. Some are holding handmade signs and placards with borders of hearts or flowers or stars drawn on them. They're waiting for a glimpse of someone famous, I know, because I've been on the other side of makeshift holding pens just like that one, dozens of times before.

Someone in the movies or TV? Maybe fashion? Not business or politics, it's pretty clear from the captive demographic.

A road sign on a nearby building reads *Great Eastern Street*, and I work out, shocked, that we've reached the outskirts of central London. The Barbican's not far from here. Jamie's walked almost two icy city miles in bare feet.

Without warning, Jamie suddenly moves away from me towards the kerb, as if she's about to step off in front of the taxi that's only inches away. Instinctively, I run forward and grab her by the shoulder to stop her being run over... only to have *my right hand catch fire*.

I look at it there, burning faintly on Jamie's shoulder, phantom flames licking hungrily up the back of my hand, a pale, corrosive luminosity moving slowly up past my wrist, past my forearm.

Mercy's left hand — when she hung in the demon Gudrun's grasp on the catwalk in Milan — flamed the same way.

I can't tell if I'm freezing, or burning up.

I am one huge sucked-in breath of anguish, but I can't rip my hand away. It could be fused to Jamie's body.

Inside my head I hear a whisper: *Look*.

There's so much hatred in that voice, like dark honey. Hate and honey: a startling contradiction.

The thing that's possessed Jamie is female. And I know I've heard that voice before in a different place. A human place. In another life, when I was another person.

I'm in so much pain and terror I can't think properly. I search my mind for clues, trying to put faces and voices together, but nothing comes to me.

It's not someone I ever knew well.

And it's not Mercy, I know that. But it's someone like her.

Not Mercy, no, the voice drawls inside my skull. *But someone who knows her, yes. A* friend.

She spits that word *friend* with so much loathing I know the truth must be the opposite.

Who are you?

I can't push the words out through my clenched teeth, but inside my head I'm screaming them, and she hears, turning her head to look at me over her shoulder. She stares at me through Jamie's unblinking hazel eye and I wonder what the creature looks like when she's not hiding. Beautiful, I'm sure. Not in the way that sells magazines or movies, but elemental, like Mercy is, or that demon inside the Argo was. Strong. Terrifying. Like a myth made real.

Where's Jamie gone? It's an effort even to think the words. It feels like I'm blacking out on my feet.

There's a burst of harsh laughter. *The same place you do when Mercy has need of your body,* she replies. *Submerged, like the drowned; held under by a power that will always be greater — because we were created to rule over you. Look around you, Gia Basso. I'm giving you both what you want. The answers are* here. *In the flesh.*

It's almost impossible to rip my eyes away from my burning hand or move my head, but I roll my eyes left and right, up and down the wide boulevard running between us and the hotel across the way. I gasp at what I see. It's the only sound I can force out of my throat, which is arched and taut as if I am screaming.

Everything looks different now.

I know it's because I'm touching her — the monstrous thing hooked tight inside Jamie's living, breathing body. The demon inside Jamie is letting me see the world through demonic eyes. It's as stunning as the scene I witnessed on the isolated bluff outside Craster: worlds within worlds.

What was there before, on Great Eastern Street, is still there. But there's so much... more. There are things here now, impossible things, all superimposed upon the physical world. Buildings built upon and *through* other buildings, people moving through other people, wandering animals, drays pulled by draughthorses clattering straight through approaching cars and minivans, women in headscarves and long overcoats pushing wooden handcarts filled with salvage along phantom stretches of cobblestone marked by gaslight, spruikers in bowler hats and ragged three-piece suits, screeching gangs of little boys in waistcoats and short pants, in shirt sleeves and breeches, fighting over a scrappy leather ball in the street. Life upon life upon life, time upon time upon time, all jumbled together.

The noise. The stench.

I cower from the sheer overload of sounds — mechanical and human — and the odour of packed-in, desperate lives spent in unsewered streets. Years of jumbled sounds, voices, smells; it's overpowering. All the more so because I know that most of it is... phantom.

This is what life is like for us, she hisses, *the Exiled. This is the dominion and the power that was promised to us by our rebel King. This boundless...munificence.*

Jamie throws a clawed hand out at the streetscape seething with wraithlike things and, distracted, I don't see her until the moment a slack-faced, bowed-over old woman with a sack of something lumpen slung across her shoulders suddenly approaches me from the right ... and passes straight through me.

I throw my free hand up protectively at the moment of contact, feeling a sensation like thousands of icy, piercing needles bursting upon my skin, unable to shield myself from the awful sensation of being run through.

The woman doesn't reappear. It's like she's been atomised.

Just because she touched me, I destroyed her.

The thing inside Jamie laughs again.

Every street, every place, in this barren, benighted, sucked-dry world of yours is more than what it appears — didn't the great Gabriel teach you that? You're in the landscape of nightmare now, my dear, the voice like dark honey says into the space behind my eyes. *The landscape which was Lucifer's inheritance and his 'gift' to those who loved and served him, from which nothing is ever lost: energy returning to energy, a closed loop that only seems to grow more imperfect, more chaotic, as time passes.*

And in the landscape of nightmare, human — demons and angels are not the only ones to wield power. Tell the one who is twice-dead that, this time, I am owed. And I never forgive a debt — great or small.

I never forgive.

There's a sensation, an instance of parting, and I stumble backwards, released from the demon's burning, magnetic hold.

Then Jamie turns her face away from me and raises her right hand to shoulder height, fingers spread outward, palm downward, and the ground begins to ripple like water.

16

Small waves at first.

Then the ripples build outward from Jamie's outstretched fingers, shivering in larger and larger swells, wave after wave rising higher, as if reality is elastic.

All the streetlights for blocks around flicker before extinguishing. But I can see, because Jamie seems to light up from the inside, casting a grey-silver glow like a corona around her small body.

Then the shaking begins, and the terrified screams of 'What's happening?' are soon swallowed by the intense roar of falling masonry, of asphalt, steel and mortar tearing apart.

People are running everywhere for cover now, trying desperately to dodge the rain of heavy debris falling out of the sky. Some are instantly pinned, screaming for help; others lie still where they fall.

I run forward to assist a woman who's dropped to the ground only metres away, but I'm pitched off my feet as the first of the waves hits the façade of the hotel opposite with a convulsive *boom*. I smash painfully onto my arse on the pavement, the earth suddenly opening up in a jagged, shattered line from where the creature controlling Jamie still stands, all her energies concentrated on sending shockwaves into the ground.

Struggling to kneel up, I see that the huge gash that's opening along the surface of Great Eastern Street seems to pause for a moment at the doorstep of the luxury hotel opposite before streaking up the face of the building like lightning, shattering the glass-fronted double doors instantly. The gash continues snaking upward, live and questing, the crack forking and splitting without warning so that now there are two cracks seeking left and right around the window frames of the swaying, buckling hotel.

It's like the fractures are seeking...something.

Abruptly, unnaturally, there's no more movement and it's shockingly silent — save for the trickle of sound from settling masonry, and the weak, muffled cries of the wounded.

Squinting up through the dust-filled haze, I see that a window on the top floor of the hotel is now framed by a ragged V of cracks.

A small glow ignites inside the room, then another, moving closer to the glass.

The figures of two men, one tall and broad-shouldered and youthful, one powerfully muscular, move into the framed window and stand there looking down at Jamie's small, pink-clad figure staring defiantly up at them from across the street.

The shorter, craggier one is holding the light sources in his hands, trying to angle the light down into the street so that he can see Jamie more clearly.

The way the taller one is standing — arms loosely crossed, head slightly tilted to one side in enquiry — speaks to me of recognition, although he can't have seen Jamie before. Shaun said she hadn't left the house in nearly two years, and never in her bandages.

Jamie's just torn up the streetscape below him. Yet the younger man's body language indicates he is relaxed and unafraid, possibly amused.

The craggier man wrenches open the hotel window in one

smooth move just as the first emergency service vehicles roar onto the eastern edge of the scene, setting up powerful search lights and sending personnel flooding across one half of Great Eastern Street in search of survivors.

As he leans out of the hotel window to get a better look at Jamie down below, the bright lights pick up the hard contours of the man's face and the underside of his broad jaw. There's a splash of bright blood-red colour across his pale throat... *in the shape of outspread wings.*

Instantly, I forget everything — the soreness of my muscles, the cuts, bruises and scrapes all over my body — and stumble backwards into the shadow of the laneway just in time to be sick against the wall of the chemist. I retch until nothing's coming up anymore, but still I gasp and heave.

Finally, wiping my mouth with the ragged cuff of my cardigan I hit Shaun's number and croak, 'It's him. *The tattooed man.* I think I found him. He's here.'

I'm still on the phone to Shaun — who's shouting at me to grab Jamie and *run, RUN for St Leonard's, got that? The big redbrick church just off the Shoreditch High Street. Look for the steeple, the steeple! I'll be waiting* — when Jamie crumples sideways to the ground before my eyes like a puppet that's had its strings cut; her body narrowly misses toppling into the great ragged trench at her feet that the demon created through her.

For a moment, I think I see the thing that took Jamie over shimmer and stretch in the air before me — a tall, winged creature of silver-grey gauzy light, long wing feathers trailing along the ground, her patrician features and intricately bound coronet of hair turned towards me in profile — before she shreds into thin air.

Where, *where*, do I know her from?

I half-carry, half-drag Jamie back through the maze of dark streets that lie between the devastation and the church. When I stumble onto the footpath below the church steeple Shaun roared at me to look out for, he's already there waiting in his lopsided blue hatchback that rides low to the ground and doesn't look big enough to hold him, let alone all three of us.

When he gets us both inside and Jamie's sprawled, unconscious, across my lap in the back seat, her heavy bandages scratching the painful grazes on my thighs, Shaun and I just stare at each other for a while before he starts the car.

'I knew,' he says hoarsely as the engine judders to life. 'I was watching the news and I didn't see neither of you in the carnage, but I just *knew*. I wanted you to call so badly — and then you did. Damn you, I'll never get used to it. I don't understand what's happening. But I trust Jamie. She doesn't lie.'

Shaun swings back around to face the windshield, gripping the steering wheel so tightly his golden-skinned knuckles are white. 'I trust you, too,' he mutters, 'as hard as that is to say. You've given me no reason to do that, in the past. But I do. If you're both saying this shit's real — it's *real*.'

My throat is very tight as I stroke the side of Jamie's bandaged face and instead of saying *thank you*, and the thousand other things I could say to this good, kind man, who is possibly the only person left in this world who cares about Jamie or me, I say gruffly, 'We need to get her home. She would hate to be seen like this. It'd be her worst nightmare come true.'

Without another word, Shaun starts the car, and we leave the silent bells and pitch-black streets of Shoreditch in our wake.

☙

Shaun shifts Jamie's dead weight in his arms as if she's no heavier than a throw blanket and lets us into her house with the spare key she once gave him; '*In case anything ever happens to me*, were the words she used,' Shaun says matter-of-factly. 'I think this counts as one of those times.' I feel a stab of sorrow as I watch him disarm the back-to-base alarm system, and I follow him up the stairs with a heavy tread.

'Just lay her down on top of her bed,' I command before limping around the house to gather warm water and towels, antiseptic and bandages.

Shaun and I crouch down to study the soles of Jamie's feet, which are raw and filthy and cut up from her impromptu night walk through East London. Though not as bad as Irina's were that time Mercy caused her to leap off the roof of a moving limo and outrun her own security team in bare feet just to reach a demon-spawned apparition in the road that looked like Ryan Daley.

Jamie doesn't even stir as I clean her cuts and grazes as best I can, bandaging her feet firmly before Shaun tucks her back into the bed she left hours ago in the fever grip of a demonic dream.

'I don't think she needs a hospital,' I whisper, looking down at Jamie lying so small and still in her big bed, only her bound head showing pink above the covers.

'She wouldn't want to go anyway,' Shaun murmurs. 'Unless the scar tissue in her throat is threatening to stop her breathing, you can't pay her good money to set foot in a hospital. She just needs some rest. She's tougher than she looks. She's had to be.'

Jamie's breathing is steady and audible as we head downstairs together, Shaun's powerful frame filling the staircase in front of me. It's shocking how much I've gotten used to him being around.

Feeling suddenly self-conscious I say, 'I'm just going to see whether there's been a message from Bianca St Alban.'

Shaun shrugs, letting me take Jamie's usual seat as I fumble for the power button. Jamie's powerful central processor hums to life. Having sat here for hours beside her over the last few days, it doesn't take me long to input her passwords and go straight to the icon that represents her arcane messaging system. There are almost a dozen emails from Bianca, waiting with a red *high priority* logo beside them, and a bunch of other things from web addresses with weird suffixes I've never even heard of.

Shaun leans closer to read Bianca's messages over my shoulder as I flick in and out — each message progressively more terse and annoyed than the next. The sandalwood and citrus tang of him, his physical proximity and body heat, start to make me feel hot and panicky, like my skin is too small to hold everything that's inside. I know that it's just Shaun — and he's the last person who'd hurt me, he's proven that over and over — but the room feels claustrophobic with just the two of us in it and the feeling of wanting to scream builds inside me.

Even after all these years, I still can't bear to be touched, or watched. I don't think that will ever change. Not now that I've been broken and re-set in irreversible ways.

Working with Irina was perfect because around her and the storm that seemed to follow in her frenetic golden, long-limbed wake, I was invisible. I could interact with fifty people and no one would remember me even being in the room afterwards. I called it *hiding in plain sight*. I was a master at that.

But Shaun *sees* me. He always has.

'Give me some space, for heaven's sake!' I finally snap, and Shaun stands and stretches, asking calmly and evenly if I want a coffee. I nod without looking at him and he leaves the room in the eerily silent way he has.

Hugging myself, relieved to be alone, but perversely missing the warmth and bulk of him, I read Bianca's last message again.

Where ARE you two?
In case you missed the last nine messages, I said:
I'VE GOT A BLOODY ADDRESS FOR YOU.
Call me!

I look at Jamie's wall clock and work out that it's just after 6am where Bianca is.

Flicking out of Jamie's inbox, I hit the video link to Bianca at the exact moment Shaun pads back into the room with a cup of steaming coffee for each of us.

Bianca doesn't pick up, even though I dial her three times straight, letting each call go until the system kicks me out. I see that there are a handful of missed calls from her to us during the course of the night.

'Nobody's sleeping these days,' Shaun murmurs wryly around his mug.

'Where could she *be*?' I say, my teeth clinking against the rim of mine. I suddenly feel very tired. There's something I'm forgetting here — something important — but for the life of me, I can't work out what it is. It's like the adrenaline that flooded through me during the earthquake burned out all my synapses. The connections I should be making seem just out of reach.

Completely out of ideas, I try dialling Bianca one more time.

'Did you ever find that bird?' Shaun asks suddenly over the sound of the ringtone.

'What?' I ask, glancing at him over my shoulder, wary.

'So Jamie tells me you're looking for this bird, right?' Shaun insists from where he's sprawled in his chair, pushed way back now so that he's not sitting too close to me.

My throat constricts at his thoughtfulness and I can barely squeeze the word out. *'Bird?'* I turn back to face the screen because it's safer than looking into his amber eyes. 'Come on, come on,' I mutter at Bianca's frozen, gorgeous photo avatar as the dial tone continues to blare through hidden speakers in Jamie's study.

'Cibyyl?' Shaun prompts. 'That was the name of the bird you were looking for, right?'

Cibyyl.

As I stare at Shaun the dial tone abruptly cuts off, and in the silent room, all I can hear is the sound of his breathing because I'm *not*. My breath is caught up somewhere high in my throat, like a bubble.

'Rabbleknowledgenet!' I exclaim, wondering if this was the important thing I was struggling to remember. 'How do I get there, Shaun? Quickly, man!'

I scramble out of my seat and Shaun takes over at the keyboard while I perch in his chair, unable to follow the rapid sequence of screens he's opening and closing with his big, callused hands.

'It's a private web buried way down in the Rabble platform,' he explains as he continues typing. 'Jamie got me onto it because I do a sideline in, uh, complex personal security projects — retrievals, deliveries and the like. *Ask and ye shall receive* is pretty much how Rabbleknowledgenet works — that is, if anyone's around and can be bothered replying. It's an honour system — you scratch my back, I'll scratch yours — like a kind of blockchain hive mind. Everything you ever wanted to know can materialise in there. The lyrics to a 1970s cola jingle, how to breach the security systems of a small sovereign state — it's pretty much available to you if you ask politely enough and can pay the necessary price. Everything's seen as a challenge. *Nothing is inviolate* could pretty much be the motto.'

'You know you lost me at *private*,' I mutter, chewing on my right thumbnail at the time it's taking to access the thing.

'I was exactly the same way until Jamie showed me how much I was missing just noodling around in the surface web,' Shaun murmurs. 'Here it is —'

He shows me a rectangular box with a blinking cursor in it on a plain black background dotted inexplicably with things that look like cute cartoon heads of garlic.

Shaun types a long, complicated-looking password into the box. Instantly, the page of repeating garlic heads dissolves into a background of hot pink — a sign that Jamie's managed to customise even this far-flung corner of the virtual underbelly — and I read the words printed there in bold, stark black letters:

Cibyyl says: I just want to be noticed.

I stare at the message for a long time, struggling to work out what it could mean. By whom? How? *When?*

It's a bit vague, and a little off-key. Exactly like Cibyyl's singing is. It might not even be from her. But something tells me that it is.

I actually stand and grab Shaun by the shoulders from behind, shaking him in the grip of a fierce excitement. Getting someone noticed?

Now *that*, I can do.

I can barely move Shaun. It's like he's made of warm stone.

At the feel of my hands on his shoulders, Shaun turns his head of bright curls and looks up at me through his long, dark gold lashes and I startle a fleeting look on his face that brings that rush of hot, uncomfortable feeling right back before I lock it down again.

Shaun's expression goes bland.

I drop my hands.

What I'd seen on his face? Quizzical, patient…affection. It's the face Shaun wears around me when he thinks I'm not looking.

He *likes* me.

Shit, maybe it's always been more than that.

Instantly, I have the stretched-too-tight feeling of panic and fear. Maybe he's *always* liked me and that's why I ran, and why he reacted to my reappearance in his life with so much fury. But what happened to me all those years ago short-circuited any expectation that I could ever have anything *normal*. Even with a man as extraordinary as Shaun.

No walks in the rain, no hand-holding. None of it.

Not for you, I tell myself with a feeling like razor blades in my throat.

I swallow, stepping back even further, wrapping my arms around behind my back in case they should reach for him again.

Then I remember, and my body goes hot as if there's electricity flowing under my skin, not blood. 'Shaun! *Who was staying at the hotel —*'

But an insistent electronic ringing noise suddenly cuts through the air, causing Shaun and I both to flinch away from each other.

Shaun flicks out of Rabbleknowledgenet and we see that Bianca St Alban is trying to connect to us.

17

'Not to put too fine a point on it, where the *fuck* have you been?' Bianca snarls, her electric-blue eyes raking my face. They narrow on Shaun before flicking back to me. 'I've been trying to reach you for hours, Gia. You asked for *my* help, if you recall.'

I have to stop myself from lashing out in return because, even before *the thing* happened, I've always defaulted to attack mode. It's a flaw in my programming.

My reply is studiously neutral. 'This is Shaun Kassmeyer,' I say, indicating Shaun beside me.

Bianca continues to ignore him, although her cool blue eyes flicker briefly in his direction because Shaun's looks are so out of the ordinary no one would ever fail to glance twice.

'Where's Jamie?' Bianca snaps. 'I need her. The boffins in Switzerland have some verification instructions I can't make head or tail of. Oh, and did I tell you I have an *address*?' Her voice is heavy with sarcasm. 'The account that received the bulk of Spartak Skorobogatov's worldly wealth is registered to Charybdis LLC at a commercial bank in the Bahamas. It's a one-man company owned and operated by an individual called Buster Strang. Ring any bells?'

I don't reply because I'm too busy mentally scrolling through all the names of all the famous people I've ever brushed up against at all the fashion weeks. No bells are ringing. Buster Strang could be a vacuum cleaner salesman or stand-up comic, and I almost say that when Shaun pipes up with, 'Jamie's in bed.'

There's a smile playing around the corners of his wide, expressive mouth as he looks at Bianca and I see that he appreciates how beautiful she is when she's angry. It's like anger takes her general luminescence to a whole new level, and Shaun's never been afraid of a challenge.

Even though they're not physically in the room together, the air feels combustible. I experience a sharp pang that I mentally stamp all over in metaphorical steel-capped hunting boots.

Bianca pretends Shaun hasn't spoken, her face haughty. 'You and Jamie call me back when the two of you can stay awake long enough to focus on the task at hand. While people like to make out that all I do is attend cocktail functions and film premieres, I actually have an empire to run.'

She lifts her hand to disconnect us, but Shaun speaks again.

'The Hotel Darlie,' he says. 'You were asking where Jamie and Gia *were*? If you caught the news like I did, it was three dead, eight critical, seventy-five injured at last count. Jamie was the one who "caused" it. Gia chased her on foot across East London and watched Jamie bring down a major thoroughfare, in just her nightie and bare feet, in real time.'

'All she did was raise her hands like a gospel preacher,' I pipe up quietly. 'And things came a-tumbling down.'

Bianca recoils. '*How* —?'

I explain the night's events, and devastation is in Bianca's face the way I know it is in mine. *People died.*

'I saw the footage,' Bianca whispers finally. 'It reminded me of the Lake and Milan and Paris two years ago, you know, after...'

I nod, remembering how the world's media attributed the catastrophes in Lake Como, Milan and Paris — firestorms in the night, shattered buildings, caved-in streets, scores of dead and injured — to Acts of God after Mercy fled Milan with Ryan. But Bianca and I both know they were more like the polar opposite: physical evidence of the passage of demons. And plenty of inexplicable things have happened since then: dead volcanos coming back to life, swarms of light in the sky all over the world, bridges and buildings collapsing without warning — the earth, the sky, in revolt.

Seemingly random disasters, random things — but only to those blithely unaware of the powers moving among us.

My voice is barely audible. 'We've witnessed a few Acts of God ourselves in the last few days...'

Bianca nods absently. 'How bad is Jamie?' The heat has gone out of her voice now. It's all the apology I'm going to get, I know.

'She's still out,' I say. 'But we think she'll be fine. Her vitals are strong. Just a few surface cuts and grazes. When she's awake, we'll call you together, promise. But I'm not going to wake her. Not even for you.'

Bianca nods before suddenly focusing her extraordinary eyes squarely on Shaun and he leans forward so that she can see him better. There's that pang again as I register how good they look together, and how hard they're looking at each other.

Like ice meeting fire, their eyes clashing.

'Who *are* you?' Bianca's tone is less waspish. 'Can we trust him?' she says to me, like Shaun's not sitting right there in front of her.

'Shaun is Jamie's guardian angel,' I say huskily. 'He's taken care of her since she lost...'

'A functioning life,' Jamie finishes soberly from the doorway. 'He's my rock and my lifeline to a world I am now completely terrified of. *I would not be alive without Shaun Kassmeyer. I* would have ended it months ago. You can absolutely trust this man, Bianca St Alban. Anything you want to tell me, you can tell him.'

Jamie limps over on heavily bandaged feet, squeezing Shaun's right shoulder with a scarred hand. He rests his own on hers for a moment and I see that Jamie has changed into one of her signature fluffy pink tracksuits, the collar zipped right up under her chin. The pressure bandages across her face are gone and her brunette wig is firmly centred on her head; the plastic face mask she's now wearing causes her facial scars to shine under the bright-white study lights.

'You must be feeling the cold right down to your bones,' I say, getting out of my chair to make room for her, pulling up a spare seat just behind Shaun.

Jamie nods, knowing that I know exactly how she's feeling. 'What happened?' she croaks around at all of us.

After I explain how she sustained the damage to her feet, Shaun and Bianca take turns describing the scenes of chaos around the Darlie Hotel.

'I was *there*,' Jamie says in tones of quiet wonder.

'You kind of... caused it,' I reply neutrally.

Jamie turns and looks at me, insisting, '*She* caused it. She was burning me up from the inside. So much anger and hatred, it was like I was bathing in a river of acid. I felt like I was dying as she made me *do those things...*'

'Mercy — when she takes over — is kind of the same,' I whisper. 'There's no way you can stop it. You're just a conduit for something — bigger. And you don't know how you can stand it and still be alive...'

'She could have killed me,' Jamie says raggedly. 'Should have. But she didn't. She held back, deliberately. I felt that.'

From the screen, Gia looks from me to Jamie in confusion

as she says, 'The Darlie's even been on high rotation across the financial news channels. The finance minister of a small European nation was staying at the hotel with his mistress. The cameras caught him stumbling out into the street in just his underwear. It's quite the scandal on the continent...'

I sit bolt upright, suddenly recalling what I was about to ask Shaun when Bianca dialled through.

'Who *else* was staying at the Darlie besides the finance guy?' I ask hoarsely, remembering the large captive crowd of women, camped out in the cold patiently waiting. 'Someone famous was there. Male. Most probably loaded. Most probably young, hot.'

I see again the outspread wings inked in blacks and reds across the thick throat of the man who'd leant out of the top floor hotel window. Had he seen me? I shrink down involuntarily in my seat at the memory, scrubbing at my arms, remembering the familiar, hateful contours of his big-boned face. How often had I seen them in nightmare from just that angle?

My skin feels icy as I say, 'I know why we were brought there.'

'Why?' Jamie, Shaun and Bianca demand together, their eyes turned on me in a way that makes me want to vanish again.

What had the creature said?

Look around you, Gia Basso. I'm giving you both what you want. The answers are here. In the flesh.

Two men. One a human agent.

But the other?

'There was a young man standing in the top-floor window looking down at us,' I say, and I know the distress is etched plainly in my face. 'Who *was* he? He's the key to everything.'

For a moment, everyone is silent.

Then Bianca replies, puzzled, 'It was Kit Tyburn.'

Jamie's shoulders go rigid with recognition as Bianca continues speaking. 'Kit Tyburn was staying at the Darlie. The worst of the structural damage to the building was centred around his suite, they're saying. He's lucky he didn't topple right out of the building onto the ground below, they're also saying. The floor beneath him was minutes from giving way when they got him out. The roof and entire top level came down not long after — the cameras caught the whole thing pancaking into the level below. He could have died.'

'*She* wanted him to die,' Jamie murmurs.

'Kit Tyburn?' I say, struggling to place the name. Like Buster Strang, it rings no bells. But I was in self-imposed exile in Craster for over two years. No TV, no radio. Empires could have risen and fallen in that time.

'Kit Tyburn,' Bianca drawls, sounding faintly disgusted, 'is only the biggest R&B star in the world *right now*. He's a gun-packing, culturally-appropriating, five-time Grammy-award-winning "artist" — I use that term loosely — with a face and body like a platinum-blond angel. He's also a self-obsessed, womanising, misogynist arsehole who hasn't even turned thirty yet. I know, because he propositioned me on a mutual friend's maxi-yacht off Cap Ferrat almost two years ago and I told him to go to hell. But that's a sordid story for another time.'

'Well, that's certainly ironic,' I whisper. 'Telling Kit Tyburn to go to Hell. He might know a thing or two about that.'

'Sorry?' Bianca says. 'I didn't get that, Gia. Can you repeat what you just said?'

'*@therealKit*,' Jamie murmurs, staring at me with the same haunted expression I know I'm wearing, 'can that really be *him*?

Is that why we were there? And who was *she*? The one who tore up Great Eastern Street just to lead you to him?'

'I think I knew her from somewhere,' I say, troubled. 'I didn't get a good look at her — it was like she was made of some kind of... of *afterlight* — but there was something about her profile, before she vanished, that I swear I've seen before...'

'What are you two *talking* about?' Bianca's voice is exasperated.

One of the other computer terminals in front of us flares to life as Jamie's fingers start flying across the keyboard, searching for new information.

'*I just want to be noticed.*' I say, over her rapid-fire typing. 'That was the message Cibyyl left for you in Rabbleknowledgenet, Jamie. Shaun got us in. Can you trust the source?'

'You can trust it,' Jamie snaps, preoccupied, her fingers not pausing for a second. 'If it says it was Cibyyl, it was Cibyyl. Or whoever administers that video channel of hers. It would have to have gone through a chain of filters before that message reached me via Rabble. I called myself "Mercy", remember? I didn't exactly invite her to send me an email back.'

Jamie's searches pile up before our eyes. I read the car crash snippets of gossip about Kit Tyburn over her shoulder and I know Shaun is doing the exact same thing because his eyebrows are somewhere near his hairline.

'The male equivalent of Irina Zhivanevskaya wouldn't get into half as much trouble as this guy,' I murmur, appalled. 'Who runs his PR? Who's supposed to be keeping him on a leash? He's out of control.'

Jamie shrugs. 'Out of control sells records. Eighty-eight million followers and counting, baby.'

Bianca waves her hands at the three of us, trying to get our attention. 'Hello? I'm still here? I can't see what you're doing.'

Shaun murmurs, 'Kit Tyburn — he's the same guy who wants the same Cibyyl you two want? The same Cibyyl who's impossible to find?'

Jamie and I both nod and Shaun frowns as he says, 'Now, see, coincidences like that make me very, *very* uncomfortable.'

Bianca's expression narrows on the three of us through the screen when she can stand it no longer. 'Pony up!' she shouts.

I explain about Cibyyl; about how she's like a beautiful, folk-singing ghost — except for one tweet that some guy called *@therealKit* sent out into the ether a few days ago that pretty much trumpeted disgruntled *lust*. 'She owes him in some way,' I murmur.

'Jamie's just showing us how *@therealKit* is the social media identity of the artist-slash-arsehole commonly known as Kit Tyburn,' Shaun explains. 'The same Kit Tyburn that almost died tonight at the Darlie.'

Bianca frowns, still not seeing the connection.

I lean forward, excited. 'Okay, so let's say Cibyyl caught the attention of the biggest R&B star in the known universe, because he or his entourage are, what, basically trawling the web twenty-four hours a day looking for hot young babes to ravish, and "Kit" sees Cibyyl singing in basically her scanties and sees how beautiful she is. And he wants her, badly. Being who he is, he likes new, pretty things. And he wants them *now*. He's like the human embodiment of instant gratification.'

'So what?' Bianca queries, still confused.

'Remember the Argo?' I ask.

'I'm trying to forget the Argo,' Bianca snaps. 'And how a casual business acquaintance of my father's appeared to be *harbouring* a major league demon who tried to smash me into pieces from two storeys off the ground.'

'Say Kit Tyburn is Satan,' I say slowly.

'Every woman I know is saying Kit Tyburn is Satan,' Bianca scoffs. 'As in: *Not now, Satan. I've got a headache.* You can buy tee-shirts that say those exact words. Kit Tyburn treats women like actual garbage. Several assault and false imprisonment charges have mysteriously been dropped against him over the last year because his management paid for them to go away. No major luxury hotel chain will have him these days, which is why he was probably staying at a boutique hotel-slash-dump like the Darlie, trawling for women while he's in London on a promotional tour. His 'Kitty Burners' have been out in force all over Europe this week. Wherever he is, there's a drove of them. London is supposed to be his last stop before he heads home to the United States. Where have you *been*, Gia?'

'Craster,' Shaun and I say at exactly the same moment. We both look at each other and burst out laughing.

'What? *Where?*' Bianca says in confusion.

'You're not understanding me,' I say, still breathless from laughter. 'Kit Tyburn — like Spartak Skorobogatov was — is the *actual* Satan. I'm guessing he's Lucifer's current bodily ride. That's why Jamie and I were "brought" there. Whatever that thing was that took Jamie over, it — she — led us right to him. She wanted us to know who Lucifer is pretending to be — *right now*.'

'Because she *hates* him,' Jamie murmurs. 'I felt it. She wants him destroyed and she can't do it herself. She's not strong enough. She might never be. That, by itself, is eating her up.'

Jamie shudders. 'Not strong enough? She felt like a hurricane. But she still can't do it on her own. That's where I think Gia — and Mercy — come in.'

Bianca's eyes are wide and unfocused with shock. 'Kit Tyburn,' she splutters finally, 'selfie king, serial lip-syncher, public fornicator, fad dieter and dedicated nudist, is *the Devil*?

No, really? I feel...dirty. He *touched* me.'

'Not when he met you at Cap Ferrat,' I reassure her hastily. 'The timing's all wrong for that. Spartak had probably just come into the picture at that point. Kit Tyburn wasn't the actual Satan when he accosted you on your friend's yacht. But think about it!' I insist over Bianca's gagging sounds. 'He's not going to take over someone anonymous, is he? The actual Satan is going to want access to *everything*. He's going to want to be doing it bigger, better, brighter, faster and louder than every other human being on the planet. Money, girls, guns, toys, fame, *looks*. Kit Tyburn has it all. If you were forced to live in our world, you'd want to be Kit Tyburn because it's literally *access all areas*. Everything's on tap, all the time. Mercy didn't fall for just anyone, back in the day. Lucifer was the physical embodiment of charismatic perfection. And this Kit dude is the same on earth, right? I mean, I'm looking at his photo right now. He's like some pouty blond god with abdominals of chiselled marble who can't seem to keep his shirt or pants on. It's like Kit Tyburn was pre-fabricated just for Lucifer's use. You couldn't find a better fit. Better even than the Russian, because Tyburn has serious *profile*. But given enough time, Lucifer's going to burn through him too, the same way he burned through Skorobogatov and left the dregs to some demonic underling. Based on how quickly Lucifer degraded Skorobogatov, we probably don't have a whole lot of time. The clock's *speeding up*, not slowing down. We have to get to Kit Tyburn before Lucifer abandons his body for a new one. We know where he is right now — so we have to *move*.'

Bianca's mouth falls open as she mulls all this over.

I think about the two armies of winged giants that stalked the Galleria Vittorio Emanuele in Milan two years ago, each seeking to annihilate the other. One lot had seemed more beautiful than the sun, and, like the sun, had emitted light as if it was some essential part of their being. The other had possessed an eerie, gleaming beauty marred — without exception, every male, every female — by disfiguring scars, exactly like that thing inside the Argo. They all had burning handprints across their faces, necks, torsos, limbs and backs. To denote the exiled, I know now.

Lucifer had to have one, too; somewhere hidden. Whoever had marked him had spared his face because the Lucifer I saw in the front row in Milan had been perfection itself. I could not tear my eyes away from him in his sharp, three-piece suit, textured tie and wing tips. He'd been glorious.

I stare at the half-naked image of Kit Tyburn that's open in front of Jamie, which is pretty glorious too. 'Actually,' I murmur, tilting my head to try to work out the twisted black, Gothic script tattooed up Kit Tyburn's left ribcage, 'Tyburn looks a bit like a teenaged girl from some angles, but otherwise...'

'It's bonkers,' Shaun snorts, crossing his arms.

'I know,' I exclaim, wondering what language the tattoo is in, 'it's utterly *mad*. The concept that these creatures can just, I don't know, *step into people* as if they're trying on clothes. But say Kit Tyburn *is* the Devil and he's bored and insatiable and fancies a go at this girl who's caught his attention. He's thrown a whole lot of cash her way to get her undivided attention and still she's nowhere to be found, and the Devil always gets what he wants, so it's like this terrible itch in his crotch that's only getting worse —'

Bianca drawls, 'So we need to get him the girl? We need to bring her to him?'

I shake my head. 'Or the promise of that, because we can't put her in actual danger. That would be morally reprehensible. She looks like some defenceless forest creature as it is.'

'You want to bait and trap…the Devil?' Jamie pauses midway through typing, looking at me over her shoulder in disbelief.

I nod vigorously. 'He's still here in London, isn't he?' I make a clashing-of-cymbals gesture with my hands. 'We say we'll bring them together at an agreed place and time and then…'

'And then what?!' Shaun's tone is incredulous. 'If you and Jamie are right, he's the fucking Prince of Darkness, yeah? *He will rip your head off.*'

'That's Mercy's lookout,' I say vaguely, refusing to be cowed. 'She'll have my back. I'm just the delivery girl, the vehicle, if you like.'

'"Mercy",' Shaun growls, 'will be too busy running "Lucifer" to ground to take care of you. I've seen her in action, remember? She will burn you up alive just to get at him. And I care what happens to *you.*'

I have to look away from him then.

'I can find out where Kit Tyburn is right now,' Jamie murmurs as if Shaun hadn't spoken, fingers already flying. 'That's easy enough.'

'And then what?' Shaun shouts in frustration, waving his hands in the air.

What Bianca says next stops us all in our tracks. '*I* can do that, Gia — bring them together.' Her voice is very quiet. 'I'm the Crown Princess of Logistics, aren't I? That's what the financial press calls me. The St Alban Group can deliver anything to anywhere. It's in our mission statement: *We can reach everything and everyone.* With your help, Gia, Jamie, Shaun — we'll give the Devil and his dead muse what each of them want.'

৪১

It doesn't take us long to come up with a plan to get Cibyyl noticed. But it does involve somehow contacting the elusive indie chanteuse again and getting her to London from wherever she is while Kit Tyburn is still in the country.

'Where is he now exactly?' Shaun rumbles, rubbing his eyes. None of us can sleep, even though we badly need to.

'Holed up at a model-slash-actress's mansion in the Cotswolds with his extended entourage,' Jamie answers as she types our agreed message to Cibyyl into Rabbleknowledgenet. 'Do you want to check it before I press *send*?'

'Read it aloud,' Bianca commands. So I lean forward and read:

Contact Bianca St Alban via the number below, URGENTLY, who will fly you out to London by private jet from wherever you are for a photo shoot at the St Alban Group's Warehouse B, Coniston Wharf, Tilbury Docks, tomorrow night at 9pm.

'It's a bit clinical,' Bianca murmurs. 'I don't think Cibyyl will get a sense of all the wheels that we're turning for her here. How about you add: *Everyone in the whole world is going to know who you are as soon as the shoot is over. Guaranteed.* That's more attention-grabbing.'

So above the untraceable private number Bianca's wangled from one of the unseen lackeys that flit about her, always, like persistent, bloodsucking insects, Jamie types what Bianca's just said, verbatim, shooting the message to Cibyyl out into the ether.

There's no response for hours.

Shaun, Jamie and I take turns at the computer terminals while Bianca calls through impatiently at regular intervals to find out what's going on; there hasn't been so much as a single missed call to the private number she nominated in the message.

'I followed your instructions to the letter,' Bianca's almost babbling at one point when I'm alone in the room, glumly staring at the garlic-covered Rabbleknowledgenet window left open on one of the screens, blankly waiting.

'It will just be me and him, essentially. He'll do all the photography himself so that he doesn't scare her off. *She looks skittish* — that's exactly what I told him, *skittish*. The shoot has to be small and intimate so that Cibyyl doesn't baulk and do a runner. But after that? *Kapow*. We're going to tie the final images of Cibyyl into a new fundraising campaign for an abused women's shelter in the United Kingdom. Brilliant, right?'

I nod, not really listening, the blinking cursor in the sea of garlic heads mesmerising my bloodshot eyes. I rub them with my fists as Bianca exclaims, 'Jamie's face, you know? That's what gave me the idea. It breaks my heart every time I see her. If she'd let me, I could change her life. I decided we had to hang Cibyyl's story on something the public can get behind, something with real heart. And if the campaign actually *does* help the shelter, we've achieved two good things. I've already called in every favour I was ever owed in the fashion industry to set this up quickly, so this Cibyyl had better not stand us up.'

I struggle to keep from nodding off as Bianca adds, 'Every major fashion blogger and magazine editor — print and online — has been primed for an imminent, newsworthy scoop. I've had people in my office drip-feeding the idea all over the place that something *huge* is brewing in fashion/philanthropy. We're going to make Cibyyl and her fabulous facial structure and delightfully off-key stylings the biggest, fastest, blanket-coverage overnight star the world has ever seen. Mondial Publishing and the syndicated fashion magazine empire run by the Costa International Group are ready to devote print, social media and screen time to the campaign. By the end of the week it'll be all over TV ads, bus shelters, buses, railway stations, cinemas, shopping centres, billboards and the sides of apartment buildings. Anywhere you can paste a larger-than-life-size image up, it'll be covered with Cibyyl's face. Everyone in the world really will take notice.'

'Even bloody Lucifer himself?' I yawn.

'Especially *bloody Lucifer*,' Bianca drawls and the words sound strange in her French-inflected accent. We're going to appeal to his white-blond, winner-takes-all, atavistic leanings, big-time.' Bianca leans forward, her big blue eyes and forehead looming into the screen as she stares at me.

'Get some sleep,' she urges softly, before cutting the call.

I must sleep for a long time, because when I next open my eyes, my right arm — where it's twisted somehow under me *and* under one armrest of Jamie's gas-lift chair — feels dead, like it doesn't belong to my body. I have to massage it fiercely to bring the blood tingling back.

The air out in the hallway seems lighter now, and the others must still be sleeping wherever they're sprawled out in the house, because it's absolutely silent as I stretch and yawn, my breath visible in the frosty air of Jamie's study. Shivering inside my worn cardigan, I tap at the keyboard to bring the hibernating computer terminals back to life.

I let out a loud scream when I see what's written on the middle one.

Shaun runs into the room with a wild, just-woken-from-sleep look in his catlike eyes. 'What is it?' he growls, scanning the room we're in, the lightening hallway beyond. 'What did you see?'

I turn stiffly to let him read the words printed there in stark black letters on a background of hot pink.

Cibyyl says: I'm only going to show up at the place and time you say if Jamie Suggitt is there.

18

'No,' Jamie says, frowning down at the message on the screen. 'It's out of the question.'

'How does Cibyyl even *know* about you?' Shaun's tone is fierce. 'Rabbleknowledgenet is supposed to be completely anonymous. I don't like it.'

'Someone in the food chain must have let on that this is my account,' Jamie rasps, shaking her head. 'There's no other way she could have worked it out and I'm going to have to fix that — fast. But I can't go with you, Gia, I'm sorry. I've just been out of the house, and see how that turned out! Half a city street came down. I can't be part of it. It's not safe.'

'It will just be Bianca, me, the photographer, Shaun...' I cajole. 'Small, brief, intimate and non-threatening. Not like some of the week-long circuses I've been part of.'

I think of the 'photographer' that we've agreed on. When Bianca nominated Tommy Taffin, global brand manager for Milan's legendary Atelier Re and one of the most influential men in fashion, to do the behind-camera duties I leapt at the chance to see him again. In cutting all ties and turning my back on 'fashwan', I had to give up on him, too, and it hurt. I didn't have so many real friends that I could afford to lose the ones I had.

'Tommy's the gentlest, most lovely man, Jamie,' I insist. 'It's always been a complete mystery to me how he's survived this long in fashion. You'll be completely safe with all of us there.

Especially if Shaun's there, too, running personal security for you.'

I give Shaun a pleading look. The one he returns is piercing and I shiver under his gaze.

Jamie shakes her head so fiercely her wig shifts a little. 'No,' she says, more harshly this time. 'I'm not doing it. I can't.'

I get Bianca back online and she can't budge Jamie either, whose expression is shuttered.

'Anyway, how's Cibyyl even going to know if Jamie's there or not?' Bianca exclaims. 'Am I right in saying that no one has seen a picture of Jamie since that monster...'

Jamie suddenly pushes up out of her seat and leaves the room.

Bianca's voice is sober as she peers out of the screen trying to see where Jamie went. 'So how do we do this, Gia? Really?'

'We proceed.' My reply is terse. 'You're right — Cibyyl can have no idea what Jamie Suggitt looks like now. So *I'll* wear Jamie's pressure mask if I have to and say that I'm her and we get on with the photo shoot as planned. Quick and dirty, before Cibyyl can ask any questions.'

'I'll maintain a tight security cordon around the warehouse,' Bianca adds. 'Just the five of us — you, me, Shaun, Tommy and Cibyyl, with no one else allowed inside. And I'll send a car for you at 7pm to ensure we're all in place and singing off the same song sheet before she arrives. You'll need to help with the set-up, Gia: drop sheets, lights and so on. Tommy can't do it all on his own, and he'll want to bounce ideas off you because you used to style as well. Tommy's really missed you. He told me that, when I called him.'

'Just the *four* of you,' Shaun corrects us, suddenly rising from his chair. 'I won't be there. Jamie needs me more than Gia ever did.' Bianca's eyes widen slightly at the bite in his words. 'Jamie's mental state — you can't possibly understand what it's taken to get her even this far, doing all these things with people who, at the end of the day, amount to strangers…'

He glares at me and Bianca before pivoting on his heel and leaving the room.

I crawl into bed after Bianca signs off and sleep for hours, waking, startled, to feel Jamie's hand on my shoulder. She's sitting on the edge of my bed, and the afternoon light has already gone from the hallway between our two bedrooms.

'I'm sorry,' is all she says, her synthetic wig backlit in the glow of the bathroom fluorescent, her face in shadow.

I sit up hastily. 'None of us want you to do anything you're not comfortable with. We were wrong to put the screws on. You've been through enough.'

'You need to get ready,' she says, rising. 'It's getting late.'

She presses something soft into my hand and my fingers trace ridges and seams, an eyehole. 'Shaun says the car will be here soon. He's on his way over now — to sit with me, he says. He doesn't want me to be by myself because he knows that I don't like to be alone — not anymore.'

When I worked in fashion, getting dressed on a daily basis was like putting on armour. Spikes, heels, metal, chains, quilted leather, winged eyeliner, white eyeshadow, precision-contoured brows, structural hair, the more outrageous the better, because looking like an iron-clad, spike-covered bitch gave me absolute licence to *be* one. I would put invincibility on every morning and take it all off again before crashing into bed, alone, every night. Rinse and repeat, for seven long years. Now it all feels like it happened to another person. I'm not that woman anymore.

Getting ready now, in Jamie's cramped, icy bathroom, is an entirely different story. I pull on some semi-clean indigo jeans, my dark green plaid flannel shirt, navy jumper and navy oil slicker, and braid my hair tightly into plaits that hang halfway down my back, finishing with a half-hearted slick of foundation that doesn't begin to cover my numerous farm-acquired freckles. I shove the pressure mask Jamie gave me into one of my outer pockets.

No one will be looking at you tonight, I tell myself as I pull on a heavy pair of socks. *Being the equivalent of human wallpaper might stop things like Lucifer from seeing you coming.*

I walk down the stairs, and pause outside the kitchen door when I hear Shaun and Jamie arguing with each other in low voices. Standing in the shadows near the powder room, I can just make out Jamie saying, anguish in her voice, 'They don't play by the rules, Shauny. They have absolute contempt for human life. I *felt* that. But I was *spared*, God knows what for, by that thing that got hold of me. What if something happens to Gia and we're not there to help her?'

Shaun's answer is firm. 'You don't want to do it, so we're staying put. What could happen at a silly photo shoot? Someone gets a feather in their eye? Gia's a big girl now — she can take care of herself. She proved that when she left me the first time. And she's got a few new tricks up her sleeve, courtesy of yours truly.'

'I'm being selfish,' Jamie moans into her hands. 'But I can't go outside again. I can't, *I can't*. It's not safe.'

'We're staying here,' Shaun insists.

I count to twenty before I pull on my heavy boots and walk briskly into the kitchen. Jamie's hands come down and her head whips around and she tries to pin on a smile as she hands me a cup of her awful coffee that's made with so much love. But the smile doesn't stick, and no one says anything.

My hands are so cold I can barely close them around the novelty bright pink mug that screams *She's the Boss!*

'Don't worry about me,' I mutter finally, taking a quick, too-hot pull of my drink so they don't see my teeth chattering. 'We're just going to take a few photographs of a pretty girl and then I'll be home.'

When I say the word *home* it feels true. More *home* than Craster ever was, or living out of a suitcase in all the six-star gin joints across the world over the last seven years.

But there's such a feeling of dread in my heart that I blurt out suddenly, 'Guys, I'm so afraid.'

I am. I feel as if I'm standing on the edge of something vast and terrifying. One push and I'll be lost. I want to tell them how I woke just now, my head tight and pulsing as if the claws of some giant bird of prey were hooked deep into my skull. But I can't get the words out, so I take another scalding mouthful of my coffee.

Jamie shoots Shaun a haunted look before taking the mug out of my trembling hands and putting it on the counter, taking my icy fingers in hers. 'You're going to be fine,' she says with forced-sounding cheer. 'And, anyway, I've told my angel he's not to go anywhere near you tonight, and he agreed that he wouldn't.'

The thought that Jamie has some kind of direct line to her angel makes me shiver.

'That will have to do then,' I whisper, gathering her gingerly into my arms — even though my entire body rebels, like it always does, at touching another living human being.

I give her a quick hug, feeling her brittle body go stiff with tension. The two of us are like damaged shopfloor mannequins, craving human contact but at the same time deeply repelled by it.

For once Shaun isn't rolling his eyes at all our talk of angels. As I meet his gaze over Jamie's shoulder, he looks away, posture tense, knuckles white. He's torn, I know he is, but I might have irreparably damaged any loyalty he ever felt to me, the first time I walked away from him all those years ago.

The doorbell rings and I step away from Jamie, giving her twisted fingers a quick squeeze before heading towards the front door. I wrench all the chains and locks open, seeing myself out before they can stop me leaving — or I stop myself.

౩

I don't remember much of the car ride except for the splendidly upholstered isolation, and the miles of pretty Christmas lights appearing all over the city though it's still weeks too early. Bianca's arranged it so that the internal panel is up and I can't see the driver and he can't see me, and he doesn't speak, which I'm grateful for. When we draw up to the St Alban Group's warehouse — overlooking a generous stretch of the Tilbury Docks — I first have to pass a human cordon of bespoke-suited security guards. I get a hard frisk for my troubles before they let me through the hangar-style doors and haul them shut behind me.

Inside, the light is bright and warm and golden. Every pendant lamp in every gantry hanging high overhead is beaming down. I see Bianca first, fussing around with an arrangement of wooden crates in front of a drop sheet splattered artfully with paint in grey and white tones that I vaguely recognise from a past advertising campaign for Atelier Re's pricey handbag line. There's a scattering of different light sources on stands, cameras on tripods and tall, light-diffusing umbrellas, some white on the outside, some black. When I finally spot him —

the slender young man with a narrow black fedora pushed back on his cropped dark blond hair, wearing a grey fitted suit with the most perfectly cut and pressed stovepipe pants that are just the tiniest fraction too short on purpose — tears spring into my eyes. I feel them spill over and run down my cheeks.

Tommy doesn't see, because he's still turned away, and I hear him say in his light, silvery, Boston-inflected accent, 'Where do you want the shoot-throughs and how many, Miss Bianca?' And Bianca — in a signature Chanel fantasy tweed jacket, silk pussy-bow blouse and jeans — looks straight across at me with a smile and says, 'Why don't you ask Gia? She'd have a better idea than I would.'

Then he's flying across the distance between us the same way I'm sprinting towards him and we're crushing each other in a hug so fierce it feels like my bones, or maybe my heart, is breaking and I'm sobbing, 'Tommy! Tommy! Tommy!'

All he can get out through his own tears are, 'I thought you were *dead*, you complete bitch, leaving Milan without saying goodbye and then vanishing — vanishing! — into thin air. Irina, the hard-hearted cow, *wouldn't. Even. Return. My. Calls.* I thought you'd *died —*'

He pushes away from me to see me better, although he doesn't let me go, exclaiming with wet lashes, 'You're like a low-rent, chain-dressing, stable hand Dorothy just landed in Oz in godawful duck boots, I don't believe it, *look at you.*' He flaps one hand at me. 'This, *this*, ensemble is horrific —'

I'm laughing through my tears. 'But it's warm. And comfortable! Don't underestimate how good comfort feels.'

'Better than skinny?' He laughs.

I nod, scrubbing at my face with the backs of my hands. I take a step back to drink in his sharp three-piece Savile Row tailoring, the black velvet of his sleek, shawl-collared jacket, the bright white of his oxford button-down shirt, his textured skinny black tie and high-shine sockless loafers.

'Nothing tastes as good as comfort feels!' I reply finally and then we're giggling together like I never walked away, and nothing's changed; although everything has, and forever. Demons walk this world now, above-ground at all hours, in soul-jacked human skins. It will never be the same.

Only most people don't know it — yet.

Tommy takes one of my hands and draws me over to the wooden crates in front of the back drop. He tilts his head the way I've missed so terribly but hadn't realised until this moment. 'Could it be better, do you think?'

I nod, hauling away a couple of the smaller crates, feeling a certainty flow through me that I'd forgotten I could feel. 'More drop sheets? Preferably grey. It needs to be about *her* — not about the raw timber, or the set. It has to seem almost as if she's... floating.'

Bianca — heiress to billions — hurries off to see what she can find further inside the building.

'I brought some looks — they're on a wheelie rack in the office. We can work through them with the girl, when she gets here,' Tommy says as we lift, carry and arrange the array of umbrellas and lights around the small set. 'We need to work out the level of background light,' he mutters to himself the way he always used to, 'the fill lighting, figure out where the black flags are going to be, the angle of the soft box...'

I catch him up on what I've been doing. 'Cows, root vegetables and preserves, essentially,' I say as Tommy stands back to gaze at the two large timber crates we've placed side-by-side on their short ends in front of the paint-splashed back drop. He squints at the array of umbrellas we've placed around them. 'It's a bit industrial,' he adds, unconvinced. 'I'm still not feeling it.'

'Wait till you see the girl,' I reply, stepping forward to tweak the angle of the nearest parabolic umbrella. 'It won't matter where or how you shoot her. She will transcend her surroundings like a flaming phoenix.'

'Oh, goody,' Tommy grins, the grin fading as a walkie-talkie blares to life somewhere in the depths of the warehouse.

'Mademoiselle St Alban?' I hear a tinny voice squawk in French, the disembodied voice drawing closer. 'We have a problem.'

Bianca strides out of the gloom with an armful of dusty fabric under one arm, shoving the walkie-talkie she's holding into the loose, long hair around her right ear. 'What problem?' she snaps back in English for the benefit of me and Tommy, looking at the two of us with raised eyebrows. She lets the bundle of drop sheets in her arms fall to the ground at our feet.

'The girl is here,' the man on the other end replies, in gruff, French-inflected English this time. 'But there is a man with her. Big. Dangerous build. Like the cage fighter. He says his name is —' there's a static squawk, then, '*de Haut Rive.*'

'Daughtry?' Tommy wrinkles his nose sharply. 'Like the rock band? The rock band's here? No way.'

Bianca and I shake our heads. '*De Haut Rive* — the High Bank, or something like that,' I translate. 'It's French. The language you only ever learned to swear fluently in, Tommy.'

'I like the sound of him already,' Tommy murmurs back. '*Big, dangerous* and *French* have to be three of my favourite descriptors of all time.'

He picks up one of the grey drop sheets and arranges it across the wooden crates so that, all of a sudden, they just about blend into the background of ombre-toned grey paint behind them. I give Tommy a silent thumbs-up and mouth, *Much better.*

Bianca says into her walkie-talkie, 'Is the man armed?'

There's a long moment of silence, and the crisp reply comes back, 'No. Not armed.'

The three of us look at each other.

'Oh for goodness sake, let him in!' Tommy exclaims finally. 'What could happen with two dozen three-hundred-pound gorillas with guns and batons standing guard at the door? And you could freeze a grown man — even a big, *dangereux* one — with just your magnificent eyes, Gia darling. That hasn't changed, even if the rest of you has. *And not for the better.*' He gives me a wink to take the sting out of his words.

Bianca snaps into the handset she's holding up to her carmine-coloured mouth, *'Allez! Vite.'*

Then the hangar doors slide open with a clang and a blast of arctic air.

19

I only remember to pull the hot pink pressure mask over my head and face seconds before a tall, pale, willowy woman with a cascade of wavy, honey-blonde hair falling loose around her shoulders enters the echoing warehouse with an even taller man in tow.

Through the single eyehole in Jamie's suffocatingly tight pink mask, I can just make out that Cibyyl is wearing the exact same kooky outfit she wore in her music videos — grey, knitted, sleeveless dress and rainbow arm-warmers, plain black ballet flats on her long feet — like she only owns the one set of clothes or was scared we wouldn't recognise her in anything else. The big, tawny-haired man she's with is wearing a beat-up pair of black jeans, a plaid lumberjack shirt in a faded red tartan that strains across his big shoulders, and boots that appear to be constructed from the whole furry skins of wild animals, held together with leather ties; like battered mukluks, only shorter.

'They both look like they got dressed in the dark,' I mumble through the mask, which smells faintly of Jamie's rose-scented perfume.

'Oh, I don't know,' Tommy whispers beside me. 'All he needs to anchor his wild frontier man outfit is a huge, furry Davy Crockett hat. I likey.'

As the big man turns his head to the woman beside him

to point out something high up in the overhead catwalks, I see that his dark gold hair isn't actually short, but worn in a long, tight plait down his back with some kind of sharp, double-ended wooden stick — like a deadly weaver's spindle — jammed through the base of it, near the nape of his neck.

It doesn't take long before the two of them are standing in front of the three of us, and the skin on my body goes taut in recognition of what she is. It would explain the faintest luminescence that seems to be coming off her pale skin, like she's sweating *light*.

Beside her, her green-eyed companion appears to be standing in shadow.

It could be the Argo and Great Eastern Street all over again. There's a power in the room; I can feel it. The light that bathed her in her videos didn't come from clever lighting, I realise with a chill. It all came from *her*.

They can't hide what they are.

But I think I'm the only one here who can see it. Mercy has changed me in some irrevocable way. I take a step back, light-headed and suddenly afraid. 'I think we might have made a mistake,' I mumble under my breath. 'Jamie's not here. They're not going to deal.'

Bianca gives me a sharp, quelling look before holding out her right hand and saying graciously in her best Swiss-finishing-school voice, 'I'm Bianca St Alban. Thank you for making your own way here. I trust it wasn't too difficult to find.'

Cibyyl doesn't meet anyone's eyes. And she doesn't take the hand Bianca offers; she doesn't even seem to register it suspended there in front of her. The tall man with Cibyyl places his big hands protectively on her shoulders, giving her a gentle *you can do this* kind of shake, before answering in a smoky, faintly French accent, as if Bianca has been talking to him all along, 'Jean de Haut Rive.' The man's voice holds a tinge of amusement. 'But people call me *Daughtry* because it's easier, you know? It was no trouble.'

Bianca frowns, lowering her hand, disconcerted at the blonde woman's refusal to take it.

Up close, I see that Daughtry has a heavy silver chain around his neck, interwoven with small, smooth discs of black onyx or obsidian; it seems a curiously sculptural adornment for someone so woodsy-looking. A similar bracelet encircles his left wrist. I look up from surveying the tanned, strong column of the man's throat to find his green eyes locked on me, a small frown between his strong, arched eyebrows. His gaze on me is piercing. I go hot beneath his steady scrutiny, even though most of my face is covered by Jamie's pink mask.

He can't know, can he? I lift my chin defiantly and the big man finally looks away as Bianca indicates Tommy beside me.

'This is Tommy Taffin,' she says, 'one of the top men in fashion who will be your photographer today.' Tommy inclines his head, staring boldly at Daughtry, who doesn't look the least bit discomfited at Tommy's frankly lascivious up-and-down appraisal. Daughtry seems totally at ease inside his own skin, which isn't something I often saw with the good-looking men in Irina's orbit. This one doesn't preen, and he doesn't fidget. Instead, he's still and watchful in a way that reminds me very much of Shaun. Despite his just-crawled-out-of-the-undergrowth appearance, there's something almost military about his bearing.

Bianca indicates me last. 'And this is —'

'*Not* Jamie Suggitt,' Daughtry states in his deep, husky voice, his generous mouth turned down now at the corners. He runs his green eyes across the bandaged contours of my face again — almost as if he can see through the fabric — and

I flush hotter beneath the mask.

Cibyyl's head goes up and she turns a frantic gaze on Daughtry, shaking her head furiously like a mute, distressed child.

Daughtry takes his hands from her shoulders and gently turns her around to face him. 'You're sure?' he says, as if in answer to something she's said, although she still hasn't spoken a single word aloud.

Cibyyl gives an emphatic nod, her honey-blonde bangs falling around her heart-shaped face. I think of the Archangel Gabriel's innate majesty, power and poise — how around him, time, all of creation, seems to stop — and I realise there's something very wrong with this angel, if that's what she is. This one is diminished or... damaged in some way. I wonder what's happened to make her like this.

'Then we're going.' Daughtry's hands fall to his sides and he addresses me with an expression of reproach in his dark green gaze. 'The instruction was quite specific that Jamie Suggitt be present. It is a matter, you understand, of trust. No Jamie, no photos. We were quite clear in our message.'

Then, shockingly, the two of them are turning and walking away — Daughtry's big hand hovering protectively in the small of Cibyyl's back — and Bianca freezes in consternation for a moment before actually running after them in her high-gloss kitten heels calling out, 'Wait! *Wait!* You haven't even heard about the campaign we've lined up for you. It will be historic! Groundbreaking! Wait!'

I look over at Tommy ruefully and rip off Jamie's face mask, my mousy brown hair standing up all over the place in wisps, knowing that we've blown it.

'What actually just happened here...?' Tommy says,

confused.

I explain about the message Cibyyl left for us on Rabbleknowledgenet that asked specifically that Jamie Suggitt be present for the photo shoot.

'I think Cibyyl's one of them,' I murmur. 'You know, like at the Galleria in Milan? The ones capable of death and fire?' Tommy was there too, that night, the two of us narrowly escaping serious injury in the desperate stampede to get out.

Tommy shakes his head, still bewildered. 'One of the shining ones with wings? Or the...other ones?'

I lift my shoulders in a shrug as the huge hangar-style doors slide open again, bringing another icy blast of air from outside. 'Whoever, whatever, she is — she's going, going, gone and we've just lost our best chance of getting close to Kit Tyburn.'

'Not yet we haven't,' Tommy murmurs, nudging me. 'Look.'

Startled, I glance across to the open doors to see that Cibyyl and her big minder have not yet managed to leave the building because a small knot of people, struggling and scuffling just outside, is blocking their exit. A powerfully built man is trying to push his way inside the warehouse, letting out a shout as he spots Bianca halfway to the open doors.

My heart plummets, just for a moment, inside my chest.

Shaun.

'Bianca St Alban!' Shaun calls out, the harsh exterior lights flaring gold off his curls.

Bianca strides forward, peering at him for a moment before barking at her security team, *'Let him in!'*

'You said to expect *one woman*, Mademoiselle St Alban, and now there are all these strangers —!' One of the burly security guards outside gives Shaun a hard shove in disgust.

Shaun stumbles and I see his shoulders bunching, ready to shove the bodyguard back, when a small, frail figure wearing a pink face mask identical to the one I'm clutching in my hand comes into view. She places the fingers of one hand on the sleeve of Shaun's beaten-up black leather jacket. He immediately goes still.

Bianca pushes her way forward through her security detail, waving at all the big, burly types to clear the area around the doors.

Jamie Suggitt is suddenly framed in the entryway, dwarfed by the high ceilings and milling people around her. She's wearing a shapeless, baby-pink woollen cardigan and a turtle-necked, ankle-length, dusty pink dress, every inch of her covered by heavy fabric. She's like a character from a horror movie, come back from the dead to wreak revenge. Even Cibyyl and her minder move back reverently to allow Jamie to pass through the doors towards me and Tommy. Cibyyl's dark, wide-set eyes with their impossibly long lashes track Jamie's thin figure as she crosses the floor towards us with hesitant steps.

The way Jamie's hunched over, darting quick looks up from under her lashes, I know she's thinking about all the space around her, and how anything could come at her from anywhere. I've been the same. It took me over a year not to completely freak out in new surroundings. In the early days, I spent a lot of time in locked toilet cubicles trying to get my emotions under control. My breathing quickens now in sympathy as I watch Jamie draw closer.

Eighteen months. She's barricaded herself away inside her fortress-house for eighteen months — and yet she's here in person.

I caused this.

She's so very brave.

'You came,' I say, wanting to take her hands, but knowing

it wouldn't be welcome.

'I want to hide,' Jamie rasps, unable to meet my eyes. 'But I couldn't stay away. Something told me... I had to come. Shaun wasn't happy about my change of heart — I was almost ready for bed, I mean, look at me, I just threw on whatever I had that was clean — but, well, here we are. We made it. Better late than never, yeah?'

She flinches as Bianca's security team pulls the doors closed again with a loud *clang*, sealing the seven of us inside.

As Cibyyl and Daughtry make their way back towards us, Tommy says, suddenly brisk and businesslike, 'Right. Now we can begin. Kill most of the overheads, Gia, Bianca — let's get to work.'

It's the strangest photo shoot I've ever been part of. Tommy and Bianca are making a conscious effort not to stare at Jamie — who's hovering nervously on the sidelines wringing her gloved hands — while Shaun just glowers at everyone. But especially at Daughtry. The big stranger's got to be six foot seven, at least, and his hands are thick with calluses like he regularly knocks heads together for a living. I can see Shaun wondering if he could take the man down in a fight, and I'm hoping he's not going to start one just to find out.

Cibyyl, meanwhile, is sitting stiff and wide-eyed in a sleeveless, bejewelled and feathered metallic-gold Atelier Re gown with a plunging neckline, looking as wooden as the crate she's perched on while Tommy tries to elicit some emotion from her very beautiful, but very blank, face. She still won't look at anyone directly, except Daughtry — and when she does look at him, her eyes are pleading.

To top it all off, every shot Tommy has taken of Cibyyl so far has come out ruined.

Calling time for a moment, Bianca and I peer into Tommy's laptop screen in consternation as he scrolls through take after take, showing us how not a single image is usable.

Even Jamie, hugging herself tightly, draws closer to see.

In all the pictures, Cibyyl is either a blur of light or a smear of movement — even though she's barely moved a muscle since she sat down in front of the backdrop. In some pictures, she looks like the girl-next-door seen through a badly applied Vaseline-covered lens; there's so much fog around her face it's almost impossible to make out her features. In others, she's only a vaguely human shape, as if she's been caught whirling on the spot.

Tommy's frustration has long since eclipsed his sense of awe. 'They don't, uh, photograph very well, do they? You'd think it would be the opposite.'

'Surely there must be just *one* you can use?' Bianca exclaims in dismay, unsure exactly what the problem is because neither Tommy nor I have seen fit to tell her what we're really dealing with here. Bianca looks from Cibyyl's glittering, rigid figure to the light-smeared images filling Tommy's screen and shakes her head in disbelief. 'I don't understand it,' she mutters.

'You can't *make* them do anything,' I tell Tommy resignedly.

'Not even dial it down?'

I shake my head. 'It's like they operate at a different frequency from us. Trust me.'

'Then what you're trying to achieve here is *impossible!*' Tommy says, exasperated. 'You know what the schedule is like at this time of year, Gia darling. It's madness. We've just come off Paris and are gearing up for the February shows. Juliana absolutely backs the cause we're trying to promote here — violence against women is fundamentally *abhorrent* to her — but she wasn't too happy about the timing. I have an invitation-only trunk show to oversee in New York tomorrow evening and we've got bupkiss.'

Bianca looks from Tommy to me, unable to follow the train of our discussion. 'What are you two *talking* about?'

Daughtry wanders over from where he's been watching from the sidelines. He asks in his deep, sexy voice, 'Is there a problem?'

Tommy glances up at him sharply. 'We've been at it for *hours*, big boy, and she's sitting there with the expressive range of a concrete garden gnome in possibly the most expensive couture dress in the world! I can't capture *anything*. It's like she's doing something to my equipment —' Tommy's voice drops, 'or she's giving off something that resists...'

Tommy doesn't finish the sentence. It's clear from the expression on his face that part of him is still sceptical it isn't just an equipment malfunction issue; although he's tried every camera and lens he brought with him from Milan.

'It's because she's afraid,' Daughtry says quietly. 'It took a lot for her to come here; to be seen like this. When I first found her, she was half-wild, you understand, almost mad with pain and rage and fear. She wanted to die — but Death would not take her. Instead, he told her to help him find and destroy a common adversary: Lucifer.'

Tommy snorts. 'You speak of "death" as if it's a person.'

Jamie and I exchange troubled glances and I don't tell Tommy that he was there, in Milan, Death himself. Walking among us clothed in eternal youth and power, picking and choosing who would go, and who would stay.

'*They can only kill or be killed by each other*,' I murmur, recalling something Mercy once said in a corridor in Milan, when she was pretending to be someone else. 'And Azraeil wouldn't do it?'

Daughtry shakes his head. 'Lord Azraeil would not. *Could not*,' he amends. 'His province is *our* kind, Gia. Not his own. Her pain is beyond his to remedy.'

I am weirdly comforted to have confirmation from Daughtry's own lips that Daughtry is one of us. Even by the standards of the male models I used to hang out with, Daughtry is an outlier, built on an otherworldly, almost angelic scale.

Bianca blinks rapidly in confusion as Daughtry adds, 'She was once tortured to the point of death by Lucifer and two of his most powerful demons. Which is why we're here — she came back solely for Lucifer. Only the promise of vengeance holds her together. Sometimes I think her mind is gone, and only the *animus* remains. Your goal is hers. She will do all she can to bring him down.'

'*Bring him down*?' Bianca utters in disbelief. 'The woman won't even answer to her own name!'

Daughtry says quietly, 'That is because *Cibyyl* is not her name.'

I look across at the dazzling creature dressed all in gold who, underneath, is not so very different from Jamie, or from me.

'Of course it isn't,' I say briskly. 'But Satan's not going to rise to the bait on the strength of these pictures,' I remind everyone, jabbing my finger at the light-stained images, row after row, on Tommy's screen. 'He likes beautiful things and we can't use a single one of these. You need to speak to her, Daughtry. Do something.'

Jamie leans in to get a closer look at the photos, and Daughtry abruptly raises his hand as if he's going to touch her.

Jamie flinches back immediately.

'Can *you* talk to her?' the big man asks, bending a little to look into Jamie's rapidly blinking eye. 'It would help a great deal.

She did ask specifically for you. You have a common…friend. She wanted very badly to meet you. You were all she spoke of as we made our way here tonight.'

Bianca, Tommy and I exchange glances, intrigued.

Jamie stares at Daughtry for a long moment, then gives a curt nod.

'Go to her then,' Daughtry urges. 'Please.'

Jamie works her gloves off her fingers, handing them to me. I shove them in one of my pockets.

The five of us — Shaun, Tommy, Bianca, Daughtry and I — watch Jamie walk past the camera on its tripod and lower her birdlike frame tentatively onto one corner of the drop sheet-covered crate Cibyyl is perched on.

Jamie murmurs words of reassurance we can't hear before reaching for the other woman's hands.

Shaun shoots me a look of apprehension.

The instant Jamie takes Cibyyl's long fingers in hers, both women go rigid.

Their gazes are wide and staring — fixed on each other.

Jamie lets out a long, low cry of pain and I remember Mercy's voice when she first touched me in the farmhouse at Craster — like a breath of fire in my mind; all the memories I absorbed from a life I never even lived, that I will never now forget.

Shaun runs forward to pull the two women apart, but Jamie snarls through clenched teeth, 'Stay back!'

'What's happening?' Shaun pleads.

'We're *talking*,' Jamie rasps, in the grip of some fever.

'What?' he exclaims.

I grab Shaun by the arm. He tries to shake me off angrily, but I hold on. 'This is how they show you,' I say fiercely. 'Jamie has to know who she's dealing with.'

Cibyyl moves so suddenly that her hands are around the base of Jamie's throat. Bianca gasps.

'What is she *doing*?' Shaun shouts, straining in my grip.

'Wait!' I beg, though I'm filled with misgiving. '*Watch.*'

In one abrupt move, the creature that calls herself *Cibyyl* rips the mask from Jamie's face and we all gasp to see Jamie the way she is now — hair in crazy tufts as fine and thin as a baby's, skin covered with red-raw scars and craters. Her naked face resembles melted wax.

Beside me, Bianca makes a shocked sound and starts to sob through the fingers that she's laced over her mouth.

With reverence, Cibyyl places her slender hands around Jamie's ruined face and touches her forehead to Jamie's, crooning something in a weirdly resonant voice. The two of them stay locked together like that, rocking, forehead to forehead, and Tommy sees something, at last, that he can use.

'*Before* and *After*,' he whispers. 'But which comes before? And which comes after? This is perfect.'

He runs forward, camera raised, and begins shooting the two women in close-up, from every angle — their faces still touching, the tears on Jamie's cheeks catching the light like diamonds.

Daughtry and I have to physically wrestle Shaun to stop him grabbing for Tommy's camera and smashing it to the floor. 'He knows what he's doing,' I gasp as Shaun continues to fight me. 'Let him do his job.'

As Cibyyl pulls her face away from Jamie's at last, Tommy calls out, 'Bianca? Gia? I have an idea I need your help with.'

We watch Jamie and Cibyyl head back to the office with Bianca, both of them draped in dusty drop sheets, their bared necks and shoulders exposed to the cold air. Tommy has taken dozens of portraits of them, cheek-to-cheek, the camera unsparing on Jamie's acid-scored skin, Cibyyl's luminous beauty. There are portraits of each woman face forward, in profile, in close-up, and at a distance. Eyes open, eyes closed, swanlike necks extended; every image is heartbreaking in its own way.

When Shaun sees the final pictures laid out on Tommy's lap top, he understands at last what Tommy has been trying to do.

'*Before* and *After*,' Tommy repeats quietly, 'only sociopaths or demons would fail to be moved by the two of them together. 'This one —' Tommy taps at an image of the two women, eyes wide, cheekbones touching, looking out at the viewer, the line of Jamie's bared neck deformed with thick red scars, the line of Cibyyl's as pure and lineless as a young child's — 'is the first one we go with. Now. Tonight. Get it out on social, and everyone in the world will be talking about them by tomorrow morning. *Everyone*. Even the Devil will have to take notice. Cibyyl will be everywhere.'

'But so will Jamie,' I point out, troubled. 'I'm not sure this is what she wants — to be seen and known in this way.'

'This is for Jamie as much as it is for Cibyyl. There's no reason a woman as beautiful as she is needs to hide or wear a mask — *she's done nothing wrong*.' Tommy has a sheen of tears in his own eyes. 'Now put Cibyyl into the system,' he commands me. 'I'll do the same. Make her very findable. We want to know the minute *he* sees it.'

I nod, taking out my phone to give Cibyyl the kind of high visibility she couldn't begin to dream of. Tommy and I start uploading the image of Cibyyl and Jamie everywhere. While we're bent over our devices, heads together, we see the likes and comments begin to rack up in their dozens on all the platforms, sites and accounts we've seeded it to.

'*Go*,' Tommy mutters, shooting the image out to his

own followers, who number in the millions. The hearts and comments and shares and reposts snowball as we watch, our heads pressed together.

#Cibyyl #Jamie #ShelterMeUK we type and post and type, *#Stopviolenceagainstwomen*

Behind me I hear Shaun say, 'I still don't understand how you managed to get photos of Cibyyl when you couldn't get a damned thing before, Tommy?'

'She needed to be reminded,' Daughtry interrupts quietly, 'of what it means to be human. Her own suffering — it can be all-consuming. Like a fugue through which no one can reach her. Some days, I think she still believes she's there, on the verge of destruction; that she's still being tortured by Luc, by his demons. She has to be reminded to fight. You have to understand she wasn't always like this. She was *strong*. But Luc and his *daemonium*, they almost broke her.'

Shaun is about to ask something else when Daughtry holds up one of his big callused hands, his face troubled as he scans the huge warehouse space.

There's something coming.

Both he and I can feel it.

My breathing starts to accelerate, fast and ragged. She's like the sharp point of a blade sliding between my ribs, and I stumble forward.

'What's wrong?' Shaun exclaims, gripping my arm as I sway dangerously on my feet.

I dimly register Daughtry's head going up, testing the air, the smooth, wooden weapon he usually wears in his hair already in his right hand like a crude dagger.

When I exhale sharply, my breath streams out in a dense white cloud — like an escaping soul — and Shaun shies away, horrified.

Daughtry turns slowly towards me, his lips drawn back from his teeth in a snarl.

'Move back.' I swing a shaking finger at the three men ringing me. 'You'll want to give her *room*.'

Then every light in the place goes out and I know what's coming and my skin... illuminates. Silver-blue waves of energy begin to pour off it, visible in the darkness.

I bow my head.

This time I let the black waters take me willingly. I welcome them, feeling them close over me as I am enveloped in her pain, and mine.

20

Gia's head snaps up, an unholy light in her eyes, and I growl at the man she calls Shaun.

He flinches in recognition, but bravely stands his ground.

'Let her go,' he pleads hoarsely. 'How can you call yourself *Mercy* when you're killing her every moment you're in there?'

Through Gia's agency, I shake my head, the pale blue-silver fire pouring off our shared skin, lighting the darkness.

'She is my voice and my vehicle,' I rasp, 'and she understands the bargain. *She is willing*, and I will take only what she can give, and no more. Whatever I am now, I am no murderer of innocents. She is my friend.'

I turn to the other two men, my eyes roving across the bone-white, wide-eyed face of the one she calls Tommy, settling on the big man with the sharp, spindle-shaped weapon raised in his right hand against me.

'Where is Cibyyl?' I growl. '*Mastin*, I would talk with your charge.'

'*Habominacion!*' the bigger man roars, his accent thick with rage. 'Get thee back to Sheol or be returned to God.' He slashes at the air with his pointed weapon and my laughter rises, ringing from the rafters in painful waves to make them all cower and tremble where they stand.

'I *am* Sheol,' I roar. 'Sheol is *in* me, by the will of Azraeil. I am Death's purpose, and his right hand. Your weapon has no power over *me*. I am a wraith — yes —' the word comes out like a serpent's hiss, 'but I was never born of woman.'

The *mastin*'s green eyes instantly flare wide in shocked understanding of who and what I am.

The gatekeeper — for that is what he is, a *mastin*, one of the rare few who stand between the unwary living of this world and the teeming dead, who are able to speak with us when others cannot, who can open and seal doors between worlds — gets down on one knee and bows his head reverently.

'Where is she who would face Lucifer at my side?' I whisper in a voice to rend steel.

In the silence that follows, I feel Gia sway dangerously. Without her, I am truly the abomination Daughtry says I am; just another voiceless wraith in a desperately haunted world.

But Gia's losing what hold she ever had on me. I am power without outlet now, without direction; I feel as if I'm blowing apart. The only thing stopping me from atomising into a billion pieces is *her*. I fray and shred and fracture here, where under the violet sky of Azraeil's domain I am whole and myself and free.

It is too cruel, the dissonance between me and this world I once walked through with my love.

'*Where has he gone?*' I scream at them all and they cover their ears in terror at my voice. '*Where?*'

Gia staggers again, as if she would fall.

Long-fingered hands, as hard, smooth and unmarked as polished marble, suddenly grasp us by the forearms to hold us steady. I look into the face of the tall, blonde woman. Only her dark eyes are the same, and they rake Gia's face desperately for signs of me.

'Is it really *you*?' Her words tumble out through a wide, sensuous mouth I do not recognise. 'What did he *do* to you?'

'I'm here now,' I murmur, unwilling to describe for her my last moments as a woman on this earth. 'We are together again.'

I touch her face, and she closes her fever-bright eyes.

My touch, at least, is familiar, if not what I have become.

Beneath my touch, Cibyyl seems to shimmer before blurring in outline. Then her long blonde hair, her face, it all melts away, to the gasps of the humans in the room.

I face the Archangel Nuriel — whom once I saved from the black waters of Lake Como where the demons Ananel and Remiel kept her chained for their own pleasure while they awaited Lucifer's return.

Like me, Nuriel has suffered terribly.

She is no longer human in appearance, but has shifted into her true form — dark-haired and dark-eyed, inhumanly tall, slender but powerful, broad-shouldered. She wears a torn and sleeveless shift so bright it seems made of light; the ends of it flutter in the icy air around us. Marks left by demons stripe her face and torso and limbs. She wears them deliberately, like the medals of a hard-won survival.

'Luc nearly destroyed you.' I touch her cheek with the back of one of Gia's small hands. If I could still weep, I would.

'He *killed* you,' Nuriel cries, tears of light spilling out of her dark eyes.

'All he did was *change* me,' I insist. 'I'm still here. I'm still *me*.'

I touch the scars on Nuriel's face, which only serve to make her more beautiful to my eyes. 'You did not go home?'

She shakes her head violently. 'I will never return. Not while Lucifer walks this world. I cannot. He chains me to this place. While he lives, I am not free.'

I shake her fiercely. 'Yet Azraeil tells me you entered Sheol — seeking to die.'

Nuriel's eyes glitter in memory. 'I was…lost for a long time. Daughtry found me wandering among the dead and brought me to Azraeil — who would not help me. He said that I should become what Luc most craves, and then —'

She makes a fist of her right hand, smashing it into her left palm. 'He said Luc must not be allowed to do unto their kind —' she throws her arms wide to indicate the silent band of humans ringing us at a distance, 'what he did to *me*.'

She begins to shake beneath my hands, and I reach up to stroke her scarred cheek before gripping her hands in mine. 'Azraeil was right not to help you,' I say urgently. 'There is no end to pain, my love; no end to suffering. Only vengeance remains to us now. I have need of you, *soror*. Everything, even time, is borrowed. There is nothing that will stay. *Listen.*'

There is a hollow roaring in my ears — the call of the sweet river that runs through the Valley of the Shadow of Death — and I have to struggle to make myself heard above the black waters that have taken the place of my heart and flesh and blood. 'Jeremiel will stand where Selaphiel cannot — for our brother Selaphiel will never return to this world which almost destroyed him. For one brief moment, Raphael, Gabriel, Uriel, Barachiel, Jegudiel, Michael, Jeremiel and you, my love, *you*, will sing me to sleep again inside a human body so that I may enter the Devil's house undetected. *Nothing of me must escape.* He thinks me gone forever. Let him keep thinking it until the moment I finish him.'

I raise the fingers of Gia's hand and Nuriel sees the telltale silver-blue fire flowing down between them like molten liquid. 'What Luc will see will be *you* — the prize, the one that he burns for, and craves. His perfect woman, in a way I never was. You will be accompanied by a dowdy, expendable female companion no one will notice: *Gia Basso*. What Lucifer will see will be two frail human women. And he will welcome us into his house — and then he will die.'

'You can't let him touch me again!' Nuriel pleads. 'None of them can touch me again.'

I grip her fiercely. 'I swear it. I will bear it all for you. You are my way in, my key. Beyond that — stay or leave — the argument is mine. Luc has robbed me of the life I hoped to live with the one I love, who loved me even when I didn't know who, or what I was. I am the sword of Azraeil and I say: *There will be a reckoning.*'

As the words pour out of me, I feel the painful dissonance in the air around us grow, almost seeming to fracture the icy air. Gia's breaths come in choking fits and her heart shudders in the narrow cage of her chest.

There is no time — there never was.

'On Gia's word,' I hiss, 'I will be freed and we will meet him *together*, Nuriel. We will be two, the way we were before I was lost to the serpent who came between us, all those long years ago. I will make it right, my love. For you, for me. For Ryan.'

My fingers on Nuriel loosen and I prepare to step away into the roaring void that will separate me from my love every day that he still breathes.

But the man, *Shaun*, interjects clearly and fiercely, 'I'm coming with you.'

I turn to look at him with blazing eyes — all of me burning blue-silver — and the man recoils from what he sees, for I am monstrous: a hollow-eyed, burning girl.

'The *mastin*,' I snarl, indicating the tall one with the tawny hair and eyes like polished jade, 'possesses shortcuts through this world others of your kind can only dream of. Look to *him* for a way in.'

With a jerk of Gia's head, I indicate the sharp stick clenched in the *mastin*'s fist. 'There are other means to enter the lion's den, human, but the first approach must be made by the lambs — and the lambs alone.'

'Wolves,' Nuriel rasps, turning her own burning eyes on Shaun, her dark hair streaming and writhing about her face like a snarl of living serpents. *'Wolves dressed as lambs.'*

My own laughter is harsh. 'What else to take down the lion of the world? He will expect pleasure and receive only suffering. It is fitting that we two be the fork in which he is caught.'

Gia sinks to her knees suddenly, and the breach between this world and the next becomes a howling gale that pulls at me. She is at breaking point. As am I. I cannot stay.

I have difficulty focusing on Nuriel's heartbreaking face above us as I say, 'It will not be long, my love. I will be with you, when it is time. Trust in that.'

Nuriel grips Gia's fingers harder, but I can already feel the bonds between Gia and me loosening.

'You know that we may not survive this.' Her words are bleak.

'I know it,' I say, as Gia closes her eyes, ready to step back into the river and release me; release herself.

'Wait!' the *mastin*, Daughtry, shouts, moving closer.

I focus on him with difficulty, as if I am in the midst of a sandstorm.

'How will I find *you*, wraith,' he thunders, 'in order to strike at the Devil? I can only find a person in this world whom I have first *read*. Someone I have known from something of theirs I have placed my hands on. You have no substance, you have no possessions; you cannot be known, you cannot be read. Nor can the Devil! Without me, your chances of success are so much less. This —' he holds up the sharpened stick in his hand, 'can dispatch wraiths and demons to Azraeil's demesne, almost as well as you can. You know what my kind can do. You *need* me by your side.'

'And *me*.' Shaun's dark gold gaze is feverish where he stands shoulder-to-shoulder with the *mastin*. 'You forget that Gia will be with you. And the man who hurt her badly will be there. Gia will be among monsters. She is the vessel that will hide you. Who will protect *her*?'

I turn my head to look at him and the man, Shaun, shrinks back as my searing gaze rakes his face.

I *feel* it then — his absolute love for Gia.

An emotion as constant and hopeless as the love Ryan once felt for me.

So.

She does not know it; nor will he ever willingly tell her.

It is a complication I do not need at this — the eleventh — hour.

Daughtry makes a hypnotic figure of eight in the air between us with the weapon of worn but polished wood in his hand. 'All I know, wraith — all I have ever known since once I walked the bloodstained fields of Lisieux and Bayeux in times past — is to send the dead and demonic back to where they can do no harm to the living. It has been my life's calling. *Let me help you.*'

'Let *us*,' Shaun adds fiercely. 'We will be the element of surprise no demon will see coming.'

I pull away from Nuriel's grasp then, and instantly the sounds of the black river rise up, shrieking, in my ears. And the world is all light, or I am, and my voice is the world, shaking them all in this room to their bones.

'You wish to read *me*, Gatekeeper? You wish to know who *I* am? By this, will you know me, and find me — wherever I may be. You will be marked forever, Knight. But then, you already were.'

I step out and away from Gia's body so that, for a moment, I am revealed as I am now: a tall and shining wraith with hollow eyes, as insubstantial and silent, as deaf and dumb, as air. Without weight or substance. An imprint of someone who once lived, breathed, *loved*. A ghost girl.

Without Gia, I am a spent breath, a silent movie, a memory; nothing more.

I see the woman, Bianca, mouth *Mercy* — recognition and fear in her dark eyes as they lift up and up, to take me in. I see the remaining eye of the young woman, Jamie — who speaks with Death himself, who loves the shining Prince of All Souls with a devotion as deep as it is hopeless of ever being returned — go wide with awe.

I see the man, Shaun, catch Gia's unconscious body before it falls to the ground, cradling her tenderly against his broad chest. So beloved, in a way I will never again be in this world.

My pain and my sorrow rise and rise.

My love, I scream in a voice that only Daughtry can now hear, *Where have you* gone?

Daughtry stands tall and unafraid, as I flicker and burn before him in my true form, raising his hand confidently, palm outward as if he would meet mine and I were still human, and capable of common touch.

His dark green eyes are wide and fascinated as they gaze on me, for I am beautiful in a way that is now, and will forever be, elemental.

He steps forward and I smile, raising my own hand, whispering for his ears alone, 'By this, Knight, shall you know me,' and I plunge — *straight through him*.

He is that howling, jetstream, raceway tangle of skin and bone, nerve and muscle and blood that all humankind is. I read him and know him the instant he knows me. We meet at the core of us, and I am burning him alive with the knowledge of *who I am*.

You will never forget me now, my words echo inside his mind. *You will never forget who you are in this moment. Wherever I am in this world or the next — you will find me.*

The *mastin* shudders, caught in the weave of me, his green eyes stark with pain.

If I were archangel still, or demon, Mastin, I add, a touch of acid in my voice that licks along his already convulsing nerves like fire, *you would already be dead.*

Then I am through and out, and I am gone.

℈

I wake to the feel of Bianca stroking my hair, the tears that are falling from her eyes wetting my face. Her long dark hair is a warm, scented curtain around me, but I can feel all of them leaning in close, watching me with concern: Tommy and Shaun, Jamie.

My friends.

For a moment I close my eyes, aware of how much it is I have to lose now.

'Where is the angel?' I gasp finally, re-opening my eyes with difficulty because all I want to do is sleep. 'The warrior?'

But the words come out strangled and strange. I sound like I'm drowning, not speaking.

Bianca puts her fingers against my lips to quiet me. It is an effort even to breathe. Everything burns from the inside out.

'They're gone,' she sobs. 'I'm not sure how I'm going to explain it to my security detail, but Cibyyl — I mean, *Nuriel* — and Daughtry just *vanished.*'

'That stick,' Jamie adds in an awed whisper. 'After Mercy broke up into all these tiny pieces of... light, Daughtry opened some kind of hole in the air with it and then he and the angel just stepped through and —'

I roll my head sideways with difficulty, looking to Shaun — the eternal sceptic — for confirmation. He nods reluctantly to say it's all true.

※

I don't remember much of the journey back to Jamie's place.

I know I'm lying across one of the seats and Shaun's in the car with me because my head is — inexplicably — cradled across his denim-clad, muscular thighs. And he's stroking my hair — the biggest hard-arse street fighter in the western world is stroking my hair. And even more surprising is that I'm letting him. I don't have the energy to even come up with my usual defensive *Don't touch me.*

I close my eyes, knowing that Jamie, Tommy and Bianca are sitting beside each other, across from us. Talking in low voices.

All the people I like best, in one place.

I sigh, or imagine I do. Everything *hurts.*

The town car moves again, fast, then slowing to a stop-start crawl. Tilbury Docks is miles from anywhere, but it feels to me as if the driver is following the entire course of the River Thames in getting back. There are so many turns and switchbacks that I think that I doze. Waking, then dozing, for what feel like hours.

Finally, I hear Tommy ask to be let off at a hotel in the heart of the West End — his spiritual home when he's in London. 'This isn't goodbye,' he warns everyone angrily as the door opens to let him out. 'And don't you dare say another word, any of you, or I will *howl*.'

I get a sense of his cologne around me, then a warm tear falls on my cheek that might be his — I can't be sure — before the door slams shut. I'm too spent to open my eyes, even though it might be the last time I ever see him.

I feel regret; I think I sleep.

Sometime later, the car slows abruptly and Bianca barks through the intercom, 'What's happening, Jean-Michel?'

'*Les journalistes*,' the driver's disembodied voice replies in disgust as he gives three blasts on his horn, steering slowly through what must be a thick press of bodies outside. I hear open palms slapping the surface of the car. I know from having lived through situations like this before that we are walled in by a crowd of eager men and women clutching cameras and microphones.

It's so familiar that I murmur, 'Irina.'

Bianca's answering laughter is curt and unamused.

'They're camped out on your doorstep, Jamie,' I hear her say. 'You can't go home now — you won't even make it to your front door! They will tear you apart for an angle. Baring your face to the world was extremely brave, but it's made you notorious.'

Jamie's reply is harsh with fear. 'I have to get home, Bianca! It's the only place I'm safe. My things are in there. My entire life is in that house now.'

The car rocks as people start bashing on the windows. 'Jamie Suggitt! Jamie Suggitt!' is repeated over and over.

'We know you're in there!'

'Care to comment?'

'Who's with you?'

'What's caused you to break your silence after all this time?'

'Do you think his sentence was too lenient?'

'What are your thoughts on chemical castration?'

'Give us a picture, love! We know you want to!'

Jamie lets out a long, low, wounded moan through the hands covering her face.

'*Stay with me,*' Bianca insists in a low voice. Maybe I'm the only one who really hears the deep loneliness and uncertainty in her words. 'At least until all this blows over?'

'What have I *done*?' Jamie whispers, appalled, as the noise outside grows more deafening. The car comes to a complete stop, unable to move forward anymore.

'Jamie, love,' Shaun says, still stroking the side of my face absently as if I'm a house cat, 'being with Bianca right now might actually be the safest place for you. She can protect you around the clock.'

'*But my things,*' Jamie chokes as the car rocks on its tyres, axles protesting.

'*Mademoiselle?*' Jean-Michel's voice interrupts tersely through the internal speaker. 'I can go no further. I need instruction.'

'I'll bring them all to you,' Shaun insists, leaning towards Jamie over my prone body. 'Anything you need, whatever you want — I'll bring it over. Nothing's going to stop me getting through all that. They don't care about someone who looks like *me*. I'll just bum-rush them and they'll go flying like skittles.'

The driver gives another three sharp blasts on his horn, but the pummelling of fists on the windows, on the sunroof, the shooting-star flashes of light and shouting only grow more intense.

'Bianca's rich,' Shaun adds. 'She'll have people, walls, things to keep you safe that you won't have at home. If you insist on *being* home those reporters outside will try to take your windows out of their frames to get at you. They will disable your alarm and surprise you in the shower. I'm telling you, go to Bianca's if you know what's good for you. You're a sitting duck here.'

'It wasn't supposed to be about *me*,' Jamie whimpers.

'*She couldn't have done it without you*,' I try to say from where I'm lying, but none of them hear me. Being close to Jamie's peculiarly human, wounded energy enabled Nuriel to *be* almost human, just for a while. It enabled Tommy to take a usable picture. I try to tell them all this, but the words won't come out.

'I will take care of you, Jamie Suggitt,' Bianca says fervently. 'I'll see to it that you get strong again — that you are *yourself* again. Whatever it takes. I promise you, you will be safe while you are with me.'

Her words have the sense of a vow.

'All right,' Jamie says finally. 'Just for now. Just till all this attention…blows over.'

I dimly register Bianca's instructions to the driver, the feel of the armoured town car reversing back the way it came, away from the feral tabloid press pack, before I am lost to the night.

21

The car stops again and one of the windows of the town car slides down. Cold night air streams into the vehicle. I shiver fitfully where I'm lying curled up, my knees almost touching my chest, facing into Shaun's big body.

'I'm seeing a residential London street with a boom gate on it,' Shaun whispers down at me in tones of fascination. 'Crash barriers. Guards with guns. We're in the beating heart of the city, right? But it's like Bianca lives in a different *country*.'

'Good evening, Miss St Alban,' a clipped, male voice states from outside the car. The speaker leans in through the opening, bringing the smell of damp wool and aftershave with him. 'I'll need the names of the four individuals with you. Are they all proceeding to your address directly?'

'Yes, Dennis,' I hear Bianca reply. 'I'll get my security team to contact you as soon as we arrive with all the relevant details.'

There's a brief pause, then the man outside asks more gently, 'Will you be requiring me to call for any...medical assistance?' I feel his eyes on me.

'I have a personal physician on standby,' Bianca says smoothly, her tone broaching no further enquiries. 'He assures me he can be here in under ten minutes, at any time. Have a lovely evening, Dennis.'

'And you, miss,' the man replies, a tinge of doubt in his hard voice before the window of the town car slides up almost soundlessly and the car moves forward again.

'You live in *Kensington Palace Gardens*?' Jamie's voice is as accusing as a pointed finger. 'Houses here cost upwards of *fifty million pounds*.'

'We picked ours up for significantly less,' Bianca demurs. 'Papa bought ours in a divorce-induced fire sale.'

'You've got your own personal security post at the end of your street?' Shaun sounds impressed despite himself as he twists to look back out the rear window at the way we've come.

'Both ends, actually.' Bianca's reply is distant, as if she's lost in thought. 'Diplomatic protection is required for the Israeli and Russian embassies, not to mention the Czechs and the Slovaks. I forget who else. But not for me, specifically. I'm just a private citizen.'

The car stops again to accommodate the opening of another set of heavy iron gates. I hear more male voices outside the windows, someone conversing with the driver of our car before we proceed.

Shaun whistles as the car rolls to a stop. I feel his entire body shift as he cranes his neck to look out the window.

'I can't repay you,' Jamie mutters as the two passenger doors simultaneously swing outwards from the middle and a blast of night air forces its way into the car. 'My entire home would fit inside your gatehouse. I'm here under protest.'

'You're here as my treasured guest,' Bianca replies carefully in a neutral voice. 'The family's rarely here — the run of the house is entirely yours, Jamie; treat it like your own. The staff are paid to practise discretion. Nothing they see here will get out into the public domain; you'll have complete privacy, time to rest and heal. And there's an indoor pool, gym, sauna, a theatre. Computer equipment.' She dangles the last two words casually.

Jamie's tone is mutinous. 'I want my own gear.'

Bianca replies soothingly, 'Let's get Gia off to bed and then I'll show you where everything is and how it all works, all right?'

I feel Shaun slide across the leather seat towards the open door, taking me with him. He lifts me easily as he stands, holding me against his broad chest and I could be a little kid again. I have a faint memory of one of my foster mums lifting me out of her hatchback after a visit to a friend's farm, late one night. I must have been about four or five — back when I was cute and small and did what I was told. That phase hadn't lasted for long, but that feeling of being safe, of being cherished, is what I'm feeling now. It hasn't happened so often that I can afford to be blasé about it and I stir fitfully in Shaun's arms. In wordless reply, his hold on me tightens.

As Shaun strides across a cobbled driveway with me tucked up against his chest, he whispers, 'You should see this, Gia. The...*house* is four storeys high — eight windows on every floor! — with an extra set of dormer windows set into the roof and at least six chimneys. It's a fucking *palace*.'

I crank open my eyelids, just for second, seeing from a crazy, tilted angle the storybook façade of a huge red-and-white brick Queen Anne-style manor house with a slate tiled roof and so many sash windows I can't count them all. The bit of front garden I can see surrounding the circular front drive, a whopping great ornate cast iron fountain in the middle of it, is mathematical in its neatness and precision.

'How many bedrooms are there?' I croak through parched lips, and Shaun relays the question to Bianca who is striding ahead up a sweep of stone stairs leading to a door surrounded by a carved stone door case.

'Eighteen,' she says over her shoulder as the door magically opens of its own accord to let the five of us inside.

'One of the smaller places, then,' I murmur with a touch of acid that's lost on everyone but me as the world slides back out of view.

જ

'*He's made contact.*'

I frown. Just drawing my brows together causes little darts of pain in my screwed-tight skull.

I struggle to open my eyes and see Jamie sitting beside my bed — *whose bed?* — morning, somewhere. The daylight is weak and struggles thinly through the filmy lace curtains drawn across the tall, deep windows of the huge bedroom I'm lying in. I turn my head slightly on the fat, feather-stuffed pillow and survey the entire room in silence, seeing expanses of wood-panelled wall in every direction. The effect is broken in pleasing ways by the occasional tasteful period chair, settee or chest of drawers, and a huge, white, marble fireplace that's directly opposite my king-sized bed, complete with a real, crackling fire. There are two doors leading off to other rooms on either side, and the floor is covered in an elaborately patterned Persian carpet in rich tones of gold, blue and red. Above the picture rail that runs around the four walls of the room, there's a painted frieze of photo-realistic, fluffy white clouds against a duck egg blue sky. The white ceiling is a riot of ornate plasterwork. This mansion must be absolute murder to keep clean.

'It's finally happened,' I murmur dryly. 'I really have died and gone to heaven.'

Jamie — her features moulded by the usual clear plastic face mask she wears by day — doesn't smile as she repeats, 'He's made contact.'

Her words make no sense. A whole chunk of time seems to be missing.

To buy myself time to work out why I can't remember where I am and what I'm doing here — the only familiar thing about this whole situation being the woman in the chair beside me — I say, 'Help me sit up.'

Even the feel of Jamie's soft pink cashmere jumper against my cheek is painful as she pulls my pillows upright and helps me lean up against them.

Seeing my confusion, Jamie raps in a staccato voice, '*Cibyyl*. Photo shoot. Bianca's house. You've been asleep for over a day. Kit Tyburn's seen the photos and he's still very much interested. His exact invitation via social was charmingly brief and to the point. It went something like: *You and me at Buster's. I will make you my Queen for all time.* Cibyyl's already had over eight thousand death threats since his tweet went out. It's been wild.'

I frown at the jumble of words, hurting my head all over again.

'Cibyyl hasn't responded yet,' Jamie adds. 'We were waiting for you to wake up and advise us on the most attention-grabbing way to say *Yes, please with bells on*.'

I do a *gimme more* gesture with my fingers, the backs of my hands resting gingerly on top of the lemon-yellow Egyptian cotton sheets swathing my aching body.

'*Buster*, it turns out, is Buster Strang —' I sit up straighter, recognising the unusual name from the mysterious offshore bank account we'd linked to Spartak Skorobogatov. 'Sole shareholder and director of *Charybdis LLC*. He's Kit Tyburn's manager — the man who discovered the *real* Kit Tyburn as a baby-faced teen before Lucifer took him over. No one's seen Buster Strang in public for three months now — the gossip sites are buzzing with speculation regarding his whereabouts, but no one has reported him missing, so that's all it is: speculation.'

Jamie snags a slim electronic tablet up off the floor and starts scrolling through photos of a sprawling, white-walled, nineteen-thirties mansion on a green-foliage-covered island. She shows me an aerial view of the massive terracotta-roofed colonial-style house and twelve-car garage, pointing out a clay tennis court, croquet lawn and separate, glass-walled conservatory wing. There's a grey, rectangular concrete structure located at some distance to the main buildings on a far corner of the island, right above a natural inlet. Jamie taps on it.

'It's not clear what this smaller building is for,' Jamie says. 'It doesn't even look like the others. It's a much more recent addition to the estate. Tackle shed? Sauna? Panic room? Could be anything.'

Jamie leans forward so that I can better see the windowless grey outbuilding. My skin prickles at the sight of the place. If you wanted to keep someone close, secure, but not necessarily want to have to *look* at them on a day-to-day basis, a bunker like that would be perfect.

'That would be my first port of call,' I murmur. I find that I'm hugging myself.

Jamie nods. 'I've got to say, for us, the timing fits. Buster knew Kit best — it makes sense that Luc somehow got him out of the way in order to completely appropriate Kit Tyburn's life. We know that Strang still owns this island in the Florida Keys — Riley's Island, it's called — that Kit Tyburn has been spotted entering and leaving multiple times in the last few months. There are loads of recent pictures of him and a revolving entourage swaggering in and out of the place like they own the joint. It has to be Luc's base. Strang's compound is the only home on the whole island. See these?' Jamie flicks through a further swag of photos. 'They're all taken from above. We've checked the externals out from every angle and the estate looks unbelievably secure. Pristine views in every direction, only approachable by that guarded, single-lane bridge, or from the water. You'd need an army to get into the place uninvited.'

'Any pictures of the inside?' I ask.

Jamie shakes her head. 'We've got no idea about the internal layout — how many levels there are, how many occupants. I've got friends trying to help themselves to any security footage they can find, but they're not holding out much hope. I don't think the estate's cameras are switched on anymore, if they even still work. Luc probably fried them — accidentally or on purpose.'

Jamie leans forward in her armchair. 'What should we tell *@therealKit* via social?' she urges. 'Bianca's anxious we reply as soon as possible — she's afraid he'll lose interest. *The world is filled with beautiful women*; that's what she told me to tell you. You're better with words than I am. Give me something I can get out.'

I think about how Cibyyl is like no other woman on earth, and that Luc somehow recognised that, beneath the surface kook.

'*First light* — ' I murmur so quietly that Jamie has to lean forward to hear what I'm saying. 'Mercy once had it; even Luc before he fell. And it's what Nuriel carries with her, always, no matter how damaged she might be now. Even in the videos, it was there, leaching out into every frame. They can hide it, Mercy showed me that in her memories, but it's so much a part of what they are that they don't — or they don't properly know how to, unless they're reminded.'

Jamie's eyes widen in sudden understanding. 'That's why Nuriel touched my skin?'

I nod. 'The *elohim* aren't as inherently sneaky as we are. In some ways, they're a lot more naïve than the people they're supposed to be watching over. It was the reason we couldn't take a decent shot of Nuriel until being with *you* reminded her to dial it down.'

'My angel has it too,' Jamie whispers, nodding. '*First light*. So that's what it's called.'

'Right,' I say, wondering again if her angel is who I think it is, 'which means Lucifer won't lose interest until he has Cibyyl under his control and that "interest" ends up killing her. The jumble of memories Mercy once showed me — of an angel in chains at the bottom of a dark lake, bleeding light from her terrible wounds — they make sense now. Nuriel — as Mercy was once — is the one who got away from Luc.'

'He *knows* what she is?' Jamie says, troubled. '*Who* she is?'

I shrug. 'Perhaps, at a subconscious level. Maybe he can't be sure — it's probably why he wants her so badly that he threw so much money in Cibyyl's direction. It was a calculated gamble — a lot of people would jump at the chance to be bought for twenty million dollars. To Lucifer, that much attention-grabbing filthy lucre has no intrinsic worth. If she'd been human, he figured, money would have drawn her to him, no question. If not, Cibyyl must be something else altogether. Remember, she didn't bat an eyelid when he wired her that enormous fortune — didn't go to him, didn't even react. *Money doesn't push her buttons*, he's thinking now, *so what does? What does she want?* Sure, the world is full of beautiful women, but I don't think Luc considers any of them truly worthy. He must run through them like old newspaper. I'd bet good money he gets bored easily. No ordinary woman is ever going to come close to being Lucifer's equal, right? But a demon might. *Or an angel.*'

For a moment, I'm reminded of the statuesque blonde

demon, Gudrun, who'd so obviously been with Luc in Milan, and wonder what became of her.

Jamie sits straighter, comprehension lighting her twisted features. 'He can't be sure if Cibyyl's one of his or...'

I nod again. 'You're sure Kit Tyburn's no longer in London? This isn't some kind of trick, some test?'

Jamie shakes her head. 'One of the official music news sites had images of Kit Tyburn being mobbed by fans and paparazzi at Heathrow yesterday, minutes before heading back to the States by private jet after his terrible "near-death" London ordeal. It's obvious Luc wants *Cibyyl* to go to *him*. Home-ground advantage, love. If she goes in there,' Jamie swallows audibly, 'he's going to make sure she never comes out again.'

I close my eyes, exhausted by the simple act of sitting up.

Finally I say, '*I will tear down your walls to die by your side*. Got that? That's what Cibyyl's reply should be. Sufficiently romantic with the kicker that every word,' my laughter resembles pained coughing, 'is *true*. Or it will be. I'm going to see to it.'

Jamie squeezes my hand, stands up and hurries out of the room.

I'm about to sink back down beneath the cooling sheets, feeling chilled right through to my toes, when I hear someone else enter the room and stand beside me. The warm sandalwood and citrus smell of him is so familiar the corners of my mouth lift involuntarily.

'Oh no you don't,' he rumbles down at me. 'It's taking you too long to bounce back between bouts. A saltwater recovery session first, I'm thinking, followed by stretching, light weights and gentle sparring. Bianca's got the lot — she's got a saltwater indoor pool and her home gym is state of the art. I've brought some protective chest guards. Up and at 'em, soldier.'

My eyes pop open in shock.

'There's no such thing as "gentle sparring",' I growl. 'It's an oxymoron.'

'Counter-terrorism, hostage rescue, close-quarters combat, covert operations,' Shaun ticks off on his fingers. 'That's the kind of territory you're about to cover. No one beats the clock lying in bed.'

Then he lifts me up in his strong arms and carries me out of the room, protesting.

∽

'*No one* sees me in a bathing costume,' I repeat through gritted teeth, my arms crossed tightly over my chest. I'm wearing the only 'plain' black bathing suit Bianca St Alban claims to own, although there are still a couple of large oval cut-outs centred over my ribs, making it less of a one-piece and more of a two-piece. Built like an underfed teenaged boy, I know I look ridiculous in the scanty bands of fabric.

The air in here is steamy; the heat rises off the surface of the azure pool dug into the foundations of one rear wing of Bianca's home. There are bare-breasted marble statues in grottos and outsized Chinese urns covered in dragons standing all around the pool, which has a viewing gallery above it, supported from below by columns carved out of a glossy, veined, dark green marble.

'Look at the nymphs,' I command Shaun haughtily. 'Not at me.'

I can hear his sigh from where I'm hunched in the shallows near the art deco-style fan of entry stairs, my toes curled into the tiny mosaic tiles that give the saltwater pool its extraordinary colour.

'All right, I'm turning around,' Shaun snorts, crossing his arms so that the navy jersey he's wearing pulls tight across his shoulders, straining the length of his long, strong back. His body almost seems more familiar to me now than my own, and I have to force myself to look away, focusing instead on the distorted view of my legs through the water.

'The temperature isn't ideal,' Shaun booms, oblivious to my traitorous thoughts, 'particularly if you've got any areas of inflammation — but I want you to get in, chest-deep. Then start jumping on the spot; lift those knees. I want lots of pace.'

After I've obeyed half-heartedly for a while, Shaun directs from the side of the pool, 'Now *run* — from side to side. I'm not looking, but I'm not deaf either. You're not going to get away with any half-arsed measures, even with my back turned. I'm counting the "jumping" you just did as a warm-up, that's all. That was pathetic. I'd call it *girly* — even by your standards.'

Snarling, I push hard through the water, my fatigue-loaded body aching. After a while, the heat of the water starts to dissolve the tension in my legs and shoulders and arms. I'm getting tired, but I no longer feel like a giant clenched muscle, and I start taking in the surroundings of the swimming pool with greater interest. It reminds me a little of the Grand Saloon at the Argo, because there's the lower level where the pool is, but also that genteel upper viewing level; the two tiers surrounding the pool are separated by a forest of marble columns, with interesting private grottos set well back beneath the gallery, filled with recliners for conversations and trysts. It's fantasy-land stuff, just like the rest of the mansion, built on a scale that doesn't seem human.

'Out,' Shaun commands after I do a few more sets of scissor kicks, stretches and aquatic sit-ups off the sides of the pool, my face screwed up into a giant grimace. 'You're going

to carbo-load now as if it's the last meal you'll ever have —'
he pauses for a moment as we both register the awful sting of
truth in his words, '— then you're hitting the gym.'

Later, after Bianca's sent a high-end colourist-to-the-A-list to
turn my light, natural hair colour a mid-range, unremarkable
brown, I study myself inside the St Albans' fully-equipped
private gym with its long feature wall of mirrors that reflect
back every angle of my sallow face and bruised-looking eyes.
I've never had hair this colour. I don't even recognise myself.

Shaun shows me a short, narrow, cylindrical rod about the
length of my forearm, cast from clear perspex. With one end
pushed into the tips of his index and middle fingers, he puts
his arm back against his side to hide the rod against his body,
along the inside of his arm.

'You're going to wear this in a lightweight tote bag,' Shaun
says. 'If anyone does a pat-down on you, they're not even going
to glance twice at the tote you've got slung over your shoulder.
There'll be a concealed pocket for the baton up one side of the
bag. It will look like part of the bag's structure — just a thick
internal seam of some kind. Bianca's got a pair of cargo pants
she can lend you; they're the most complicated pair of trousers
I've ever laid eyes on. There are so many outer pockets and tabs
on those things, the security guards will be too busy going
through them to work out you've got a weapon in your tote.'

Shaun flips the hidden staff back up into a right-hand grip
and brings it down through the air into his palm with a dull
smack. 'The short staff is hard enough to break bones with, but
it won't be picked up by a standard metal detector and it isn't
technically an outlawed street weapon. All positives.'

'It's like that thing Daughtry was wearing in his hair,'
I say with sudden insight. 'Easy to hide, not made of metal,

potentially lethal.'

'Yes,' Shaun replies, darting me a shrewd sideways glance. 'In the right hands. And I'm going to show you how to use it. But, first, I want you to drop to the ground and give me thirty push-ups and not a bleeding word about how you're feeling, I don't give a rat's arse.'

ॐ

It's near midnight and I'm so wired by the exercise, Shaun's words of warning, and my searingly hot shower, that I feel too awake, too painfully alive, to sleep.

Prowling around the opulent bedroom in a pair of borrowed silk pyjamas, courtesy of Bianca's never-ending wardrobe, I finger the fabric of the dark olive cargo pants earmarked for me to wear. There *are* a stupendous number of pockets, but I'm still not sure they're enough to help me pull off concealing a weapon on my body. Feeling self-conscious, I lay the pants back down and pick up the tote bag with the built-in pocket up one side made especially to hold the perspex baton. I slip the baton from its resting place in the bag; stabbing and slicing at the air with it the way Shaun showed me how to do.

There's a movement in the corner of my eye and I feel my face colour in embarrassment as I lower the baton.

'Who am I kidding, right?' I say, turning to see Jamie leaning against one of the connecting door frames. She's wearing her bright pink face mask and is, weirdly for this time of night, in street clothes. There are even shoes on her feet.

I cock an eyebrow at her in curiosity as she says in a hushed voice, 'Get dressed. We're going for a walk.'

'Uh, okay.' I look around the room for the clothes I wore to the Tilbury Docks a couple of nights ago, already pressed and laundered by a phalanx of largely invisible housekeepers who've kept out of my way.

Jamie comes forward into the room and tugs me by a pyjama sleeve. 'Not those clothes,' she says, shaking my street clothes out of my hand. '*Those* ones. And remember the bag. The bag's vital. Shaun told me to remind you — you go nowhere without that bag.'

She indicates the cargo pants, the baton and the tote — which I'd discovered contains only a tube of sparkly lip gloss, a small tan leather purse with a couple of hundred pounds in it in crisp fifties, a glossy romance novel and a disposable phone — and I go still, realising that it must be time. Of course it is. It can never wait. *They* have all the time imaginable, but every moment they're in the world could be the end of it.

Suddenly clumsy with fear, I slip awkwardly out of my pyjama bottoms and into the cargo pants, sliding the perspex baton into the special pocket in the tote, which cradles it snugly without being too tight. There's maybe half an inch I can get my grip on above the concealed pocket, meaning it will slide out quite easily if I need it. Shaun was right. Being clear, the baton is pretty much invisible.

I shrug out of my pyjama top into my own black tee-shirt, following that up with the black cashmere hoodie that was folded neatly under the cargo pants. I slip my feet into heavy socks and my hunting boots because I'm going hunting. This is exactly what they were made for.

When she sees that I'm dressed, Jamie quickly braids my still damp mid-brown long hair into the tight Heidi-style plaits I wore under the wig at the Argo. 'To get it out of your face,' she rasps. 'The last thing you want to worry about when you're up against Satan himself is your hair, love.'

Then she takes a small plastic box out of the pocket of her

own pants and gestures for me to tilt my head back. With more practised movements this time, she slips a pair of contact lenses into my eyes. 'Brown this time,' she murmurs. 'To blend in with your new hair. The less you stand out, the less likely they'll be looking at you long enough to know that you're the real threat.' She reaches into the pocket of her track top and takes out a pair of hipster tortoiseshell spectacle frames big enough to swamp my face, slipping them onto the bridge of my nose. I shoulder the tote bag, which has an eco-friendly slogan on the outside; the concealed weapon gives the bag enough structure to hang nicely without seeming stiff.

'You're her *PA* slash *Stylist* slash *Publicist*, got it?' For a second Jamie stares into my face with a troubled frown, then leads me quickly out of the room, placing her finger against her lips. From Jamie's expression, it's clear that Bianca doesn't know my time Chez St Alban has just come to an abrupt close. Bianca's just going to wake in the morning and find me gone from her charmed life the same way I fell into it. All that will remain will be an empty guest bed in an empty room, and a handful of faded and discarded clothing on the floor.

I feel a pang of momentary sadness at all the promises I've made that I may not live up to.

I may not live.

The thought interferes with my ability to breathe. I've tried not to come at that notion head on over the last few days. But I did know, when I signed up for this, what the price might be. My eyes have been wide open the entire time — the way I've lived my entire life. I've always hated surprises.

Jamie walks us swiftly along the main corridor on this level before turning into another corridor and taking me down a narrow, winding staircase that leads into a glassed-in conservatory-style breakfast room dappled with moonlight at the back of the manor. We don't encounter anyone as we cross a black-and-white-tiled floor towards some French doors, ducking around lush potted palms and white wicker furniture to get there.

Strangely, the French doors are unlocked. The whole world seems asleep; there's no breeze, no noise. It could be a world empty of life. Standing at the back of the manor looking out across the severely beautiful formal *parterre* garden that stretches away from the house for at least half an acre, my gaze is drawn towards a Victorian-era iron and wood gazebo. The gazebo has a sloping dark green roof — shaped kind of like a circus tent — and carved wooden columns painted white with contrasting dark green highlights.

The gazebo is open on all sides and is the size of a bandstand. There's a warm light shining from within it that isn't moonlight. It's gold with a touch of pale blue at its heart. And it's moving about the gazebo restlessly, as if the light is...pacing.

I know whose light it is.

'Holy fire,' Jamie whispers. 'First light, you called it. He's waiting.'

She reaches for me without her usual hesitation and hugs me fiercely.

I can barely make out her next words, Jamie's shaking so hard. She's speaking straight into the top of my shoulder, her voice muffled. 'You come back as soon as you can with your smart mouth and your hard eyes and your kind heart. You're one of us now, you understand? One of *the League of Broken Women*. That's what we call ourselves online — all the broken sisters who aren't ready to lie down and die yet. Now that I've found you and Bianca, I'm not letting you go, you hear? You don't have to be alone — not anymore. You'll always have a home, a place, with us. No matter what happens, *you remember that.* There'll always be help, safe harbour.'

I understand from Jamie's tearful rambling that she's hoping I'll survive whatever I'm walking towards.

I pull back and look into her masked face, damp with tears. I know, because I touch her cheek through the elasticated weave before raising my eyes towards the graceful iron and wood structure standing at the far end of the property. My gaze sweeps across the *parterre*, which contains, at its heart, a lozenge-shaped pond surrounded by eight *plats* or ornate garden beds constructed from clipped hedges in baroque scrolls and whorls, the entire rectangular space bisected by elegant gravel walks. It's a garden from another time.

Jamie pushes me away, saying raggedly, 'Your angel's waiting.'

Giving her hand one last squeeze, I place my foot on the central gravel walk, facing towards the pond, and start walking towards the light.

Part 3

In any life, given the same choice, I would choose you.

22

His broad back is towards me, and I'm almost close enough to reach out and touch the ends of the long, dark red hair falling down his back when he turns and regards me with the slow smile and bright green gaze that never fail to bring heat to my face.

Standing in the light the Archangel Gabriel casts, the worn floorboards of the gazebo, the entire moonlit world, are as nothing. He's my sun. I couldn't look away even if I wanted to. My entire lonely, blighted life I would live over again for just this moment.

'They are gathered,' he says without preamble, holding out his hand, smooth as fired porcelain.

I hesitate, remembering that punched-inside-out feeling of being nothing more than sentient particles, the barest essence of being alive.

I'm so horribly afraid that I'm not ready, that I will fail Mercy when she needs me most.

Gabriel can see that fear in my eyes as I ask, 'You're taking me...*to* them?'

I'm not sure I even said the words out loud, but he nods, his eyes so kind that my own flood with tears. 'There is no other way.'

As the tears spill over, slipping under the frames of my fake glasses, tracking down my cheeks, I place my hand in his, feeling it tighten as I shatter into pieces.

I survive it, of course I do. A moment that is the *slowest fast* I may ever feel.

Whooping for breath, trying to overcome this scraped-thin feeling of having just been brought back together from a great distance, I fall to my hands and knees on wind-bent, salt-laden grass, head down; my surroundings are a storm of purple-black buzzing pinpoints in my eyes.

For a moment, I fear I've gone blind. But then my sight clears and I push back up onto my haunches and realise that I'm once again facing the ruins of Dunstanburgh Castle in the dead of night. Between me and the eroded ruins — like a broken crown, or withered fingers reaching up into the sky — there's that gleaming cluster of vaguely human shapes, shifting and moving like a restless sea.

Only this time, they're held back away from me by a loose ring of shining beings, all built along mythical lines.

I lift my head to look into each of their faces and have to remind myself to breathe. Seven male, one female; the best dream of all the ancients, come to life. All archangels, all *elohim* — most holy, most high. Each one different, each one heart-stopping; in sleeveless raiment so blinding that their features and outlines constantly shift and blur and change before my eyes. All wingless — for they are not at war with me, or the dead gathered here.

I see them and know them, as they do me.

Michael — burning black eyes and short black curls. *Viceroy of Heaven*, Mercy once called him. *The Commander of the Army of God.*

Gabriel — emerald-eyed and flame-haired. Our emissary since times past, somehow appointed to me, at this time, to be my strength and my comfort.

Raphael — the healer. Sable-eyed, dark-haired and olive-skinned, ready laughter curving the lines of his generous mouth. The one who loved Mercy so much that he devised a way to hide her from Luc — the one who'd exiled her, desiring her death — for centuries. Raphael's *way* is the reason we are all here now.

Jeremiel — wreathed in glory, silver-eyed, auburn-haired, with a bell-like voice who alone calls out in welcome, 'Gia Basso, well met.'

Barachiel — dark-eyed, with long black hair like a starless night, whose province is lightning. It seems to play within the folds of his shining raiment, between the long, strong fingers of his hands as he considers me, unsmiling.

Jegudiel — waving, dark gold hair about his shoulders and a steely, forbidding expression in his brown eyes that softens even as I watch. Though he, too, does not smile, but considers me narrowly, as if I am being weighed in a balance. What had Mercy called him? *The scourge.* He is like the threat of punishment made real.

Uriel — who could *be* Mercy, so identical do they appear, save that he is male. I blink as I look up into his face, and he smiles in genuine amusement, the corners of his mouth lifting at my astonishment.

'*His* little joke,' Uriel murmurs before the smile fades again.

Last of all is Nuriel in her true form, her loose dark hair in waves about her face, livid scars striping her body, her unquiet mind reflected in her troubled gaze. My fellow traveller, ready to be sprung like a weapon. Just as I am.

I stagger a little as I rise to my feet within the circle, pushing the spectacle frames that have slipped down my nose back up onto the bridge.

Gabriel steps forward and puts out a hand to steady me, and I'm not ashamed to admit that I cling to it, and to his warmth. It may be the last time we ever meet.

'Where *is* she?' Barachiel turns to Gabriel with a hint of impatience. 'Unlike the followers of *Shaitan*, we do not claim to be legion. We borrow from the flow of time to be here, to achieve this thing. Time moves inexorably forward. What is asked of us *does not stop.*'

Jegudiel turns on Raphael almost menacingly, fists clenched with distaste. 'Never again, you told us, brother. And yet we assemble once more to wreak the unspeakable upon those who have suffered enough.' He looks at me pointedly and I colour with shame to have even this glorious creature perceive what I am: one of the manifestly broken ones.

Michael, a touch of anger in his strong features, growls, 'Look! She comes. *Look there —*'

He stabs a hand in the direction of the ruined castle behind him and even the gathered wraiths go still. They turn as one shining mass towards the lone figure that emerges from between the crumbling drum-shaped towers of the Great Gatehouse, dressed in luminous black.

The sea of dead divide, bowing, as she moves among and through them, the power and will of Azraeil himself gathered in the clenched and shining fists by her side, for she is their paladin, their commander. Death's will, here on earth.

The dead may not understand what they are, but they understand — at some fundamental level — what she is to them.

The *elohim* part to allow Mercy to enter our circle and there is sorrow in all their faces as they gaze down on her. It's clear that some of them did not fully understand, until this moment, what was done to her; what she has become.

'*Soror*,' I hear them whisper with regret, one by one.

'She has passed beyond our understanding,' Gabriel murmurs. 'Yet she is as she always was — singular and perfect. Her like will never be made again. She is paradox.'

Mercy is like a light-limned crow in our midst, strangely insubstantial and dreamlike against the might and solidity of her towering, collected kin.

Barachiel, moved by unspeakable pity, even reaches out one hand to her, but she can only shake her head ruefully, a bitter smile lifting one corner of her mouth; her look saying, *I am beyond even touch now.*

Mercy stands beside me, one corner of her wide mouth lifting in greeting, and the wind of the afterworld moves her dark hair, lifting the folds of her jet-black raiment in a way that it cannot move any of us who still live.

It's as if she stands in a vortex while the entire living world stands still. And from that chaos, she surveys us all with her dark, quick eyes and we see that her will is as adamantine, as hard and resolute, as it ever was.

It's true that she is herself. Even the death of her physical body could not change that.

Mercy's lips begin to move and I know that she's addressing all of us, but I'm the only one who can't hear her. When I steel myself to touch her — so that I might hear and understand — Gabriel's emerald eyes flick to me and he raises a hand in negation.

'You will know her touch soon enough,' he cautions. 'You are valiant — we perceive this — but do not ask for more pain than you can bear, Gia Basso.'

There's a sudden ripple of disagreement at something Mercy tells her brethren.

Uriel shoots me a sharp look and blusters, 'You cannot delay it! The moment you have entered Lucifer's house you are to let that child go! You are to see her *safe*. She is to fall away — go as fast and as far as possible. How can she be asked to do anything more?'

But Gabriel grasps him by the arm and shakes his head. 'As Nuriel, and as Mercy, have — Gia has invoked the *Lex Talionis*. She has her own reasons to remain.'

Uriel's eyes widen in astonishment. 'Gia remain in a nest of demons? What reason could she have to stay beyond the moment she looses Mercy on Lucifer like a plague?'

Gabriel's reply is quiet. 'She invokes wild justice upon one of Satan's own. That is reason enough.'

Raphael raises his hand, cutting Uriel off. 'Luc's *daemonium* have largely scattered about the four corners of the earth now, it is true; most have shaken off Lucifer's iron control after so many long, cold years. But Astaroth, Balam, Beleth, Amon and Caym still stand with Luc — five of his strongest demons — and who knows what other abomination, demonic or human. Gia cannot remain while... Mercy —' Raphael openly falters as he speaks her name, 'does her... work.'

Uriel's dark eyes flick back to me. 'Release Mercy then *flee*, Gia Basso,' he urges. 'I cannot counsel you more strongly. When demons and the will of the archangels collide, you may not survive.' His gaze flickers towards the shining throng beyond our circle as if to emphasise the choice I am making.

Mercy and I glance at each other as I shake my head. 'Gabriel understands why I agreed to help. I have my own reasons. And I know what the risks are. No greater sacrifice and all that.'

Uriel looks at me, then grimly to his kin.

'The slipknot?' he queries. 'Never before — in all these

years — has Mercy been given a trapdoor, a means of escape. We must agree a way for Gia to unleash —' his mouth twists in a way that mirrors Mercy's own wry expression so closely that I almost laugh, 'the beast within.'

Mercy says something then that I don't hear, and all eight of the gathered *elohim* nod in approval.

'It is agreed, then,' Jegudiel says with a touch of impatience.

Barachiel reminds everyone almost bitterly, distaste clear on his aquiline features, 'Time *presses*. Let it be done.'

Gabriel bends and looks into my face.

'*Deus ex*,' he murmurs. 'Those words will be your slipknot. Say them aloud, and she will loosed upon him.'

A peal of laughter escapes me then, I can't help it. I speak enough Latin and Italian to know precisely how perfect those words of release are.

'I suppose she is —' I find myself smiling broadly, 'a kind of god. At least to all of them.' I wave my hand at the shining, restless dead standing beyond Gabriel's shoulder. 'And I'm the machine from whence the avenging power is supposed to emerge — though you're all too kind to actually refer to me in that way. So I'm to get Lucifer alone, then...*pow*?'

Uriel makes a sound not unlike a snort, which only makes me like him more. The towering archangel and I seem to share the same slightly twisted worldview. 'Corner the Great Deceiver and say the words aloud,' Uriel agrees. 'That is all. Leave the "pow" aspect of proceedings to Nuriel — and to this one.'

He inclines his head in Mercy's direction with exasperated affection, but in his eyes there is a great, unspoken grief.

Something complex and unspoken seems to flow between Mercy and Uriel then, some kind of understanding. Then Mercy puts her hands out to me, palms up. As I turn to face her reluctantly, I see them glow with that intense silver-blue fire that has the power to burn me from the inside out.

'It won't feel that way,' Gabriel whispers above us, 'but you are enough to bear it. *You are enough.*'

'I eat pain for breakfast,' I mumble, seizing Mercy's hands fiercely before I can change my mind.

At the point of contact, heat begins to flower between us and I feel my lips draw back from my teeth in a snarl as it builds and grows.

Around us, the eight *elohim* link their hands, and begin a low, quiet hum that raises every hair on my body; it makes the silent dead actually sigh in unison like a summer breeze soughing through grass.

An agonising scream bursts forth — but not from me.

It's the sound of Mercy shrieking in torment and it's the only noise I can hear for the longest time. It's like the sound the universe might make being born from a single word, from a mote of time. I find myself weeping uncontrollably, begging for her to stop.

Mercy's pain obliterates everything, and her eyes are wide and blind with it — and with fear. She is being unmade. What's worse is that, this time, she *knows* she is.

And I realise she's been rendered down in this way many times before — but it's clear she was never conscious, never sentient, when they did this to her across all those human lives. Not the way she is now. Mercy can feel herself unravelling, being broken down, twisted and bent and compressed into a new shape.

From one life to another, her people sang her in and they sang her out, and she never knew what it took to get her there because she was never conscious. And they would move her again and again until the day she began to wake *as herself* inside a stranger's body to the knowledge that something was very wrong with her.

Gabriel was speaking words of reassurance to Mercy, I realise, not to me, because my pain is bearable. She's not taking me over this time; they are somehow tuning Mercy to *me*. I'm not the one that's being reconfigured — made small enough, unobtrusive enough, to be tucked away inside another living being. They're making her undetectable to Luc and his kind. In a way, they're making her as demon-proof as she'll ever be.

This, whatever it is, is actually bearable, as if the initial feeling of being bathed in fire is gradually diminishing, gradually cooling. But whatever they're doing to her is tearing Mercy apart all over again. It's not like when she simply steps into me and takes me over by brute force. They are twisting and remaking *her*; they're breaking her down into the barest essence of what she is — to fit me.

And they know, having seen the barren wasteland inside, that there is plenty of room within me to hide her.

Beneath Mercy's agony, I begin to make out eight separate voices. All are singing in a language that existed before all life did. It's so beautiful it raises gooseflesh on my skin; elements of the song are almost recognisable until it veers into languages I know have long since been lost. It's a song through which all the tongues of angels, and of humans, run like a river, as they were, as they are. The air shimmers with pain and beauty and wonder, the eight voices weaving in and out in dizzying counterpoint, some strands of the melody higher or lower than the human voice is even capable of.

The expression in Mercy's eyes is a form of pleading — that I will remember the words and bring her back to life.

She was lost for so long.

Her eyes beg: *Don't let me be lost again.*

In my grip, her silver-blue-limned form begins to waver and grow indistinct. She's like the imprint of someone who once was. A ghost girl. A memory flickering out of existence, that's being deliberately extinguished.

It's horrific, and that horror is echoed in the faces of all the gathered *elohim*.

I find myself still weeping as I struggle to grip Mercy tight, turning my head away sharply as she grows brighter than I can bear to look upon before scattering into nothing more than a cloud of fine, silver-blue mist.

The song of the *elohim* rises until it seems to echo back at us from the skies, and with it that cloud of energy draws up and up until it is a funnel that collapses into a fine rope, just a thin, skein of twisting, silver-blue energy. I rock forward as it pierces me through, disappearing at the point where it enters my sternum. I feel it seeking the scar that I know is knotted into my soul, moulding itself to it. Going into hiding. Scar laid against scar.

I feel her there, and suddenly find my clenched fists grasping at nothing but afterlight.

I'm the only person standing now inside the circle. I feel the scar inside me pulsing faintly and wonder if, across all those lives, those other women could somehow sense Mercy hidden there like a hard little kernel, this knot, pulsing away beneath the skin. I rub at my breastbone absently. I am the machine being wheeled out; the Trojan Horse in the final act of its brief life.

She is gone into me completely, as if she never was, and I hear one of Mercy's brothers whisper, head bowed in grief or benediction, 'It is done.'

23

The gathered wraiths move away, as if my living energy has been tempered by something noxious — as mixed and muddied now as a pool of disturbed water.

'Do you get a...*sense* of her?' I ask the gathered archangels, still rubbing at my chest, unable to believe Luc won't somehow feel Mercy within or around me.

The gathered *elohim* turn their piercing gazes on me and shake their heads, Michael growling, 'Eight are needed, and eight are here. Nothing of her can escape unless and until you will it —'

'Let no demon touch you,' Jeremiel interrupts. 'They will read you and divine your intentions.'

'Nuriel will draw their gazes,' Barachiel adds. 'Stay in her shadow, be watchful. The moment Lucifer and Nuriel are alone —'

'Say the words,' Michael cautions with a grim set to his mouth. 'Nuriel and Mercy will be enough, Gia Basso. They must be.'

'Together, they may achieve what none of us has ever been able to do,' Gabriel adds.

'We have always been finely balanced on disaster,' Raphael murmurs and I hear the pain and apology behind his words. 'For every first-order demon that falls, it seems, a power of angels must first die. And unlike the *daemonium* — whom Luc can fashion out of blood and bone and filth according to his whim — we cannot make our own kind, or be remade. All these years, we have never been able to strike at Lucifer where he dwells without suffering unspeakable losses — but now *you* can. He will not expect danger to come from this quarter — from two frail, unarmed women. One of whom happens to be harbouring the might and will of the great Azraeil himself.'

'Do what it is you have to do, Gia Basso, and *run*,' Uriel adds, frowning. 'If Mercy were here, in my place, she would tell you the same.'

But they see in my eyes that I do not expect to outrun what it is that I mean to do, and Jegudiel's steely grey gaze softens on me momentarily before he turns and addresses his kin. 'Azraeil has already claimed Gia for his own. Like "Mercy", she has been marked and she will be called. The fate of these ones —' he scans the shredding, restless, confused wraiths drifting across the plains and valleys surrounding Dunstanburgh Castle, 'will not be Gia's. We must be content with that.'

Then Jegudiel grows in brightness, so that I am forced to shield my eyes, before scattering into motes of light. I am left buffeted by his passing, blinking at the space where he was.

One by one they take their leave in the same way, until only Uriel, Gabriel and Nuriel remain. The night seems so much darker without the others. I find myself shivering uncontrollably, suddenly terrified at what is expected of me.

'Use Gia as your pattern at all times,' Gabriel cautions Nuriel, whose eyes appear clouded, focused inward on remembered pain. 'She has more native cunning than even *we* possess. You must be the perfect simulacrum of a human being — fleshy, dense, opaque, unpredictable. You're just an unknown singer — young, uncertain, naïve — who has somehow caught the attention of the most infamous young music icon of his generation. Don't just stride in there blazing holy fire the way I know you want to. Don't underestimate the raw power of surprise —'

Uriel cuts Gabriel off. 'You need to be captured by the security cameras on the bridge, Nuriel. They need to see two human women approaching the island on foot. Only then will they open the gates. They will be completely disarmed if the two of you show up with only a shopping bag between you...'

'But where have we come *from*?' I argue when Nuriel continues to say nothing, anguish etched in every line of her face. 'They're going to be suspicious, Uriel, if we just suddenly appear on the bridge that separates the mainland from Riley's Island. Assume Luc's got people watching the approach to Buster's place. Unlike you lot, humans can't just appear and disappear at will. We've got to have come from *somewhere*.'

'Then you'll have come from the direction of Key West International Airport,' Uriel says thoughtfully, 'disgorged there like all the other tourists. The airport is only a couple of kilometres away from Riley's Island.'

Gabriel opens his mouth as if he's about to speak, but Uriel holds up one of his hands in a *zip it* gesture that makes me want to laugh. 'Catching a taxi from the airport is a good idea!' Uriel insists as Gabriel shakes his fiery head in disbelief. 'Luc's not going to expect an archangel to come by cab, Brother...'

I can't contain the peal of laughter that escapes. 'How does an archangel know about security cameras, airports, tourists, *cabs*?'

Uriel frowns at me, but his brown eyes shine with amusement. 'Because I am ancient, Gia Basso, and I *have* been paying attention all this time I have been abroad in your world. I have some understanding of how things work. Almost enough knowledge as Mercy has to get by. Almost.'

But then his voice goes quiet, and I have to strain to hear his next words. 'Mercy and I searched an airport in Tokyo once, looking for Ryan Daley. And now she searches for him again...'

Uriel shakes his head, refocusing his shrewd, dark gaze on me. 'And if faced with a choice between ending Lucifer's reign forever and saving the life of *that boy*, Gia Basso, what would Mercy do? You know her better than anyone on this earth — as far as someone as ornery and impossible as she is can be known. Can she be relied on, do you think?'

Gabriel shoots Uriel a warning look with blazing green eyes. 'We were created with the right to *choose*. Mercy will do what the circumstances demand, and with that we must be satisfied.'

'Her poor choices are what have brought us to this pass,' Uriel growls.

'She has changed,' Gabriel insists, and I get the sense that this argument has played out many times before — across lives and centuries. 'Beyond all reckoning. She is not the same creature that fell.'

Uriel doesn't reply, instead stooping for a moment to fetch up something from the ground. It hangs, small and incongruous, from his hand. I blink as he gently hooks my dropped tote bag back onto my shoulder before tilting my face up with one finger and studying me intently. Behind my owlish glasses, I feel the strained lines of my face melt under his appraisal.

'What do you see?' I whisper, dazzled by all of them, their proximity, the strangeness of this night. His features are so strong and beautiful and familiar — although recast along such stern male lines — that my breath catches in my throat in wonder. Mercy was one of them, once. And she gave all that up to keep Ryan alive. I don't know if I could have made the same choice. To have power and beauty and grace beyond measure and then to give it all away — it staggers me.

Uriel looks at me for a moment longer with a quizzical half-smile on his face before he straightens and murmurs, 'I will tell you the next time we meet, Gia Basso — so be sure there *is* a next time,' before he, too, vanishes into motes of light.

Nuriel looks down at me then with a look of such bleak sadness that I take a step back.

'*Soror*,' Gabriel reminds Nuriel sternly, and I go cold as her true form begins to blur and ripple and shrink before my eyes; her hair grows longer and straighter and lighter, her form less athletic, less martial, more waiflike, skin paler, more matte, millimetre by millimetre, shift by shift. It's a process both deeply fascinating and deeply horrifying and I want to look away, but I can't.

It's like there is a *legion* inside her.

When she's done adding and subtracting to make herself more like Cibyyl and less like herself, she is human in scale and aspect, only a couple of heads taller than I am.

She's the kind of feminine, pale, demure-looking blonde with pert, perfect breasts that is exactly Luc's type. Only her dark, wary, wounded eyes are the same.

But there's still something the faintest bit *off* about her. There's a surface glimmer of light around her that seems to seep out of the pores of her skin and I point that out despairingly.

'It's never going to work,' I say. 'Not when she looks like *that*. We won't even make it across the bridge. She's glowing like a torch. She needs to . . . '

'Hold the light inside,' Nuriel murmurs. 'The way Mercy can by knotting it down, deep. Help me, Gia. Take my hand.'

I do that, reluctantly. And as I watch — Nuriel's burning hand gripping mine tightly like an anxious child's — the surface glimmer of her skin fades and fades until it is almost, but not quite, gone.

'That will have to do,' I say, lifting the back of Nuriel's hand and studying it in the darkness.

Something in me really has changed, I know it has, because I will always see them now, always. Demon or angel, I will see them. It's as though Mercy's tripped something in me that can never be reset. I'm awake to them now, the way most people never will be.

Gabriel bends down to look into both our faces. 'Astaroth, Balam, Beleth, Amon and Caym, even Luc,' he says, 'will be dulled by the cold, by the poor protection that their human shells afford. Their new-found freedom — of mobility, agency, anonymity — carries a steep price. There will be a moment — just after they are expelled from those bodies — when they are terribly vulnerable...'

'I've seen it,' I breathe, dimly remembering that creature in the Argo struggling to pull himself back together after shucking off Spartak Skorobogatov's mortal body like a corn husk. It had been a vision from hell — filtered through Mercy's sharp gaze.

Gabriel nods, his dark red hair falling down across his shoulders, his eyes a green so bright it should not exist in this world. 'Strike them at their weakest,' he urges Nuriel before looking down into my face with such grave tenderness that I can't breathe or look away, my heart lodged somewhere high in my throat.

'You who have felt no hope,' Gabriel murmurs, 'are *ours*. It has always felt to you as if there was no love, or it was fleeting and mutable and never enough. But I say to you, that we walk with you, always, Gia Basso. That in gifting us with your courage and your loyalty, your tenacity and ferocity — your *life* — there will always be enough love. More than you could ever want. It is your constant, and our promise to you.'

Then he seizes Nuriel and me by the hands and we are gone from the castle grounds before I can draw a single, shuddering breath.

ॐ

The change in temperature, the ambient warmth in the night air, hits me straight away — even before the bright lights do. As I lean down over my knees, dry-retching for air and equilibrium, the solid ground seems to ripple beneath my feet and the lenses of my fake glasses fog over.

Gabriel's parting words are in my ears. 'Around this wall you will see the cab rank Uriel spoke of. Stand under the cameras for a moment; be observed. Hail a cab and ask to be taken to Riley's Island. The rest will be up to you. We will do what we can, when we can.'

Then Gabriel's gone; I know it from the change of pressure in the tropical air around me, and I squint up at "Cibyyl" from where I'm bent over the tarmac that still radiates heat from the day just passed.

'What time is it?' I say out of the side of my mouth.

'Near midnight,' Nuriel murmurs, and there's a flinty quality to her voice that so much resembles simple human anxiety that I want to reach out and touch her reassuringly. She's still wearing the plain grey tee-shirt dress, flat shoes and kooky rainbow arm-warmers from her music videos, her long hair worn forward across her shoulders, blonde bangs falling into her big brown eyes.

'You know you could do so much more with your general *look*,' I whoop finally, forcing myself to stand upright. I hear the sounds of voices and passing footsteps nearby and hook my left arm through Nuriel's right. Her skin is unbelievably hot, as if she's running a high fever. It almost hurts me to touch her. 'You need to dial it down,' I remind her, shouldering the tote bag so that it sits a little higher on my right side. 'We're just a couple of girls, here for a good time, not a long time. Hold it together, darling. We're on.'

We move around to the front of the Arrivals pick-up zone, blending in with the light flow of foot traffic, and come to a stop beneath a cluster of security cameras. I point in a few different directions for extra effect while Nuriel stands slightly apart from me and the rest of the waiting people, hugging herself tightly in silence.

'Buncha losers!' I hear a man yelling in a strong Barbadian accent. Seconds later, a couple of big guys in baggy pants, gold chains and designer tees shove roughly between me and Nuriel. Out of the corner of my eye, I catch the mouth of dude in the rear drop open as he checks out the babe he's just pushed past. He back-pedals for a moment, staring hard at Nuriel, clearly torn.

'*Fingasmits!*' a man's voice roars, drawing closer. 'Come back here!' The second runner gives himself a shake before sprinting away.

I turn to look at the approaching cab driver. He has a neat moustache and goatee, short dreads hanging around his face. He appears to be in his late twenties or early thirties — a little shorter than Nuriel, a little taller than me — and he's wearing a short-sleeved maroon and white checked shirt, cargo shorts, open-toed leather sandals, and about half a dozen colourful friendship bands around each wrist.

He's puffing a little from running as he mutters, 'Thieving, malicious!' coming to a stop beside us. 'Lost the fare,' the man adds, his brown eyes widening as he checks out Nuriel's face, before his eyes flick back down to the ground respectfully. 'You need a taxi to get around Key West? I can take you.' He points at a bright purple SUV parked haphazardly across the main drive from where we're standing.

'We've got no American money,' I blurt, realising with a sinking heart that the best-laid plans of the archangels hadn't included much local folding. 'Only British pounds.'

'I take pound, sugar,' the man replies quickly, his eyes taking quick, dazzled, glances at Nuriel's face. Around us, I see a few other people doing the same, one of the men standing near us fumbling eagerly for his phone.

'Do I *know* you?' the cab driver quizzes Nuriel, clearly trying to work out where he's seen her before. 'Micah Gittens,' he adds, holding out his right hand to be shaken.

In her usual way, Nuriel looks down at Micah's hand like she's not sure what it's for, so I grab it instead and grip it firmly before releasing it. Micah re-focuses on me with difficulty, blinking as if he's been staring into the sun for too long.

She's too damn *pretty*, I realise, as I clock the flutter of movement and talk around us. It's a cat-and-pigeons situation right here. If her face has been especially designed to turn Satan's head, it's going to turn anyone's. 'Kit Tyburn' will probably find out we've arrived before we even leave the terminal building and we'll have lost any element of surprise. 'We just need to get to Riley's Island as quickly as possible,' I say hurriedly, pushing my sweaty spectacles back up my nose, smudging the lenses even more.

I see a man standing not six feet away snap a furtive picture of Nuriel, before he sees me glaring and shoves his phone back into a pocket of his jeans. If he works out that the latest internet sensation has somehow made it from London to Florida at pretty much warp speed, we'll soon have a crowd. We have to move.

Micah's face has fallen at the mention of Riley's Island — a mere five-minute drive from the terminal — but before he can back away in search of a better fare, I reach into my tote and hastily pull out the tan purse. I fold his fingers over it. 'There are two hundred pounds sterling in here,' I say crisply. 'You can have it all, Micah Gittens, if you take us to Riley's Island right now.'

I hook an arm through Nuriel's, propelling her in the direction of the purple cab.

Waving his hand in apology at all the traffic we're holding up, Micah hurries us across the concourse, shoving the purse back into my hands while using his keys to unlock the SUV.

'You sure they on the island know you're coming?' he says as he opens the back door to let us in.

Nuriel slides in first, tension in every taut line of her slender body.

I get in next, nodding as I look up at Micah standing by the open passenger door. 'She was personally invited.' I jerk my head in Nuriel's direction. 'I'm just her frumpy assistant.'

Micah frowns. 'The police been out to Riley's Island many times. Even made the *Keys News*, I remember. People coming and going — people who told people they would be there, then they ain't, they're nowhere t'all, you know what I'm saying? Now two like you? Need to be extra safe. Funny things going on, on that island.'

Then he shuts the door and minutes later we're turning out of the airport and left onto South Roosevelt Boulevard.

The Atlantic Ocean is a dark, moonless presence to our right as Micah pulls his SUV in under a row of towering palms dividing the roadway from a narrow pedestrian walkway overlooking the sea below. He points to a narrow single-lane bridge, not twenty feet away. 'To get onto Riley's Island, you're gonna go through a security checkpoint right at the end, okay? Big steel gates, wise guys, the whole drill.' He screws up his face and makes hulking big gorilla arms and shoulders to illustrate his point. 'There are cameras. Dogs. Buster's always been real particular about security. But...'

'He hasn't been seen for a while?' I finish softly.

Micah turns and looks at us in the darkness. 'Like I said, he's nowhere t'all. Not just Buster. Girls, pretty as you two. They go in, they don't come out. But no one can say for sure they were ever there. Always no proof, just hearsay. The police go in and everything looks spick, span, orderly — just another rich man's house, you know? No sign of struggle, no sign anyone even been living there. You sure you don't want me to keep on driving? Plenty of nicer places 'round the Keys.'

Nuriel's response is to open her passenger-side door to signal that the discussion is over. We both watch her lurch out onto the walkway beside the road, stumbling into the shadow of one of the tall palms some distance from the car, hands over her face like she's crying — or praying. I slide the small leather purse onto the armrest between the two front seats.

'I can't take two hundred pound, it's too much, dear,' Micah mutters, as he frowns at Nuriel's hunched outline beneath the trees.

'We don't need money where we're going,' I insist. 'You'd best head off now, Micah. You never saw us. We were never here either.'

Micah's brown eyes on me are troubled.

The car engine doesn't start up again until I set foot on the bridge with its tall set of automatic steel gates, topped by razor wire, barring the end of it, two guard boxes of stainless steel and glass facing each other just inside them. As I turn to give Micah a wave, I catch the whites of his eyes as he does a slow U-turn. He's still looking back over his shoulder at us as he drives back the way we've come.

24

'Nuriel!' I hiss into the trees. 'Please let's go before I lose my nerve completely? I'd like to get the slaughter and mayhem over with while the night is still young.'

The salt-laced air is warm, but I can't stop shivering.

After a moment, Nuriel straightens as if she's come to a decision and crosses the hard shoulder of the road towards me, linking her arm through mine. Her skin is still fever-hot to touch, but gives off only the faintest gleam in the dark. I can feel how hard she's trying, all the coiled tension inside her as she struggles to lock her light away. In this moment, she's probably the most human she'll ever be.

As we walk forward to the bridge together, banks of floodlights along the entire span suddenly flare brighter, turning it an eye-searing white.

I shield my eyes with my left hand, the glare bouncing off my plastic lenses, gut twisting with the fear that some trigger-happy clown is going to start taking pot shots. We're so exposed out here. Our shadows stretch out before us, weirdly attenuated, and I have to force my feet to keep moving. Time becomes elastic, the road going on and on. The sweat pours off me, making my tee-shirt stick to my skin.

But Nuriel seems to grow taller as we progress, as if she's remembering what she's capable of, what she used to be. The light flares in the ends of her long hair, illuminating the pure, hard lines of her face. Beyond the gates, I glimpse a watchful shape emerge from the guard box on the right, then the one on the left, each man resting the flat of one hand on the assault rifle slung across his torso.

'Human,' Nuriel mutters immediately.

I nod, having come to the same conclusion only a beat behind her. 'In that case, just stand there looking achingly beautiful and leave the talking to me,' I whisper in return, my lips barely moving.

We reach the heavily spot lit area in front of the barred gates after an eternity of walking. I'm drenched in sweat as if I've sprinted the entire distance, though it's been less than a kilometre at most. In contrast, Nuriel's flawless, lit-up features could be carved from marble. Even under the harsh lights she's radiant, something completely apart from the rest of us. She sweeps her heavy fall of honey-coloured hair away from her face, giving the two men behind the gates a better view of her arresting features, swan's neck and perfect breasts. As they move towards the bars from their side of the gates, I approach them as well, pasting a huge, goofy grin on my dial and waving my hands over my head excitedly like I'm landing a chopper.

The men are only a couple of feet away now and I'm rocked by an intense feeling of relief that neither of them is *the man* — the one I've imagined beating to death with just the length of clear perspex and the fat romance novel hidden in my tote bag.

High on adrenaline, I cock my right hip, cross my arms and say in my best sing-song *East Enders*, 'We're here to see "the real" Kit Tyburn, gents? We're expected, like?'

The two men give me cold, lizard-like stares for a moment before one of them returns to the guard box on the left and the gates begin to part smoothly. I have to resist giving Nuriel the double thumbs-up like an overexcited kid.

The two guards step forward through the open gates, rifles

swinging slightly as they draw closer. They look down the length of the bridge in the direction of Key West before their suspicious gazes alight back on us: two oddly-dressed birds who've fetched up in the dead of night, looking well up for it.

As the men stare at Nuriel, I see a moment of pure confusion pass across their hard faces. She's a vision, a mirage, the loveliest thing they will ever see in their lives, guaranteed.

'Who's asking?' one of the men rasps finally in heavily accented English, as though he's struggling to wake from a dream. He's only just above average height, but built like a cube of muscle; his face and head are close-shaven, and he's dressed all in black and fully menacing, just like Skorobogatov's goons at the Argo.

'*Cibyyl*, you know, love, the indie singer and next big thing?' I give a girly snort-giggle, trying to channel *bubbly airhead* as I push my big, hipster spectacle frames back up my nose and flap my right hand near my face like I'm fanning myself. 'The girl who just broke the internet? I'm her PA slash dresser slash publicist? We was *invited*, love?'

A flash of recognition crosses the security guard's face as he considers Nuriel with deep-set, hooded eyes, licking his lips as if she's something good to eat.

'Why don't you check with one of them higher-ups?' I can't resist saying. 'Your boss won't thank you for making him wait! You know what a temper he has. Got an itch in his pants, that lad, and I don't blame him. I mean, *look at her.*'

At an impatient signal from the other man, Cube stumps reluctantly back into the guard box on the right to make what I'm guessing is an urgent call back to the main house while the second guy — taller, with a wiry build and close-cropped black hair — starts circling the two of us, his gaze immediately dismissing me, the plain bint in the oversized face furniture.

He ogles Cibyyl unashamedly, eyes running all over her like a pair of wandering hands. But all she gives him is an imperious, unblinking *Go to hell* stare that would put even Irina to shame. The man actually looks away first, a faint blush on his high cheekbones.

Then he squints at me as if he's only just remembered what he's supposed to be doing out here, and raises his hands in my direction like he's reaching for a couple of ripe melons. He squeezes the air between us and I back up in haste.

'Whoah there, buddy!' My laughter sounds strained, even to my ears. 'Looking, no touching, mate. We're *ladies*.'

The Cube stumps back out of the guard house on the right at that moment and swings the muzzle of the semi-automatic he's wearing up into my face. 'No touching, no enter,' he drawls, waving at his compatriot to deal with me while he gets on with a full body search of Nuriel.

His expression goes dreamy as he walks towards her, flexing his thick fingers like he's about to play the piano.

I close my eyes at the taller man's approach, fearful of the violations that are about to occur, when the ground begins to tremble beneath my feet. It's so faint at first that I think I'm imagining it, until there's a sudden sharp retort like the distant boom of cannon fire, or something cracking.

My eyes flash open as one of the security guys yells, '*Ty che, b'lyad?*'

I recognise one of Irina's favourite profanities. Which makes these guys as Russian as the hired muscle at the Argo.

But there's no time to wonder about it now, because bigger shocks start transmitting up through the ground into my feet.

It feels like Great Eastern Street all over again and I hiss in Nuriel's direction, 'Are *you* doing this?'

There's another sharp retort, louder and closer this time,

and I rock on my feet, hands and arms shooting out to steady myself.

Nuriel's headshake is barely perceptible. Her dark eyes are so wide and watchful now they seem black; her posture so steady she might be floating just off the ground. But I can't look down to check, because I'll fall. It's taking everything I've got to stay on my feet as the side-to-side rocking of the bridge goes into overdrive, like a waking animal trying to shake us off.

Somewhere behind us, the bridge is giving way.

Nuriel's hand shoots out and grasps me hard by one elbow.

'*B'lyad!*' the other man shrieks as the two guards fall at our feet, roaring in fear.

A large crack opens between us and the thrashing bodies on the asphalt. It snakes across the bitumen like forked lightning. Through it, I can glimpse the darkly churning sea. The noise is immense.

Then the metal halide light banks overhead fail simultaneously, exploding outwards in blistering sprays of metal and glass, and we're plunged into instant darkness. Hot fragments of glass rain down painfully into my hair.

The gap widens, the lip of the broken roadway rising before me as the men try to grab for my ankles across the parting span. I lurch backwards, tipping, halfway to falling on my arse on the wrong side of the gates, when Nuriel loops an arm like an iron band under my armpits and —

Vaults us up and over the gap.

It lasts forever, for the blink of an eye.

There's so much effortless power in her it steals my breath away.

I imagine I hear the sound of giant wings as we pass over, and I know I have felt this before — flight. Mercy made the same sound leaping off the ground in the Argo. She — we — fell on the demon Hakael from above like cold fury. The sense of *déjà vu* I'm feeling is dizzying. She'd been in me, at the wheel. We'd done it together — torn him apart. I feel intense nausea at the fleeting memory.

All I get is an impression of the men's pale and terrified faces at least eight feet below us as we sail across the widening breach in the darkness, nothing but air beneath my wildly cycling legs.

Then I'm back on solid ground — there's not even a jolt as my feet touch the earth — and Nuriel propels us forward through the open gates at a run, her arm still around me like a vice. The fearful, flighty creature who wouldn't even meet my eyes at the warehouse is gone. Nuriel's steeliness, her absolute lack of fear in this moment, remind me so much of Mercy it's uncanny. I can see how, once, they would have been like sisters.

I rub at the hard nub beneath my breastbone. The ground on this side of the rift is completely still, reassuringly solid. At a look from my companion, the heavy security gates behind us swing shut with a groan — the mechanism forced backwards along its tracks by Nuriel's will alone — barring the two howling, terrified Russians outside the island estate.

She slows to a walk on the lamp-lit, paved carriageway that leads in a series of sinuous, terrain-hugging curves up to the main house. She doesn't look back again, but over my shoulder I catch sight of the bridge peeling away in sections from the Key West end, the destruction an unstoppable chain reaction like the spine of some giant prehistoric beast collapsing. The section beneath the two men falls away, and they drop straight into the water with the rest of the debris, their screams lost in the roar of falling concrete.

I blink and swallow, unable to tear my eyes away from

the space where the bridge had been. Not even the supportive concrete pylons remain. The Atlantic has taken everything, and the island is an island once again. Between us and Key West now lie hundreds of metres of open water.

'That should — what is the term you people use? — *buy us some time*,' Nuriel murmurs, her eyes never leaving the road ahead.

I turn back and study her profile fearfully, realising that when the *elohim* make judgment, they carry it out. Absolutely and without hesitation.

'If it wasn't you who did that to the bridge,' I whisper, '*who was it?*'

Her eyes flick upwards in reply and I see, above the trees, the sky glowing a bright crimson.

'Whoever did that,' she replies tersely.

I flinch as a wailing alarm splits the night air.

'*Ours not to reason why, ours but to do and die* — isn't that what you English like to say? Friend or foe,' Nuriel rasps, 'the chaos can only be to our advantage and we must use it. Lucifer is already under attack.'

She picks up her pace, stalking up the driveway lined with lush, tropical foliage towards the fire raging in the distance. I have to take three running steps to keep up with just one stride of hers.

As we come close to the end of the curving drive, I see a natural, grassy plateau, encircled by tall palms. Through the gap in the trunks up ahead, I catch sight of Buster Strang's sprawling colonial-style mansion already well alight. Flames lick out of multiple chimneys, roar up the whitewashed walls. Even as I watch, the fire engulfing the main house begins to branch out — moving like no fire I've ever seen. It spreads out in arrow-straight lines across the manicured emerald lawns, racing towards the showy, glass-fronted garage to the right of the house before climbing up the floodlights surrounding the clay court to the rear. From somewhere inside the mansion there's the sound of an assault rifle going off in a series of erratic bursts, followed by a bloodcurdling scream. Then I hear an explosion of superheated glass— probably the conservatory wing going up.

It's as if the fire is sentient. It streaks across open green spaces devoid of viable fuel. The flames fork and split all over the place, like that crack that almost tore the front of the Darley Hotel into pieces, as if the fire is searching for something specific. There's another burst of uneven gunfire from within the tree line somewhere close by and I see a burning man stagger out of the undergrowth, his rifle still clutched in one hand. He falls face-first onto the edge of the lawn and lies still, and I could swear the heat spikes in intensity for a second.

Before my eyes, things that shouldn't burn — an elegant stone fountain, a grouping of cast iron garden chairs and tables — are all consumed by these questing flames that have a corrosive tinge of silver-grey at their heart.

Demonsign.

Nuriel sees it, too, and her dark eyes, brilliant in the firelight, narrow dangerously.

She shakes me off like an irritant. I have to run to keep her in sight as she plunges through the line of palms bordering the plateau, each one going up like an outsized sparkler: *boom, boom, boom.* Even the floral border of the circular drive is ablaze, the inferno sucking up all the oxygen, taking everything in its path. There's a huge flash of light as something to the rear of the garage goes up — maybe an electrical transformer or some kind of generator — and I'm almost floored by the sound and the shockwaves that follow.

I shield my head, watching in awe as the resultant fireball shoots at least forty feet into the air before abruptly extinguishing as if something's sucked it right out of the night sky. So much energy — gone in an instant. I can't make sense of what I've just seen.

I rip the fake plastic spectacle frames from my irritated eyes and let them fall to the ground. 'This wasn't part of the plan!' I scream in Nuriel's direction, my voice all but lost in the roar of the flames. 'You're supposed to take me with you. *Wait!*'

Nuriel ignores me. She's halfway across the hard forecourt in front of the main house when she stops dead, her gaze scanning the scorched lawns surrounding the circular driveway. Abruptly, she turns her face towards the open ocean to the south, before pivoting towards the southeast corner of the island. Her expression hardens, and I know that she's somehow pinpointed the bunker without having even seen it. The nondescript concrete building that was in Jamie's photos, overlooking the sea, must be somewhere beyond the trees.

Still some distance away along the drive, I'm overcome by a fit of coughing; the heat is so ferocious it's like an impenetrable wall. Weeping, struggling to push forward, I can feel the skin of my forearms peeling and blistering as I hold them across my face protectively. The hard, hidden nub below my sternum begins to flare and pulse, as if Mercy is coming awake and pleading to be set free. But there's no way for me to reassure her that she hasn't been forgotten. I just need to find him — find Lucifer — before I let her go.

I look up at the distant façade of the burning house and see frantic shapes moving in the windows on both floors. A human torch suddenly charges shoulder-first through one of the white-framed upstairs windows in a rain of broken glass and I'm still screaming hoarsely as the burning figure falls headfirst over the blazing balcony railing onto the paved forecourt below. Facedown on the ground, it jerks once then goes still.

I rip my gaze away from the still-burning body as the front door of the mansion bursts open. Three huge, muscular Dobermans race straight for me in formation. Like something out of a horror film, their coats are on fire and their teeth are bared in anguish. They are mere metres away when each beast gives a weird, mid-air twist-flip — as if all three have been lifted simultaneously by an unseen hand — before falling to the ground. Across the threshold of the open front door, another man in black collapses and lies still, and the intense heat seems to ramp up another notch as if everything that dies only fuels the fire.

Beyond the trio of dead animals, the man who fell off the upper balcony — legs and arms splayed at unnatural angles, still burning as if he's been immersed in some kind of accelerant — abruptly rises to his feet in jerky bursts, drawing himself awkwardly together like a busted marionette. His face is caved in from the impact, lips and nose burnt away to reveal the white of teeth and underlying bone. Despite his multiple, horrific injuries he lifts his head in my direction and starts lurching towards me brokenly.

I'm so terrified that, for a second, I seem to lift out of my own body, seeing the whole scene from above. It's impossible. He should already be *dead*.

I back away fearfully. But behind me, there's a roar, as more and more trees inside the tree line catch fire. I can't move forward, and I can't go back.

All I can do is watch as the man who shouldn't be alive keeps coming.

I almost say the words then.

I almost scream: *Deus ex!* Just to save myself.

But before I can form the words, the burning man dragging himself towards me seems to run into an invisible wall. His hands fly up, palms out in a position of surrender, as if he can't push through it. Then he starts to jerk and convulse, plunging to his shattered knees on the hard pavers only metres away from where I'm standing. My hands are over my face, and I'm screaming so hard that it feels like I've torn something in my throat.

A dense cloud of grey-silver mist starts to jet out of him, the broken body already peeling away from what's really inside. The man slumps sideways on the ground and finally lies still while over and around his body this buzzing, keening cloud of energy struggles to reform, almost close enough for me to touch.

The bodies that are human or animal will just succumb, a voice in my head tells me soberly. *But the ones that harbour demons...*

That's what I'm seeing — a demon desperately trying to escape the dying body it had taken refuge in.

What was the word the Archangel Gabriel used?

Succubus.

The succubus is fleeing. So much energy trapped in such a frail vessel.

This is the weakest the demon may ever be. If only I had a way to kill it.

'Nuriel!' I scream and she turns her head, her eyes meeting mine through the boiling cloud of angry energy between us.

But I realise with horror that the heat — the heat that's everywhere — will sustain the demon long enough to come after me. The *daemonium* crave the heat and this situation — where fire seems to be actively searching out human life while it takes everything in its path — was tailor-made for demons.

I can't even take a step back, frozen by the knowledge that when it becomes itself again, that thing is going to rip my face off.

'Nuriel!' I scream. 'Do something!'

Backlit by head-high flames, her nostrils flare as she roars, '*Caym*. I would know his signature anywhere. Lucifer cannot be far.'

Her ringing laughter is bitter, and she seems to be speaking to herself more than to me when she says, 'Even when he is not with me, Luc is there — like a wound that will not close. *The Destroyer* — he whom we once named the "son of morning", the most beautiful of us all — I cannot shake him off. The flames cannot burn away the corruption at the heart of this place.'

She turns her head again towards a line of burning palms at the southeast end of the island. 'Lucifer left his long confinement to bring affliction directly to this world — let this place be his last stand. Let him die as he left me to die.'

Then she breaks into a run, passing through the flames beyond her with ease, untouched by any of them. Her long, golden hair streams out behind her like a bright flag and she is as sleek and swift, as powerful and elemental, as the day she was made. I know she's already forgotten me, is already lost to sight, when I am crash-tackled to the ground.

25

Big hands turn me roughly and all the years instantly vaporise.

I could be back there — in the clearing that smelled of resin, plant life and heat in the summer I turned eighteen. The season has always, ever since, reminded me of death and dying.

Tree branches filigree the sky menacingly, just as in the woods near Mama Kassmeyer's house, and, just like then, the man I've been searching the world for drives his heavy knee into my abdomen.

The air rushes out of my body with a *whomp*, and I'm small and pinned and helpless all over again. The tote bag that holds the weapon I brought here to kill him with is trapped under my body. There's not even enough wriggle room to hook it up from under me.

I've been cursed since the day I was born. How did I ever think I could win?

Hot tears of rage spill from my eyes.

All these years, I've been so deluded. Just living would have been the best revenge; I see that now. Just living.

Far, far away from here.

He frowns down at me; firelight burnishes the gleaming, shaved contours of his head. He has the same powerful shoulders and thick, corded bull's neck — ropey with veins and intricate inkwork — that I remember. Maybe his nose is a little more broken, and his breath, over the stink of smoke, is even more sour. But the tattoo that has haunted my sleep in nightmares has lost none of its crispness or definition. It's probably the last thing I'm ever going to see in this life, and the irony hurts me more than trying to draw breath with his full body weight crushing me into the ground.

Icy with shock, the entire world reduces down to the black and red death's-head moth hovering just inches from my face. The man poised above me swallows, and the moth jerks in a parody of flight.

It takes the frowning man a couple more beats, but then his pale, bloodshot gaze widens in recognition.

'*Your eyes* — ' he breathes. 'No one on earth has eyes like yours.'

I lash out at his face then, fingers like talons, heaving my head and shoulders off the ground in a last, desperate attempt to tip him off me and roll to my feet the way Shaun taught me to. But I'm already down, it's too late — the element of surprise was his all along — and the man grabs both my wrists in one of his big fists. I've suddenly got nothing left to give. I'm all locked up with nowhere to go.

This is it. It would take a miracle at this point, but Nuriel has gone and left me. And what are we, really, to the *elohim*? Our lives and preoccupations must appear as brief and weightless to them as smoke.

The man stares down into my tear-drenched eyes. Between the stinging, acrid air, the crying and the fall, I must have lost the brown contacts Jamie put in for me a lifetime ago.

He knows me for exactly who I am, the same way I know him — there's no more subterfuge, everything is laid bare now — and his lips draw back over his teeth in a grin.

The man strokes a crooked forefinger down the line of my cheek with his free hand, lifting my chin and studying my face first from one side, then the other. Acid bile surges up in my throat.

'I knew this day was coming.' He leans in so close that his knee feels like it's breaking me in half. 'When the papers said you didn't die of them things I done, I knew you'd be back. I haven't made the same mistake again. Been waiting for you, darlin'.'

He suddenly grabs my face with one hand and squeezes it so tight I'm going blind with pain. 'And this time, girly? I'm doing it properly. *This time you die and stay dead.*'

Then his thick hands are around my throat, his thumbs hooked in around my Adam's apple. The flame-seared sky overhead goes black and purple around the edges, and my head rings, tight with my own desperate blood. I'm starting to lose consciousness as he bears down with all his weight, fingers gouging into the muscles of my throat until there's no more air and my eyes are bulging out of my head.

It occurs to me that I'm dying.

It's that simple. And I know that Mercy will die with me because I was stupid enough to think I could take on this monster single-handed — just me and him in a fight to the death that I decided I could walk away from, victorious.

How naïve was I?

I make a choking noise that's lost in the roar of the flames and he leans closer, his nicotine-stained teeth only inches from my face. 'What, bitch?' he laughs. 'I didn't catch that. *Say. It. Again.*'

With each word, he smashes my head into the ground. I feel the bag shift beneath me, the hard staff working its way out from under my body.

There's not enough oxygen left now to even form the words that would unleash Mercy like a dog of war. I couldn't free her now to save myself.

Tears leak silently out of the corners of my eyes as my rapist kills me for a second time.

Mercy, I'm so sorry, I think as the world fades.

The man — whose name I don't even know — feels me weakening. He abruptly changes his grip around my throat so that it's now one-handed. With the other, he starts tearing at my clothes, baring my bony chest to the burning air as he fumbles with the waistband of his trousers, yanking at mine, cursing at all the complicated ties and buckles. He rips the bag that's still looped around my shoulder down my arm because it's stopping him from getting at my bra.

'I'm gonna do it to you again,' he grunts. 'Do it to you while you *die*.'

Almost blind, the fingers of my right hand close over the exposed end of the baton and I grip it tightly in gratitude before bringing it up and across the side of the man's face with all the strength I have left.

He rocks back, roaring, blood streaming into one eye as time —

It seems to speed up and slow down all at once.

I feel as if I can see everything that makes up the world — all the tiny motes and colours and particles it consists of — and all of it is hurting my skin, burning across my vision. Even with my eyes open, I can see small darts of energy zig-zagging across the surface of everything; like the bright blood staining my attacker's teeth as he rips the baton out of my right hand and smashes me in the face with a closed fist. My senses will never be so alive as in this moment — the instant before I die.

I turn my head sharply from the next blow and catch

Azraeil just standing there, out of the corner of my eye.

There's such a look of sadness upon his youthful, beautiful face, his long hair spilling like moonlight down his shoulders. His hands are empty and weaponless, loose at his sides. And I imagine how he will take my hands in his, when it is time.

I feel the ties between my soul and my body beginning to slacken — the spiritual, the corporeal shifting apart — and I close my eyes; it will soon be over, I am being called. It doesn't matter what is done to my body now — the essential part of me, what makes me who I am, will soon be free.

I know it will be all right — when I am in Sheol.

But there's a sudden vengeful hiss overhead — a drawn-out sound of such rage and dire warning — that my skin tightens again in fear. The sound is followed by a stream of words in a language so bestial and foul that I know it was no tongue ever devised by the *elohim*. It is the idiom of Lucifer. The speech of the fallen.

A promise? I overhear Azraeil's deep, gravelly reply in the space behind my eyes. You *make* me *a promise?*

There's something like laughter, or incredulity, in his words.

What is said in return resembles the noise a predator would make tearing out the throat of its prey; a reply both violence and rage-filled.

But then I hear the demon say quite clearly: *Not for you, 'brother'. Not now. You cannot stay while she yet lives — and I will make certain that she does so long enough to bring about what we both desire. You are compelled to leave the living be. It is the 'law' that guides you, is it not? Go.*

It's a woman's voice — dark and bitter, achingly familiar.

I open my eyes in shock to see that Azraeil has indeed gone — banished or warned away — and that standing above the man who is killing me all over again is the tall, winged creature that tore apart Great Eastern Street. She's made entirely of silver-grey light and is at least seven feet tall; growing more substantial as I watch. It's as if smoke is pouring into her outlines, giving her colour and form, second by second. Her eyes — a startlingly rich sapphire blue — never leave mine for a moment.

The demon stretches silently behind my attacker, unfurling her giant wings that are taller than she is. For a moment, they remain outstretched as if poised for flight; the long primary feathers catching and reflecting the nightmarish light. Then she relaxes the central vanes, and the end feathers trail upon the burning ground, untouched by the flames all around. This time, the demon appears so much more real and solid than the first time I saw her. I can only just make out the night sky through her now; and suddenly even the stars are gone, blotted out by her solidity. She is as real as I am.

And I realise now that the fire is somehow feeding her. Or maybe she *is* the fire.

The demon raises her right hand and, as if it was there all along, there's now a short, sabre-like sword in it with a wickedly curved blade and curved hilt. She points it at me — above the man's head — and the weapon is like the sinuous horn of a great beast but made entirely of the same stuff she is. Silver-grey flames lick down across its surface towards me as if drawn by my living energy.

Our eyes meet above the head of the man straining to take me as I die, and my eyes beg: *Kill me. Please.*

In my head — words like fire appear.

Yes or No?

Whatever my answer, I know there will be a price. In this world, or the next, I will owe this demon a debt that will demand repayment. Demons neither forgive nor forget. It is the rage that drives them. I will be bound to her in a way I do not yet understand — across worlds.

I try to nod in answer to the demon's demand, but the effort is too much. If the demon takes my life, I know that Azraeil will have to return for me and it is the best I can hope for. Then the torment of my body, at least, will be over.

There is a crow of triumph from the man poised over me as he wrenches my stubborn zipper open at last.

He shifts position hungrily and I don't even have the strength to turn my face away from what he is about to do. I tell myself it won't matter anymore.

Yes, I answer the demon inside my head. *I will pay your price. Do what you must.*

There is a sound then — like the wind rising through the trees. A hurricane gathering, to sweep me up.

I wait for the killing blow to fall, my eyes wide upon the demon's own — her bright, jewel-coloured eyes — while the stupid, oblivious man continues tearing the fabric down around my hips.

Focused on his own pleasure, he has no awareness of the winged creature silently poised behind and above him with a weapon of flames gripped in her hand. She lunges down towards my head and I tense beneath him.

When is anyone ever ready to meet Death? No matter how beautiful, how grave and courteous he might be?

Make it quick, I beg silently.

But the demon shifts suddenly, changing the angle of her blade before driving down then cutting upwards, burying her sabre deep in the man's chest.

My eyes fly wide in shock at the same instant his do.

For just a moment, the tip of the blade burns through the

torso of the man poised above me. Just a shining, silver-grey point cleaving the heavy matter of him. Death in the form of a hairline breach, a thin luminous line. As the demon holds the weapon steady, her outline grows brighter as if she is drawing from the flesh she is joined to.

And I realise that that's exactly what she's doing — every thing living that dies here tonight is somehow *feeding* her. She's found a way to survive in this world that even Lucifer — in his state of desperate, soul-jacking symbiosis — may not yet have worked out. She's stealing this man's electricity, taking it from him while he still lives. She's evolved into some kind of demonic predator that can survive, above ground, *outside* a human host.

Over me, a howl of anguish shatters the air.

'Go,' she hisses as the man's body begins to topple forward off her blade. 'You are confined to the lake of fire until such time as you are called again, Peter Allen Masters. *Go to the place you have prepared for yourself.*'

For a second, I think I see him, Peter Allen Masters — such an ordinary name, unbefitting of a monster — now as grey and insubstantial as mist. He's just a suggestion of a man rising to stand, lost and confused, over his own mortal remains.

Then time seems to restart, or speed up, and the spectre blows apart, scattering. Blood fountains from the lifeless body onto me. Writhing, I turn my face from the iron heat of the torrent as the man's body falls across mine. Blind blue eyes are turned in my direction as I push frantically at the heavy corpse, shoving it off me in a fever of nausea. I surge out from under it, rolling away to lie retching in the scorched grass under a blood-red sky.

Beyond me, the roiling, shrieking cloud of energy that Nuriel identified as Caym has grown denser, more manlike in aspect.

The other one — the female — turns sharply from where she's standing over Masters' dead body, the vicious sword of burning matter still grasped in her right hand. She strides towards her shrieking, boiling brethren...taking all the fire with her.

Fire comes down from the trees, pulls up out of the ground. The flames climb the trailing feathers of her wings, the billowing hem of her gauzy, sleeveless gown. They play within her outstretched fingers, the ice-blonde coronet of her braided hair, leaving only ashes all around. She is incandescent now, wreathed in flames. I've never seen anything so terrifying — not even when Ryan doused Lucifer with petrol, setting him alight beneath the dome of the Galleria — *because the demon and the fire are one.*

Around me, the landscape is now still and blackened; just a smoking terrain littered with twisted human forms, burnt beyond recognition. All harvested, I realise, sickened to my core, by this creature for her personal use.

She stretches again, the vanes of her wings momentarily extended, caressing the air, secondary and axial feathers streaming in the fiery updraft of her own passing, as she walks away from me on pale bare feet. She crosses through the heavy drift of ash on the ground towards her demon brother, Caym, leaving no footprint, trailing tendrils of fire.

Recognition tugs at me again. Something about the way she moves, the way she does her hair. Her unearthly blue eyes. But the way she burns yet is not consumed is hypnotic, and the memory of where I first saw her in this world will not come.

Over her shoulder the demon hisses at me, 'You carry the "sword" that will sever Lucifer from this life, Gia Basso. Leave Astaroth, Balam, Beleth, Amon and Caym to *me*. All that is required of *you* is to deliver accursed "Mercy" unto him. Arise and go now, as swiftly as you can. I will clear your path of those who would do evil unto you. But I would deal with this one first. There are matters… outstanding.'

Dark laughter fills the space inside my head as she croons wordlessly, her stride never slowing for a moment, *Caym, my love, I am coming.*

Pushing myself up off the ground and tugging frantically at my clothing to cover my nakedness, I see her reach the male demon who is moments away from pulling his fractured light together.

Caym wears nothing but a loincloth that rides low across his narrow hips and everything about him is awesome in scale. He rolls his head of shoulder-length mahogany curls from side to side, ready to lift his chin and open his eyes. His bare torso, heavily muscled and tattooed all over with a dark looping script that I can't read, is marred by a giant's gleaming handprint upon his right breast.

It is the mark of the exile. Proof he is a first-order demon. One of the very first who fell. One of the strongest.

Two giant, glorious wings, taller and wider than Caym himself, unfurl behind him to sweep the ashes that lay thick on the ground. He gleams with that sickly grey-silver light that cannot help but draw, and unsettle, the eye.

I can barely breathe as Caym lifts his chin. His beauty is breathtaking — both ascetic and primal. Something about his strong-boned features reminds me strongly of Mercy.

Caym's pain-filled gaze begins to clear and I see that his eyes are a fearsome dark red in colour, like drying blood. He struggles to focus on the burning vision standing before him, the hand holding the lethal sabre drawn up behind her back, hidden in the bright, constantly shifting feathers of her flaming wings.

Caym's cruelly beautiful mouth tilts up at the corners in recognition, widening into a smile of admiration. It strikes me how absolutely unafraid he is of her, of anything in his physical environment. He doesn't flinch or step back from the burning figure that fills his vision. Instead, he moves towards her and murmurs, 'Gadreel.'

It's a deep, thrilling sound, like a caress, and I actually shiver at the name, which sounds like a snatch of ancient music. Caym's lips draw away from his long, inhumanly pointed, razor-sharp teeth, rendering him even more monstrous-beautiful. 'You have returned at last.'

'As I promised to, brother,' she purrs, a smile playing about her full lips. 'I have thought long upon his betrayal and made my peace with it — and with you. With *all* of you. I have returned with my final reply. I have returned to be the empress of you all once more.'

'The offer stands,' Caym growls. '*They* —' he indicates me in the distance with a lazy tilt of his head, and I shrink back instinctively to kneel among still-warm ashes, 'are not our equals. Among their many faults, they are too easily broken. To take possession of such weak vessels, the way Luc insisted we must, has rendered us slow, powerless, limited, earthbound, nothing more than mere golem: creatures of clay howling at the gates. But *you* have only grown in power and beauty — the air thrills with it. Tell me your secret.' He opens his palms mere millimetres from the burning, shifting flames pouring off the surface of Gadreel's skin as if warming his eternally cold hands.

'Share with me how you are able to hold this much power around and about you so far from the lake of fire and *we*, together, will rule our fractured, scattered, lessened people. Let you and I take this world for ourselves and turn the old order on its head. It was a mistake to leave the dark places and clothe ourselves in flesh; many of us told him this — you, loudest of all. And for that dissent, were you were banished from his presence, sent to wander the earth in penance. Despite all his worldly "power", however —' Caym indicates the smouldering ruins behind him dismissively, 'Luc is the weakest he has ever been. The time to strike him is *now*.'

Fire plays in Gadreel's wide, sardonic smile. 'This I have already perceived.' Her murmur is as low, thrilling and seductive as Caym's own. 'And I would be your consort, as I was his? Place my hands below my husband's foot? Is that it? On the same terms as before — you to be "king", I to be "queen" and subject to your whims, however perverse they might be?'

Gadreel's laughter has a painful, biting edge to it and I flinch as she drawls in a parody of Lucifer's voice, '*Thou must be married to no man but me. For I am he am born to tame you?*'

Caym's blood-red eyes narrow. 'Is it not the natural order? Man to be the head of the woman? Is it not written? It was the reason he so easily sacrificed "Mercy". She would not abide by his terms the way you would. You will be my queen — that is true — as you were his. To rule under me.'

It's the wrong answer; even the dumb, powerless creature of clay that I am can tell that.

Gadreel's reply is very quiet, but no less piercing for it. 'But that is where you — all of you, my people — are so very wrong. We are not *men* — who were not made in our image, and stand separate and entire from us. We were created *equal*. We were not tasked to bring forth life, but to govern it. The rules as they were set for this accursed sphere by unlearned men of old *do not apply to our kind*. I refuse to abide by your terms as I refused to abide by Lucifer's in the end. I grew tired of them. The secret I have learned, my foul and murderous brother, in my travels through this lonely world, is that *no one* stands above me. *I rule with no one. I — and I alone — am enough.'*

Gadreel moves so swiftly that all I see is a fiery lash — like the tongue of a whip unfurling — and then a blur of flame. Caym's voice bursts forth in a howl of indescribable anguish as Gadreel buries the blade of her sabre deep in the shining scar over Caym's right breast, holding it there. Drawing on him. Hers forever more.

Their mouths are inches apart as he gasps her name aloud one last time, absolute bewilderment etched upon his face. She twists the blade deeper, her savage grin never wavering. She leans in towards him, pushing down. And I imagine, sickened, that she might even kiss him.

There is a blinding instance of light then, a blast wave of intense, lung-searing heat as the heretic energy of which Caym was made returns not to God — but into *her*.

Huddled on the ground, my forearms thrown up over my face, I don't have to look to see that she has somehow absorbed him into her — increasing her own power. She is monstrous with it, bloated with energy. In this moment, she possesses the strength of *two* demons.

Power thrums in the air between us, as I look up.

Gadreel seems so tall now against the star-littered sky, as powerful as a burning stone colossus.

I draw breath sharply, seeing her at last for who she is. 'I *know* you,' I whisper, recognising her as the woman I once knew in Milan as Gudrun, Mastro Giovanni Re's immaculate, red-lipped personal assistant. She'd been with Lucifer when the roof had caved in that night at the Galleria.

Gudrun — Gadreel — raises her hand, levelling the tip of her burning sabre at me, and her words are like a dagger between my eyes.

Did I not tell you to get to your feet, woman? Her voice issues from everywhere, and nowhere, all at once. It's outside me and inside me; in the ground, the sky. The sonic afterfeel of it is shocking.

Divine 'Mercy' — there is that harsh, dark laughter as she says the name — *is all that matters now. Deliver Azraeil's revenant unto Lucifer. I will clear the way.*

Reeling, I reach for the bloodstained baton on the ground beside me. Barely able to stand in my torn and burned clothing, I follow Gadreel across the charred lawns in the direction of the grey bunker that overlooks the sea, my weapon gripped tightly in my right hand.

26

In the half light, I see a hint of turbulent dark water and open ground in the distance, the farthest edges of the island that face the open sea. Gadreel and I are about to step out of a forest of flame-blasted trees, when a luminous streak falls out of the sky above us, screaming her name.

Gadreel's wings open with a clap and rush of air that seems to shake the ground, and she soars upwards to meet it with an answering scream that splits the sky.

Beleth!

Gadreel and Beleth meet in a fiery burst of energy, twisting and grappling high in the air. They rise in a series of ragged spirals through the stark, charred canopy of dead trees, gripped in a parody of a lover's embrace. One is a creature composed entirely of a living, corrosive flame, the other of a silver-grey, nacreous light, their faces and torsos — his muscular and unclothed, a shining handprint on his lower back — only inches apart. Two sets of wicked blades are trapped between their straining bodies, so far off the ground now that they might be distant stars.

I'm looking up, so I don't see the third one — the third demon — until he's already on top of me. There's just a glimpse of large, cat-like eyes the colour of verdigris, an onrush of air almost strong enough to knock me off my feet, and then — *crack*, a fleeting moment of intense silver-blue light at the point where the demon's outstretched fingers meet the soft skin of my throat.

His touch feels like an instance of eternity; of absolute power.

But it's the demon — not me — that is cast down to the earth.

It's as if he hit an invisible wall, or some kind of force-field, that's around...me.

I blink in shock to see the winged titan sprawled on open ground. The force of the impact with me has propelled him back beyond the tree line. His wings are tangled beneath his body and he's lying directly between me and the grey bunker in the distance.

Somehow I put him there — *simply because he touched me.*

In a flash, he's on his feet again, his luminous wings outspread like the hood of an enraged cobra as he comes at me a second time. He's so big, and moving so quickly, that I've got no time to do anything except scream and throw the baton I'm holding up in front of my face as if it will do any good.

But there's another crackle of live energy as he is repelled again, falling to one knee fifty, maybe one hundred, metres away.

He leaps to his feet immediately, shrieking, '*What are you?*'

The demon's muscular chest rises and falls as if he is in the grip of some wild emotion; pointed teeth bared and glistening.

'There is something,' he spits, '— written in your flesh. A complex signature I do not recognise.'

I surprise myself by stepping forward towards him, the baton in my trembling hand held out in front of my body. The moon finally breaks through heavy cloud cover as I approach the demon slowly. He is naked save for loose, silver-grey trousers that swathe his powerful legs and lower body. He bears no dark markings on his face and skin and could be *elohim* still with his shock of russet curls and surreally flawless beauty. But when the demon drops his stance, sweeping both hands up from the ground and over his head in a curved, wavelike-shape as he surges to his feet, I see the long, razor-sharp quills that protrude from his back and the glowing handprint that's wrapped around the base of his neck as if a hand gripped him there just before the moment he was exiled.

Between us now there is a seamless web, a frozen, breaking wave of energy; only the faintest trace of silver-grey light plays across its surface to show that it is even there. He stands tall behind it, watching me warily, and I wonder how it is that a deadly winged titan like this — a primeval being at least seven, eight feet tall — could be the slightest bit afraid — *of me.*

We face each other, separated only by that humming wall of energy, while Gadreel and Beleth wheel and spiral and shriek far above our heads.

'*Exorcizo te!*' the demon facing me bellows, the fingers of his left hand outstretched in my direction. Startled, I realise that he is using ancient words of exorcism against *me*. It occurs to me suddenly how deeply weird that is.

Of course, nothing happens because I'm not possessed; I'm just a kind of sentient carrier. The demon goes rigid with shock as I continue to stand there, my baton held out before me shakily as if I could somehow poke him to death.

I come closer, and the demon steps back further behind his protective force field as if I could actually do him harm.

'I'm not possessed,' I say slowly, fascinated by him despite the terrible danger he represents. 'There's nothing that can be "exorcised" from this body.'

I gesture at myself with the end of my weapon, knowing

every word I'm speaking is the truth. Mercy is so tiny, so hidden, as to be undetectable, even to a creature like this.

'But you are *mortal*,' the demon snarls, his face half turned away as if he can't bear to look at me because I'm something new under heaven, and therefore grotesque. 'What makes you proof against *me* — Astaroth, Prince and Duke of Hell, Commander of Legions? Your body is inviolate; it is as if made from glass. I can gain no purchase upon your flesh. I grow cold. Yet you are unassailable, inviolate — as if already inhabited by another. Yet you are not. So I say again, if you are not possessed —' His voice drops to a piercing whisper. '*What manner of being are you?*'

I stalk back and forth before the protective shield he has thrown up between us and he raises his head, tracking my movements with his gleaming, pale green eyes as if he can't help himself. Through the thin film of naked energy I see that his frown mirrors my own. We are struggling to comprehend each other across an unassailable divide.

'You see that building over there?' I ask, answering his question with one of my own. The demon's verdigris-stained eyes flicker briefly in the direction of the concrete bunker behind him before returning to me. 'I need to get inside it. I need to get to Lucifer. I carry a message for him.'

'You seek...Lucifer?' Astaroth's frown grows heavier in bewilderment and it strikes me how strange it is that he and I are having a kind of conversation.

I nod casually, though the baton in my hand is visibly shaking. 'If you try to stop me, Gadreel will annihilate you. She'll annihilate you anyway. She promised Azraeil as much, and she's very much a creature of her word.'

'*Gadreel?*' Astaroth growls dismissively, mirroring my pacing behind his protective shield of energy; his long wing feathers trail upon the ground, the outline of him curls and shifts in the night air as if the edges of him are slowly dissolving. 'She possesses but a fraction of my power. And Azraeil is a weakling — not even *elohim*, so limited are *his* powers.'

'Gadreel has evolved,' I insist. 'I saw her destroy Caym not five minutes ago, and she will take Beleth apart, too, I guarantee it.'

Astaroth's reply is flat with disbelief. '*You lie.*'

I wince as a piercing shriek rings out high overhead.

'Look, Astaroth, mate.' I point upwards with the weapon in my hand. 'That's not the sound she makes when she's happy to see someone. *I've got no reason to lie.* You're about to meet your maker, whether you're up for it or not, and you'd better have a bloody good explanation unless you walk away from me — from all of this — right now.'

The demon goes rigid at my words and, by his absolute stillness, I know he is really listening.

'Me giving you a heads-up like this? There's nothing in it for me,' I add gently. 'You aren't proof against the power of *three* of your kind. Three first order demons. That's how strong Gadreel soon will be. She's as powerful as she was before but she's also somehow *subsumed* Caym — I watched her do it — and will shortly do the same to Beleth. I don't know how long it lasts for — all that lovely power — but she's pretty much indestructible right now.'

Astaroth is silent for so long I almost miss his answering whisper. 'How is it possible that she not only opposed Lucifer to his face and prevailed, but even... *thrived*?'

'There are ways to survive in this world beyond simple possession,' I reply, hoping the demon can't see how badly I'm trembling. 'And she's worked out one of them all by herself. If you step aside, if you go now... you just might survive the night. You, Beleth, Amon, Balam, Lucifer — Gadreel has you all marked for destruction and she intends to see it through. There is nothing more valuable to her right now than a freshly dead demon, the older and stronger, the better. I'm telling you the truth. She wants all of you returned to God. Tonight.'

Astaroth makes a spitting sound. 'You are telling me to flee?' His voice is incredulous.

I nod, uncertain why I'm giving this one a chance — maybe it's the wild, sorrowful intelligence in his cat-like eyes; the eyes of an enraged, long-caged animal. And, in a way, he has been. He made a stupid choice a long time ago and paid for it with all of time itself. But if I were not somehow proof against Astaroth, if two separate and distinct types of energy were not holding us apart right now, I know I would already be dead.

The demon draws himself upright to his full majestic height. 'What do you want from me in return?' he murmurs.

'Nothing but to be left alone,' I respond just as quietly. 'It's the same answer that I always give the Archangel Gabriel, and that he always ignores.' A shadow moves across Astaroth's face at the name of his lost brother.

'Just leave me alone and we are square,' I say. 'We are done and dusted. From here on out, you and me are nothing — it goes no further. You stick to your corner of the world, I'll stick to mine. Everybody happy.'

'But — don't you understand? — I will be in your debt, woman,' Astaroth hisses, shocking me by letting the humming curtain of energy between us fall. There is nothing now but four feet of warm night air and a perspex stick between us. I could reach out and touch the shining skin of his hand. And I badly want to. He's one of the most eerie-beautiful things I've ever seen, right down to those long, inhuman, razor-sharp spines bisecting the space between his wings.

'Even between demons,' Astaroth says hollowly, 'there is honour. A life for a life. Even *we* abide by that when our own lives are at stake. We do not forget our debts, as we do not forget our debtors.'

The night sky is suddenly lit up as bright and searing hot as a high summer's day at noon, and I'm rocked on my feet by the wave of energy released at Beleth's passing — it can be nothing else. The heartstopping scream that shatters the sky above signals the victor.

'She's coming for you,' I point out through gritted teeth, the sonic afterbite still ringing in my ears.

We both hear her gathering speed like a falling meteor.

Astaroth!

Astaroth's wings suddenly flare wide as he lifts his head, scenting the air.

Then he does something completely unexpected.

He says, 'Laters,' in the perfect simulacrum of a London East End accent before blowing apart into a billion tiny pieces, streaming around and about my body as motes of warm, nacreous light before dispersing — as if in warning, or thanks.

I shiver at the feel of him against my skin, but in seconds find myself running flat out across open ground towards the bunker before Gadreel can punish me for letting the very unsettling Lord Astaroth — Prince and Duke of the Legions of Hell — slip through my fingers.

ॐ

There isn't a breath of wind as I enter the open threshold of the small concrete building standing at the extreme southeast corner of the island. I squint, spooked, at the open room stretching away before me, the corners and edges in absolute darkness; I'm unable to make out the dimensions of the space. In the diffuse moonlight spilling through the doorway behind me — the only source of light — I can barely discern the tangle of junk in the room: a clutter of folding sun lounges and outdoor umbrellas nearby; piles of fishing and boating equipment a little further away; the glinting edge of a chrome art deco drinks cart near my right hand. Anything could be hiding in here. I break out in a cold sweat at the thought of what could come at me from the darkness.

You'll never be brave enough, says the small voice of sabotage in my head. And the voice is right. I'm completely paralysed by fear.

But behind me there's a sudden roar — like the sound petrol would make being thrown on a bonfire — and Gadreel's standing behind me. Just behind her, the once-open threshold is now sealed off entirely by a wall of liquid flame that cascades upward, against the laws of nature.

No one in or out unless I will it, she murmurs into the space between my eyes, almost as if she's talking to herself. *Not that eternal meddler, Gabriel, nor that mouthy troublemaker, Uriel. None of them may pass on pain of destruction.*

Every hair on my body stands up at the feel of so much raw power crammed into this small space. I find myself sweating heavily in a room now drenched in red light, the baton slick and slippery in my right hand; I spot, at the very back left corner of the storage area, a darker circular opening in the brushed concrete floor, surrounded by a simple iron hand rail.

Stairs that lead down.

I swallow convulsively.

Of course, I think. *It would all have to end in the cold, dark ground.*

Gadreel's voice in my head is bitter. *In this world? It always ends in darkness. Keep moving, woman, or I swear I will wrench the revenant out of your body with my own hands and 'release' her myself — even if it kills you.*

Numbly, I begin weaving through piles of junk towards the staircase, gasping when I stumble across the naked body of Kit Tyburn half-sprawled beneath a nineteen-twenties-era writing desk, discarded like so much rubbish. Facing me is that dark tattoo that runs up his ribcage — which seems far more prominent than before — and I bend closer to make it out, saying aloud the word that is written on his skin in black ink:

Haereticum. Heretic.

I shiver.

Jamie had told me that Kit Tyburn was the most famous music icon of his generation, a kid with more Top 10 songs than his actual human age, but Lucifer's left him crumpled on the ground like a fast-food wrapper.

Crouching, I feel for a pulse in the guy's neck and am relieved to feel a faint one, flickering just beneath the cold, clammy surface of his skin. But he's pale and unmoving — just as Irina had been when Luc had ripped Mercy straight out of Irina's body.

I wonder where the real Kit Tyburn has gone, and whether he'll wake up again before his body dies. As I hesitate over his sprawled form, Gadreel hisses, *Move.*

I turn and look up reproachfully at the fiery apparition bent over me but she just raises the tip of her blade in warning, levelling it directly at the space between my eyes.

When I reach the top of the stairs and look down, there's not a single light on below to cut through the darkness of the descent. But as I begin to feel forward gingerly with my toes, I find it's impossible to miss a single stair on the way down because they're illuminated by a demon made of fire, impatiently lighting my way from above and behind.

The winding staircase is irregular, cut out of the rock itself. As we go deeper, the smell of the sea grows as overpowering as the chill: an icy damp that seeps down into my bones and lodges there, making every movement clumsy. Disoriented by a series of sharp switchbacks, I stop for a moment to regain my equilibrium, and Gadreel passes the flat of her flaming blade across the fine hairs at the back of my neck in warning. I can feel the heat of her weapon there, the threat very clear: I'm a mere handful of follicles from total annihilation.

I know it's only the strange kernel I carry inside me that is keeping me alive right now.

Woman, Gadreel whispers. *Don't try me.*

Sweating and shaking with cold and fear — I can't be sure where one ends and the other begins — I continue my slow, crablike descent down the steep stairs, my back to the uneven stone wall. Some sections are so narrow I trip and stumble over my own feet, barely catching myself from falling through space.

Abruptly Gadreel says, *Only a few steps further. You won't see me, but I'll be watching. When Lucifer stands directly before you — say the words and let her fall upon him —'*

'Like a plague, yes,' I say a touch acidly. 'I got the memo.'

Then do it. Her disembodied words stab at me.

The light of her goes out so swiftly and completely that I almost fall down the last flight onto the slick stone floor below. Swinging around wildly, jabbing at the air with the baton in my right hand, I realise I've hit some kind of passageway. Water seeps continuously down the walls; I can feel it on my fingertips when I touch them.

It's pitch-black now, and I'm groping forward in the darkness for an eternity, starting at every scuff my feet make upon the slick ground, the clatter of loose pebbles underfoot. But then the rod in my hand hits something hard and smooth and I realise in horror that there's no more passage, just a closed, solid steel door.

My dark-blinded eyes finally make out a thin border of light seeping around the edges. I feel for the doorhandle, which is a submarine hatch-style wheel set directly into the centre of the door at waist height, the circular edge of the handle cold, smooth and heavy in my hands. Then I turn it. And as it swings open away from me, I scream — because I see him in profile, kneeling on the bare, stone floor, eyes wide and staring into the heart of the open sea.

I'm looking at some kind of undersea viewing chamber.

One entire wall of the huge stone space is made of a thick, transparent, seamless material, as clear as glass. There's a field of coral before me, lit up bright as day by weird, fast-moving streaks of phosphorescence in the water — like drowned lightning playing out there — the colourful field of coral dropping abruptly into a dark abyss in the distance.

We must be at least a hundred feet below sea level. Panic crowds my airways as I jam the weapon in my hand into the back of my waistband and run, sinking to my knees, instinctively throwing my arms around the kneeling, rocking male figure. But he won't yield or bend.

He's rigid; his muscles are like taut wire.

He doesn't even react as I say his name, over and over, shaking him, trying to turn his face to mine. But he might as well be made of stone.

He's utterly changed. He's how I imagine a prisoner of war would look: starved and beaten, filthy and abused, barely alive. But I know it's Ryan Daley because how many times have I traced the bones of his face in my dreams, wishing he were mine — absolutely — the way he was only ever Mercy's?

He's still shockingly tall — six foot five if he's anything — but emaciated to the point where he shouldn't still be breathing. His dark hair hangs in tangled and matted rat's tails just past his gaunt shoulders. It's been weeks since he's seen the sun, I'm guessing, from his extreme pallor and the weeping sores on the exposed parts of his skin. And though it's icy in this chamber — as cold as the depths of the ocean the chamber looks out upon — Ryan is dressed only in a ragged flannel shirt and torn and dirty trousers that are too short for his rangy frame. His feet are bare, almost black with cold, the nails broken or torn away.

I come around him so that I'm staring into his dark eyes. But even though he's looking right at me, he's not seeing me — he's seeing someplace else, sometime else.

I can tell this from the stark changes in the muscles and hollows of his face —smiles give way to anger, then confusion; outright terror to grief. But he's so weak, from malnutrition or the intense cold, that his howls are silent, his entire battered frame wracked by them, his cracked lips stretched wide over grey-looking teeth.

I shake him by the shoulders, taking shallow breaths to block out the rank, animal smell of him. But Ryan does nothing but rock back and forth on his knees, his arms wound tightly around his body. He holds himself as if, at any moment, he might fly apart.

I've known that feeling. I've lived it.

'What's wrong with you?' I plead in anguish. Tears stream silently down Ryan's skull-like face, his dark eyes turned dully inward on some personal grief. 'What do you see?'

There's the suggestion of movement in the cold air around us, just an eddy.

He sees this. Gadreel's voice is the darkness, and even Ryan flinches at the whip-like lash of her words.

He sees nothing else — but this.

Then the stone room I'm kneeling in is gone and I'm lost again in the moving roar of taxis and buses, tourist rickshaws and cars, the intense smells of spice and heated bodies, the cries of flower sellers thronging a temple complex entrance in Asia somewhere. But this time I'm not her — not Mercy. This time I'm watching from a point above and behind her as Mercy and Ryan enter that temple to *Kālī*: the blue-skinned, four-armed goddess of Time and Change, Power and Destruction, eternal slayer of demons. I want to scream at them to run, but horror holds me fixed in place, robs me of my voice. And what voice does one possess, anyway, inside another's nightmares?

Then I find myself standing at a point behind them, still observing, still waiting, as Ryan and Mercy study the garlands of skulls and flowers around the neck of the massive raven-haired statue. They point out to each other the long, fanged teeth in *Kālī*'s mouth, the skirt of human arms about her waist, the bloody scimitar and severed head grasped in her hands. The intense smell of incense and jasmine is almost sickening, but part of me still recognises that I'm kneeling in a cold, stony chamber far below sea level with my hands gripping Ryan Daley.

Two realities, one superimposed atop the other. But the temple memory has taken over — overpowering the present — and it's like I'm smoke, like I'm standing just behind Mercy and Ryan in the last moments of their lives together. Just waiting.

I'm *Gadreel*, I realise with a sick surge of dread. I'm seeing what she saw.

There's a lick of fire along my nerve endings as if in silent confirmation and I know that I'm bearing witness to what was done to Mercy all over again because Gadreel had been there, though already banished. I'm seeing her rival's destruction through Gadreel's eyes, feeling an awful surge of savage joy that is entirely Gadreel's as the twenty-foot statue of *Kālī* seems to come alive in front of Ryan and Mercy, toppling towards them.

It's already too late as they move back in terror because they can't know this, but the watcher assigned to keep them safe is already dead. They are unprotected, ripe for the taking, doomed.

I feel the terrible confusion of Ryan's and Mercy's thoughts as the statue shatters into pieces, blowing outward, debris hitting them both. They cry out in simple human pain and terror. And then Lucifer is standing there — not as he was that day he sat in the front row of a fashion show in Milan, urbane, charming, human in aspect — but as a fiery, roaring, beast-headed creature, wings outspread in fury, weaponless hands outstretched to grasp Mercy by the upper arms, pulling her to him at last.

'It's been too long,' he purrs.

I watch as she goes rigid at his touch — as paralysing as live current — unable to struggle. She can't twist, move or breathe for the pain, the human threshold for pain being so much less than that of the *elohim*.

'Did I not say, my love,' Luc smiles down upon her beneath his hands, 'that harm would come in many guises, many forms?'

'*Mercy!*' Ryan screams as she is taken up by the beast, still lying stiff and unmoving in his arms. She is borne upward towards the sacred patterns painted in flaming reds, golds, blues and greens upon the temple ceiling as if he might crush her mortal body against them.

I watch demons step out of the bright murals painted upon the walls, two to hold Ryan fast, two to scour the living from the temple grounds. By turns they are cyclonic and formless, by turns they take the form of animal-headed men or ancient gods come to life. The screaming and chaos and bloodshed inside that place of worship makes me — *makes Gadreel* — smile with open delight as Lucifer explodes up through the multi-layered roof of the temple, shattering stone and plaster, shearing straight for the hot, humid skies overhead, leaving Ryan shrieking and thrashing in the grasp of the two demons far below.

I *am* Gadreel as I soar through the gaping wound in the temple roof, following at a safe distance. Looking down, I watch Ryan grow smaller and smaller on the ground. Looking up, I see Lucifer and Mercy doing the same, fast moving away from me. He is twisting her in his arms as they spiral upward towards the energy-giving sun, as if forcing her to perform one last dance. It is a parody of the way they used to move together through the skies — unfettered by anything, by any code — bent solely on each other and an all-consuming love.

The echo of Gadreel's terrible jealousy is palpable in my veins. She strains to hear what Lucifer whispers into Mercy's ear, but knows she can go no further or she will be detected. Lucifer has waited for this moment for millennia. It is time to end it — past time.

And suddenly it's *me* howling in joy as I watch Lucifer tear apart Mercy's corporeal form with bare and burning hands far, far above the teeming streets of a backwater city in a nothing province of a fly-speck country in Asia.

She is already dead before the pieces of her body hit the ground, while Ryan Daley howls and howls in the grip of demons. Mercy is no longer there.

'The Devil does not make the same mistake twice,' I watch the memory of Astaroth snarl in Ryan's ear as he and the demon Amon wrestle Ryan Daley right out of the flow of time until the loop of memory… it starts again.

27

Ryan is in the grip of a living nightmare.

All he sees is Mercy alive, her hand in his, then dying — over and over in an endless loop that he's trapped in — unable to work out where *now* begins and *then* ends.

As Lucifer murders Mercy again with his bare hands, I shriek in horror, seeming to crash back into my body from a long way away, scrambling and pushing to get away from Ryan and his awful, ensnaring grief.

I scrub at my mouth with the back of my hands, knowing I'm going to be sick if Gadreel makes me watch that again.

But Ryan has watched it, Gadreel purrs from the darkness. *Continuously. Since she died. He bears it and bears it because it is the only way he can still be with her. Pathetic, aren't they, humans?*

She addresses me as if I'm one of them and I shake my head in rejection. But Gadreel ignores my cries of protest, projecting the last happy moment of Mercy and Ryan, alive and together, upon the walls of the undersea chamber as if to mock my denial. That scene of them with their backs to me — so happy, so filled with life and possibility, hands clasped tightly — plays across the thick acrylic window that is the only thing keeping the sea from flooding into this room. Their giant images mock me in this suddenly claustrophobic space. It's like a tomb.

I shut my eyes tightly and plead, 'Make it stop! Make it go away! For him, for me, Gadreel, *please.*'

There's a change of pressure in the air so abrupt that I can feel my eyeballs bulging out of my head. There's no air left to breathe. It's like I'm being turned inside out by a giant, unseen hand.

I plunge to my knees on the stony floor, all the veins in my arms and hands standing out starkly as if my flesh is shrinking tight to my bones.

And one of the lights streaking eerily through the water resolves itself into a ball of intense silvery-grey light that plunges straight towards us, growing larger and brighter all the time until winged Lucifer steps out of the depths of the sea and into the chamber drawling, 'Show yourself, *demon*.'

Maybe Gadreel is feeling coy because while Ryan and I twitch and convulse where we kneel with our heads bowed before the Devil himself — whose silver-grey wings graze the ceiling of the chamber and trail upon the stony ground — she chooses to remain hidden. Swirling and eddying around the room somewhere at my back. Biding her time.

Lucifer comes to a standstill before me and the air grows arctic. I can't stop shaking. I can't even lift my head to look at him, and maybe he reads this thought straight out of my head because he whispers, 'Then look on me, woman,' and suddenly I am — I'm staring up into the most singular face in all of creation.

His beauty is almost blinding. I am transfixed by it. And I know that Lucifer is himself again as he was made — snake-hipped, broad-shouldered, perfectly balanced in form and symmetry, save for the glowing scar in the exact shape of the Archangel Michael's handprint right in the middle of his bare, muscular chest.

The Devil, long golden hair fallen forward around his face,

eyes as pale as living ice, bends low and reaches for me, just a feather-light touch to the hollow between my clavicles, but the *crack* of energy that instantly flares between us makes him recoil as if punched in the throat.

'What trick is this?' he growls. 'What have you done, Gadreel, to make her impervious even to *my* touch?'

Then Gadreel is in the room with us — a being of red flame, flames pouring through her fingers, running between her bared and pointed teeth, her extended wing feathers, through the tight braids that encircle the crown of her head — and Lucifer smiles with pleasure at the sight of her. It's obvious to him that she possesses a new kind of power; I can tell by the way his gaze has suddenly sharpened, both with desire and naked greed.

He stretches lazily, rolling his leonine head upon his shoulders, basking in the red heat of her. 'Did I not foresee this moment? That you would return to me at last?'

'Stronger than ever before,' Gadreel agrees with a faint answering smile.

Lucifer drifts closer towards her then, beyond where Ryan and I kneel, twitching and choking, and the pressure upon us seems to ease in his passing. I gasp like a drowning person coming up for air. Beside me, Ryan does the same.

'And how could I stay away?' Gadreel adds playfully, and I shiver at the deep, seductive timbre of her voice.

'You have come to prove me wrong, I see.' Luc's reply is like a breath of fire along my nerve endings as he circles his prodigal lover warily. 'You have found a way to build and hold power that you would now share with your liege and master. That is why you have returned.' Statement, not question; his arrogance is breathtaking.

'I have a gift for you, yes,' Gadreel murmurs.

'*Woman.*' Breathing heavily, perspiration running down

my face, I struggle to focus on Gadreel's burning eyes. 'Say the words.'

Lucifer's wide mouth curls up at the corners as I shake my head. 'She's a defiant little one,' he whispers and the pressure in the air bears down on me more fiercely. I am being squeezed by a giant fist. I can't even cry out, simply toppling sideways as Ryan has done. We both lie rigid on our sides on the slick floor, curled around the pain.

The two winged demons look down upon us as from a great height. 'Say the words.' Gadreel's voice is almost gentle now.

I don't know how I find the strength to do it, but I force through my lips and gritted teeth, '*Not. Deal. Only. For. Her. Not. For. You.*'

Lucifer's look of amusement instantly darkens. 'What "deal" does she speak of?'

'She holds the secret,' Gadreel replies airily. 'It was placed in her for safekeeping so that it could be delivered unto you entire. But the human claims she can only speak it in the presence of that weakling, Nuriel, whom I lured here for you, my love.'

'Then, by all means, let us oblige the creature.' Lucifer turns and raises his right hand at the clear wall before him. 'Bring her!' he roars.

I find myself suddenly on my feet, held rigid by unseen forces, my gaze directed at the coral ocean again. The streaks of lightning in the water zigzag and clash furiously before resolving into the struggling figure of a winged female bound in fiery chains, her long, dark, curling hair like seaweed around her contorted, fine-boned features. Nuriel's true form.

On either side of her drifts a hairless, heavily-muscled demon, each bearing so many tattoos that only his gleaming eyes and the bright shining scars of his exile are visible among the seething words and runes etched into his living energy. The demons' silver-grey wing feathers trail and billow about them in the deep water.

Gadreel's voice is like an in-drawn breath. 'Amon,' she murmurs with a sound like satisfaction, 'Balam, my darlings, well met.'

She turns to Lucifer as grey-eyed Amon and violet-eyed Balam display Nuriel's chained figure before us in the water. All that separates Nuriel from me is a single pane of manmade material, but she could be as remote to me as the moon. As she thrashes and struggles to pull away from her captors, Nuriel won't even look at me. Why won't she look at me?

The pressure of Lucifer's gaze feels strong enough to crack my bones. 'Speak the secret, *filth*. I have need.'

Gadreel gazes down into my streaming eyes. 'Speak,' she insists kindly, as if my troubles will be over if I just say the words.

I gesture at my throat as Ryan continues to writhe at my feet. Gadreel raises her right hand as if directing an invisible choir to draw breath, saying more harshly, '*Speak.*'

The pressure eases. 'I do it for Nuriel,' I choke out, 'or I do it for no one. That was the deal, Gadreel. You twisted the truth. You didn't —'

I realise suddenly that she was never working with the *elohim*. Gadreel was only ever for herself. The answering gleam in her eye as she looks down at me is like laughter.

'*Then you do it for no one!*' Lucifer roars, raising both his hands above his head impatiently.

It happens so quickly that all I glimpse is Nuriel struggling violently with the demon to her right — Balam — throwing one loop of the fiery chain encircling her body over and around his head and throat, before pulling down with all her weight. She twists with all her power, wrenching herself out of Amon's grasp as Lucifer shrieks in anger, stepping towards the acrylic pane, unable to see who has the upper hand but making no move to pass back through it into the cold, cold ocean.

The light through the viewing window builds and builds as if the sun has fallen into the water and I half-cover my eyes. There's a muffled roar and a concussive *whump* as Balam is destroyed — his passing shaking the vast pane and leaving a ragged hairline crack in it from top to bottom. There's a confused impression of twisting limbs and wing feathers, smears of light, of Nuriel's mouth stretched wide in agony as Amon grasps one fiery loop of the chain around her body in one of his heavily-marked fists. And then nothing but that eye-searing light again, and then — she is no longer there.

It is only Amon staring straight at me through the seamless pane. He runs his long, purple tongue across his razor-sharp teeth lasciviously as he crosses his arms, covered in tattoos that blur and shift and change. I shudder at the unspoken threat as he, too, steps through the window and is suddenly in the room with us; perfectly dry, but affected by the smallest tremor in his heavily-muscled limbs. It's a tremor that also afflicts Lucifer. They're growing colder by the moment, and their desperation is rising, I can feel it.

Lucifer turns from the window abruptly, pointing his right hand at me so that I am drawn toward him as if magnetised, my feet not even touching the ground. I drift before him and he does not try to touch me now as he hisses, 'Speak the secret you carry, Gia Marie Basso, or I will remove every bone from your body piece by piece until you drown in your own blood.'

As I hang there, suspended, tears run down my cheeks.

Nuriel is dead. The plan has gone to shit. She was supposed to confront him, with me, and live. She was supposed to survive her last encounter with Lucifer in defiance of every torture he inflicted on her at Lake Como.

'You betrayed her,' I choke, glaring up through my tears at Gadreel.

Gadreel seems to shrug. 'It was a trap, yes,' she replies. 'All those whom Lucifer ever loved or desired cannot be allowed to survive. I am the apex. There can be no other. He is mine.'

'She was ever jealous.' Lucifer's voice is indulgent as he manipulates the air with small movements of his long, elegant fingers. I am studied from every angle, hanging before him, helpless; the perspex baton I brought all the way from London completely useless against a singular adversary like this.

I shudder as Lucifer's eerily perfect, otherworldly face stops only inches from mine. '*Speak.*'

Defeated, I breathe the words at last.

Deus ex.

Lucifer turns and looks at Gadreel, puzzled. 'What "secret" is this —' he begins to say, but I don't hear any more as my heartbeat goes through the roof and the linkages between Mercy and me begin to dissolve.

It's as if time is speeding up and I am a vast open desert pummelled by an intense and sudden storm — a storm to end all storms — and the seed that is in me bursts into life, the burning strands that emerge from it climbing and twisting and growing, streaming forth. The last thing I can recall is my body flying back, away from Lucifer, from Gadreel, through the air, before I hit the wall and the lights go out.

※

'Hello, my love,' I say as golden Lucifer stares at me, taking a step back in open horror. Immediately, he composes his features, but I felt the extraordinary spike of his fear, just for a moment, and I smile.

'I killed you,' he murmurs.

'You did,' I whisper, a sound as terrifying as steel striking stone. 'Most definitely. Twice.'

I stalk closer, seeing him take me in fully as he steps back towards the burning, watchful form of that traitor, Gadreel, whose part in all this has yet to be fully played out.

I am myself as I was created — seven, nay, eight feet tall — but insubstantial, the red light in the room striking through me. I am clothed all in black now — black as the feathers of my sweeping wings — and I catch Amon shifting uneasily at the corners of my sight.

Once were archangel, once were human. Now wraith! Amon's thoughts crowd the atmosphere of the stone chamber and I turn my head for one moment to look at him. Amon's grey gaze skitters away from mine.

I turn back to survey Luc. 'Where is he?' I say pleasantly. 'Give him to me and I will be kinder than you deserve, *Shaitan*.'

Lucifer's eyes flicker. Beyond him, Amon stirs. Something passes between them.

'Take her!' Lucifer screams at the two demons at his back, but as Amon surges forward towards me, the air between us seems to ripple apart from this small point of *nothing* that's growing — first along the vertical, then the horizontal.

As the rift begins to grow — the air temperature dropping below freezing — there is a glimpse of an overarching dark-violet sky scattered with bright stars against which is outlined a great stone fortress, bounded by water on three sides. Two men sprint from the base of the fortress through the rift towards me — each man holding the spindle-shaped weapon that marks the *mastin* or gatekeeper.

And the ones that Gia calls *Daughtry* and *Shaun* fall into the room, spinning quickly to place themselves between me and the demons Amon, Lucifer and Gadreel. Both men are breathing heavily, and their movements grow clumsy from the intense cold. Daughtry has difficulty even swinging his tawny plait back over one broad shoulder.

Three facing three; the power in the room is so unbalanced as to be laughable. 'Three demons versus a disembodied wraith and two men?' Lucifer's smile widens, grows fearless and dazzling once more. I can feel Ryan struggling to draw breath, somewhere on the edges of this room — the faint pulse of his heart singing to me — and my longing is almost my undoing.

Time — there will never be enough.

'Knight,' Gadreel hisses from behind Lucifer's shoulder. 'I see you and know you. Leave now, or die.'

'Fair warning, demoness,' Daughtry replies tightly in his smoky, faintly French accent, now shaky with cold. 'But we made a promise to the wraith that we would stand with her against the Dark Prince, and we do.'

'*Hanamel!*' Luc roars and it is my turn to smile at the absolute look of shock on his face when nothing happens.

When Raphael had originally devised a way to hide me from Lucifer in a string of random human lives, he reasoned that if I could not remember or utter my own name, I could never be found. But to have my own name spoken in my presence would cripple me — render me helpless. It had been both Raphael's gift, and a curse which could not be undone. Until now.

'*God's gift? Grace and gratuity of God? Compassion and Mercy of God?*' I reply, my laughter harsh. 'Just plain *Mercy* will do well enough these days. When you destroyed my corporeal body, my love —' I see Lucifer's pale eyes flicker with the memory, 'the flaw that Raphael knit into one small portion of my soul — my true name, the name that eluded me for centuries, the sound of which could drive me to my knees and turn me deaf, dumb and blind — was destroyed. Raphael's curse no longer binds me. My own name — Hanamel — can hurt me no longer.'

Lucifer runs at me then, howling, but the *mastin* raise their simple weapons of wood and rapidly draw a complex, perfectly symmetrical two-sided glyph in the air. It hangs there, and through its loops and whorls I see the *motte* upon which the grand stone castle stands — the fortress of the *mastin* in Sheol since time immemorial. The threat is clear to all of us in the room. *You may not pass.*

Lucifer stops dead in his tracks, although his eyes flicker in the direction of Amon at his back and I see the man, Shaun, tense as he catches sight of Gia Basso's crumpled body to our right. She is lying against the back wall of the chamber, one arm trapped at an unnatural angle beneath her slight body.

Then Amon atomises in an instant and when he reappears — between Lucifer and the glyph — he has Ryan Daley gripped in one fist like a rag doll, the end of a short, shining blade protruding from Ryan's abdomen.

I know the look of horror on Shaun's and Daughtry's faces is mirrored on my own, and the shining glyph — the glimpse of the great castle that stands at the heart of Sheol — melts away. There is only one world again.

Bright blood is on Ryan's lips as he whispers haltingly, 'Merce. *You look so beautiful.*'

His body shudders on the end of Amon's blade. I can feel the matter and the spirit of Ryan beginning to peel away, one from the other. Without help, he will die. And in the dying, he will call Azraeil to him from wherever he may be — re-weighting the balance of power in this room.

I smile, but there are unshed tears in my gentle reply. 'Love transcends all worlds, Ryan Daley. It will never be over between us. Even death is no barrier. We will be together soon enough.'

At my words, Lucifer's silvery eyes grow almost black with anger.

'*Amon!*' he shrieks. 'What have you *done?*'

Amon turns to survey his master in shock and his grip on Ryan falters. Ryan lets out a groan that makes me hiss in anguish, my black wings flaring wide.

'Until I destroy the wraith utterly, the boy *lives,*' Luc snarls. 'She is death's right hand. To destroy him now *is to give her what she wants.*'

I watch Amon wrench Ryan off his blade, throwing him against the back wall of the chamber. Ryan lands with a shocking sound, lying still near where Gia Basso lies, and Shaun's eyes dart to the right, distracted. In that instant, Amon surges forward, reaching for Shaun's throat and Shaun brings his spindle-shaped stick up between them, sketching something clumsily in the air before man and demon disappear entirely from the chamber.

Daughtry stumbles forward towards Lucifer, but Gadreel steps between them and the big man stops short of the burning demon's reach. 'Take them —' she indicates Gia and Ryan lying barely alive across the room, 'and go. Live to fight another day of your interminable life. This is no argument for mortals to settle. I can say no fairer.'

Lucifer's eyes gleam as he studies the shivering *mastin* narrowly over Gadreel's shoulder. 'But open season on you, *Knight,* when we demons are done here. Fair warning, as your kind say.'

Daughtry looks to me for confirmation and I nod. *If only*

one of us can survive this, let it be Ryan, I say into the space behind the big man's eyes. *He lives. He must.*

'No tender goodbyes,' Lucifer spits. 'Take them and go, Knight, or find yourselves, all three, wraiths in Sheol this night.'

Daughtry backs awkwardly away towards Gia, his breath coming out of him in short, pained gasps that stain the air white. With one more searching look at me, he grasps Ryan's and Gia's wrists in one big hand and, with a rapid movement of the sharp double-ended spindle in his other, all three mortals fall out of the world and are gone.

The sound of Lucifer's laughter rings, true and seductive, through the stone chamber.

'Didn't your "master" tell you? *You* can't kill me because *he* can't. You're the useless agent of a wingless archangel, the Great Eunuch of all the greatly exalted *elohim* — a creature created without the power to finish what he started. Death is no greater than evil,' Luc snorts. 'Azraeil has ever been misguided. Death is a dark horse running in oblique parallel to all that matters in this world. Death cannot stop *me*. Nothing can stop me. He's not even here in your hour of need, wraith, because he's so busy running after the human dead that he cannot be present to keep me from destroying his protégé — his so-called "weapon" and "right hand".'

He turns and looks at Gadreel. 'Kill her,' he says simply, and I stand my ground as Gadreel comes at me with her burning sword shaped like the sinuous horn of a great beast, atomising at the moment her blade meets the energy of which I am made.

I reform, whole and unharmed, across the room before the wall of clear acrylic with the hairline crack running up its face.

Lucifer cannot hide his shock, but Gadreel's expression is a more complex thing. I can almost see her thoughts shifting and re-calibrating, as if I have proven something which was only theory.

'It is true that my powers can no longer compare with yours,' I murmur. 'Indeed, they cannot be measured on the same scale. It is a subtle thing you have wrought in me, Lucifer, my love. By destroying my human body you rendered me immortal — in the way all human souls are immortal.'

I see Gadreel's eyes widen as she drifts almost imperceptibly away from Luc. 'Kill an angel or a demon and they are gone forever,' she murmurs as if thinking aloud. 'Returned to a heartless God. But kill a *human* —'

'And they gain more than the world they left, yes,' I hiss.

'But what use is such an empty immortality?' Lucifer spits.

'I had hoped you would tear each other apart so that nothing of you remained,' Gadreel addresses me, as if Luc is no longer in the room. 'But there is still a way.'

I nod, saying, 'I know it,' and Lucifer turns to look at her sharply as if sensing a new duplicity.

'But open season, no matter what happens,' Gadreel adds.

'Fair warning,' I agree grimly.

Then Gadreel collapses into a ball of flame, as red and vicious as a suspended, unsleeping eye, before vanishing into motes of light that within seconds are nothing more than an afterglow.

She is no longer in the room, and I know that matters will remain unresolved between us until she can find a way to destroy me utterly. A problem for another time and another place.

There is an achingly familiar bravado in the way Lucifer holds his head high, his gaze upon me unwavering. 'You make a pretty ghost, *Mercy*,' he sneers. 'But you can't destroy me and I can't destroy you. Stalemate, then. We no longer cohere.'

'We never did, demon,' I say quietly. 'It took you killing me the first time for me to realise that.'

The light of which Luc is made begins to draw inward, begins to gather up as Gadreel's light did. I will lose him if I do not move quickly. He is weak, but he is the Devil. And there are yet enough dark places and warm bodies in the world in which to hide.

So I make time stop then, the way Azraeil showed me was possible.

For a moment, I let the raw power surge in, let it build, let the door to the endless rooms of arcane knowledge fly open. I hold this moment of time separate and apart from all others so that none but *I* am outside it. I suspend not only time, but life itself, because I can.

I raise my open hands high, calling down the singular power that I have been gifted, standing framed before the kind of bright, living Eden Luc and I would once have been entwined in, together. I spread my black wings wide across the last view he will ever have of this world, God willing.

I am death passing over.

Haud misericordia! I cry.

No mercy.

The sound of cracking is immense. I feel the pressure build at my back as the fissure in the vast window behind me widens. Within that stopped bubble of time, I imagine Luc's mouth forming a scream.

And water pours in through the breach I have opened — not the cold waters of the Atlantic, but the hot, black waters of the river that is Sheol's heart's blood. It is true that I cannot kill him, not now. But I can hold him prisoner in Sheol — forever, if I have to.

The waters rush around me and through me, reaching for him as surely as I once pulled him into my arms.

I open a bridge between two worlds and let the river at the start, and end, of time drag Lucifer, drag me, down, down, down into the Valley of the Shadow of Death.

Epilogue

When I open my eyes, I'm right there — in that clearing filled with long grass and twisted yew and oak, the air dense with the scent of resin. When I come to, there's a sharp crust trapped between my skin and the cold, cold soil.

It's like lying on a bed of nails.

I try to move, but everything hurts. There's something wrong with my right arm. It won't respond when I try to shift it so that I can push myself up.

I gasp in pain as I roll and sit up awkwardly, bracing myself on my left hand, my right hanging useless like a dead thing. As if I've fallen through a black hole in time, I know where I am.

I'm sitting fully clothed in that clearing where I was taken by that monster just shy of my eighteenth birthday; the hard perspex baton still jammed at the base of my spine. I go cold when I realise that there's an emaciated man drawing shallow, panting breaths beside me and I look down at the wet mess of Ryan's abdomen and cry out in horror. He's been run through with something both deadly and burning. Ryan's not going to make it if I don't move now.

I stagger back through trees I haven't seen for years, cradling my shattered right arm with my left. I know I'm retracing the run I tried to make before that man chased me down, all those years ago.

I come out of the wooded edges of her sprawling, cluttered farmstead, tripping up the front steps of her sagging wooden veranda. As they always did, a cast of desperadoes — animal and human — come spilling out the front door as I stumble up to it.

'Help me,' I croak and all the faces crowd around me as the sky begins to whirl overhead. 'There's a man called Ryan, in the clearing. I think he's dying.'

'*Gia*,' Mama Kassmeyer breathes as if I've never been away. 'Darling, show us.'

And her foster son — the big, beefy one with Down Syndrome whose name I never bothered to learn — lifts me up in his strong arms as if I weigh nothing, and I take them to where Ryan is.

Acknowledgements

With thanks to my loving husband, Michael, and our beautiful, constantly hilarious children, Oscar, Leni and Yve — who put up with my uneven cooking and general disorganisation on a daily basis, but continue to love and humour me, regardless.

With thanks also to my dear friend and editor, Hilary Reynolds, who has ushered my chaotic stylings into the world on more than one occasion since we first worked together in 2008. The next feast of dumplings is definitely on me.

While this is a work of fiction, it was written for all the Jamies: the ones who survived, and the ones that didn't. Every female life matters.

I also wrote this for all the readers of the Mercy books over the years who have reached out to me from places as far away as South Africa, the Netherlands, Brazil, Singapore, the United Kingdom, Canada, Portugal and the Philippines with questions and comments and enthusiasm. *Wraith* is for you, with love and gratitude for embracing the freakiness and just going with it. There are no rules.

Sharp-eyed readers will have noticed Nuriel deliberately misquoting from 'The Charge of the Light Brigade' by Alfred, Lord Tennyson on page 259 and Gadreel quoting from Act II, Scene 1 of William Shakespeare's *The Taming of the Shrew* on page 276.

All of the names, characters, descriptions and events in this book are entirely fictional, and all opinions expressed by the characters are expressed by the characters; whose preferences and attitudes are also entirely their own. Any errors are entirely mine.

Certain authorial liberties may have been taken with those buildings and places that do actually exist in the real world and, for those, as always, the author apologises and begs your leave.

About the Author

REBECCA LIM is a writer and illustrator based in Melbourne, Australia. Rebecca is the author of seventeen books, including *The Astrologer's Daughter* (a Kirkus Best Book of 2015 and Notable Book, CBCA Book of the Year for Older Readers), *Afterlight* and the bestselling *Mercy*. Shortlisted for the Prime Minister's Literary Award, Aurealis Award, INDIEFAB Book of the Year Award and Davitt Award for YA, Rebecca's work has also been longlisted for the Gold Inky Award and the David Gemmell Legend Award. Her novels have been translated into German, French, Turkish, Portuguese and Polish. She is a co-founder of the *Voices from the Intersection* initiative.

CPSIA information can be obtained
at www.ICGtesting.com
Printed in the USA
LVHW041652070619
620540LV00001B/135/P